DAY OF INIQUITY

A Prophetic Novel of the End Times

by

Wm A. Stanmeyer

D1564479

St. Dominic's Media
P.O. Box 345
Herndon, VA 20172-0345

(703) 327-2277 • FAX (703) 327-2888
http://www.sign.org

DAY OF INIQUITY

A Prophetic Novel of the End Times

Published and Distributed by:

St. Dominic's Media
P.O. Box 345
Herndon, VA 20172-0345

Phone   703-327-2277
FAX   703-327-2888

http://www.sign.org

Cover design by Tina Isom - Artworks, Ltd.

Library of Congress catalog number: 99-7176

ISBN 1-892165-06-6

PREFACE

DAY OF INIQUITY is a frightening but compelling ride from tonight's news into the apocalyptic world that some see coming to pass here and now, week by week. Bill Stanmeyer has done his socio-political and biblical homework and has kneaded a super-loaf, which will intrigue, educate, and spiritually nourish you. It will also challenge you to cherish, while you can, all you prize and hold dear in this life, even as you seek to renew your spiritual roots and become real prayer warriors.

This work is fictional, but its social, political, and religious contexts are real. The author develops his characters carefully and deliberately, until they become alive in his pages. They give you a glimpse of behind-the-scenes events which few people know about, because our press and electronic media yield to economic and other pressures and thus fail to educate and inform us on the actual underlying causes of events. Two years ago I became aware of these socio-political contexts when I heard the respected newsman Edwin Newman, by then retired from NBC, narrate a 1989 study of the coverup of John F. Kennedy's murder. Later I saw the acclaimed 1995 documentary video, "Cover-up in Oklahoma," which interviews credible witnesses, cites authoritative studies, and exposes hard facts ignored by government investigators. The urgency of this book is made crystal clear by the January 1999 issue of "The McAlvany Intelligence Advisor" (1-800-528-9556), a brilliant newsletter which everyone should read. My awareness of the religious context of *DAY OF INIQUITY* was heightened by books like Dr. Tom Petrisko's Call of the Ages and periodicals such as "Catholic Prophecy Update," published by Signs of the Times Apostolate, Inc. The Great Sign, urgent prophetic messages and visions given to Sadie Jaramillo is particularly helpful as well.

Mr. Stanmeyer seeks to call readers to faith and to challenge them to intensify their prayer in what has become total spiritual war. His story shows how the world has become an illusion which distracts people, at their spiritual peril, from the only source of everlasting life: Jesus Christ. The biblical setting of *DAY OF INIQUITY* is "The Revelation of John," the last book of the New Testament, written by Saint John the Evangelist while exiled to the island of Patmos during a Roman persecution. Now, 2,000 years later, some wonder whether God is about to establish His Kingdom through events like those depicted in this book. The Bible makes it clear that the context is universal spiritual war between God's servants and those who choose to serve the fallen angels in rebellion against Him, trying to set up the kingdom of Lucifer. God has allowed them to be rulers of this earth for a time, and they give power and wealth to those they choose (Jeremiah 27:5; Luke 4:5-6). God permits His servants to be attacked but preserves their souls by the blood of the Lamb (Rev. 5:9; 7:13). Finally, hastened by the prayers of His saints (Rev. 8:2-5), God intervenes through His faithful angels by an escalating series of punishments directed against His enemies (Rev. 9:4; 14:9-11). God's servants will be tested and some will be killed (Rev. 6:11); but those who pass through the great trial will not suffer again. They will stand in front of God's throne and serve Him always (Rev. 7:13-17) and He will renew the heavens and the earth (Rev. 21:1).

In his December, 1998 bull *Incarnationis Mysterium*, the Holy Father Pope John Paul II decreed that the Great Jubilee of the Holy Year 2000 would begin Christmas Eve, 1999. Holy Years are special times of forgiveness and mercy, which John Paul regards as significant steps towards the fullness of Christ. Consistent with this book's call for us to become prayer warriors, John Paul notes that the Father "is now doing something new, and in the love which forgives he anticipates the new heavens and the new earth ... let faith be refreshed, let hope increase and let charity exert itself still more." The Holy Father urges that this sign of charity must open our eyes to desperately poor peoples upon whom the shadow of death is being cast. "The human race is facing forms of slavery which are new and more subtle than those of the past; and for many people freedom remains a word without meaning." As the century of martyrs now ends, may the hearts of the faithful, like some of the characters in this book, admire and follow the saints' example, with God's grace, should circumstances require it. This story's powerful episodes showing Mary and the angels active in the world should motivate us to intensify our prayers for the intercession of the Mother of God, to obtain abundant grace for all Christian people.

I pray that this riveting novel of total spiritual war in the apocalyptic age which we share may move each of us out of our spiritual comfort zone of mere weekly worship and occasional prayer, and to personal commitment to fight in this greatest spiritual battle of all time!

Maranatha! Come Lord Jesus!

Fr. Jim Anderson, M.S.A., J.D., Ph.D.

INTRODUCTION

This is a work of fiction based on many recent private revelations about the End of the Age. Much of this book was written before certain now-public events came to light and made parts of the book plausible. But there is no intent to call attention to any real person by using his or her name or by depicting him or her, in this book, as having certain physical, moral, or intellectual qualities.

As in most fiction, the settings in the story are a composite of real and imaginary locales. Needless to say, the White House exists; but the author does not know whether there are secret tunnels under it. There are modern office buildings in Brussels; but the author has no knowledge whether the world's largest computer is in one of them. Somewhere in Europe or America there probably is an actress like Dolores Montalvo, a pilot like John DeSanto, a priest like Father Michael Kanek--but in describing these characters, the author had no specific real person in mind. At the time the manuscript is being finished, there is, to the author's knowledge, no such person as the Chairman of the Council of Europe; when this book reaches its audience, there may be such a person--but that fact is no reason to believe he bears any resemblance to the Chairman this book depicts.

The story mentions some scientific developments which have taken place or will take place. The HAARP project in Alaska, the Y2K computer problem, low-orbiting surveillance satellites, SmartCards, microchips--all these are real. The author's knowledge of them comes solely from public sources, such as newspaper articles, conversation with experts, essays on the Internet.

There are many science-fiction, mystery, and spy novels whose skilled authors display marvelous attention to detail and weave realistic plots. But very few of them grasp the genuine supernatural: the struggle between God and Satan for the free allegiance of every human being, played out in every generation, experienced in every human soul, soon to be finalized as events of history rush to their climax. For unlike the bizarre preternatural characters in popular novels that depict the unseen realm, in the real universe supernatural beings such as Lucifer and his demons, Michael the Archangel and other angels, and the Virgin Mary do exist. They are as real as your neighbor next door or the car in your driveway. At this very moment, all of them are active in this world. *They* are not imaginary.

Though the human characters in this story are fictional, the plot is based on predicted fact: I have taken many of the messages recorded by modern mystics, who describe apocalyptic events at the End of this Age, and woven them into the lives of imaginary people. Beyond private revelation, which a person is always free not to believe, the public revelation of Sacred Scripture, disbelief in which is *not* an option, also forms the factual basis for this book. So the persons are fictional; but in my opinion much of what they live through in this story will take place.

I am aware that some Catholic priests eschew making any favorable comment about the messages which numerous modern mystics assert come from Heaven. This story is not a brief for or against the truth of such claims. Everyone must evaluate the internal evidence in the messages, consider what fruit they produce, and ponder the growing evil of our age. Even if a person denies that any of the messages are of divine origin, he could still benefit from a story that shows how the events the messages describe might take place.

Let us hope that every reader will react to these events as well as do the good characters in this story. No harm will be done if we pray more, fast more, or do more penance. So, to benefit from this story beyond its modest entertainment dimension, suspend your disbelief and absorb it as if it is true, as if it will happen soon.

Perhaps it will.

Wm A. Stanmeyer

January 31, 1999

Feast of St. John Bosco

DEDICATION

To all those good people who have been willing
to take messages from Heaven and pass them
on to others on earth, often at substantial
personal suffering.

* * * * * * * * * * *

St. Michael the Archangel, defend us in battle, be
our protection against the malice and snares of the
Devil. Restrain him, O God, we humbly pray, and
do thou, Prince of the Heavenly Hosts, cast into Hell
Satan and all the evil spirits, who prowl about the
world, seeking the ruin of souls.

ABOUT THE AUTHOR

William A. Stanmeyer has been a law professor at Indiana and Georgetown law schools and currently does estate planning and Internet home-based business development. His other works include *THE SEDUCTION OF SOCIETY: Pornography & Its Impact on American Life; CLEAR AND PRESENT DANGER: Church and State in Post-Christian America;* and *THE BEST KEPT SECRET IN AMERICA: How to Retire at Any Age ... Even When the System Crashes*, which sold over 250,000 copies. Married for 33 years, he and his wife Judy have five children. They live in Great Falls, Virginia.

PROLOGUE

The Woman walked slowly up the long golden ramp. There was a bright radiance around her like the sun. Her gown resembled a beautiful wedding dress made of white light. Her manner was perfect mix of regal dignity and childlike humility. Her hands held a globe-like blue, green, and brown sphere. Behind her, one to either side, their demeanor mixing dignity and humility reflecting hers, walked two powerful beings who looked like men. A Person sat on the Throne, concealed by brilliant light. The Virgin Mary approached the Throne of God.

At the top of the ramp ten yards from the base of the Throne, the Woman and her two companions stopped. They bowed. As she straightened up, a voice came from the Person on the Throne, the friendly, kind, loving voice of a parent speaking to his little girl. The voice was also strong, authoritative, protective, infinitely powerful. "What do you desire, My beloved daughter?"

The Woman lifted the colored sphere. Within it was a kaleidoscope of events that had occurred recently on earth: a Judge driving his car home in rush hour, saying the Rosary...an old woman in a hospital, offering her pain in reparation for sin...a college student declining another beer so he could leave the party early and make it to Mass...a wife and mother offering her struggles raising three little children while her absent husband worked two jobs to support them...a doctor after a long day at the clinic, stopping at his church to pray...a man in church alone at midnight on a Friday night, meditating and praying in adoration before the Holy Eucharist...and thousands of other prayers, mortifications, and acts of charity. The Woman held the sphere out toward the Throne, as if to offer a gift.

"I would like to plead with You, Heavenly Father, to extend the life of Pope John Paul II into the time of the Tribulation. And I would like to ask, in addition, that You appoint Saint Michael the Archangel his special Protector for this time."

"I am pleased with you, My daughter, and with the gift you have brought. What you ask is granted."

Immediately a human-like figure emerged from one side of the brilliance around the Throne. He resembled the two beings with the Woman, but he was taller, his shoulders were wider, and he appeared significantly more powerful. He had blonde hair and well-defined strong-jawed facial features. His uniform resembled that of a Roman gladiator. An enormous sword hung from his wide belt.

Michael the Archangel walked forward gravely, bowed before the Woman, and took his place at her right facing the Throne. "Thank you, Father," she said simply, humbly. Then the small party bowed, turned, and walked slowly down the ramp.

CHAPTER I

(1)

"Mr. President, Sir--there is a call for you on the secure line."

"Who is it?"

"A European, calling from Brussels. Says only that he represents 'the Chairman.'"

The President's hand tightened on the phone. He was not ready for this call. He took a long breath, as if waiting an extra five seconds would make the caller go away, and groped for the button under the desk. He wondered whether to activate the recorder.

"I'll take the call, Lieutenant," the President finally brought himself to answer, without pushing the button. There was a double click on the line.

"Mr. President." It was an imperative.

"Mr. Chairman--how are you?" The President feigned cordiality.

"Fine, thank you. But--to get to the point at once--I am not pleased with the delay. You are falling behind my timetable." His tone was irritation on the edge of anger.

"Well, Mr. Chairman, we...uhh...we have had some recent successes you might not have heard about and--"

"Perhaps. Your delay has caused me to question your commitment. So I am sending one of my personal aides to discuss this matter with you directly and obtain certain assurances of loyalty. I am a practical man, Mr. President; if you want what I have promised, you must perform your end of the bargain."

The President controlled his own irritation; *The gall of this man! Fall behind his timetable!* But he lacked the courage to say anything. The Chairman of the Council of Europe continued, "You will be contacted within the month, during the time when your wife is on her Asian tour."

"Who is the aide you are sending?" asked the President.

But the line had gone dead.

(2)

Dolores Montalvo was well known among the wealthy families of Europe. Born of a philandering American father and beautiful but shrewish Spanish mother, she had inherited her father's strong build, her mother's breathtaking beauty, and the self-centered amorality of both. She was five foot eight, with perfect figure, tanned athletic legs, and a striking face with high cheekbones and wide brown eyes, framed by long auburn hair.

Attached to the Spanish Diplomatic Corps, the senior Montalvo educated his daughter at various European schools and, during a four-year stint at the Embassy in the United States, at Georgetown and later at Catholic University, the latter for its excellent Drama Department, not its slight veneer of religion.

Later, in the intermixed world of European fashion, finance, and politics, she found it easy to trade beauty and talent for advancement. A fairly good actress, she won supporting roles in a few successful movies filmed in Italy. Over the course of a jet-set decade she was "romantically linked" with three of the most influential men on the Continent. Each of these relationships lasted a couple years; the first a jealous wife broke up, the second Dolores exited out of boredom, and the last ended through the decision of the unmarried nobleman who was to be her next trophy. He had been so bold as to offer what he called "reciprocal fidelity": if she would promise faithfulness, he would as well. When she told him she would never allow *any* man to bind her with such medieval rules, *he*, in a spasm of momentary good sense, walked out on *her*.

The first conquest had netted her some assets; the second, the title of Countess. But the fish that got away took both his fortune and his rank with him.

Now she needed money to maintain her two villas, her Ferrari and Mercedes, her servants, and other creature comforts. Long a Feminist, by her thirtieth year resentment at her father for his repeated infidelities and at other men for "using" her--with her ready permission, even as *she* used them and their money, though she would never admit her own hypocrisy--had grown, like a cub into a lion, into general hatred of men.

At a party in Brussels she chanced to meet an old acquaintance who introduced her to the new Chairman of the Council of Europe, a man in his early fifties, with broad shoulders, a round face and very short black hair. She noted something strange and peculiar about his eyes: they were dark brown, nearly black, and seemed to emit a strange power, though muted for the moment.

Having a sense of diplomacy, she knew one does not scare the fish before she gets the hook in; and after the last fish got away, she had resolved never to reveal her true intentions to a man until it was too late for him to save himself. So when the Chairman made some flattering remarks about her looks, comments that from a lesser personage she would have called "sexist," she chose the high road and simply expressed polite thanks. He followed the compliments with the suggestion of possible well-paid employment, a prospect which made her agree to a private meeting.

Later in the week, in a interview in his office at one of the major banks, the Chairman offered a plan to use her acting ability, earn substantial income, and, as she saw it, get revenge on men.

"You have certain attractive qualities," he told her in what both knew was gross understatement, "that can be very useful. I am putting together a world wide group of high-level associates to advise political, economic, and religious leaders how to improve their programs. You can work with us as an International Liaison. The compensation is excellent--one million dollars for successfully completing your first assignment. That should help you pay for your villas and your fast cars," he added, watching her closely. "The chance to have significant influence on Europe and the whole world is very real. You may start immediately."

She accepted, dismissing her puzzlement as to how he had known her financial needs. He gave her a cheque for $250,000.00, a down payment to stimulate her willingness to take risks--and a key to a numbered safety deposit box in the Bonded Warehouse at the edge of the Zurich airport. There, he told her, she would find $750,000.00 after successfully completing her assignment. He admonished her in no uncertain terms not to disappear with the money unless she had been successful, intimating he had ways of locating her.

Then for an hour they discussed tactics, preparations, and "the target." The Chairman did most of the talking, spelling out exactly what to do when she gained access to the target. It was like following a script and he was the film director. She was amazed at his intricate planning and grasp of detail. He even had arranged a diversion in the building so that she could get access to "the target" without security staff knowledge. It was almost as if he were guided by some sort of higher intelligence.

He finished his instructions with a warning. "I want him to make a firm commitment either way. He has been too much a straddler, a compromiser. He has no real loyalties--except to himself. This quality is good, because it makes him open to my proposal--but it has its downside, because he may think his commitment to *me* is just as temporary as all the other promises he makes--which he slips out of when they no longer serve his needs.

"I want it made absolutely clear," he added, his dark eyes flashing as his voice rose, "that he must be loyal to *no one*, in Heaven, on earth, or under the earth--*except me!*"

She shuddered inwardly at such a strange choice of words and at the intensity of his outburst, but she controlled her emotions and said nothing.

"Of course, Ms. Montalvo," he added after a pause both to regain his composure and to let his point sink in, "paint what he covets in the most attractive of terms."

"Do you want me to seduce him?" she asked.

"I have no doubt you could. That's up to you. But if you decide to entertain him for an hour, it must be *after* he fully agrees to our terms. You will be able to compel him to demonstrate his loyalty by deeds, not just words..."

He stood up to signal that the interview was finished. She rose also. He walked around the desk, bowed, took her hand, and kissed it. "But of course, Dolores," he added, using the more personal form of address as he looked into her eyes with a glance that was almost hypnotic, "you might ponder whether a woman of your...abilities ...should not have a man far tougher than he."

(3)

Theodore Patrick--"Pat"--Greene sat on the tenth floor balcony of his apartment at Prospect House and gazed out across the Potomac at the night lights of Washington, D.C. From his tenth floor vantage point he could make out major landmarks, the Jefferson Memorial, the Washington Monument. The scene was beautiful. He savored the moment, both because of the twinkling sparkle of the lights and the sense of self-satisfaction that engulfed him. He poured a second glass of *Pete's Wicked Ale*, a sudsy brew, and looked again at the check.

It was a $50,000.00 advance from his publisher for his proposed book on science, government, and the impact of secret research projects on the environment. Coupled with regular stipends for his monthly column in *Discovery* magazine, the royalties from his first book, and the offer from the *New York Tribune* of $100,000.00 for the next year of his monthly feature on investigative reporting, this check, he felt, had put him over the top. *It's the big leagues, now, Patty me boy,* he thought. *You have definitely arrived.* He downed a big gulp of *Wicked* ale.

Of course, there was a small fly in the ointment. Or two, to be exact. One was Vanni, his girlfriend. Her new attitude. They had hit it off well when they first met, a year ago, she an executive secretary with BDR, a Fairfax, Virginia-based defense contractor; he the hard-charging investigator trying to pin down a story about some sort of government research project in Alaska called "HAARP," that was going to poke a hole in the ozone or the ionosphere or something. He had to pass her desk--security checkpoint, to you military types, he had mused--and he paused to make the acquaintance of a blonde bombshell, Marilee Van Niesen.

Actually, she had stopped him: he had failed to pin his little "Visitor Pass" card on his lapel properly, where it could be seen; and for all she knew, she was dealing with an enemy spy on a mission to steal all the secrets in the whole damn company. "Hold it, buster," she had exclaimed with force disproportionate to her five-foot-five frame. "You can't go in there until I see some ID. What's your name?"

"Bond...James Bond," he had said, displaying his best roguish smile. She hadn't thought it funny and told him to be seated, right across from her on that sofa over there where she could see him, while she called Reception downstairs to verify that he had even come in that way--the only legitimate way.

Reception was busy with a flood of calls, so the wait expanded to a quarter hour, enough for him to "break the ice" with Miss Bombshell, and by means of his well-developed Irish wit and considerable genuine charm, thaw her somewhat. The delay also gave him ample opportunity to measure her with his practiced eye when an errand to the xerox machine in the adjoining room pulled her out from behind her desk. She walked right by him and he almost whistled out loud. On a scale of one to ten, he had told himself, you're at least a nine; knock off fifteen pounds, babe, and you're on the cover of *Playboy*.

The interview with Mr. Big, though superficially cordial, did not go well. Despite his best attorney-doing-cross-examination style, all he got was an adroit mix of "classified," or "don't really know," or "We sold the program to E-Systems," or other dead ends. *Damn!* he had thought, *there must be something here, this guy is so eager to tell me nothing.* Save for getting the numbers of some patents, the interview was about as revealing as a turtle shell. But on the way out, he stopped by Ms. Bombshell's desk and applied the charm again. She yielded to it this time and agreed to let him call her.

So, over the ensuing months he had been able to salvage something out of that dead-end interview, namely, a growing romance with Vanni, as Marilee Van Niesen preferred to be called. He had been enormously relieved that she was not just another dumb blonde, of which he'd met plenty, the kind whose sound-bite conversation never gets beyond mindless drivel and whose notion of a lasting relationship is a weekend at a ski resort. Once he passes the Big Three-O, a guy's gotta start looking for someone who could maybe be his *wife* and even a *mother*. He was excited to discover that she had a bouncy personality but also a serious and even deep side; that she was well read for a 28-year-old in the television age; that she too was getting tired of the "singles scene," because both the process and the people were superficial; that she was a good conversationalist; and best of all, that she seemed intrigued by an investigative reporter/writer who genuinely wanted to dig down to the Truth.

All went smoothly until Vanni "got religion," as he put it. How it happened, he didn't know; maybe it was her grandmother, maybe it was some sort of airborne virus. About five months back she just started going to Bible Study and talking heavy stuff about "spiritual meaning in life." Worse still, she must have swallowed an overdose of cant about the "End Times," because she started turning their dinner table talk to speculation about apocalyptic events. He figured he'd have to endure her quirks, just as she would have to live with him flying radio-controlled model airplanes, if--when--they got married. Small price to pay, he figured, to win a woman who's bright and virtuous and, even if a bit *zaftig*, could pass for a model. But he didn't *like* the price, if only because he was too much the skeptic to believe in prophecy, whether by Nostradamus or John the Evangelist.

He figured he had to go with her to those study classes, lest she meet some stud there who looks like Samson and starts whispering quotes from the Letter to the Romans, or something, into her ear. Granted Vanni's susceptible condition, Samson with a halo over his head might beat out James Bond with a bottle of *Pete's Wicked*. He pondered giving her more boxes of chocolates; maybe the imaginary Samson wouldn't make a pass at a babe *thirty* pounds too heavy. But he rejected that ploy, since the girl was now into aerobics, had lost most of the surplus fifteen, and now could gobble down a ton of Lady Godivas and still sweat them all off by noon. She was actually evolving from a "nine" to a "ten"--and his amorous feelings were keeping pace--though he had not tried to bed her down--and she had to go toss a monkey wrench into it with this "personal relationship with Jesus" stuff that she babbled about. She had started hinting that Mister Wonderful, whoever he would be, needed the same relationship with Jesus. And Pat wasn't ready for that, not by a long shot.

So that was one fly in the ointment. The other fly had come along the same day as he and Vanni met: it was that damn turtle interview, in which BDR's Mr. Big gave him the run-around, a bunch of gobbledygook about the HAARP project being just a small Airforce experiment upgrading over-the-horizon radar. He hadn't let on that he already knew, both from surfing the Internet and from a private source, that something sneaky--and maybe dangerous--was going on out there. The problem was how to figure it out without getting zapped.

Then other assignments had come up and forced him to put the HAARP investigation on the back burner. By now too many months had rushed by. He knew he had to find a shortcut to get it back on track...He took another swig of ale and watched, absently, the landing lights of a nearby 727 descending at a rapid diagonal left to right in front of him, toward Reagan National Airport. His mind turned to the "private source," an old friend from his grad school days, when they traded friendly jabs in a club he and a few of their buddies had created, "The Honest Debate Society"...Father Michael Kanek. Probably gotta call him again.

He had liked the priest, because Kanek never pushed his faith on anyone and the guy did make a lot of sense. The problem for Pat Greene, he had admitted to himself, was not the theory of Christianity--if you're going to believe in *any* God, he had decided, the Christian one was the only one that made any sense. Hell, this Jesus person was so...*concrete*. Here's a fellow, he had come to realize, who goes around doing *practical* things like changing whole jugs of water into wine...feeding 5,000 hungry men...walking on water...curing people with leprosy...giving sight to the blind...raising a man from the dead and then *predicting* and actually *doing* it for *Himself!*

How could anyone make that stuff up? Those Apostle guys were just not that bright. And besides, they all had been willing to *die* for their testimony, which most people living in the same city as their killers had ample ways to check out. If the stories were a bunch of lies, everybody would know it, and most of the disciples would have cracked under torture within a couple days--they wouldn't have conquered the whole damn Roman Empire in a few hundred years.

No, Patty me boy, he had admitted to himself after one long discussion with Father Kanek and other Honest Debate Society members, one an atheist, another a devout Catholic, a third--a pretty blonde like Vanni, he recalled--also a Scripture-quoting Evangelical, *the reason you don't want to accept Jesus is that you don't want the rules He imposes.*

Anyhow, all that's not the point right now. He got up, grabbed the now empty beer mug, and walked from the balcony back into the living room. Gotta call Kanek, he decided; maybe a priest with a Ph.D. in electrical engineering, a guy who did his dissertation on Modern Applications of Tesla Electrical Theory, or some such rarified topic, could give him the full scoop on this HAARP thing. Either that, or I gotta break into E-Systems at night. Now *that's* an assignment for the real James Bond!

He rummaged in his personal phone list and managed to come up with Father Kanek's phone number at the University. When he called he was told the Father had just left for a visit at the University of Stuebenville, but that the switchboard would take a message, and that the Father did call in frequently for messages. So he left a request that Father Kanek call him immediately at his home.

Then he dialed Vanni. He figured he had to keep daily track of the girl, or he'd lose her; but he had to recapture the initiative--get *her* to come to some meetings where *he* decided the topics and who participated, so that she couldn't drag him into a circle of people that made him uncomfortable. Maybe he should try to re-assemble The Honest Debate Society.

"She's out?" *Damn!* "Joanie, you're her roommate. Got any idea where she is?" Joanie wasn't sure, but she remembered Vanni saying something about..."A Christian book store?" *Double damn!* "Well, would you please ask her to call me when she gets in?...No, that's o.k. I'll be up late."

Ah, an exciting Saturday evening in Washington, D.C., he mused: typing a chapter in a book...waiting for phone calls from a priest and a Bible-crazed woman...and drinking ale alone. He scowled at his empty glass and walked over to the refrigerator for a refill. *Triple damn!*--no *Pete's Wicked* left!

(4)

Dolores Montalvo, now calling herself Desiree Morgan, was back in the United States, hair dyed blonde. She rented an apartment in Arlington, across the Potomac from Georgetown and only ten minutes from the White House. Within two weeks she had been hired onto the White House staff, with the title of Deputy Assistant for

International Liaison. She was surprised at the lax security in the headquarters of what was supposedly the world's only "real superpower"; but she did not question whether her ready access was the work of the Chairman's agents, whom in any event she did not know, or the fumbling incompetence of the amateurs who managed the screening process.

Whatever it was, no one checked her concocted resume, which had enough subtle inconsistencies to raise eyebrows and perhaps fears about her reliability. Anyone shrewd enough to read between the lines and add information easily available from Interpol would have uncovered the true identity of the fictitious Desiree Morgan: the multi-lingual Dolores Montalvo, beautiful, intelligent, avaricious, amoral, a person with plenty of cash purchasing power but no apparent means of support--a woman who would compromise any cause or person, especially handsome men, for the right price. Even in ethically rootless Washington, she was not the type to bring to the inner councils.

A month after joining the White House staff, long enough to learn the layout of much of the building, she received a phone call from the Chairman. He spoke quickly in French, only two sentences, partly a question: "This is the Microchip Division of Securite Internationale Ltd--is this Pentagon Research and Development?" to which she responded, also in French and just as quickly, as she had been instructed, "I'm sorry, you must have the wrong number; I do not have that number," and hung up.

The Secret Service recorders, if they were on, would note nothing incriminating. Besides, how many Americans can understand fast-paced French?

It was time. The active phase of her assignment had begun. The target was the President of the United States.

* * * * * * * * * * *

CHAPTER II

(1)

He found the letter in a pile of mail in his box. Someone at the Jesuit House of Studies outside London had mailed it. He opened it to find, to his surprise, a second envelope, slightly smaller. The return address was simply, "Vatican City, Italy." The envelope was sealed in wax. The wax bore the imprint of the Papal Seal. The Pope's ring.

Heart pounding, he opened it carefully. Written in Latin, the letter was short, to the point, and not hard to translate.

Dear Father Kanek:

When I am in the U.S. in a few weeks, please meet with me personally at the Franciscan Priory at the University in Stuebenville, Ohio. Do not mention this request to anyone except the Father Superior, who will give you a private room and arrange a place for us to meet.

In Jesu,
John Paul II

(2)

The Priory, a large two-story building shaped like a cross, had three main wings extending toward the north, west, and south; the shorter wing, in which the Chapel was situated, extended east.

It was 11:00 p.m., the night before the Pope's scheduled visit. After the last Franciscan community prayers, the Chapel was empty, darkened except for small dim yellow night lights at the rear and side exit doors--and the flickering candle in a red glass holder near the Altar. Actually, the Chapel was not entirely empty: a lone Person waited patiently at the center of the altar.

The rear door swung open and a black-robed figure walked slowly into the gloom and quietly up the center aisle, his lips moving wordlessly.

He did not *see* the Person a short distance ahead; but he knew He was there and, as he reached the first pew at the front end of the main aisle, he genuflected slowly. "We adore Thee, O Christ, and we bless

Thee," he whispered reverently, "because by Thy cross Thou hast redeemed the world."

After a moment, he rose and slid into the pew on his left. He did not know what the Lord had in store for him, but long ago he had decided to do His will, wherever it led. He had hoped to be a simple parish priest and just preach the Gospel to husbands and wives and teach catechism to children and be an instrument of grace for many souls. But his intellectual gifts had motivated his superiors to assign him to Georgetown University, with the directive to teach science and conduct research and writing in the area of electrical phenomena, the subject of his Ph.D. dissertation and subsequent graduate studies at MIT. He recalled that in that environment he had hoped to preach the Gospel to faculty and students. Indeed, he had become part of a serious graduate-student discussion group, "The Honest Debate Society," where he and other a few others interested in genuine intellectual discussions, not just the reciting of "politically correct" slogans, had met monthly to discuss--with civility--serious issues. But that was well over a decade ago.

He forced his mind to dismiss both reverie about the past and speculation about the twists and turns of one's life, and to turn to the prayerful task at hand. He knew the Pope did not spend his time on trivia and that he, Father Michael Kanek, had been singled out for some kind of important assignment.

For an hour he prayed, first the Rosary, then the remaining time in adoration, then thanksgiving, then satisfaction, and finally petition. Prayer was like any other human activity, he had discovered; humanly speaking, you do better if you practice specific proven techniques, just as in playing golf or piano. There was a major difference, of course--the need for God's guidance and help--but there was a similarity to sports or music there too, in that you learned under the guidance of a coach or teacher. Still, the parallel was not exact, because in prayer the Holy Spirit worked *through* you and the "results" were entirely in the hands of God.

When he turned to the easiest form of prayer, petition, he simply pictured in his mind Jesus standing before him--*as in actual fact He was*--and asked...not only for light, for courage, but as he had begun more and more often in recent months, for his parents, for his brother in the FBI, and now for the Holy Father himself. He had a premonition that tomorrow would change his life forever.

As with every other serious hunch that came to Michael Kanek in his adult life during prayer, this one would be accurate too.

* * * * * * * * * * *

The Franciscan Superior of this small community, Father Sean O'Bannon, was a portly man with a ready smile and genuine concern for every person he met. Like Michael Kanek, he was a "late vocation": he had done well at Yale Law School years earlier and practiced law for a time in New York; but he'd grown weary of the materialism pervasive in big city dog-eat-dog legal practice. "*Billablehoursuberalles*," he had begun to call it, coining a horrible neologism with more than a grain of truth in it.

So he had begun to question his life's purpose and goals and, after considerable soul searching, yielded finally, as he said, to the "Hound of Heaven." To shrive himself of his billable- hours sins, he embraced Franciscan poverty, harboring the hope--forlorn, as it turned out--of a life working with the poor, perhaps including, as he jestfully remarked more than once, some people who were not poor until his law firm filed suit against them.

But, much like Father Kanek, who yearned to be a parish curate and ended in the science department of a big university, Father O'Bannon had professional credentials that fairly shouted to be used. So it was that he rose through a flurry of minor assignments and after six years in the priesthood, at age 45, found himself in this small town in northeastern Ohio, the Prior of the monks' Franciscan Community, which provided many of the teachers at the local college which it ran.

He had received a terse message from a Papal aide, saying that His Holiness wished to meet with a priest who would identify himself and that His Holiness desired one hour of private consultation with him.

The two had met the day before, minutes after the visiting priest arrived. As was the custom among the monks, when an important visitor appeared, they dispensed with dinner time public reading of a spiritual book and permitted casual conversation, so that the visitor could sit at the head table with Father Superior and share news of his travels in the outside world. The two priests were good conversationalists, and despite the distracting excitement that each felt about the Pope's mysterious request, they hit it off well, trading "old war stories" about life in their secular careers and, later, in the seminary.

Now they walked down one wing to the door of what in a hotel would be the Presidential Suite. This being a Franciscan monastery, the luxury of a Hilton or Hyatt was absent; but the Pope's temporary quarters did have two rooms, unlike the average monk's. The inner was a standard bedroom, but carpeted, a concession to creature comforts expected by visitors. It was exactly like a small hotel room, the only additions being a *prie-dieu* facing a large Cross on the wall, and a Douay-Rheims, not Gideon, Bible. The outer room, where the meeting would take place, had chairs and sofa much like a large family room in any affluent suburban home.

They reached the Pope's temporary quarters and Father O'Bannon knocked once. A deep pleasant voice bade them enter. The monk opened the door, bowed slightly to the large figure in white standing across the room in front of a wide desk, and said, "Your Holiness, this is Father Kanek--as you requested."

"Come in, Father Kanek," the Pope said warmly, in slightly accented English. "Thank you, Father O'Bannon," he added, and the monk bowed slightly again, and without a word quietly closed the door and left.

"Father Kanek," the Pope repeated to the priest, who remained motionless, mentally almost paralyzed, just inside the door, "do come in." Obediently, the priest walked slowly forward, his mind a rush of feelings and thoughts. *I'm meeting the greatest man of this Century,* he thought. *And he's probably a Saint as well.* He started to go down on one knee in front of the Pope to kiss his ring, but John Paul took his hand in a strong grip and pulled him back to his feet.

"Your Holiness," he said, "this is such an honor. I am--well, I am not worthy--"

"My son," interrupted the other with a smile, "we can dispense with your expressions of humility, which I know are genuine. Let us walk outside, and I will explain..." He gestured toward the patio just beyond two french doors behind the desk. Father Kanek exited behind him and they stepped down two wide steps and onto the patio; he was still in awe at the moment but relieved at the Pontiff's gentle warmth.

"What languages do you know?" the Pope asked as they ambled slowly along a hedged garden path. It was a surprising question, but this Pontiff, so traditional in his teaching, had been spectacularly unconventional in his pastoral activity.

"Besides English...well...Latin, Spanish--and my grandmother taught my brother and me quite a bit of Polish."

"Fine. As we talk, I will shift more than once from one language to another," said the Pope. "Respond in whatever language I use.

"There is a reason for these shifts," he continued in Polish. "It is possible that there are remote listening devices, ones that the good Franciscans have no knowledge of." He gestured toward the woods seventy-five yards away. "If there are, we'll make them work to decipher what we're saying."

"Holy Father, this--this is all very confusing," Kanek responded in Polish, wanting to enter the conversation but unable to think of anything sensible to say.

"Yes, it is," said the Pope, continuing in Polish. "But I can explain quickly. There are certain people in Rome--some are even Bishops--who want me removed from the Papacy. There have been attempts on my life that have failed. They may try once more. They may succeed, but they could fail again. If they do, then, in frustration, they will try to force me to resign and probably couple their effort with a forged letter of resignation. The Lord does not want me to resign, but they may orchestrate an apparent resignation."

These blunt predictions shook Father Kanek badly. He knew that the "progressive wing" of the Catholic Church hated John Paul's firm commitment to traditional teaching--their attitude was common knowledge. He had heard it rumored that certain secret societies had infiltrated some seminaries and their agents actually had worked their way through to Ordination and, in due time, a few might have advanced to become Bishops. He was well aware of the cryptic comments of recent Popes since Vatican II, to the effect that "We have opened the windows to the Church--and the smoke of Satan has come in!"

But *this* prediction was something far more sinister. If the Pope were correct, it would mean a concerted conspiratorial effort to subvert the Church--coupled forgery and kidnapping--all with the collaboration of--and perhaps instigated by--men who are, supposedly, ordained priests of God and even Princes of the Church!

"Holy Father," he began, "May I ask how you know this? Could it be that this is more conjecture than fact?" He feared he might be overstepping himself to doubt the Pope's analysis; after all, the man was brilliant, and during the breakdown of Communism he had shown himself a master of geopolitical intrigue. Indeed, Bernstein and Politi's book, *His Holiness: John Paul II and the Hidden History of Our Time,* which he had read some months before, made a powerful case that the Pope had been one *cause* of Communism's collapse. So the opinions of a man of such acumen deserved great respect. But at the same time, perhaps old age was blurring the Pope's perceptions somewhat.

"A fair question, my son," said John Paul, choosing to take no offense at the priest's inquiry. Continuing, now in Spanish, as they turned a corner along the path between the hedges, he said: "The truth of my answer you will have to take on faith. Of course, humanly speaking, I pay close attention to men's words and especially to their actions and I make it a point to notice little coincidences. After awhile, I became suspicious of certain Princes of the Church who seem to have their own agendas. But I do not rest my conclusion on my own grasp of sometimes ambiguous events; rather, I will tell you, with all solemnity, I know *some*--not all--of the events to come because *Jesus Christ has appeared to me and told me!"*

Again Father Kanek found himself groping for anything sensible to say. He felt like an amateur swimmer in deep water far from shore. Conversationally he determined to try to stay afloat, while his mind groped for something intelligent to say. He clutched at one of the Pope's statements.

"Why did they fail in their past assassination attempts?"

The Pope smiled, though gravely. "Because, my Son, enough prayers of the remnant Faithful have enabled Our Lady to win from God some additional time for me, despite my enemies' plans--and she has sent Michael the Archangel to assist my personal Guardian Angel." He lowered his voice. "It is very humbling..."

Then, again shifting languages, the Pope added in English, "A month ago one of the two top assassins in Europe--you Americans call him a 'hit man'--managed to elude the Swiss Guard and make his way to the door of my personal quarters. He could have finally broken through the door and shot me while I slept, and most assuredly that was his intent. But--Michael appeared before him, stated just one sentence--'You have gone too far!'--and struck him across the forehead with his sword, killing the man instantly. I know this happened," he added, sensing the priest's doubt, "because God showed me the whole event in a dream that very night, even as it took place." He paused, then spoke in a low, almost childlike voice, "God is so kind--He even removed all fear, so that I was rested when I awoke.

"But the *proof*, my son," he added in a firmer tone, "is this: when I opened the door to my room that morning, lying there dead on the hallway floor was the armed assassin. The only mark on his body...was a welt, like a burn, on his forehead. The police and their doctors have no idea what killed the man. I do know."

"I believe you, Holy Father," Kanek blurted, feeling foolish because the logical part of his mind told him it did not matter whether *he* believed the Pope or not.

"Yes, you do, and that is good." The Pope had moved into Polish again. "But the *lesson* in all these events is what prompted our meeting. The lesson is that evil is intensifying, for the Mystery of Iniquity must have its Hour. There is not much time left before the Era of Mercy will close. A terrible time is coming, a mix of the Hour of Evil and the Era of Justice. Many mystics have predicted it: 'the Chastisement,' they call it. And when that Hour comes--it will be soon--we must have the Faithful prepared."

They rounded another corner and approached the patio. "I am going to ask you to cooperate with Our Lord, Father Kanek, in two matters. As when Jesus asked His apostles to follow Him, He did not force their wills--and neither will I. I will not command you under obedience, but I will *ask* you to accept the assignments I will offer you."

"Of course, Holy Father," Father Kanek stated, quickly and sincerely, also in Polish. "I do."

"But my son," said the Pope, changing to Spanish, "I appreciate your eagerness, but first you must hear the requests, and *then* you may accept or decline." They were silent for a time, mounting the stone steps to the brick patio, and then walking slowly back into the room. Then the Pope resumed.

"My son, I have written an Apostolic Letter," the Pope said, pulling an envelope from his pocket, "to the Universal Church. At the time I am deposed, as I believe is likely, and before the College of Cardinals elects a new Pope--or a man who will *appear* to be Pope but will actually be an imposter--you are to publish this letter in as many magazines and newspapers as will accept it, and also publish it as a small pamphlet and distribute it through the network of Remnant church communities forming even now. This letter is my statement to the world, my last effort to teach them before the Warning and the Great Chastisement hit." He handed the envelope to Father Kanek. "Will you undertake this assignment?"

"Of course, of course Holy Father," said Kanek.

"Good. Second," continued the Pope, this time in Latin, "I have decided to ordain you as a Bishop, keeping the fact *in pectore meo*. And," he added immediately, not permitting any response until his entire purpose was laid out, "if you accept, I will do it *now*, while we are alone in this room. You are aware, of course, that the essence of this Ordination is simply that a Bishop pray to the Holy Spirit and lay hands upon the ordinand--as many of our brothers did behind the Iron Curtain during this terrible century."

As John Paul expected, his short comments had left the younger man utterly flabbergasted. He knew he had to give Father Kanek a moment to digest it all. So he continued, in English, "In my travels, Father Kanek, during the past five years I have been quietly ordaining priests such as yourself as Bishops, but keeping that fact *in pectore*. I always give them a copy of the Apostolic Letter I have given you--with the same instruction. My intent is to ordain twelve. You are the eleventh. I hope to finish before the Warning and the Great Chastisement."

"Holy Father, I--well, I--of course, I accept. I would not be worthy of the priesthood if I were to resist the desire of the Pope himself. But I feel I must tell you that I know at least half a dozen other priests who would be a better choice."

"Possibly," said John Paul, smiling slightly. "But I am sure you would agree, Father, that the decision should be between the Holy Spirit and myself." Without waiting for an answer, for there could be none, the Pope walked quickly to a table near the door to his bedroom, picked up a long thin piece of cloth, a *stole*, placed it over his shoulders and strode back to Father Kanek a few paces away. "The short form of Ordination of a Bishop," he stated, "begins with a prayer to the Holy Spirit."

He stood before the priest and closed his eyes. In prayerful recollection he paused as if in deep thought, then began in Latin, *"Veni, Sancte Spiritu, reple tuorum corda fidelium, et tui amoris in eis ignem accende..."* and continued invoking the Third Person of the Trinity. Then he opened his eyes, raised his hands,, and placed them upon the forehead of Father Kanek, who stood silent, awestruck. "By the power of Jesus Christ vested in me as Bishop of Rome, I ordain you Bishop in the Holy Roman Catholic Church, in the line of Apostolic Succession, going back through my predecessors even to the Apostles and Saint Peter himself...in the name of the Father, and the Son, and the Holy Spirit. Amen.

"Now, my son--my fellow Bishop," he added, a slight tear in his eye and his voice quivering, "I will impart my Papal Blessing and our meeting is over."

As the Pope raised both his hands, and said, *"Benedictio Dei omnipotentis, Patris, et Filii, et Spiritu Sancti, descendat super te, et maneat..."* a brilliant light appeared behind him, brightening the entire room. Sensing its source, the Pope turned. He and the now Bishop Kanek beheld the figure of a being like a man, nearly seven feet tall, dressed as a Roman gladiator. *The source of the light was this being's body: it appeared just as solid as any other object in the room, but made of a material not found on earth.* The man-like being had light blonde hair and strong square-jawed features. From his belt hung a long sword.

"Do not be afraid," he told them, "I am Michael the Archangel. I have come to strengthen you."

Father Kanek, almost numb with awe, was amazed that John Paul took control of the situation. "The Scripture says," the Pope stated firmly, "that we should 'test the spirits'--so I ask you, Michael, to join me in a confession of faith. Let us recite together the Apostles' Creed."

"With great joy," replied the apparition. And the Pope summarized the Creed, affirming his belief in God, the Father Almighty...in Jesus Christ, the only Son of God, who was conceived by the Holy Spirit, born of the Virgin Mary, and was crucified, and so on. Joining John Paul, Michael recited the Pope's paraphrase *simultaneously* and, when the two bishops paused and genuflected to honor the crucifixion, Michael did as well. The Pope added that every knee should bend in Heaven, on earth, and under the earth to the name of Jesus Christ, and then ended with the Glory Be to the Father. Michael spoke, simultaneously, every word. *No demon would say those words,* thought Father Kanek. John Paul was satisfied that the apparition was from God.

"Your Holiness and Your Eminence," Michael resumed, in a tone of utmost respect, "I have been sent to strengthen you." He stepped closer to them, reached his right hand out, with his thumb made the sign of the cross on the forehead of each, then placed one large hand on the upper forehead of each man, looked up as if to see through the ceiling and roof of the building to a world beyond, and said, "In the power given me by God, I bless each of you with strength and courage, in Jesus' holy Name."

At that instant a river of warmth coursed through the bodies of both men. They felt energy, power, like the rush of oxygen an Olympic runner feels after an intense workout.

"You are now each seven years younger," said Michael. And disappeared.

* * * * * * * * * * * *

CHAPTER III

(1)

The President sat at his desk watching the 11:00 News and playing solitaire. There was a knock at the door.

"Come in," he said absently, staring at the television images, snippets of that week's criminal trials. The door opened and a silhouette of a woman stepped through the shadows and quickly closed the door. The glow of his desk lamp did not reach her face and its glare on the playing cards made it hard to see her clearly.

"Who are you?" the President asked, reaching for the button under the desk top. Press it once, the recorder is activated; twice, and the Secret Service is alerted. He could see only a tall female. He felt a twinge of fear. He was about to press the button twice.

"The Chairman of the Council of Europe sent me," she said softly. "My name is Dolores Montalvo. I am the aide the Chairman mentioned to you in a phone call some weeks ago." She noted his right hand was concealed by the desk top. "No need to call for Security, Mr. President. I am not armed." The statement was not entirely true.

He smiled, relaxed, brought both hands together and placed them palms down atop the playing cards spread out on the desk. "Well, come all the way in." She moved forward tentatively, as if uncertain. The door she had entered was in the shadows; now as she slowly moved into the center of the room, the circle of light from the desk lamp illumined her high heeled shoes, shapely legs, a black skirt cut two inches above the knee, a wide gold belt with large black and gold buckle, black long-sleeved blouse with white lapels and three white buttons, and long blonde hair framing her lightly tanned face. Dressed fashionably, except she was not wearing stockings, he noted. No matter, she was stunning. He scanned her up and down appreciatively.

No gun, he thought--*but plenty of charm.* He did not see, because it was hidden behind the belt buckle, a slim pouch of soft leather that hooked onto her belt, slipped discreetly behind her waistband. Nor did he notice, under the sleeve of her right arm, a slight cigar-sized bulge, secured by two rubber bands, one at the wrist and the other a few inches up her forearm.

"Mr. President," she said, pausing a few feet in front of his desk, "the Chairman wishes me to modify the main point of his offer. It is more lucrative than he has made to any other head of state."

"Why is that...?" he asked, trying to maintain his composure as he drank in the visual wine of her beauty, and, on the reflective level of his being, wondered hungrily about the offer.

The incongruity of the situation was utterly lost on him. Most Presidents would have insisted that any emissary come by appointment during the day and state her message in the presence of a trusted assistant--just to cover himself. But his passions were stirring and he relished the thought of what he might do with the control he believed he had: push the button and in two minutes she's in handcuffs, and, if he wanted, held *incommunicado* indefinitely. A strong negotiating point, he felt, arrogantly dismissing the possibility that he could be in danger.

For this President had successfully skirted along the edge of impropriety so often that he had come to believe he lived a charmed life. Then too, his political intuition told him that what she was leading up to should not be heard by anyone else. If there are no witnesses, then one need not deal with them later. As for being alone with her, well, he had always been able to charm women, and he was supremely confident he could handle this one.

Finally he remembered good manners and momentarily wrenched his eyes away from her. "Why don't you sit down?" He gestured toward an easy chair facing the desk a few steps to his right. She walked to it, sat down, crossed her legs and leaned back slightly, seeming not to notice that sitting caused her skirt to ride higher up her thigh. He did notice.

"The Chairman has already offered you *one* of the Ten Directorates to be set up," she began. "Now he is willing to refine the offer: *you* may choose *three* Directorates, as long as they are contiguous. But you must keep to the timetable."

His mouth dropped open slightly. He was dumbstruck for a moment. This was generous indeed. But she went on.

"I see by your expression that you realize the power you will have in the New World Order. You will be like a king. But in return, you must make a firm *irrevocable* commitment."

"Of course," he said, smiling. "You have it."

"That is too vague," she said firmly. "I have specific language you must agree to. And there is something you must do. Then, when we have completed business," she added suggestively, "there will be time for other things." As she spoke, she deftly retrieved a folded piece of paper from behind her belt buckle, leaned forward to hand it to him, and watched his expression intently as he read:

Agreement

"I, _____, do solemnly swear allegiance to the Chairman of the Council of Europe above any other claim by any person, country, or God."

_____

Signature

The lower part of the page contained an equally terse statement:

"In return for the foregoing commitment, I, Chairman of the Council of Europe, do solemnly promise the Signatory above that I will designate him as Director over one of the Ten Directorates to be established."

It was signed by the Chairman of the Council. After the moment it took him to read this cryptic contract, Dolores quickly stated: "This is the same form of Agreement he will be using with the other Directors."

"I have no problem with this," said the President, "as long as we agree that it will not be made public until *after* the entire Plan is implemented, and--" he realized that the Chairman could not give *all* the Directors the choice, since two could desire the same region--"you also agree that I am the first to choose Directorates."

"Of course. The United States is the most important country, so that goes without saying," she responded. But she felt he was too quick to accept, and she remembered to keep to the script, so she reiterated the main point in a different way. "Mr. President, when you sign, there is no turning back. You will have abjured your past, any competing claim for your loyalty, whether by country or even God Himself--if there is one." She had given him an unambiguous choice.

She saw a trace of fear cross his face, so she continued, "Needless to say, the past is irrelevant, whereas the future--whether your years as a virtual king--or the next hour with me--will be times of great power--and pleasure.

"Of course, you are free not to sign, but you must also fully understand," she said firmly, "that if you feel you cannot sign, we will get someone else. I cannot say what the Chairman will do, but I do know he has information you would prefer to keep private. If that information becomes public, you would be forced from office. Unlike your critics in the United States, the Chairman is not a person you can fool..."

Their eyes locked for a few seconds. She chose to remain silent: let him blink first. After a few moments, he picked up a pen, inserted his name in the blank, scratched out the word *one,* wrote above it *three,* put his initials in the margin to the right of the change...and signed.

"Good," she said, maintaining her outward calm, though her heart raced. "Now, there is one other thing." She retrieved a small cylinder from the same pouch as had produced the paper. She pulled on both ends and it opened, revealing a small glass tube not unlike a thermometer, but pointed at one end. "You have been briefed, I believe, on the experiments with the microchip?"

"I am aware of them," he answered, not sure where she was going.

"Fine," she said, sliding forward to the edge of the chair, a movement which pulled her skirt higher. "Well, as a strong proponent of a National Identity Card, you must recognize the superiority of the Chip. Every one of the Chairman's followers will be taking this Chip under the skin in his right hand--it is a sign of loyalty and recognition.

"You cannot plausibly tell your countrymen to accept the Chip unless *you* show them leadership. So I want you to take this Chip. As you probably realize, this"--she held up the thermometer-like-device--"is a hypodermic." She showed him the pointed end. "The chip has been micro-engineered. It is like a thread. When I inject this under your skin, there will be no more pain than when a nurse draws blood. Put out your hand." She stood up and leaned over the desk.

"Now, Dolores," he said, raising his hands palms out, as if to push her away, "I--ah--I'm, uh, not sure I want that just right now."

She leaned closer. Her face was within two feet of his. He felt the magnetism of her beauty and, despite his emotion, realized she had him trapped. By signing the Agreement with the Chairman he had lost any way out. She made that point immediately.

"Mr. President, a moment ago you signed a contract with the Chairman of the Council of Europe, the most powerful man in the world." She salted her words with a slight touch of contrived anger.

"Now it is *he*--not just myself--asking you to carry out his wishes. If you renege on this first request, I will be forced to tell him that you are not dependable. The Chairman will not give you a second chance; he will get someone else." *Pull the lure away,* she thought, *and you learn how hungry the fish really is.*

"What is in that thing?" he asked, pointing to the hypodermic. "What does it do, once it's inside you?" He was trying to buy a bit of time, while his mind raced to find some method to have it both ways.

"What's in it? Beyond the fact that it's a mini computer chip, I'm sure I don't know," she said truthfully. She did not know *what* was in it; but she did know what it would *do*. She chose to answer only half of his question. "Probably the same things the 'SmartCard' contains--you know, personal information like medical records--but, Mr. President," she returned to the issue, "it *doesn't really matter.* You have told Americans they need a National Identity Card; this is an advanced form of such a card. You know the Plan is to persuade everybody to take the SmartCard and then move them on to the Chip. Do you think *you* should be exempt from the rules you make for others...?"

Mentally he answered Yes, as his conduct during his life showed; but he would be embarrassed to state the fact, and he noted the anger in her voice. He had interpreted her demeanor to be soft-core seduction, or at least a libertine display of feminine charms designed to dazzle him; and he admitted she was successful. But the emotion of anger would not be a good prelude to getting her to cooperate in the adjoining room once the "business" side of the meeting was finished. He had to find a way to calm her down.

"Do *you* have this Chip implant?" he asked.

"Not yet. But when the Chairman says it is time, I will take it. But," again with her unassailable logic, "what *I* do is irrelevant. It is *you* who have signed a contract, *you* who expect the Chairman to make you de facto King of thirty percent *of the whole world*--and yet you will not carry through with his first request!" Her dark eyes flashed as she thrust the hypodermic back into its tube and started to close it.

A voice in his head seemed to paraphrase her threat, *If you refuse, you will never get another chance to rule--and the Chairman might reveal the skeletons in your closet. You could even be impeached.* Having lost spiritual discernment years earlier, he did not recognize the voice of a devil.

"Wait! all right. You are correct, of course. Go ahead," he said, "do it quickly." He extended his arm and placed the hand on the desk.

She picked up a decanter of brandy from a shelf behind her chair, spilled a couple ounces onto some tissue, rubbed the top of his hand as if to sterilize it, dosed the needle the same way, and skillfully injected it. He looked away, across the room, and winced as the needle entered. She compressed the plunger slowly, then carefully withdrew the needle, wiped it with the tissue, blotted a drop of blood from the top of his hand, quickly replaced the instrument in its container, and put the container into her belt-level pouch. In less than a minute, he had taken the Chip. *The play is over, Mr. President,* she thought triumphantly. *Now I write the script for the sequel.*

He stood up, angry that a woman had beaten him in one contest, determined that he would be victor in the next. It would be a pleasure to put this sassy female in her proper place. "Business is done. It's time for other things. Go into that room," he pointed to a side door that opened to a bedroom, "and take off your clothes! Or, better yet, start right here!"

"Mr. President!" she exclaimed, pretending to act surprised. "That is--not proper. I will not!" *Suddenly the seductress is a nun!* he thought. He savored her seeming discomfort as his passions mounted.

"Then perhaps I need to call Security," he said menacingly. "You could have an 'accident' on the way to the airport, and the Chairman could just find himself some other secret agent!"

"No--please," she answered in a husky voice. She paused a few seconds, as if pondering her options, and kept a worried look on her face. She sensed that he was distracted enough by his mounting excitement not to notice what she was about to do. So, with a sigh, as if trapped, she spoke slightly above a whisper: "I will do what you say."

She bent her head and shoulders forward slightly, put both hands on her belt buckle, and loosened it, as if to start removing her skirt. At the same time, with a practiced move he did not detect, her left hand reached under her right wrist, grasped the tube attached to her forearm, and pulled it just a few inches forward into the palm of her right hand. The next moment, while her left hand seemed to struggle with a recalcitrant zipper, she raised the right slightly and pointed it toward him. She aimed at his right hand, only a few feet from hers, and pressed a button on the device. The thing was a transmitter, set to emit a low-frequency 116MHz electrical beam.

There was a barely audible hum. Extremely low frequency electricity entered the chip in his hand, spread through his nervous system and disrupted it, like static interference with a radio signal. The effect was dramatic. He heard crackling inside his head. He stiffened up. A blank look crossed his face. The transmission was short-circuiting his body's electrical system. Lethargy, fatigue, sleepiness--all hit him like blows from a heavyweight. He fell back into his chair, strength draining. *I'm having a stroke!* he thought, in panic. He tried to raise his hand to reach for the desk button, but couldn't. She stood impassive, seeming a long distance away. He tried to call to her for help, but he could not speak. He was in a daze, virtually paralyzed. She continued to aim the transmitter at his hand. She held the button down and counted to herself. When her count reached 50 seconds, she released it and returned the device to her sleeve. He was unconscious.

"I've seen cattle resist an electric prod longer than that, Mr. President," she sneered. "You're not very tough." *In his next life, he'll come back as a mouse...and I will be a cat.*

Then her eyes darted to her watch. She did not know how long he would remain unconscious. At least an hour; perhaps all night. She knew that if the Secret Service caught her, the transmitter would be useless against a man who did not have the chip implant. Though athletic, she had no martial arts skill, and in any event the guards would be armed. She could not fight her way out and the chances of charming a guard were nil. If even one saw her, he would apprehend her. And if she were captured, the President's anger that she had rejected him would be boundless. She had to escape.

She fastened her belt, hurried to the door, exited, and closed it softly. In the corridor she moved toward the service stairs as rapidly as silence would permit. Before descending, she took off her high heels and held them in one hand. Anyone using an elevator at this hour would draw attention. She found that even the servants' stairs were carpeted and she made her way to the basement without detection; there she ran barefoot along another long hallway illuminated only by occasional low-wattage night lights in the baseboard. At the end was an office two doors away from her own. It was locked. But the Chairman had provided her with a master key and the lock posed no challenge.

Once inside, she flipped on the overhead light for a moment, glanced around, saw the typical furniture layout, flipped the light back off, and groped her way along the left-hand wall to an empty closet. She slipped in and sat down on the floor, back to the door, with the soles of her feet pressed against the baseboard of the far wall opposite the door.

Gathering her strength, she pushed her feet against the baseboard as hard as she could. There was a *snap!* as if a trigger disengaged, and the floor beneath her tilted down. She slid forward into darkness and fell four feet onto a thick mattress. Once her weight was off the teeter-totter trapdoor floor, it swung back into its horizontal position and locked in place--*gug-lick!*

There are tunnels under Washington, D.C. Many are innocuous enough: small repair corridors for plumbing, heating, electrical, and phone lines and pipes, running like a complex spider-designed maze among the many big buildings. But others, it is rumored, run from the White House, the Congress, the Treasury, and other high-level Government buildings. They were started before the Civil War and expanded greatly by a few ensuing Presidents. It was all secret, of course, since the escape-route purpose would be thwarted if reporters made their existence public. If a utility contractor or construction worker chanced to come across one of their few entrances, he was transferred to another job and frequently received substantial "hush money" for his silence--along with serious threats of harm to himself or his children if he should let slip anything he knew. Money and fear having powerful ability to silence a wagging tongue, this bribery-threat system worked well until the Cold War. At that time greater caution compelled the Secret Service to install the trick floors such as the one she had just used. Even so, the older agents worried that *egress* could enable a determined terrorist to get *ingress*, and they urged that the tunnels be walled up. But sometimes a President could use the tunnels deliberately to get someone *into* the White House, and no President would give the order.

Now Dolores Montalvo groped her way along the tunnel escape route. Every fifty feet there was a light switch exactly five feet up from the floor. These worked like restroom faucets in better hotels: press it down and it turned on for twenty seconds, then went off. She pressed the first one she found. Dim light went on above her. She walked briskly forward. The first light, now behind, turned off. But she'd located the next.

She moved this way under the Executive Office Building, took a right turn, descended a ramp to a lower level, and, she estimated correctly, approached Pennsylvania Avenue. She had memorized a map of this part of the labyrinth and followed the corridor leading out of the next right-hand turn. She stopped to catch her breath at the next light switch and looked up, relieved to see on the wall the logo, *PA Above, H-A Right 300.* She surmised that the Hay-Adams Hotel was three hundred yards to the right. She almost ran that distance.

At a dead end, she found herself under an apparatus that she guessed might work just like the teeter-totter trap door that she had sat on in the basement White House closet. As the twenty-second light behind her went out, she found and pushed the next button. In the gloom she studied the wall before her and the ceiling above. *How do I get this thing to open?* she wondered.

Then she saw it above her, hanging there within reach: a simple cord with wooden handle at its bottom. It looked like the pull-cords attached to drop-stairways that many Americans have in the lofts of their garages. She pulled it gingerly, not wanting to make any noise. The trap door swung down with a slight creak and became a narrow stair-ladder. Grabbing each rung at chest level, she steadied herself as she climbed. At the top was another closet. Once inside, she stepped to the side of the trap-door opening and pulled the contraption up into place. As it clicked into position she paused, caught her breath, wiped the perspiration from her forehead with the back of her hand, and looked toward the light that shone under the crack at the bottom of the closet door. She listened intently. No one speaking, but someone could be there. Slowly she turned the door knob and peered through the thin vertical crack. No one there. It appeared to be a storage room. She put her shoes back on and crossed the room quickly. Again she carefully opened another door. A hallway, sub-basement level. She walked briskly toward the end. An elevator. Take it; if anyone sees you at the lobby level, she thought, they'll think you came down from your room.

The lobby was deserted except for a sleepy-looking clerk behind the registration desk, reading *People* magazine. Controlling her emotions and her pace, she forced herself to walk slowly through the lobby. The clerk looked up and caught only a glimpse of her profile. "Can I call a cab for you, Miss?" he asked, hoping to delay her and perhaps get a better look. She did not answer, but strode through the revolving door and onto the tarmac outside. No doorman at this hour. A black stretch limousine stood fifty feet away, its parking lights on, the driver, dressed like a chauffeur, complete with cigarette in hand, leaning against the left front fender. He saw her coming. "Good evening, Countess," he said pleasantly.

* * * * * * * * * * *

CHAPTER IV

(1)

John DeSanto watched the sky warily. The clouds had gathered suddenly, towering grey-black mountains tumbling on one another like a quickening horizontal avalanche. It wasn't yet tornado season here on the Illinois prairies west of Chicago, but he still felt uneasy. So much weather had been out of the ordinary, even weird, the last few years. He pressed the accelerator harder, hoping the Highway Patrol would grant him some indulgence. The speedometer needle crept up to 75...then 80. He wondered if he should push his luck and go faster.

There had been the "storm of the century" in New York, enough rain to flood a whole state. Then the "blizzard of the century" in the middle Atlantic states. There had been "killer tornadoes" that devastated Arkansas. And the hurricanes, a whole bunch, like Andrew, "the "most destructive in American history" and another--he'd forgotten the name--which was heading *away* from the southern coast and then, the same day Congress voted to fund international abortion programs, *turned around,* like a car making a U-turn, and headed straight for the Florida coast. There it trashed Pensacola.

One summer--was it back in '93?--a cloud bank hovered over Iowa, South Dakota, and part of Minnesota, *for more than a full month,* without moving, as it deluged these states, to the point that the Missouri, and then the Mississippi, rivers burst their banks and caused untold destruction. Hovered there, rained there, for over a month! Where was the Jet Stream? What about the prevailing west-to-east winds?...There had been long periods of heat in some places, unpunctuated by the usual rain. In much of the east it did not rain for two months in the summer of 1997...and crops failed in that region and, for the same reason, in many other places nationwide...while on the west coast, powerful storms repeatedly lashed the shores and the people living along the ocean. In late 1997 a blizzard buried New Mexico and killed of thousands of cattle. Then in the first week of January, 1998, an immense ice storm cut off all power for a month in most of Maine and Quebec for over a million people. "The worst that ever happened," they said. There were all the disasters from *El Nino*.

In the summer of 1998 unremitting 100° heat virtually destroyed farming and ranching in Texas. He remembered all these because his business was flying and unexpected weather changes can become matters of life and death.

Now he glanced behind him out the left side window of his speeding Blazer. The dark cloud mountains were closer. *My God, I'm doing 80 but they're catching me!* He wished he had flown, but Susan had convinced him the week's weather forecast was so stormy that driving was the lesser of two evils. He could see jagged bolts of lightning attack the earth. Behind, an especially large bolt crashed down. He counted. *One and, two and, three and, four and, five and--kkrrraaggbooommmmmm!* the thunder exploded in his ears. Less than a mile away, and deafening.

Suddenly the wind, like a wave of shock troops before the main assault force, smacked his car a glancing blow from behind. A gust maybe 90mph, he thought, gripping the wheel with whitened knuckles. Moments later the sheets of rain hit, a million fire hoses from the sky, crashing into the Blazer from the rear and washing over the top in microseconds. He reacted quickly, struggling to keep calm, as he had so many times when he flew for the Navy. No evasive action possible here. But in an instant he did what he could: switch wipers on high, lights on, punch the four-wheel-drive button...and slow down, quick! As visibility collapsed, he pressed the brakes hard. Cut the speed to where you can see what's ahead. The wind delayed his deceleration, but still he managed to cut the speed down to 60...50...40 miles per hour. Nonetheless, he was driving into a wall of water. Gotta slow down even more, somehow get under a viaduct...

Then, around a slight curve to the left, too late to swerve aside, *a tree!*--a tree lying right across the road! That wind gust knocked down a tree, he remembered thinking, instinctively jabbing his arms up before his face as the Blazer crashed straight into it.

The air bag exploded into his face even as the seat belt strained to hold him back. The equipment did its work; it absorbed much of the impact, sparing his body and head. But for a long minute he sat there motionless. The impact had left him limp, dazed, seemingly suspended outside time. He felt nothing. He couldn't hear the rain.

He could not see with his natural eyes. But then his mind saw it--the vision.

> *Before him was a huge sphere, like a globe atlas fifty feet in diameter. On it he saw rain storms, lightning strikes, fires, blizzards, rapid color changes from blue to red, hurricanes, tidal surges. Next, in place of each of these events, he saw men and women fighting...stealing...involved in repulsive acts...then the people faded, the weather phenomena returned, then stopped still, like a video movie set on "pause." At that moment, a Voice said to him, "My son, you see how the sins of mankind are so grave that they even affect the weather. Tell My people that the physical world and the moral world are all of one piece. If they do not stop their sinning, they will suffer more horrible storms. These are the beginning of punishments."*

Then the vision was gone. He could hear the pounding rain again. Instinctively he reached around the now crumpling airbag, grabbed the ignition key, switched it to Off, then punched the warning flashers on.

He sat there a long minute as sensation seeped back into his body. His neck ached. His face was raw, where the airbag had smashed his hand against it. His ribs hurt, pinched by the cross-belt of the restraint harness. But otherwise he seemed o.k. What about the car?

He turned the wipers back on and peered out the water-drenched windshield. Large branches crosswise on the hood, inches from the windshield. He had not hit the *trunk* of a tree, he realized, but the upper branches; indeed, as he put the four-wheeler into reverse and, like an elephant backing off a pile of boulders, it lumbered down, he realized he had gone slightly off the road onto the right shoulder on that curve and climbed a ways up into the tangled limbs of the downed tree.

Once free of the branches, he backed all the way onto the shoulder, put the gear in Park, retrieved a flashlight from the glove compartment, pulled his jacket hood up over his head, stepped out into the rain, and walked quickly around to the front of the car to assess damage.

One headlight out; mega dent in the bumper; smaller and less serious dents in the hood. He opened it a few inches and inspected the radiator, which with relief he noted was intact. He squatted down and peered at the ground underneath the vehicle; no apparent oil leak. Tires o.k. He listened intently to the motor. Idling fine. He got back into the Blazer, four-wheeled around the tree, and continued, cautiously on the empty highway, on toward Chicago.

Calmer now, he let his mind turn to the vision. *God, what are you trying to tell me?* Stupid question, he thought an instant later. He *knew* what God told him: human sins can *cause* the cosmos itself to react violently. Maybe like this very storm, which had almost killed him. But the real question was, *How am I supposed "tell My--God's--people" about this...?*

The rain remained heavy, but the lightning had let up. He turned the radio on and was able to pick up radio station WGN, despite intermittent static crackling. The news was not good. The storm had actually intensified as it approached the city, until its winds reached hurricane-level with gusts over 100. It had spawned at least a dozen tornadoes. Many homes and garages lost their roofs. Others were crushed by falling trees. Two ten-story buildings on the Near North Side had collapsed. Lightning struck dozens of buildings and set numerous fires. Monsoon-like rains--over three inches during the evening--left the expressways awash in water and wrecked cars. Rescue squads, police, fire trucks--all had to pick their way through pockets of rubble and wreckage. Downed power lines blacked out many neighborhoods. There had been sporadic looting.

He wondered whether they would call this "the storm of the century" or a "disaster of Biblical proportions." And he wondered about the vision.

(2)

W. Carleton Mason, III sat comfortably in a plush corner chair in the lobby of the Hay-Adams Hotel. He was elegant in costly black business suit, white shirt, and red "power" tie. He carried a small attaché case, from which he had extracted a copy of the current *Robb Report*, an upscale magazine/catalogue featuring the costly toys of the rich and famous. He had arrived from New York on the Shuttle on a day when, miraculously, Washington traffic and cabdriver cupidity were in shorter supply than usual; so he had some time to kill before his scheduled dinner appointment with the Undersecretary of Treasury.

As he thumbed the colorful pages he reviewed his situation: forty years old; executive assistant to the president of the country's largest bank; well off, but not wealthy enough; unmarried after his divorce a year ago. Ever since he graduated from Yale back in 1980 he had "reviewed his situation" almost daily; in fact, pondering the gap between where he was in life and where he wanted to be had become almost an obsession.

Very consciously he knew where he wanted to be, or, more precisely, what he wanted to have: wealth, sex, and power. Concretely, he told himself whenever the thought came to mind, which was frequently, he wanted at least fifty million dollars, at least one strikingly beautiful woman, and control over at least a multinational corporation or, better yet, the Governorship of a large State like New York. At least.

Unfortunately, his divorce had temporarily sidetracked all three. He had lost his wife Vicki, her fortune, and her father's power to bankroll him into the Governorship. He frowned, thinking of Vicki's old-fashioned reason for leaving him: only a few instances--well, one per week--of adultery. But he had salvaged something from it all: the position at the bank remained secure.

He could work hard in bursts, and new problems often sparked a rush of creative energy. One such had been his discovery of "the Millennium Bug," the generic computer problem of date-change on December 31, 1999: it was quite possible that at midnight on that date all the bank's computers would "crash" and either freeze up or start spewing out meaningless data, simply because the computer would "think" that January 1, 2000, which it would designate as "00," was the first day of the year 1900.

Quickly he had grasped the import of this seemingly trivial fact: all date-based calculations such as interest on loans could be inaccurate, credit cards could all "bounce" because the computer might "think" nothing had been paid for one hundred years on the account, even elevators and security systems might shut down. Since the Bank had over 400,000,000 lines of computer code, with dates embedded in random places, the reprogramming challenge was immense.

With a persuasive mix of charm and logic, he had convinced the Bank's Board of Directors to invest substantial sums in the project. No one knew whether they would be compliant--that was the term for getting everything fixed in all the computers--by December 31, 1999, at least not till they could do a test run of all new programs. But as more information about the Millennium Bug began to reach the public, and the danger to the country's computer systems became better known, in the New York banking community the reputation of Carleton Mason as a prescient guru had grown.

He expected, therefore, that the Undersecretary of Treasury would have some sort of proposal to use his talents. If it meant more money, more power, or could be leveraged somehow into finding a replacement for Vicki, he had already decided to accept.

(3)

Dolores Montalvo walked briskly from the plane's steps toward the entrance to the Zurich Bonded Warehouse. She showed her passport to the guard, who took his time reviewing it, his eyes mostly on her. He did not stamp it, since the Bonded Warehouse is not diplomatically "in" Switzerland, and one can discreetly visit it without leaving official tracks, if he is willing to fly out immediately after. The guard asked her the reason for her visit; she showed him the key to the safety deposit box; he called ahead to another check-point and motioned her to enter the building and proceed. She traversed that stop more quickly, and within minutes walked along a well-electronically-scrutinized corridor to a door where Herr Scheppli, the chief administrator, met her with a smile. Minutes later she sat alone at a small table in a tiny closet-like room. She opened her box. It did indeed contain the $750,000.00, U.S., in large denominations. It also contained a sealed envelope. Reflecting on her success in the White House, she wondered whether the money itself contained electronic tracing devices. She decided to take a third of it, and leave the rest for now. She opened the envelope; the note within told her to go to her villa in Spain for a week, then go to Bonn.

(4)

Theodore "Pat" Greene dug through an old college science book. Folded in the back was one page, with a simple heading, "Rules of the Honest Debate Society." He reread the Rules:

1. Only one beer. Graduate students can have two. Post-graduates can have three.
2. No gossip, no talk of sex, no talk of sports, no talk of jobs, present or prospective.
3. No crudities, profanities, inanities, or insults.
4. No monologue longer than two minutes.
5. Start and stop at set time. No longer than two hours unless unanimous agreement to go to a limited longer time.
6. Anyone who violates any Rule is warned the first time; the second time he must put $5.00 into the Refreshments Pot.
7. The person who calls the meeting is the Talkmeister; he or she resolves all disputes. The Talkmeister may be replaced by majority vote of those present.

(5)

Cardinal Eugenio Cassendi placed a call to the Chairman of the Council of Europe to ask for further instructions.

(6)

John DeSanto entered his brother's office. Since his last visit, the law firm of DeSanto and Montgomery had added a new partner. Otherwise, the townhouse office in Glenview, northwest of the city proper, looked the same. So did his brother, Matt, who greeted him warmly.

"Come on in, brother," he said. "Hell of a storm yesterday, wasn't it?"

John agreed and quickly recounted his experience. His brother whistled in amazement and called it a "close brush with death." For the moment, John did not mention the vision.

That word *death* led them to the reason for the meeting: their mother's passing, three months ago. They had found where she hid the documents, of which the most important was a Revocable Trust, now irrevocable because of her death. It left over a million dollars for a specific purpose: to publicize Marian apparitions and the messages of prayer and repentance before the Great Chastisement.

"She set up this Trust, John, and wants one of us kids to run it." He looked at a typewritten page titled, "Trustees." "Her first choice is you. Then, if you can't or won't, it's me. If I bow out, its Sis, Mary Louise. It's an opportunity, I suppose--you've always been more into that kind of stuff than I, but probably her reason was also that you've got a business that permits flexible hours but I have a law practice to keep going--"

"Matt, before we go into that, I've got to tell you something else that happened during the storm yesterday--right when I crashed into the tree," interrupted John. He described what he saw in his mind and finished with the directive, *"Tell My people that the physical world and the moral world are all one piece. If they do not stop their sinning, they will suffer more horrible storms. These are the beginning of punishments."*

His brother looked at him skeptically. "Hey, Johnnie boy, if I didn't know you once flew jets off aircraft carriers, I'd think that what you saw and heard were the product of that air bag crunching your head too hard." He paused and thought for a few seconds. "Tell me, did you ever see a vision before?" He smiled, but his eyes looked serious.

"In a word, No. It's one thing to believe it can happen--that God can give people a special insight and can talk to people if He wants--and something quite different for it to happen to *you*. But it's obvious to me that the vision ties in with Mom's Trust, and--" it was his turn to pause, "I'd be stupid if I didn't read it as confirmation of what you just told me. I'm willing to be knocked off my high horse...but the problem is, *I* don't know a Hell of a lot about Marian apparitions, beyond Lourdes back around 1858 and Fatima in 1917."

"I think you need to get with some *padre* who knows the score on these things," said Matt, "but the only priest I can think of is a Jesuit who's roughly our age, Father Michael Kanek. I got a Christmas card from him three months ago; appears he spends some of his time at Georgetown University."

"Why him? There are lots of priests out in Peoria or around here."

"Sure, 'lots of priests,'--but how many of them ever talk about the things Mom worried about--you know, the reasons why the Virgin Mary appeared, the sinful mess in the world, and that confusing stuff in the Book of the Apocalypse? Most priests are afraid to speak out about the moral collapse in our country and nearly all of them fear to talk about apparitions of Mary--even if, like Fatima, it was proved beyond a reasonable doubt--because they do not want to seem old-fashioned to our modern sophisticates in the pews."

"And there's another reason: they themselves have lost their sense of the supernatural," John added.

"Right. So what good would it do to call up the Chancery downtown and ask if you could talk with a priest who knows something about Marian apparitions? You'd have more luck if you asked to talk with one who could explain why the Minimum Wage should be raised!" He flipped through his Rolodex. "Let me call Georgetown and see if I can get ahold of Father Kanek." He picked up the phone.

(7)

The President looked at the skin on the upper side of his right hand. It had been a week since Dolores Montalvo had persuaded him to accept insertion of the chip. He was trying to forget the encounter because, deep in his heart, he admitted that she had beaten him. His mind had gone blank when he fainted and now the entire event was turning into a dream. He began to wonder whether this extraordinarily beautiful woman had really materialized in his private office so late at night. And he wondered whether he had made love to her, but for some reason he could not remember. Had he imagined the whole thing? But, despite his normally facile mind, he could not come up with a way--without seeming a fool--to ask the Secret Service or his staff director whether anyone had seen a beautiful blonde near his private office around midnight. He could imagine the snickers, behind his back, about "wishful thinking." Still, despite his moral weaknesses, he remained able to distinguish reality from fantasy--so he told himself it must have happened, and, as memory returned, that indeed he must have signed the contract with the Chairman...But he told no one about the fainting spell, not even his doctor, because he could not explain the faint and did not want any tests run that might reveal some sort of nervous system weakness.

But his hand itched, as if a sliver of hard wood was stuck under the skin.

(8)

The Chairman stared at the papers spread before him on his desk. "Four options," he mused. He had a few weeks to decide which would be most effective. Each page had only one word printed at the top. "War...Famine...Collapse...Weather..."

He took out a fifth blank page and printed on the top of it, "Y2K." Then, using a red pen, next to that cryptic inscription, he wrote, *"Trumped!"*

(9)

Just outside telescope range, an unknown asteroid sped through space. Roughly spherical, but with jagged bumps and depressions like earth's moon, its core was mostly iron with a mix of other metallic elements. Two miles in diameter, more dense than any known planet, its speed was over 20,000 miles per hour.

Like a guided missile locked on target, it was heading straight toward an intersect with earth's solar system.

CHAPTER V

(1)

"The Honest Debate Society is hereby convened!" intoned Pat Greene, with cheerful pretended solemnity. "Our last meeting took place twelve years ago"--he paused, as if to let a matter of historic import sink in, "and we have had some turnover in membership. So I would like to ask the assembled delegates to re-introduce themselves and, briefly, summarize what they're doing currently."

They were sitting comfortably in his Prospect House apartment. One had a newly-opened bottle of *Pete's Wicked Ale,* another had *Bud Light,* a couple had Coke. On the glass coffee table, potato chips and *Fritos* were piled high in a large bowl next to a flat wooden tray with three kinds of cheese dip. A smaller tray contained a mound of *Fannie Mae* creme-filled chocolates. Pat Greene gestured to the pretty blonde woman in a chair to his right. She was wearing blue jeans and a light grey sweatshirt with large blue lettering across the front, *"No Atheists in Foxholes".*

"Hi! I'm Vanni. My name is really Marilee Van Niesen, but I go by Vanni. I'm an Executive Secretary at BDR; it's a 'Beltway Bandit' company in Fairfax. In my spare time I eat all the chocolate Pat can give me and I work it off doing aerobics." The others laughed. "I also put in a little time studying the Bible." The others accepted this last point with equanimity.

"O.K., my turn," said the man in black with the upside-down white collar, seated in the chair to her right. "I am Father Michael Kanek, commonly known as 'Father Mike,'" said Bishop Kanek, happy to remember that a Bishop does not cease to be a priest. "I'm supposed to be an expert in modern electrical devices, since I convinced the Ph.D.-donors in M.I.T.'s science department some years ago to call me 'Doctor.' Right now I'm at Georgetown, where some of the natives think I'm trying to be the conscience of the *Zeitgeist.* Translated into English, that means writing and giving conferences on heavy spiritual stuff like Heaven and Hell, sin and repentance--you know, all the things we moderns want to hear about. Also teach a few classes."

"Me next? O.K.--I'm Joanie Atkinson. Vanni and I are roommates. I teach at Falls Church High School and coach the women's basketball team there. In my spare time, I take lots of extra computer courses so I have some options in case they keep paying me next to zilch and I have to leave next year. I'm not sure I'm into the heavy stuff you all probably are going to discuss, but I decided to come along for the ride, because I know Pat and he's a quality guy."

"Pat is the Talkmeister today," declared Pat, "and he assures the assembled brothers and sisters that everybody here is quality. We may be heavy, but we're heavy quality. So, fair damsel, have no fear: the worst that can happen here is that you gobble down too many potato chips. Next--" he pointed to the man on the sofa, sipping some ale.

"Hi, everybody. I'm John DeSanto. It's a pleasure to meet all of you. A few years ago I was a Commander in the Navy. Flew jets off carriers. Easy job. The *hard* part was getting the darn things back *on* the carriers. Anyhow, right now I have a small contract flying business in Peoria, Illinois and I'm married with one young child. I came out here to D.C. to talk with Father Kanek on some important matters. I got here just yesterday and he told me this meeting might address some of the things I'm interested in. So here I am."

"Finally, the caboose on this train," said Pat, "is me, Theodore Patrick Greene, known to my admirers world over, as Pat. I'm a reporter and writer, sort of a free-lance investigator. I managed to do a successful book a couple years ago on science and the environment and out of that came a newspaper contract for a series of feature articles. Right now I'm trying to figure out the inside scoop on a mysterious electrical thing our esteemed Government is conjuring up in Alaska. Another interest of mine is the use of computer chips for surveillance purposes." He paused. "I also supply Vanni's insatiable appetite for chocolate." He smiled at her and she smiled back; she knew her aerobics were beating his chocolates, and she knew he knew it, so no joke about her sweet tooth could bother her. "As you can tell, she's not an atheist."

"*Life* is a foxhole," said Vanni cryptically.

"Hey, Pat," interjected Joanie, "what's the first topic tonight? I gotta do a lot of talking so I can't keep filling my mouth with potato chips." She popped another chip in with a grandiose flourish.

"Well, Joanie, Vanni and I came up with three topics. The first is the question, 'Is God going to punish the world?' We'll polish that off in fifteen minutes," he paused to absorb their skeptical looks, "and then go to something serious."

"You're kidding! This is pretty heavy stuff for a little ol' high school teacher."

"Yup, but to make the question more topical, let me rephrase it. 'Are there so many strange events happening that a person could reasonably conclude that there's going to be a cataclysm, a punishment, or the End of the Age, or some really major change in society?'"

"Who knows?"

"I've got a friend, another priest," said Father Mike, "who thinks the spiritual world has already 'come to an end,' if you want to phrase it that way, and the physical world is just about to catch up to it." Joanie looked puzzled. So he continued, "What he means is--that in America, as a matter of fact in Western Civilization, we have lost our bearings, forgotten our past; we're groping in the dark for meaning and purpose--and, as we do, we as a society or culture are getting more and more evil. Eventually evil works its way out from the spiritual into the physical. When it reaches a kind of 'critical mass,' all Hell breaks loose."

"Let me add a point you might find interesting," said John DeSanto. "Modern planes have a gyroscope in them--it's an instrument like a little top, that spins so fast that it's always upright--it tells the pilot when the plane is tilting, so that he knows his *actual* attitude, regardless of what his senses tell him. It's easy for subjective feelings to fool a guy."

"Sort of like a person's conscience," said Vanni. "It tells you when you're about to go into a spin."

"Right. There has to be something that warns the pilot, when he's in the clouds, that he's not flying level. Another example is a compass: you need an instrument that tells you where True North is, since when the sun goes down--or, again, in clouds--you can't tell directions on your own."

"Compared to thirty years ago," said Father Kanek, "there's lots of evidence that America is 'unbalanced,' as if our collective gyroscope is broken--or that we have lost our way, as if our compass is broken."

"And when a country loses its way, its people sin more and more," said John, "and they're like a pilot who thinks he's on course but has nothing *external and objective* to guide him, so he flies straight into a mountain...by which I mean, we bring punishment on ourselves."

He paused, wondering whether to recount the storm and the vision just a week ago outside Chicago. He decided there would be no harm and possibly some good. Besides, God had told him to warn His people, and he might as well start now. But he felt he had to deal with what the others, except Father Mike, might take to be sensationalism.

"Folks, we've just met, and I don't know where you're coming from, as it were, except that Father Mike assured me that Pat has a knack for bringing together smart people who are mature enough not to prejudge anyone, or jump to a conclusion based on another person's one-liner. Father Mike told me that the reason the Honest Debate Society worked years ago--and can work now, too--is that no one gets invited into the discussion group who does not sincerely desire to understand--not necessarily agree with--but to understand the other person's point of view..."

"Let me add, John," interjected Pat, "that Father Mike and I do not agree on about half the matters in life that are important; but we get along just fine, because we're both willing to try to understand and respect the other's position. And my chocolate-eating Miss Bonbon here," he smiled at Vanni, who promptly obliged him by reaching for her second chocolate creme, "promised me that she would not hit Father Mike or me over the head with her Bible, even if we deserved it!"

"Well, to make it unanimous," said Joanie, "you guys gotta know that Vanni's halo and my horns don't clash very often. I don't mind her quoting the Bible to me, even though, to tell the truth, it's like she's pouring water onto a duck's back. We've been friends for two years. Her Bible hasn't done her any harm; in fact, since she 'got religion,' she does her share of the house cleaning on time! Also, though you couldn't tell it from her dumpy outfit, she has a figure like Miss America--so she must have done some fasting--we pagans call it 'dieting'--because when she became a serious Christian she also started to get in shape. Anyway, I get along with her and I can get along with you. I promise to keep an open mind. Just don't try to convert me on the first meeting."

"Great. Mr. Talkmeister," said John DeSanto, "now that we're all agreed to keep our minds open, I would like the floor for a minute or two to tell you all something that happened to me a week ago. It bears upon the topic." Pat nodded his assent, and John told his experience with the monster storm, the car crash into the tree, the vision and the voice, and the rest of the trip to devastated Chicago. He repeated, slowly, the words about "the beginning of punishments."

"Folks, the problem of an extraordinary personal experience--a vision--is that there is no way to *prove* that it happened. This one did happen to me. But people can't possibly believe that, unless they are first willing to believe that it is--generally--even *possible* that God exists, that He deals with us humans, that He is concerned about our sin, and that He could send us warnings about impending punishment for our sins."

"I can believe that," said Vanni. "It's all over the Scriptures. Especially the Book of Daniel and the Book of Revelation. God warned Noah before the Flood. He sent Jonah to warn Ninevah."

"As you might expect, I believe it too," said Michael Kanek. He recalled his reading of contemporary mystics, the Pope's account of the assassin's death, and the appearance of Michael, "though I have to admit, not all priests do anymore." He wished he could describe these things but decided they would indeed be too "heavy" on the first meeting, especially for Joanie and Pat.

"Well, probably Joanie and I bring up the rear in your parade," said Pat. "I have an open mind, but I'm not as sure as you three...but, for the sake of discussion, let's assume that John's experience did happen just as he said. Go on--what now?"

"If we grant that God exists, that sin eventually calls forth punishment from God, and that we Americans--as a society, no matter how good the people in this room might be--we Americans are sinning today as never before...if we grant these things, then it's quite likely that God's patience, like a clock close to midnight, is about to run out. We shouldn't be surprised if He is about to punish us."

"Why should God punish *me?* I'm living a good life," asked Joanie, sincerely.

"In the case of America," answered John, "it's not that God singles out you or me, Joanie. "He doesn't have to punish *any* individual person in this life--He's got plenty of time in the next life. But *nations*--that's something different. When a whole country, like America, collectively turns its back on God, then He can do one or both of two things--A, He can let us suffer the consequences of our own acts, and/or B, He can send direct punishments. Either way, we get zapped.

"An example of *A* would be a parent whose rebellious teenage son insists on going into the jungle alone, off the plantation, despite his Dad's command that he stay where it's safe. If the son gets mauled by a lion, it's his own fault: his disobedience had consequences."

"I think part of the problem is that we humans don't have a 'God's-eye view' of things," said Father Mike. "You mentioned a parade a minute ago, Pat. Well, it applies here, too. We're like people walking in a parade: we only see a few others parading ahead and behind us; we don't see the whole thing. But if we were up on a high building, we could look down and see the whole parade. God sees all of society; *we* see only a small segment.

"I have to admit," he continued, "that for a long time the prospect of imminent punishment by God seemed to me just the perfervid imaginings of radio preachers. You know, a few people in every generation claim 'The End is Near'--but they turned out to be wrong. And I was really irritated by the exaggerations by some, like that fellow a decade ago who claimed he knew the *exact date* Jesus was going to return. But in the last couple years, I've changed my mind."

"How come?" asked Vanni. Her Bible-study group too had begun to discuss *Daniel* and *Revelation* and the chances of God punishing the country. It was good to run into a Christian in a different church who agreed with her, even if he was a Jesuit priest.

"Lots of things. First, the intensity and perversity of modern evil is simply unprecedented. You know, cases where young mothers kill their own children...cases where 18-year-old girls kill their newborn and then go back to a prom dance...where robbers hit a 7-11, get fifty bucks, then kill the clerk even though he put up no resistance...cases where a twelve-year-old brings guns to school and kills two or three of his friends...child abuse, spouse abuse, pandemic sexual promiscuity...and on the national level, we have a government that commits sins of commission and omission so numerous I can't recount them here..."

"Second, there has been a great increase of reported apparitions of Christ and Mary in the last thirty years. While some are probably the work of overheated imagination, and some may be pure fraud by publicity-seekers, others--perhaps many--are genuine. And uniformly, the genuine ones warn of a coming Great Chastisement.

"Third, I had the privilege, just two weeks ago, of meeting with the Pope himself. Everyone knows he is a man of deep insight into current events. He is certain that we are in what he calls the 'Era of Mercy,' but that it will be followed--soon--by the 'Era of Justice,' which will be a time of great purifications." He paused, awaiting their response. He had told himself before he came over that it would be crucial not to overstate his convictions, lest they think he was arguing rather than simply informing. No one said anything, so he continued.

"Fourth, the Bible is a prophetic book. All of the Old Testament prophecies regarding Jesus' life came true. Some Bible prophecies regarding the End of this Age have recently come true. For example, Saint Paul says there will be a 'falling away'--an apostasy--in the last days. It seems that has happened in the last thirty years. I can give you other examples. But, all in all, a strong case can be made that we are either *in* or awfully *close to* the Tribulation...and the time of Antichrist."

"Paul's Second Epistle to Timothy," interjected Vanni, "says that the last days will be terrifying times. People will be self-centered, lovers of money, proud, haughty, abusive, disobedient of their parents, ungrateful, irreligious, brutal, hating what is good..." She almost quoted it verbatim. "Lots of people today fit that description, and..."

"That's pretty sobering," said Pat, interrupting her as he saw a slight scowl cross Joanie's face. To punctuate his point, he took a big gulp of *Pete's Wicked*. "I guess, as your Resident Skeptic-with-an-Open-Mind, I can agree to Father Mike's point One, I need more data on point Two, and I am willing to give the Pope credit for being smarter than I am--but that doesn't prove he's right...Hell, he could be basing his ideas on the very apparitions in your point Two. If that premise is false, then his conclusion fails as well." He took another, smaller, drink.

"But interpreting the Bible is too steep a mountain for me to climb right now. I know a guy with a Ph.D. in electrical engineering, like you, Father Mike, is not likely to be taken in by myths and superstition--but, well, I gotta admit, I haven't read the *Apocalypse* since glancing at it in Bible study back in eighth grade--before I became a freethinker. And my guess is that Joanie hasn't ever climbed that mountain." Joanie nodded agreement. "So, just give us the word on the apparitions--understanding, and I speak only for myself here, that *this* Resident Open-Minded Skeptic finds it damn hard to believe this apparition stuff. But I'll obey the rule--keep an open mind."

"Let me swing the bat first," said John DeSanto. Father Mike's been at the plate for a while and needs a rest." He smiled and the priest gestured his assent, happy to move into the conversational background. This was not a class at the university; no need to make the others feel he thought it was.

"I'll start with one that was definitely proved: Fatima. In 1917, the Virgin Mary appeared on the thirteenth of each month for six straight months to three little children. The oldest was only ten, the youngest seven. This was in a tiny Portuguese town...Fatima. The last appearance was in October, the same month as Lenin and a bunch of conspirators overthrew Kerensky, who had established a rickety democratic government in Russia. I'll summarize the proof that this did happen.

"First, these children were very young; they knew nothing of Russia, which had pulled out of World War I, and was then a weak nation--yet one of the predictions that 'the Lady,' as they called her, made was that unless many people did prayer and penance, 'Russia would scatter its errors around the world.' Humanly speaking, no ten-year-old Portuguese kid in 1917 could predict what actually happened--the expansion of Communism over more than one-third of the globe.

"Second, she also predicted 'another, worse war to come,' and that happened too--World War II.

"Third, the anticlerical town government threatened and pressured these kids, to try to make them recant, to say they had made the whole thing up--the mayor threatened to toss them in prison and throw away the key. That would scare the Hell out of most young kids but these three stood their ground; they would not change their story despite the threats.

"So, to put it in a nutshell, the messages contained information the visionaries themselves could not have invented...and other people around them put them under so much pressure to recant that for them to stick to the story was almost preternatural."

Pat cupped his chin in his right hand and stared thoughtfully into space. *Just like the Apostles' story about Jesus' miracles and Resurrection*, he thought.

"Fourth, these kids had enough sense to ask the Lady to give some 'sign,' as they called it, some objective proof that the skeptics could see, even if they could not see the apparition of the Lady itself. That sign came to be known as 'the Miracle of the Sun.'

"The children promised the townsfolk that 'the Lady' would do something extraordinary to prove she was real. By October of 1917, tens of thousands of people had heard of the strange visions and many of them came on the 13th. It rained hard all that morning. At least 70,000 people assembled in a grassy area outside the town, the location of the earlier appearances. Some of those people were reporters from local anti-clerical newspapers.

"At noon the sun came out; everyone dried instantly. The children went into a trance once again and, they later said, received a message. When that was finished--here's the miracle--*almost all the 70,000 people saw the sun spin and 'dance' in the sky,* like a Fourth of July pinwheel, shooting off huge sparks and flames in all directions, *and then seem to leave its place in the sky and rush toward them, as if to hit the earth and burn up every person in that crowd.* As you might expect, the people fell to their knees in terror, begging for mercy. When it seemed the sun was just about to hit them, it stopped--and returned back to its place, and normal size, in the sky. The whole extraordinary event was reported in local papers."

The others looked at each other, not sure what to say. Finally Joanie decided to comment. "John, that...that's pretty impressive, but, well, you know, couldn't it be explained by some sort of mass hallucination?" She offered the hypothesis, but without much conviction.

"Joanie, it's a fair question. And since we're so far removed from the actual event--over 80 years--and we have no eye witnesses or first-hand sources here, we can't really test either my summary or your theory."

"Let me jump in here," said Pat. "As Resident Skeptic, I pride myself on being even-handed in my doubts. You know, no discrimination among theories: treat 'em all with the same disdain. But Joanie, I have to say, in defense of John's account, it may take *more* faith to believe in 'Spontaneous Hallucination' than in a *bona fide* miracle. Look--70,000 people do not *all* suddenly imagine the same thing--*especially when they don't know in advance what they're all supposed to imagine.* This was not an orchestrated illusion by a stage magician. Also, if John's summary is accurate, quite a few of those folks came with such intense doubts that not only were they *not* disposed to see any 'miracle,' but if one happened, it would have to *override*, as it were, their desire to see *nothing* happen at all."

"Patty me boy, you got it!" exclaimed Father Mike, genuinely excited. "I think Pat gets tonight's 'Fair-Minded Skeptic' award." Then, more calmly, "Pat has hit the nail on the head, which should remind us what we're doing here--namely, no one is trying to win an argument or convince anyone else that he is 'wrong'--all we're doing, as regards apparitions, is putting on the record, evidence that--at least sometimes--a genuine apparition, sent from God, does happen."

"I didn't say *I* completely believe that the Virgin Mary appeared to those kids in Portugal," said Pat, "but I'm willing to admit it *could* have happened. Maybe I'd go farther, even, and say that if the Miracle of the Sun did happen, then they proved Mary was appearing to them. Still, all that doesn't mean *John's vision* a few days ago was genuine."

"No, it doesn't," said John. "But I think it does mean that one should not dismiss it out of hand, as if it were impossible."

"Aren't we getting off track here?" interrupted Vanni. "I mean, Father Mike was talking about many appearances of Jesus Christ and His mother over a thirty-year period. If Father Mike has heard about these--whether they're genuine or not--it means that lots of other people have as well...which means that someone thought these were important enough to tell other people. So, whether or not John had a vision during his car crash, it seems to me we should go back to the important ones, the 'big picture'--anyhow, I want to hear more about these others."

John DeSanto was relieved at this suggestion, since he did not like being the center of attention. So he said, "Vanni, I think you're right. To get 'the big picture,' as you put it, does not require dissecting *my* experience. But I have to admit that beyond Fatima, I'm not very knowledgeable. Some of the recent ones, like Garabandal and Medjugorje, I can scarcely pronounce!--much less tell you what happened."

"Ladies and gentlemen," injected Father Mike, "I could summarize these, but I hesitate to do so, since our 'discussion' would turn into a class lecture. That's not the format, and I think you might begin to resent my monopolizing the conversation."

"Herr Talkmeister will arbitrate," said Pat, "by putting the matter up to a vote. The Motion is to give Father Mike five minutes of monologue to answer Vanni's question. All in favor?" There were two *Ayes,* John DeSanto and Vanni. "All opposed?" There were two *Nays,* Father Mike and Joanie. "It's a tie," declared Pat. "Normally, the Talkmeister would break a tie, but in deference to the feelings of both Ayes and Nays, I will abstain, which means the Motion fails to carry." Vanni gave him a dirty look.

"That's a relief," said Father Mike. Pat Greene looked at his watch. "Well, gang, the Talkmeister hereby declares Round I over. I call it a draw: you all kept good manners and nobody tried to proselytize. It was a pretty heavy topic to kick off with, and we left some loose ends. We'll table it for now and move on to the next topic after you all get up, walk around, and stretch your legs. So I call a ten-minute time out." He looked at his empty *Pete's Wicked* bottle, stood up, and ambled toward the kitchen.

"Hey, Father Mike," said Vanni as she stood stretching her arms straight above her head. "What do you say you give me the word sometime soon on Garabandal and Medjugorje, over a cup of coffee?"

"Glad to," he answered. "On one condition: you bring Talkmeister-the-Bonbon-Supplier along. Every *Directed Study* course I teach has to have at least two students in the class."

(2)

Over Jerusalem, a huge thunderstorm raged. It was accompanied by a phenomenon never seen before: *green lightning.*

CHAPTER VI

(1)

A week had passed. The Chairman of the Council of Europe had spent most of his waking hours in meetings with heads of the now nearly subordinate member states; but he found time to seclude himself for a few quick phone calls. One of these was to the President of the United States. They exchanged brief pleasantries and then, as was his style, the Chairman came right to the point.

"Too few of your troops are deployed overseas. When the occasion arises, I want you to act quickly--send the best units, especially the Marines, overseas with dispatch."

The President agreed, of course, though without enthusiasm. He felt like a puppet. But he consoled himself with the thought that when the Plan was fully implemented, he would be the second most powerful man in the world. He did not trust the Chairman, and so he fantasized that if some accident, perhaps a successful assassination attempt, were to remove the Chairman from the scene, *he*, as the former President of the United States and by that time head of the First Directorate, would be the likely successor.

(2)

Dolores Montalvo moved easily through Customs at the Bonn airport. Once again the security guards had difficulty pulling their eyes away from her. Her passport was in order and her stated purpose for coming, which she mumbled in German, "to visit with friends," seemed plausible enough. Her assignment was a re-run of her first task, but with the Chancellor of Germany. The script was different, since his psychological profile did not suggest serious weakness for willowy blondes, as had the President's. Moreover, she was known in Europe, so the cover of a mid-level job in the German government could not be used: an actress and beauty queen does not waste her talents in such menial assignments. She would use a more direct approach.

(3)

A consortium composed of a large plane manufacturer, a major wireless communications company, and two quasi-secret Government agencies launched another low-level satellite from Edwards Air Force Base. This was the forty-fifth, one each week, some from this launch center, some from Cape Canaveral. When this satellite was correctly positioned in its geosynchronous orbit two thousand miles above a spot on earth, it would join others at various points over the globe, and additional satellites being launched every two weeks, in forming a surveillance web. When complete, this web could determine the location during the day, within as close as two feet, of every single automobile and every single person on earth. To locate every person at night, it would be necessary for all individuals to carry with them a computer chip set to a certain radio frequency; it would emit a signal that transmission towers being erected all over the country would catch, enhance, and relay to the satellite. The chip could be small enough to be concealed in a portable phone, a credit card, or, if necessary, implanted under a person's skin.

By the end of the sixth month of the year, the consortium planned to launch a total of sixty-six such surveillance satellites. After three months of planned testing, they would be prepared by September for the next phase of the Plan.

(4)

Cardinal Eugenio Cassendi paced back and forth in his study. Each time he passed the bookcase, he glanced at all the old tomes, their leather binding and gold-embossed titles visible, as the setting sun sent a final ray through the window and fell, just for a moment, on the books: Tertullian and Lactantius and other Fathers of the Church...Augustine's *City of God* and his *Confessions*...Aquinas' *Summa Theologica* and *Summa Contra Gentiles*...Ignatius of Loyola's booklet, *The Spiritual Exercises*...Bellarmine's *Disputationes*...St. Francis de Sales' *Introduction to a Devout Life*...Chautard's *Soul of the Apostolate*...and many others, ancient and contemporary.

As a young man in seminary he had read all of them. In his youthful enthusiasm he had found their message interesting, even attractive. Oh, it had seemed so real, so full of meaning!--just give himself over to God, practice the virtues, avoid the occasions of sin, pray and do serious spiritual reading daily, become a student not only of the words but the spirit of the Bible, listen to his spiritual advisor, and on, and on.

But...after Ordination, as he had moved from one assignment to another and began to climb the ladder of advancement, which in the Church is not unlike the "corporate ladder" often remarked in America, it became harder and harder to find time for prayer and reading. He began to wonder why the great writers he had once respected had enjoyed so little recognition by the world. Why could not a man be spiritual *and* have fame and fortune? More than once he had pondered the anonymity of men like Cardinal Merry del Val, close aide of Saint Pius X: In Eugenio Cassendi's opinion, Merry del Val was more able than Pius; yet the latter is still remembered, the former not at all. The Church seemed ever bent on advancing the wrong man, canonizing the wrong person, supporting the wrong, old-fashioned, philosophy...

At the same time he found he had considerable gifts of diplomacy and negotiation. His travels introduced him to the world of intellectual and political wealth and power. By the time he had reached his mid-forties, nearly two decades ago, the religious side of his life was all ceremony and no substance. If it were not for his raw ambition, he would have left the priesthood, as not a few others had when they "lost their vocation," and pursued a secular career in university teaching.

At the beginning, his conscience pricked him. More than once, those bothersome one-liners that Jesus sprinkled into His public life kept popping into his mind: *"What does it profit a man if he gain the whole world but lose his immortal soul?"* and *"I would have you hot or cold, but the lukewarm I will spew out of My mouth."* He recognized his slide and was quite uncomfortable.

So, to dispel such discomforting sayings, he embraced a form of rationalization and began to accept the Modernist critique. The Scriptures were not literal, the sayings of Jesus were the inventions of the first-century Christian community, he told himself. The Church was too old-fashioned, no longer in touch with intellectual trends, he told himself. It was important to "modernize" the Church, to reach a *rapprochement* with the World, he told himself; to adjust the ancient teachings to fit with the discoveries of science and the need to address pressing global problems such as population control and the maldistribution of wealth, he told himself. In some cases--though he did not recognize the fact--it was not he who "told himself." Such thoughts were subtly inserted into his mind by an invisible being assigned to shadow him.

He returned to his desk and sat down. The sun had disappeared. Twilight was falling. Darkness would soon be upon the city of Rome. Still he did not turn on the desk lamp. Still he pondered recent past events.

The Chairman had personally told him that within the month Pope John Paul II would be dead. Instead, the Swiss Guards had found the *assassin* dead outside the Pope's door! The man lives a charmed life! The Chairman had told him that *he*, Eugenio Cassendi, would be elected Pope and that *he* could travel to the United States, to fulfill John Paul's plans but to teach a much different doctrine. Instead, the Old Pole bounces around the United States like an acrobat on a trampoline, while *he*, Cassendi, sits stuck in this closet surrounded by books written by dead men teaching dead doctrines! Indeed, the last newspaper and television pictures showed a Pontiff who looked five to ten years *younger* than when he left! Must we wait for luck or old age, which seems arrested, to remove the Old Pole from office? Or shouldn't we take the matter into our own hands in a way less crude, more subtle, than using a paid assassin? The New Age and the New World Order could not be put *hold* indefinitely while John Paul continued his pernicious convert-making on every continent on the globe!

(5)

Michael Kanek hung up the phone. He and his cousin and namesake, Bishop Michael Kaniecki of Anchorage, Alaska, had joked pleasantly about how one branch of the family had shortened the Polish name for some reason now forgotten, and each brought the other up to date on his regular ministry. Bishop Kaniecki had entered the Jesuit Order back in the 1950s after high school in Detroit, gone through the regular training, and convinced his superiors that he had a genuine calling to the Alaskan missions. Athletic and devout, he had done an outstanding job as a missionary priest in a rigorous and demanding environment. The older priests in that desolate setting were more than a little impressed with his skill as a pilot, his courage during blizzards, and his tireless energy bringing the Sacraments to the isolated Eskimo mission outposts. In due time they brought his zeal to the attention of the Vatican committee that reviews potential episcopal appointments and, in the early 1980s, Father Michael Kaniecki was ordained Bishop.

Father Michael Kanek wanted to tell his cousin what the Pope had done a few weeks earlier in Steubenville, but something made him hesitate. It had best be recounted face to face. For the time being, until God showed him what to do different from his present activities, he had decided to keep thinking of himself as "Father" and not as "Bishop." In any event, in this conversation he wanted the Alaskan Bishop to do most of the talking; the topic was the High Altitude Auroral Research Project, or "HAARP." Yes, Bishop Kaniecki knew a good deal; yes, the electrical grid was even larger now than a year ago, as the installation neared completion. Yes, occasionally the electrical power in the whole city of Anchorage dimmed, for no apparent reason, as if whole gigawatts of power were being drained off.

Though Bishop Kaniecki had not made the connection, Bishop Kanek, because of his background in electrical studies, had: begun innocuously enough as a way to communicate with submarines all over the world, *the HAARP equipment in Alaska could modify the weather--drastically.* He knew it was tied in with similar projects in Greenland and Russia.

He wondered whether the freak snowstorm in Colorado in October of 1997...the horrible snows around Christmas the same year down in New Mexico...the incredibly terrible ice storm that hit New England and eastern Canada in early January of 1998...the triple-digit heat in Texas in the summer of '98, lasting over forty days--whether any of these were the product of these "weather-changing machines."

Oh, the arrogance of the Dr. Frankensteins of the world, the scientists who would play God! When have all their experiments done any real good? Whatever their good intentions, whatever they undertake, it seems they do harm! Or am I giving them too much credit to assume that their intentions really are good?

(6)

John DeSanto paced in his room at the Key Bridge Marriott Hotel. Occasionally he glanced out his window to the spires and lights of Georgetown University across the Potomac. It was nearly midnight and he had been reading from different books Father Mike had given him. One was a set of seven paperbacks by a layman named John Leary, titled *PREPARE FOR THE GREAT TRIBULATION AND THE ERA OF PEACE*, which recounted visions and messages received daily since 1993. Another was a large single volume by a certain Joanne Kriva, *TRIBULATIONS AND TRIUMPH: Revelations on the Coming of the Glory of God*, the transcripts of a series of supernatural messages which began in September of 1990 and ran through the end of 1994. In response to his request, the priest had offered a "crash course in Marian apparitions," along with a few meetings before John returned to the Midwest. They agreed this approach would be a good start toward arming him for the task of spreading information on the topic.

He sat down, picked up the Bible, and flipped the pages. His eye fell on Jeremiah, 12:15-17:

> Give ear, listen humbly, For the Lord speaks. Give Glory to the Lord, your God, Before it grows dark; Before your feet stumble On darkening mountains; Before the light you look for Turns to darkness, Changes into black clouds.

My Lord! that reminds me of the storm during my drive to Chicago! he thought. He returned to Jeremiah:

> If you do not listen to this In your pride, I will weep in secret many years For the Lord's flock, led away in exile.

I wonder if that applies to Pat or Joanie or the many Catholics that I'll meet--even some priests--who "do not listen"...? He closed his eyes to rest them. It had been a long day...

Once again, as at the moment of the crash, he heard the Voice, in his head, in his ears, in the room, not shouting, not whispering, just present, spread throughout his mind, as clear as if the Speaker were a few feet away in the hotel room:

If I give to you a Eucharistic miracle, an apparition of My Mother, or a prophet in your midst, and you cannot bring yourself to believe, then your heart is closed and pride is blocking grace. Then your faith is too small to be counted. In your pride you will be led away in exile. Not because you didn't believe in a sign, miracle, or messenger, but because you fail to believe in the One who sent them.

(7)

In his law office outside Chicago, Matt DeSanto finished reading the Memorandum. It had come from an east coast attorney, Jason Browning, who had done considerable *pro bono* work for various Christian groups attacked by "civil liberties" attorneys whose actions prevented religious liberty from being exercised. He had contacted Browning because a worrisome idea had come into his mind--*What if the next Pope was the Imposter predicted by so many mystics?...and he wanted to change the Church's teaching?* The questions were complex and Browning had tried to answer some of them.

The legal issues boiled down to one: if a Pope were to appoint apparent "bishops" who changed the Mass radically and the Church's traditional teachings on faith and morals, what legal remedies did traditional Catholics have? Matt was worried, as he pondered the memo's analysis: the Church was structured like a pyramid containing various smaller pyramids; the Bishop of each diocese was a "corporation sole," meaning a one-man corporation, and it, or he, owned the church property within his jurisdiction. So even though the parishioners of St. Thomas Parish, say, had contributed $2,000,000.00 for their new parish church, they did not 'own' it. On first glance, anyway, it seemed that *legally* an evil Pope could appoint evil bishops who could do evil things with the buildings and lands the laity had paid for, and get away with it.

He wondered whether civil courts would listen to *equitable arguments*. Did not the bishop hold these properties *not* for himself, but *in Trust* for the benefit of the Faithful? The Memorandum did not give an answer. Perhaps it could not be answered without litigation. He hated to think of what that might mean. Would civil courts even take jurisdiction? And if they did, would their lack of spiritual insight make the problem even worse? Would secular humanist judges see an opportunity to drive more legal nails into the body of the Church?

(8)

The parish church of San Marcos in the northwest quadrant of Madrid stood empty except for the erect figure of a tall sixty-year-old woman who knelt motionless in long silent prayer. She was responding to an inner Voice, which, the same day Dolores Montalvo arrived in Bonn, had directed her to pray for her brother's child. The Voice, whom the woman sensed was the Virgin Mary, told her to pray at least one hour daily, to pull her niece back from the brink of Hell. But weeks later, during her daily Holy Hour, the Voice stated that Dolores remained in terrible danger, since her current course of conduct had to change radically. The unresolved question was whether the power of prayer and its extra graces would move her niece's free will enough to change the direction of her life?

And so Cristina Montalvo, aunt to Dolores Montalvo, pressed on in prayer. Though once married and eager to have children, Cristina had been childless; and so years earlier she had "adopted" Dolores with the ready acquiescence of the natural mother; and, to the extent the travels of her Diplomatic Corps brother had permitted, she had tried to spend enough time with her to instill a sense of Catholic history and heritage. She had taught her catechism and prepared her for First Holy Communion. During the child's pre-puberty years, Cristina taught her piano and took her to the zoo and tried to be the example of what a Christian mother should be. She had tried to shepherd the blossoming adolescent through the turbulent teen years. But gradually her influence waned: Dolores' beauty, her parents' marital problems, travel and ensuing rootlessness, and the paganism of modern culture conspired to dilute Cristina's influence. The time finally came when, save for a Christmas gift and card and a phone call on her birthday, Dolores the actress never communicated with her aunt. But Cristina read the papers, attended her niece's movies, and was aware of Dolores' growing reputation as a very "worldly" woman.

Shortly after her husband's accidental death some years back, Cristina joined the Third Order of St. Dominic. After a six-month postulancy period, she entered the year long novice formation course.

With the intensity of the Spanish temperament, she threw herself into the spiritual practices of the Third Order: daily rosary, the liturgy of the hours, spiritual reading, fasting on certain days, frequent Confession, yearly retreats. After three years, she received permission to make perpetual profession. So she became a lay woman living a quasi-religious life in the world. She read deeply in the lives of the Saints, especially Teresa of Avila and Catherine of Siena, and gradually began to model herself, within the bounds of prudence and sound spiritual direction from an ascetic old Dominican priest, on Saint Catherine. And then certain direct communications from God began in her life...

Cristina pondered Dolores' affairs, her cars, her villas. She wondered whether, in God's providence, somehow this Prodigal Daughter, who had beauty, money, and the title of Countess--but nothing of lasting value--would come to realize she was supping with swine. Would she someday come back to those in her family who truly loved her, back to her Church, and back to Jesus, whom once as a child she had loved? Then it was that the inner Voice told her *It is late, my child; Dolores is far down the path to perdition, but there is still time if you can win the grace of repentance for her. The first grace must be to know the truth about her situation.* And so Cristina prayed.

(9)

The President signed another Executive Order. He had issued more of these decrees than any other President. Published in the ponderous *Federal Register,* unnoticed by the people, unreported by the press, this one created another set of Federal detention centers. He had decided to title them, euphemistically, Federal Transfer Centers. But verbiage aside, they were prisons, pure and simple--prisons for those who tried to resist the New World Order he was involved in setting up. They were modeled on the camps in which Japanese-Americans had been interned during World War II.

He glanced at the red welt on the back of his right hand. The itching had turned to a dull ache. He still refused the inclination to talk to his doctor about it. But he wondered whether it was becoming noticeable. Would he have to start wearing gloves? And how would he explain that?

(10)

Dolores Montalvo lay in the sun on the third-floor deck of her oceanfront Mediterranean villa on the edge of Barcelona. She wore only a skimpy swim suit, but the height of the privacy fences at either end of the deck, plus the structure itself behind her, made it impossible for admiring eyes to see her. Today she wanted no attention.

On a table nearby sat a large goblet of chilled white wine. She rarely drank during the day, but this afternoon she made an exception to dispel her sour mood. She wanted to forget the assignment in Bonn--to her mind it had been a failure, and she hated to fail. She had been unable to initiate a relationship with the Chancellor that would lead to his taking the Chip.

She wondered why he had not swallowed the bait, as the President had. True, she could not play the vamp nearly as overtly, because the Chancellor's character, accurately summed up in his dossier, was far more self-controlled. Still, though she had come on in a low key, she had displayed charms of leg and breast in a discreet way within the norms of professional fashion, yet enough to hint that she was available for a tryst after their meeting. But while complimenting her beauty, he had displayed no interest in pursuing her. She was annoyed that any man could resist. So she assuaged her bruised ego by recalling the memory of her triumph over the President and congratulating herself that she had chosen *not* to let him have her. There is no thrill in seducing a man who wants to rape you. Besides, she had not liked him at all, and as a woman who had been pursued by men of far more personal substance than the President, she was neither impressed by his advance nor awed by his rank. She understood American politicians' love-hate relationship with Feminism, but her own brand of that *ism* was apolitical. Still, the President's public pronouncements and what was known of his private life made her believe that his commitment to Feminism was not genuine. She had even concluded that he was the kind of man that Feminism rose in revolt against. So it had been a pleasure to say No and teach him a lesson.

But musing about her own skirmishes in the Battle of the Sexes was secondary, she reminded herself, to the recent assignment; and in that she had, for the time being anyway, failed: the Chancellor had not taken the Chip. He'd told her to come back sometime later.

She gulped her remaining wine, an expression of pique and bad manners that would be embarrassing had it been in public. As she swallowed, a new and frightening thought assaulted her mind. She pictured the President fall back into his chair, helpless, struggle a bit like a fly in a spider web, and lapse into unconsciousness. Then, despite herself, came images of *herself* taking the Chip when the Chairman at last commanded--and then he, or one of his lieutenants, aiming that transmitter at *her* hand, effectively paralyzing *her* mind, then laying *her*, half-conscious, on a bed, taking off *her* clothes, and--...*What if the Chairman did to me what I did to the President?--and then he or his bodyguards could...*She shuddered and closed her eyes.

CHAPTER VII

(1)

Father Michael Kanek and Pat Greene occupied one in a line of small tables along the window in the Key Bridge Marriott ground floor restaurant. They had less than a half-hour, because the former had to get back to Georgetown to teach an afternoon class; and the latter wanted to hit his word processor to finish an article that faced an early deadline.

"Mike, I've just got to get a handle on this HAARP thing," stated Pat. "I made my reputation by reporting on secret threats to the environment. From what I know--or can guess--this HAARP project could cause a greater ecological disaster than Chernobyl. In order to blow the lid off it, I need hard data."

"You're right on that," said the priest, sipping his coffee. He paused and looked around the half-empty restaurant, which because of the hotel's perfect location, was a watering hole for many in Washington's military-industrial complex. Then he leaned forward and in a low tone added, "Pat, I wrote a Ph.D. thesis on Tesla electrical theory and practice. It's right here." He pulled a thick file folder out of a small briefcase. He handed the folder across the table. "Read this, especially chapter five, on weather modification machines.

"My cousin is the Bishop of Alaska," he added. "I called him a short while ago. He says they have sporadic brownouts in Anchorage, as if something is drawing off whole gigawatts of power. I think our government is trying to control the weather."

"You mean like the experiments after World War II, planes dropping dry ice into clouds trying to make it rain?"

"Yes--but infinitely more sophisticated--and dangerous. I can't explain it all in five minutes--but in sum, the ionosphere is a natural shield against high energy particles from outer space. Beam enough concentrated electricity into the ionosphere from underneath and you can actually *lift it*--and maybe punch a hole in it. When either happens, you create tremendous disturbance in the high atmosphere winds and in the weather."

"My God! How do they control the disturbance they generate?"

"Ah--there's the rub!" said the priest. "This is probably a classic example of 'the law of unintended consequences'--you know, anything major you do can have results you did not foresee or intend. I don't think they *can* control it, with any precision."

"Do you think they care?"

"I think they care about the results. If there's collateral harm to innocent people--well, no, I don't think they care."

"What results do they want?"

"Initially, 'HAARP' meant 'High Altitude Auroral Research Project'; it was conceived as a way to transmit 'ELF' or Extremely Low Frequency waves through the earth to identify subterranean objects--tunnels, missile warheads, oil deposits--a sort of super radar or super sonar. But the scientists working on it soon realized they could modify the weather as well. Now, to answer your question: probably they first wanted just the radar capability. But I think that now some people behind this experiment want to disrupt the weather."

"But why? Just to destroy for the sake of destroying?"

"I don't think they're *that* crazy, Pat. I think there's method in their madness. My hunch is, they're onto the fact that ELF waves--extremely low frequency electrical transmissions--can disorient people, affect their perception of reality. They may have a political goal that such disorientation could help them further.

"Second, most weather modifications in the United States would be harmful to crops--you know, change the growing season, prevent whole states from getting enough rain, or maybe hit other states with *too much* rain."

"But this experiment began as a radar-enhancement effort. That's what the CEO of BDR told me, and you just confirmed it. If I write an article that suggests all this nefarious stuff--you know, secret-plot-to-cause-a-famine or something--well, all the bigwigs will hide behind the valid purpose of HAARP and call me a paranoid fool."

"I know. That's the problem with a conspiracy in modern times. It's like an onion: it has layers inside layers. And the outer layer of the conspiracy is plausible. But I don't think you should *declare* that their purpose is to cause a famine, since *purpose* is subjective. Rather, stick with *results*, which are objective. But so far, since there have been plenty of crop losses, but, fortunately, no famine, I wouldn't even raise that red flag. Too sensationalistic."

"So how do I handle it?"

"Stick with the truth--the truth about how our grain supplies are way down, about the impact on the consumer when twenty thousand chickens per day die in Texas because of triple-digit heat, day after day; the ruin of the soybeans and corn in so many states. There *is* reason to believe these electrical experiments in Alaska *do* modify the weather. It makes sense to warn people that there are too many unknown variables--that Dr. Frankenstein might not be able to control the monster he is creating. *That* kind of warning is well within acceptable journalism, especially if you mention the historical analogates..."

"Three Mile Island and Chernobyl are good examples--situations where what was a good idea, maybe, got out of hand and did more harm than good."

"Right. Draw a message out of the facts you present: remark in a low-key way that some people are buying extra food. Give a couple real-life examples. Do the whole thing right and you've performed a great public service. Maybe even get you a Pulitzer Prize."

"Mike, believe it or not, I don't give a damn about that. I love my country and I'm more concerned about what'll happen if this HAARP thing never gets the public scrutiny it should. Hell, if the people learn all about it and then they or their Congressmen approve--well, that's fine--it's the way democratic government is supposed to work. At least we walk into an ecological mess with our eyes wide open. But when you're talking about screwing around with the minds of millions of people, or destroying the food supply for thousands, maybe millions--well, that's where responsible journalism should come in. 'The public's right to know' should mean a Hell of a lot when it could come down to matters of life and death. Something as serious as this--why, we shouldn't walk into it blind."

"Which is why," said Kanek, standing to leave, "you better have a publisher who cares as much about that right as you do."

(2)

The Chairman sat in his spacious study in Brussels. Though the electronics in this new office building were state-of-the-art, the only light in the room came from five candles arranged on a coffee table in the center of the room, forming a pentagram.

The Chairman had been unknown to the general public in Europe only a few years earlier. Interpol had a dossier on him, but it was remarkably jejune. Its highlights included little more than the following: born somewhere in the Middle East, probably Syria...father possibly Jewish...mother's name known but little else, save rumors involving vice...no siblings...educated in France and England...graduate studies in Egypt, major field, computer sciences, minor in European languages. Unmarried. Age unknown because no birth certificate can be located; probably somewhere in late 40's or early 50's.

The dossier mentioned Chairman's extraordinary computer skills but did not spell out his accomplishments. During his college and graduate studies he had shown himself remarkably adept at devising and implementing "cross-pollination" applications of computer databases. He had developed software that could isolate and record thousands of telephone conversations...locate tens of thousands of moving automobiles through computer/satellite tracking...identify security-clearance candidates by computer analysis of their retinas, voice patterns, or fingerprints. Beyond these applications, he had created a program to identify everyone in a given country who subscribed to a specific magazine or newspaper, or spoke certain key words over the telephone, and then "cross-pollinate": press a few keys and, within seconds, locate all those people wherever they might be, by means of a chip embedded in their driver's license and the license tag of their car.

Secretly, he also had conducted successful experiments on implanted computer chip use. He was one of the first in the world to discover the potential for control over individuals who had taken an implanted chip. And his experiments went farther than any other: he devised computer technology using a combination of visual images, high-frequency sounds, and low-frequency electrical current both to disable a person, as Dolores Montalvo had done to the President, and also, granted the right mix of electronics, seize control, as it were, of the person's mind: almost hypnotize the subject into doing the controller's bidding.

After graduate school he formed, or joined, numerous computer companies and adroitly maneuvered himself to a position of control in all of them. In the process, he acquired great wealth.

He had concluded that it is possible to orchestrate television images and sounds, coupled with a certain electrical current, to bring millions of people even to worship an idol.

Despite long hours in university computer centers, the Chairman somehow managed to maintain nearly total secrecy about his experiments. Later, as he built an immense fortune through a conglomerate of computer companies, he continued his secrecy. Probably no individual human in the world was a close friend or even a regular acquaintance of the man. Had they been queried, those who worked for him would have had little to say about his pioneering work. As to his subjective qualities, the most they might have said, had they dared, was that he was very smart...shrewd...purposeful...selfish...ambitious...generous but always with an ulterior purpose...arrogant, though he usually managed to disguise this trait...impatient with lesser minds...full of pride...charming, even magnetic. They were all afraid of him.

In an earlier time, when Western countries' citizens still prized virtue and character, many in Europe, perhaps most, would have hesitated before transferring substantial control over their lives to such a man. But at the end of the passing millennium, public virtue had fallen to a level not very different from mankind at the time of the Flood. Though a Remnant did understand that there is no significant difference between a man with no moral character and a Frankenstein, the public at large worried little that its leaders cared not a bit about personal morality, save insofar as the appearance of probity could be leveraged into greater power than could improbity. So the Americans had elected a President who had no values; and the Europeans were in the final stages of transferring virtual dictatorial powers to the Council, which was headed by a Chairman who had evil values--a person whose one purpose in life was to gain absolute control over others.

He gazed at the five burning candles and pondered his progress to date. He knew full well that, for him, the End did justify the Means; and the End was Control.

Control. Control of information. Control of events. Ultimately, control of people. That was the goal. Control their food, control their jobs, control their money. Then, dictate what they believe. Eventually, dictate *whom they worship.*

To achieve ultimate control in a society that was in many ways decentralized and still gave lip service, at least, to democratic notions of personal freedom and limited government, the would-be Master needed to capture the Government and extend its powers to every facet of its citizens' lives. This part he knew would not be too hard: after working quietly behind the scenes for most of the century, his precursors had moved into leadership positions in the political parties of the western countries, the news media, many big universities, the banking system, and not a few multinational corporations. And in every industrialized nation the people were used to a huge intrusive Government that already managed and regulated their lives in countless ways. *In the process of voting themselves a share of someone else's money, they had handed power over their lives to the rulers who collected it.*

The harder part would be to stampede the people into giving up their remaining freedoms--motivating them to accept, even to embrace, the net of edicts, laws, rules, directives, and commands that would at last control every facet of their lives. To panic the people one needed some frightening event, a crisis of cosmic proportions, so that the danger they would flee would so absorb their attention that they would not see the greater danger ahead. Create a loud enough noise near a school of fish and they will rush away in fear--and not even see the net they swim into.

It might be harder, but it could be done. It was only a matter of orchestrating the proper series of events. But an important matter came into his mind, so he quickly picked up the phone, to handle it right now. He punched in the numbers of an exchange in Italy. His party, a man named Malin, answered. "Have you located the 'substitute' yet?" the Chairman asked.

"Yes, Mr. Chairman. A single man, a certain Giovanni Petrone, who lives outside Rome. He's a barber, about 60 years old, though he looks older. Unmarried. Lives alone. Most of his remaining relatives are up north, in Naples..."

"Don't bother me with the details," interrupted the Chairman. "Just tell me, can we capture him when we need him?"

"Yes, Sir, if you let me use four men. He's rather strong and has a quick temper; if you want him alive, and with no marks to his face or head, I need four men."

"Use as many as you want. I told you, I don't have time to discuss details. Just remember, your men must be reliable--or *you* are a dead man." There was a pause. Then the other man responded.

"I understand," said Malin. "But I should observe, Sir, that it would be easier simply to kill him--poison perhaps--and then we wouldn't need the muscle."

"I know. But timing is crucial. We need him to look as if he had just died a day earlier. We can't let him begin to decompose and using embalmers is too risky. It's better to take him alive, hold him incognito for however long we need until everything is in place, and then kill him."

"Whatever you say, Sir."

"All right. We're finished for now, except for just one more question: can you guarantee to me that he is a perfect double for Pope John Paul II?"

"No doubt about it. Dress him up in a white cassock and you'd think they're twin brothers."

(3)

After his week in Washington conferring with Father Michael Kanek, John DeSanto returned to Peoria. He called Susan and left a message for her. He promised to be home by the dinner hour.

They had met three years earlier in Chicago, shortly after he left the Navy and returned to the Midwest. By a fortunate coincidence for him, she was on the rebound from a broken romance and he happened by, just at the right time, to pick up the pieces. A computer software sales manager named Elliott Something-or-Other had successfully romanced her into believing he was about to pop the question. One night at dinner he plied her with too much wine and then made his move. Despite his artful effort at seduction, she had greater powers of resistance, even with high blood alcohol content, than he had expected: her commitment to virtue was far more than skin deep and even half a bottle of Burgundy 1968 could not wash it away. Worse still for Elliott's long-term prospects, Susan later remembered, despite her earlier fog, his efforts to pull her dress off before she slapped him. The next day, cold sober, she had called him to say the sound he was about to hear was her, "striking the key that says *Delete!*"

Not long after, John and Susan ran into each other and began dating. As a serious Catholic, he had never entered bogus romances based on ulterior purposes. His style was so low key that he did not even try to kiss her until the end of their fifth date, a disarming tactic based half on genuine shyness and half on belief that a man is more charming to a woman if he goes slow and makes her wonder whether she lacks sex appeal. In his own case, John had sex appeal aplenty: athletic build, good looks, macho Navy background, and solid character that made a normal woman with good sense drool over the prospect of a permanent relationship with a good man who might become a good father. Initially however, Susan was slow to drool, because of her lingering disgust with the maladroit Elliott Something-or-Other; but she warmed up rapidly once she realized that John DeSanto had honorable intentions. They married one year from the day they met.

Both in their thirties, they wanted to start a family; and Susan became pregnant within a few months of their marriage. By agreement with his brother and sister, John and Susan moved onto the fifty-acre country estate--erstwhile farm--on which his widowed mother still lived. She insisted they have the main house and she move into the guest house; that way they could have privacy and still be nearby to assist as her health deteriorated. Later, with his mother's death, John inherited the farm while the siblings received comparable value in cash and securities. It was one of those occasional estate settlements, handled through a revocable trust without the delay and hassle of Probate, that leaves all the heirs happy.

They finished supper in the big farmhouse kitchen, enough light coming in from the west windows as the sun set over the pond, to supplement two candles burning cozily on the table. John recounted his week in Washington and Susan listened with genuine interest, tinged with mounting concern.

"This priest your brother sent you to--what do you think of him?" she asked. Women have a way of sensing the nuance of a person and she wanted to assess Father Kanek, even if vicariously, through John's impressions.

"Sharp guy. Very smart, got a Ph.D. or something in electronics. Very well read, too."

"I know he's smart, John; all Jesuits are smart. But these days not all of them are orthodox." Susan was a traditional Catholic and, more than many lay people in the 1990's, aware of the struggle in the United States between 'the American Catholic Church' and the traditional Roman Catholic Church. She had lived in Chicago during Cardinal Bernadin's years there and her intuition had made her wonder where the Cardinal stood on a continuum between orthodox and heterodox. She couldn't figure where to place him, but his ruffle-no-feathers-ever-be-diplomatic style, while tolerating what she considered liturgical abuse and endorsing more than a smidgen of the "social gospel," and rarely promoting spirituality, had made her worry.

"He's orthodox, all right," responded John. "You can be reassured on that point. In fact, he's a member of Father Gobbi's Marian Movement of Priests, he's a real expert on the twentieth century Marian appearances, and the Pope chose to invite him to a private meeting when he was here a few months ago."

"That's good. So it follows that he is what they used to call, 'a man of prayer'?"

"I'm sure of it. When you get to the bottom line, either you are a believer in the spiritual life or you are not. If you are, then either it is the central focus of your life around which everything else revolves, or it is peripheral, like a hobby. Father Kanek's a believer--and I think he's so deep into the Marian apparitions that he must be practicing what he preaches."

"Which is?"

"That we are coming soon to an event or a period that mystics call 'the Chastisement'...that shortly before or maybe during that time, there will be an illumination of conscience, a 'Warning,' which will show everyone in the world where they stand with God...and that folks like you and me had better do a Hell of a lot more prayer and penance than we have been, for our own sakes, and for the many people we know who have lost their faith."

She poured him a second cup of decaf and then another cup for herself. He remained silent, waiting for her comment. She put the pot down slowly, thinking about the implications of what he had said.

"John, it's not going to be just spiritual, is it? I mean, this 'Chastisement' is the same thing as what Protestants call the 'Tribulation,' isn't it?"

"I think it's the same--though you could be clever and see some difference: the Chastisement might be the punishment God inflicts on His wayward children, us Christians who know better but don't *do* better--and the Tribulation could be the punishment God inflicts on mankind as a whole, who have a conscience, however darkened, and who know in their hearts the massive evils most of them are committing."

"So what's the difference in practice? What does it mean to you and me and our baby?" She gestured toward the crib in the next room.

"Honey, I know women have a greater concern for home, children, the nest, nurturing, than many men--but from my perspective, I have the same worries as you, 'cause my job as a husband and father is to provide for and protect you and my child. So, please indulge me if I get very practical with you."

"Sure," she said, wondering what this was a prelude to.

"You asked a minute ago whether it was going to be just spiritual. The answer is No. In fact, it will be both spiritual and physical. The physical side will be mind-boggling. God will give us a last chance to repent--the Warning. Many people will turn back to God but--this is amazing to me, but human nature has a perverse streak--the majority will not. They'd rather continue to wallow in their sins. God will then say, 'Enough! I've had it!' And He will send punishments, which will act as purifications of the world." He took a sip of coffee and watched her expression. It was worried.

"Probably there will be some huge physical catastrophes," he added, "such as earthquakes, monstrous storms, tidal waves. One visionary, a former corporate executive from New York named John Leary, has reported mystical messages about a comet or asteroid hitting the Atlantic Ocean...On the financial front, an economic collapse, like a Stock Market crash. There could be a nuclear war. Plagues and famines are not out of the question."

She stared blankly at the remaining crimson in the western sky. They could hear the tree frogs croaking in the small grove next to the pond. There was no wind, the air was dry, and the sunset glow reflected red off the calm surface. *Like the Garden of Eden at sundown?* she mused. *Why couldn't people be as good as the nature God gave us?*

"When will all this take place?" she finally asked.

"Honey, no one knows the exact date; but the 'signs of the times' are fairly clear. We don't know the precise day, but we can tell the *season*. I think some of it will begin by the year 2000. But--before you let that worried look cross your face again--there is reason for optimism and hope, too."

"Great! I was beginning to wonder if you could get us two tickets on the Space Shuttle for a prolonged mission!" She forced herself to grin.

"Too cooped up." He smiled in return. "I'd rather be on my own carrier--in the Pacific," he added. "But seriously, what I read and the discussions with Father Kanek all included plenty of positive stuff--reasons for optimism."

"Such as?"

"Well, for one, the messages constantly reiterate the power of prayer: we can actually affect--change--physical events. We can re-direct the thrust of unfolding history, postpone or at least mitigate these judgments of God. In more than one message to a mystic named Sadie Jaramillo the Virgin Mary emphasizes the fact that the Rosary actually *frightens* any demons that are around."

"I'd like to read that. I have to admit, I haven't been saying the Rosary every day--and when I do, often I'm pretty distracted. It would perk up my intensity to know my prayer really makes a difference."

"When I was in flight training, in gunnery school," he mused, "they always gave us an actual target to try to hit. We just didn't *shoot*; we shot *at something*. I think prayer is much the same. Of course, a person has to *believe* there's something out there to 'hit'--and he has to *believe* that he, or she, can hit it.

"But, hey, what's past is past," he added. "Most of us Catholics have been lukewarm in one way or another, at least part of the time. Spiritually, we've gotten out of shape. No point in self-flagellation. Now's the time to start getting back in shape."

He stood up, she did as well, and they both gathered up the few dinner dishes and set them in the sink. "Let's go outside," he said. "The dishes can wait." He flipped some light switches next to the sliding door and the floodlamps up under the eaves illuminated the outer edge of the deck, the patio beyond, and the swale of grass sloping forty yards down a gentle hill to the pond.

They stepped onto the deck. He took her hand and they stood motionless for a moment, absorbing the quiet cool of the night. He wondered whether he had told her too much, scared her by his bluntness; maybe he should have couched everything in conditionals and the skeptic's on-the-one-hand,-on-the-other approach, which creates no conviction because it dispels no doubts.

She had been thinking about the positive. Finally she said, "O.K., give me another reason to be optimistic."

"Sure. These messages keep repeating, again and again, that faith is from God, fear is from the Devil. They can't exist at the same time in the same person. As in the Old Testament, God keeps saying, 'Do not fear, I will be with you.' He does add, though, 'I cannot help you *unless you ask.*'"

"So on the one hand, God tells us that our whole lives could come apart at the seams--and on the other hand, He says we should not be afraid! That's a lot to swallow, at least if a person doesn't have much faith!"

"If a person doesn't have much faith," he responded, "he's up a deep creek without a paddle....Anyhow, there's a third reason for optimism: this evil time will be shortened. In fact, it already has been--because of fasting, sacrifice, and prayer."

"Anything else?"

"Yes. The angels--our Guardian Angels--will play a big role in the hard times to come. In fact, Michael the Archangel will be available to those who ask his help."

"That'd be good," she said, in understatement. "I always thought of him as God's 'enforcer' or a really tough bodyguard."

"That may be a bit anthropomorphic," he said, "but it probably has a lot of truth to it. But when Lucifer said, 'I will not serve,' and tried to con all the other angels into rebelling against God and actually overthrowing Him, Michael threw down the gauntlet: he challenged Lucifer and the others to tell him, 'Who is like onto God?'"

"His point was that they all were *creatures* and that God is the *Creator,*" she added. "He and the good angels then drove the rebels out of Heaven. They landed *here*--on earth."

"Right. Which means Michael's job is not finished, until he kicks them out and drives them down to Hell. For good. And I have a hunch he is chaffing at the bit, wanting to get his hands on Lucifer."

She thought for a few moments. Then she said, "John, you fly a lot. And when you do, I always worry that something would go wrong--and you won't come back."

"Now, Honey, you know I'm the best damn pilot this side of Chuck Yager. Besides, I'm sticking within the borders of the good old U.S. of A. No combat here. Hey, why'd you bring that up?--we were talking about angels and archangels."

"You don't see the connection, Mr. Superpilot?" He pursed his lips and nodded No. "Well, to me it's all one piece: *angels* fly...*You* fly...Therefore, you need an angel to fly with you!"

"I don't think that's good logic," he said.

"Logic, smogic. You men are all computer, no heart. As a woman, *I* understand this stuff. God gave Eve to Adam because he was too logical and needed someone who would use *both* sides of her brain, the 'heart' side as well as the 'logic' side, to help him get through life. And as *your* 'heart side,' I hereby declare that you've gotta start saying that prayer to Michael the Archangel that we used to say after every Mass."

"O.K., you win," he said agreeably. "Never can tell when I might need a celestial bodyguard." He was only half kidding.

CHAPTER VIII

(1)

Pat Greene was not enjoying his conversation with the bank manager. As an independent spirit and self-styled skeptic, he wanted to make up his own mind, not only on such theological matters as whether God had become man in Jesus, but also on such mundane things as how many credit cards he wanted to have.

This mundane decision apparently had been usurped by something called "The Bank of International Settlements," located, for Heaven's sake, in Basil, Switzerland! And Pat was not happy about it at all.

"You mean to tell me," he started back over the same verbal territory, "that I *must* sign up for this 'SmartCard' thing?"

"I wouldn't put it quite that starkly," responded Morgan Janley, the manager of Atlantic Bank's Arlington branch. "It's a new service all the banks in the country are offering. Actually," she smiled her warmest smile, "our customers think it's a great step forward in banking."

"Forgive me, Morgan," said Pat, trying to put the conversation on an informal level, "I don't want to seem argumentative--but I guess I just don't see the benefits."

"Of course, Mr. Greene, and that's my fault," she countered, controlling some irritation because she actually felt it was his fault. "I didn't explain the benefits clearly--so let me summarize quickly: the SmartCard is issued at our expense, and it contains financial information which we already have in our computer, about your account. But more than that, it actually *holds your money*--it's like a mini-Bank--so that when you swipe it across the check-out machine at Safeway, or run through a toll booth, it automatically debits your account. Saves you lots of time."

And creates an electronic record of what I've bought or where I drove, thought Pat; but he did not say it. Morgan Janley did not cook up this scheme, he mused, and it would do no good to complain to her about the loss of his privacy.

"I'm not as thrilled about that as you are, Morgan," said Pat, trying a pragmatic rationale for his resistance, "since I'm one of those guys who balances his check book rarely. It would be embarrassing if Safeway's scanner said *Tilt!* because I had insufficient funds--in this Card."

"Well, Mr. Greene, that's not likely, now is it?" she rejoined. "I would think that a successful author like yourself would always keep a 'cushion' in his account. Now let me just bet"--she flashed her warmest smile again--"you have not had more than one or two 'bounced' checks *in your whole life,* now have you?"

"No, but that's not the point," he answered, feeling he was getting the run-around. "But I guess if I don't like the thing, I just won't bother to use it."

"That may not be an option," she said evenly, trying not to sound threatening. "You see, after a three-month break-in period, all VISA and MasterCards will be cancelled, and the SmartCard will be the one credit/debit card people use." She paused, watching his facial reactions. She had been instructed to keep a list of customers who remonstrated too strongly.

"Wow! There are millions of those things circulating around out there. All over the world! You're going to cancel them all? Won't that disrupt a lot of business?"

"I suppose it might--temporarily, until people adjust. But Mr. Greene, you must understand," she said, lowering her voice as if she was about to share a secret, "*I* am merely an Atlantic Bank branch manager. The decision to do this was made, I understand, by the Bank of International Settlements in Basil, Switzerland back in late May or early June of 1998."

"Who in Heaven's name are they?"

"I'm not sure. I've only been told that they are the international oversight or supervisory body for all the banks in the world."

"So there's a bank in Switzerland that has the power to tell a Virginia bank in the United States to force a new form of credit card on its American customers, some of whom don't want it."

"Again, Mr. Greene, some people might feel the way you characterize this development is somewhat harsh," she said, once more evading his point. "After all, global uniformity in banking procedures is a good idea, wouldn't you think?"

"I guess so," he said and looked at his watch. He then mumbled something about an appointment he had to make and stood to leave. *No, I don't think so,* he thought, *especially when the thing you use, this computer card, can be used as a tracking device to locate the guy who's carrying it.*

(2)

Father Michael Kanek dropped the envelope into the mail box, addressed to Matthew DeSanto, Esq., a follow-up to a phone conversation prompted by some remarks by John DeSanto, to whom he planned to give a copy at their next meeting. After extended prayer and reflection, he had decided that the Pope's letter should be put--in confidence--into the hands of as many trustworthy people as possible. The troubling thought had crossed his mind, *What if an imposter Pope replaced the heads of all the religious orders with men and women cut out of the same apostate cloth as the new Pope himself? and these new Superiors chose to send the traditional clerics to a metaphorical Siberia?* Though he doubted that such a thing could happen, and, if it did, he doubted such a development could prevent him from publishing John Paul II's last Apostolic Letter, it might be difficult. Better safe than sorry.

(3)

The telescope rotated so slowly scanning the sky that one would think it did not move. But its single unblinking eye moved inch by inch from east to west, missing nothing within its range. Its computer-programmed camera recorded thousands of frames sprinkled with little light dots, many so faint that only spectrographic enhancement could make them visible to the naked eye.

Visual inspection by humans being less reliable than computer comparisons, the telescope and its camera attachment worked alone this cold late winter night. Everything was automatic: the aim, the focus, the shots, the prints, the evaluation of the patterns of light dots. The computer did the comparisons: this frame compared to that, yesterday's frames compared to today's, sets compared to sets. Where possible if the target area contained measurable gravity--say, the planet Venus appeared in the scan--radio signals were automatically beamed toward the planet and bounced off it, to give a reading that could measure electromagnetic intensity, gravitational pull, and surface activity.

Tonight the telescope peered into the segment of the sky containing Mars, Jupiter, and the asteroid belt. The two planets, visible to the naked eye, had provided endless fascination to astronomers: space probes had inspected them and sent back thousands of detailed photos of their forbidding terrain; and the warp and woof of much science fiction, like the landscape of Mars itself, was pockmarked with fantastic essays about life on, or invaders from, these planets.

But the less noticeable asteroid belt had not really been scrutinized. It was impossible to inspect without sophisticated instruments; careful scrutiny did not begin until 1891, with the invention of the "blink comparator," in which are mounted photographic plates picturing exactly the same region of the sky, with the exposures separated in time by only a few hours or a day. By comparing images one could detect change. Needless to say, in the post-World War II era, the rapid advance of computers greatly enhanced accurate observations and tabulations and by 1974 the estimate of minor planets--asteroids--*within* our solar system was up to fifty thousand. Some were outside the asteroid belt.

One such minor planet, Icarus, discovered only as recently as 1949, actually approached the earth as close as roughly 4.2 million miles, near enough for radar observation.

Now the robot telescope plodded on in its mapping/comparing path, recording no change, recording no change, recording no change--until--*the data seemed to show Icarus change direction.* Since this event was noted around 3:00 a.m., the equipment was unmanned. Automatically therefore, the computer printed out the following:

> *Alert! Possible discovery near Icarus. Recommend scrutinize. Check data. Repeat all automatic blink comparisons with new photographs.*

(4)

Just as he entered his room, the phone rang.

"Hey, Mike, this is your brother. How ya doing? It's been a while." Father Mike recognized the voice at once--his FBI brother, Jerry. They'd kept in touch over the years and when Christmas holiday schedules permitted, gotten together with the rest of the family at Mom's house in Detroit. But in 1996 and 97 Jerry had been in California doing whatever FBI agents do and couldn't get back. Mike was pleased to hear from him again.

"Listen, Mike, I'm at a pay phone at LAX. Taking the Red Eye out in a few minutes. Be in D.C. tomorrow. Love to get together with you, say, soup and sandwich, and have you bring me up to date on all the spiritual stuff you dabble in. Nothing worthwhile shouting about on my end, but hate to have a couple years go by without keeping in touch."

Nothing worthwhile shouting about on my end--a phrase they had half-jokingly agreed upon three years ago to mean, really, *There's something important I need to tell you--and whisper about.* The use of the phrase also meant that Jerry did not want what he said overheard and was afraid that it might be.

"Sure, Jerry, no problem. Name the place. If you buy, I'll eat dessert. If I buy, it's bread and water for both of us. Vow of poverty, you know." They both laughed.

"How about we just meet at 1:00 o'clock tomorrow at the lobby of the Best Western in Rosslyn and walk to some local restaurant? After all night on a plane, I'll need a bit of exercise."

(5)

Jerry Kanek had entered the FBI right out of law school almost twenty years ago. He was trained at a time when the Bureau still had the old *esprit de corps* inculcated by J. Edgar Hoover and his immediate successors: that the Bureau was a kind of secular religious order, bound together by unbreakable ties of honor, loyalty, honesty, etc. Like the training given at West Point and the Naval Academy, the Bureau turned out a special kind of men, and later, women, whose honesty, patriotism, professionalism, and commitment made them the top investigative agency in the world.

But that was a different era. In recent years, something pernicious had crept into the process--and the people. Perhaps it was just a reflection of the spreading moral rootlessness that infected so much of society and every social institution at the turn of the Century. He did not know what it was--only, Jerry mused, it was now a fact that *he did not automatically trust his fellow Agents.* He knew of cases where a superior had urged a field Agent to "look the other way" and not reveal evidence or not follow up a promising lead. It was rumored that in one case the Bureau *concocted* evidence to "set up" a certain target...As did the Pope, he too took note of little coincidences and paid attention to what people *did* and not just what they *said*, and he had concluded that he had better be cautious about whom he confided in, even in the Bureau.

Now he had debarked United Flight 267 at Dulles International Airport, ridden the half mile in its strange-looking shuttle buses to the terminal, and stood in the United luggage area watching the conveyor belt as it coughed up passengers' bags. Instead of crowding close to the moving belt, as most passengers did, he held back and pretended to search for a phone number in a pocket-sized Daytimer, as he watched the crowd. Thus he was not surprised, when his own suitcase came along, that another passenger, a nondescript man in brown leather jacket and blue slacks, pressed through the crowd, grabbed his bag, and hurried away up a ramp toward the exit. Instead of chasing the man, Jerry followed some distance behind, memorizing every detail of the man's appearance.

Assuming his victim would wait until all passengers awaiting luggage had left and then complain to airline Customer Service about his missing bag, the thief did not look behind him as he walked across the parking lot to his car. In the cold wind, he fumbled with his key at the car lock and Jerry managed to get close enough, still unnoticed, to discern the car license plate numbers.

Jerry smiled. *Too bad, sucker. The papers you think I have are not in the bag. They're under my shirt!*

(6)

They sat in a rear corner of the restaurant, the priest's back toward the entrance, his brother facing it. The lighting was dim but not dark, cast by 1890s lamp shades designed to create old-time atmosphere. The place was almost empty as the lunch crowd spilled out on the street to head back to their offices. The waitress, a bouncy co-ed from Georgetown named Karen, brought them their mushroom soup and club sandwiches promptly enough. She figured that probably the priest would not buy, but the other guy, who looked like a lawyer, might be a good tipper. Jerry raised her hopes further by pressing two dollars into her hand, hinting it was earnest money for a later tip, as he asked for their own full pot of coffee and her promise not to interrupt unless he waved at her.

They had covered personal and family things during a mile-and-a-half walk around Rosslyn, a trek Father Mike realized early on was meant as much to shake any followers as to get exercise and find a restaurant. This insight came in the first five minutes, when at Jerry's suggestion they entered The Best Western Hotel, which was built on a hill, its main entry on the ground level, a rear parking entry on the third floor. They took the elevator to its third floor restaurant, accepted the host's offer of a table near the door, asked for ice tea and menus--and then, at Jerry's whispered request, exited to "hit the head." Father Mike got the hint, mumbled something about too much coffee all morning himself, and followed. The men's room was one floor below, and Jerry chose the stairs rather than the elevator. In the restroom he kept up meaningless chit-chat and then, back in the hall again, he led them *up the stairs and out the third-floor rear exit,* which opened onto a small parking area and a sidewalk beyond. Thence they continued their walk.

Finally settled for lunch, Father Mike wanted to know the inside story. "O.K., Sherlock, what's this Pink Panther stuff all about?"

Jerry smiled. "Probably I'm a little over cautious, but better safe than sorry. This morning when I got off the plane an interesting thing happened at the baggage claim area." He described the theft of his suitcase.

"Why didn't you arrest the guy?" asked Father Mike.

"I thought of that. But I was torn between busting one of their small fry, or letting them think I wasn't on to them. Also--and this is the real point--I had left a fake document in the suitcase that did *not* reveal I had come across a really important one. If they have any doubt whether I know what they're up to, when their thief brings home the bacon, it won't cook--they still won't know."

"What's the real document about? And who's *they...?*" asked the priest.

"One thing at a time. Let me give you a little background. What I'm telling you--this whole conversation--is under the Seal of Confession. O.K.?" The priest nodded agreement.

"You probably heard that the Japanese have developed a computer chip so small that they can attach it to a cockroach, let the little bugger loose in the walls of a building, and use him as a listening device. As a matter of fact, it's likely that they can use the chip to *control where he goes*--immensely enhancing his value in gathering information."

"Giving new meaning," said the priest, "to the phrase, *bugging someone's office!*" They both laughed.

"Right. Now--here's the problem--the Japanese and the Chinese are heavily into industrial espionage, to get more info on what our R&D is coming up with. The Chinese are worse. So the Bureau has a Task Force trying to get a handle on whether anyone is stealing our secrets, and if so, who. I'm involved in it. And our friends from Asia routinely use bribery. Our Task Force has enough poop on some mid-level computer executives who are taking payoffs from overseas, that I got a warrant for a clandestine search of one company's files. Among other things, I came up with something I want you to read."

Jerry unbuttoned the vest of his three-piece business suit, brushed aside his tie, unbuttoned the three middle shirt buttons, reached under his shirt, and pulled out a skin-colored file folder. It contained two pages. "Read this."

In a print smaller than the remainder, a small first paragraph read:

> "The following is an internal memorandum smuggled out of the security division of a major computer manufacturer. It concerns the progress of an implantable microchip and the testing being done on unsuspecting American citizens. In order to protect our sources, proper names have been omitted."

The rest of the document, in a different type, continued for a page and a half:

"The control of crime will be a paramount concern in the 21st Century. We must be ready with our security products when demand for them becomes popular. Our Research and Development Division has been in contact with the Federal Bureau of Prisons and prison officials in three States, to run limited trials of what we have named 'The 21-C Neural Chip Implant.' We have established representatives of our interests in both management and institutional level positions within these three prison departments. "Federal regulations do not yet permit testing of implants on prisoners, but we have entered into contractual agreements with privatized health care professionals and specified correctional personnel to do limited testing of our products. We have had major successes in privately owned sanitariums with implant technology. We need, however, to expand our testing to research how effective the 21-C Neural Chip Implant performs in those identified as the most aggressive in our society. Limited testing has produced a number of results. "In the western State, several prisoners were identified as members of the security threat group, EME, or Mexican Mafia. They were brought to the prison health services unit and <u>tranquilized with advanced sedatives</u> developed by our laboratories. The implant procedure takes 20-30 minutes depending on the experience of the technician. We are working on a device which will reduce that time by as much as 80%. There seems to be no theoretical reason why, with further experience, the time cannot be reduced to as little as 60 seconds. The implants on eight prisoners in one facility yielded the following results:

- Implants served as surveillance monitoring devices for threat group activity;

- Implants disabled two subjects during an assault on correctional staff;

- Universal side effects in all 8 test subjects revealed that when implant was set to 116MHz all subjects became lethargic and slept on average of 18-22 hours per day;

- All subjects refused recreation periods for 14 days during the 116 MHz test evaluation;

- 7 of the 8 subjects did not exercise, in the cell or out of the cell, and 5 of 8 subjects refused showers up to three days at a time;

- Each subject was monitored for aggressive activity during the test period and the findings are conclusive that 7 out of the 8 subjects exhibited no aggression, even when provoked.

- Each subject experienced only minor bleeding from the nose and ears 48 hours after the implant, due to initial adjustment;

- Each subject had no knowledge of the implant for the test period and each implant was retrieved under the guise of medical treatment. "Essentially the implants make the unsuspecting prisoner a walking, talking recorder of every event he comes into contact with."

It concluded in this matter-of-fact tone and was signed by someone, probably a junior vice president, in a scrawled "executive signature" that was unreadable.

Father Mike stared at the page. "Whew! Jerry, this thing--what they're doing--is terrible!"

"You got it! Mike, here's a major computer company *experimenting on human beings* and developing the technology to turn any person into a walking listening device or, if it suits them, a zombie that they can control like a robot. I don't give a damn if it's prisoners, it's wrong to do--and they know damn well it is, which is why they do it secretly. And notice the statement, 'We have established representatives of our interests in both management and institutional level positions within these three prison departments.'"

"Interesting perversion of ethics," said the priest. "When you're hired you're supposed to give your employer your best efforts; if a prison management official is really working for an outside company *that wants to 'test' its products on your inmates*, your professional judgment as a prison official is totally compromised. As the Bible says, you can't serve two masters."

"Right. Usually lawyers call it 'conflict of interest.' But what I've got to figure out is, Do I blow the whistle on this? And if I try to, will my efforts do any good? Or do I keep my mouth shut until I have more information?"

"Are you asking *me*?" said the priest.

"Just running the problem by you. The pragmatics I gotta figure out myself. But the ethics part, well, that's your strong suit. So I'd welcome your input. And beyond that, since you're a scientist, I thought it'd be useful to trade information a little on where technology is going. Let me put more fuel on the fire before you answer." He took a sip of coffee.

"Mike, the Government has the equipment now to *set up* a target, to manufacture fake evidence and 'plant' it electronically. For example, we can park a van across the street from a guy's house, a van full of computer wizardry and high-tech transmission stuff, and--at least if his computer in his home office is plugged in--'tap in' to his files, remove them, crash his hard disk, copy all his data, or *even insert into his computer evidence that, later, we can 'find' with a warrant*--'proving' that he did what we want to nail him for."

"I'll bet you electronic gumshoes also have ways to track a suspect's car remotely by satellite," said the priest.

"We do. In fact, we can *disable* it--if not from satellite, though that's coming, at least from a distance on the ground. It's just a matter of making one of the car's essential computers inoperative. We zap it with an electrical transmission. Remember the old *Star Trek* TV stories? Well, we can use a kind of 'photon torpedo,' though small--and nothing explodes. The car just stops."

"Sounds like a great way to catch bank robbers."

"It is--but it also means that Government has a way to stop ordinary citizens whenever it wants, at least people with the newer cars, which have as many computers in them as pin-cushions have pins."

"Why's that so bad? So, you stop someone, find out they didn't do anything wrong, and let them go on their way. Like a 'sobriety checkpoint' on New Year's Eve."

"Mike, I'm not as sanguine about all these developments as you are. It's good to catch the bad guys. But if bad guys have the technology too, they can make life Hell for good guys. For instance, if a sophisticated bunch of robbers had technology to stop cars at night on lonely roads--just by hitting them with a beam of electrons when they go by--you can imagine the crime problem we'll have."

The priest looked at him without speaking. After a long moment, he said, "Jerry, I get hunches once in awhile. I have a hunch it's not just entrepreneurial robbers you're worried about. What else?"

His brother leaned forward over his plate and spoke in a lower tone, even though the restaurant was virtually empty save for their waitress, out of earshot across the room. She was banging enough dishes as she cleared other tables to make it impossible to overhear them.

"It ties in with this whole computer-implant thing...Look, here's a major computer company, with plenty of government contracts, which has compromised government officials already--and thinks this chip thing, which apparently works, will be *a big hit with Government!* I mean, they say they're wandering through this ethical jungle because *law enforcement* will want their method--implanting computer chips in people without their knowledge--to control people.

"Mike, the privacy of American citizens is being--or is going to be--totally compromised in the name of law enforcement. As it is, I walk a thin line: I can convince most judges that I've got 'probable cause' to get a search warrant, or set up a wiretap--but at least I've got to go before a judge--and the hassle alone can rein in an overzealous Agent. There are--or were other practical inhibitions too. Bottom line, though--until recently, I could say that the Bureau has been very careful to respect citizens' privacy."

The priest poured Jerry, then himself, a warm up on the coffee. "You say, 'until recently.' Things have changed?"

"Mike, if I just say the words *terrorism* or *drug money* or *money laundering* to a judge, he'll give me *carte blanche* wiretap authority--let me listen to a thousand innocent calls and never hear a guilty one, or to a thousand innocent people and never detect a crook. We can tap a line automatically, by which I mean, using voice-recognition technology, we can set it up so that if you use certain key words, our computer will record the conversations in which those appear.

"Initially, the higher-ups in the Bureau wanted this capability to identify the drug-runners who were money-laundering. Fine. But tweak the computer a bit, and you can target your political enemies--donors to the other political party--possible candidates for office--newspapers or individual reporters who might investigate you--any guy, for Heaven's sake, who mentions to his wife that he thinks his boss is sending our newest R&D to the Chinese. Doesn't matter if the guy calls from a pay phone; you put a tap on his *home* phone. And if his wife calls her girl friend or her mother during the day and reveals some of his pillow talk, *bingo, jackpot!* we got him!

"And by the way, we can listen in on a guy's conversation in his own home *even if his phone is not in use.*"

"Using lasers?"

"That's one way. You heard of it?" Jerry went on without waiting for an answer. "We've got the tech to aim a laser beam at your family room window from a mile away--turn the glass into a resonator, like a mini satellite dish--and listen in to everything you think you're saying in private. We can record everything. And you don't even know it happened."

"Maybe a person could confuse the eavesdroppers if he shifted to other languages," the priest responded. "You know--to Spanish--or, for you and me, to Polish." He recalled the Pope's tactic as they walked in the monastery garden.

"That could work--if he were talking to someone bilingual--but only the first time. Once we figured out the languages a target could use, we'd upgrade our computer program to include key words in the second language. So, if he was big enough, and thus worth the expense, we'd get him the next time round. But Mike, how many Americans can move easily into a second language? And if he didn't know we were eavesdropping, why would he struggle with a second language?

"Anyhow, let me go to another facet of this." He sipped a taste from his half-empty cup, scowled, decided the contents were too cold, pushed the cup and saucer to the side by the ketchup bottle, and reached over to the adjoining table to retrieve a clean cup, which he filled with hot coffee from the pot. "Want some more?" The priest shook his head 'no'.

"Another facet," Jerry repeated. "We can 'trap' any phone in the country that has a little chip, and most phones made since 1990 do. The computer simply dials your number, you pick up, you say Hello, no one's there, you wait a minute for someone to talk, they don't, so you hang up. Bingo! Gotcha! *Your phone's now a listening device for every conversation in the room--even if it's on the hook!*"

"Wow! That ought to give every civil libertarian a lot of sleepless nights," exclaimed Mike. "I see why you're worried." "I'm worried both because of the raw technical power of Government to learn people's private business and because these new technocrats' notion of absolute right and wrong is about as clear as their notion of marital fidelity or perennial truths--"

"--Non-existent," said the priest glumly.

"In most cases, yes. Situation ethics. 'Result-oriented.' Men and women who are like a plane without a gyroscope." *Same insight as John DeSanto had*, thought the priest.

"And, putting philosophy aside for a second, I think now you've got the context in which I can try to answer your questions." The priest looked puzzled; he had forgotten his questions. Jerry helped him out. "The questions you asked were, 'What's the real document about? and who are *they*...?' You read the real document. To answer who they are is a tougher one." He sipped some coffee, realized he had forgotten the sugar, picked up a small packet, and emptied it into the cup. Then he went on.

"The guy that stole my suitcase singled *me* out because someone knew I was investigating that computer company. It could not have been company officials, because we were plenty careful not to tip our hand. *It had to be either (a) the Judge I went to for the warrant or*

(b) one of my fellow Agents or (c) someone higher up. The higher up could be in the Bureau or maybe all of our people are clean..."

"You rule out the Judge?"

"Yes. The Judge is Irving Finegold; I've known him for years. He was a friend of Morrie Liebman, a Chicago lawyer who was active for two decades in the American Bar Association with its Committee on National Security. Liebman recommended him to President Reagan for judicial appointment and Reagan's people did a super-thorough background check on him. Finegold doesn't know it, but I was one of the Agents who checked him out. He's as clean as Caesar's wife."

"So it has to be someone in the FBI."

"Not necessarily. And the more I think about it, the more I think it may be a bigwig outside the Bureau."

"Why so?"

"Because this thing is super-secret. The Director himself put together the Task Force; there are only five Agents in it, and none of us knows the specifics of what the others are doing. Only the Director knows."

"Then it's the Director. Did you inform him of *which* company you were hitting with your search warrant?"

"He gave me a list of target firms. He has a copy. Every three or four days I report in and just say something like, 'Have finished Item Five--or Item Seven,' or whatever. I do not have to take them in order. In fact, he prefers I do it randomly. All he will know, when I call, is that I finished the fifth or the seventh company. Then I mail a report, within the week, to a P.O. box somewhere and he picks it up."

"Well, as I said, I'm an outsider to this super-sleuth stuff--but it still looks to me as if the Director 'blew your cover,' as I suppose the jargon has it. But if he did not know you were at the most recent company till *after* you were done, he wouldn't have had much time to get your suitcase shoplifter guy in place. Maybe no time. Does he report to someone else?."

"He does. And in this case, I know he did--to the President."

The priest looked at him quizzically. His mind took the next logical step: if the President authorized the theft, *he wants the chip implant program kept entirely secret.* Which means he's tied in with the people who want everyone to take a mark.

* * * * * * * * * * *

CHAPTER IX

(1)

Dolores Montalvo's villa was part of a Gated Estate on the sea side of Barcelona. The security guard at the entrance had dialed her number. "A woman here to see you, Countess Montalvo. A Cristina Montalvo. Looks quite like you but a lot older than you. Could be your mother. Shall I send her up?"

"Please do," responded Dolores, with a cheerfulness in her voice she did not completely feel. Her Aunt's call, two days earlier, had caught her off guard. Preoccupied with her worries about the Chairman and her vulnerability in his employ, alternately angry and yet somehow relieved that she had not conquered the Chancellor of Germany as she had the President of the United States, she had given little thought to her Aunt's call, on her recorder, announcing a possible visit to Barcelona and, consequently, to her beloved niece.

What would she say to Cristina? The woman was so old-fashioned, they had so few things in common...yet she did feel a tug of nostalgia and affection for the only female in her early years who genuinely cared for her. How would she deal with the religion question? She assumed that Cristina remained a staunch Catholic, and she would have to admit to the older woman that she, Dolores, had turned half-agnostic, half-New Ager.

The sound of the elevator door downstairs clanking shut interrupted her thoughts. Shaken into the immediate, she hastened to pull a blue cotton T-shirt over her bikini top and quickly stepped into a matching skirt; no point in irritating her Aunt by seeming immodest, as if that were the only sin she had committed in all these years! Then she strode quickly to the kitchen and started assembling a small wooden tray, a crock of cheese, two kinds of crackers, a couple plates, two butter knives, and some paper napkins. There was a knock. She opened the door.

"*Mijita!* Dolores! It's been too long!"

"Auntie! I've missed you!" she exclaimed in turn, surprised at her own emotion, a slight tear glistening in her eye.

The two women hugged for a long moment and then Dolores suggested they sit on the deck. She brought the cheese, asked the Aunt's preference of drinks, was told "Anything non-alcoholic, but I'd really prefer tea," and so she turned on the stove burner to heat a pot of water. She brought two glasses of ice water and plopped herself down on a deck chair at right angles from her Aunt's, with a small umbrella table between them. From their vantage point, the azure Mediterranean lay before them, glistening in the early afternoon sun. It was a beautiful sight.

They shared the view for a moment, and then Cristina opened. "You are still as lovely as ever," she said with genuine appreciation.

"Thank you," responded Dolores simply. She had decided to make her Aunt's visit as pleasant as possible, for it did offer a welcome distraction from her own irritations. "I try to keep myself up. I exercise every day."

"Do you run on the beach?" asked Cristina, observing a lone jogger fifty yards away. The villa was built on a hill, and thus the nearby beach seemed farther, and the people on it smaller, because of a seventy foot vertical one had to negotiate, by means of winding wooden stairs, before he actually reached the beach.

"When I am in town. Or I swim laps in the pool that's in the rear of this complex. But I have been travelling a good bit the last few months, so I try to use the hotel exercise rooms."

"Ah...travel...making movies...friends, I suppose, in every capital in Europe...a beautiful villa like this...oh, Dolores, your life certainly must be exciting!" The woman's comment seemed sincere, yet Dolores felt there was a question in it, a subtle probing whether this life was fulfilling, whether it had meaning.

"Yes, it is," she said with measured enthusiasm. She decided to take the bull by the horns, so she added, "Of course, Auntie, glamorous people and places come at a price--jealousies, pretended friends who would exploit, a measure of loneliness..."

"Emptiness?" suggested Cristina.

"If you will. Yes...emptiness. Men are interested only in a woman's body. Such a relationship is empty."

If you actresses did not display so much body on the covers of those swimsuit magazines, perhaps you could elevate men's interests to higher things, thought Cristina; but she overcame the temptation to sarcasm and instead said softly, "Only God can fill our emptiness, *Mijita.*"

Struggling inwardly, Dolores did not respond. She did not want to talk about God, because she had locked that spark of faith into a back room of her mind and hoped that it would die, to leave her untroubled by occasional scruples of conscience. Now her Aunt was groping for the key to the locked door. She would try to keep her locked out without offending her.

Cristina sensed her niece's struggle and turned the subject to herself. "When I lost your Uncle Carlos," she began softly, "it was like a horrible darkness had fallen down upon me. I had no children, as you know. Your mother and I were never close, and by then we lived in different cities anyway. You--you were gone out of my life, though, to tell you what I think you know, I loved you like my own daughter." She paused for a second. "So I was alone." She said it with the finality of a prison door slamming shut.

Dolores wanted to say something consoling, but she could not find the words. Cristina continued. "I am telling you this, dear Dolores, because I would have despaired, maybe committed suicide, but for God. God came into my life. Or, I should say, He had always been there, because I always believed; but now, in my moment of need, He manifested Himself."

"Auntie, I am truly happy that you overcame your despair, but during my adult life I have done very well, and--I do not wish to offend you--but I have done very well without turning to God...and now, well...God plays no role in my life."

"I am aware of that, *Mijita*," said Cristina gently. "And I am not here to force Him back in. I will not contest with you, nor will I spoil our brief time together with argument, or leave in anger."

The whistle of the teapot announced shrilly that the water was boiling, and Dolores, relieved at the interruption, rose and strode into the kitchen. A minute later she returned with a cup and a small pot of tea, a wisp of steam floating above it. She set them on the table between them and returned to her chair.

"I made the point about God, and I should add Jesus," continued Cristina, "because the day may come that you face danger or despair too, and I want you to remember me and what I said here. But now," in a lighter tone she began to turn the conversation, sensing Dolores' resistance, "let me bring you up to date on myself."

Cristina then summarized the last few years of her life: her living off a small pension coupled with modest income as part-time purchasing agent for the Dominican college in her city. She mentioned that she kept up her piano skills, traveled little, and noted without rancor that she had few close friends. She skipped speaking of Dolores' father, whom she scarcely ever saw, anyway. She remarked about injuring her knee in a fall, the reason why she now limped slightly. She did not mention her daily hour of prayer. Relieved that the focus was on Auntie and not herself, Dolores readily joined the conversation with questions and comments.

At midpoint in her Aunt's narrative, Dolores began to hanker for some exercise; so she suggested they walk along the beach, barefoot in the wet sand by the water. Cristina enthusiastically agreed. Because of the hot sun, Dolores retrieved from the front hall closet two wide-brim sombrero-style hats, which they donned as they descended the wooden stairs.

As they left the villa enclosure, a transponder chip, operating as a concealed listening device in Dolores' kitchen telephone, which had transmitted their conversation by satellite to a computer terminal in Brussels, sputtered into unintelligible static crackle. Then it went silent. The device lacked the range to pick up conversation outside the villa building. So it did not transmit the last exchange between the two women upon their return, over an hour later, from a leisurely three-mile walk along the beach.

Outside at the front gate of the complex, they stood near Cristina's rented car and said their Goodbyes. Cristina hugged Dolores, kissed her gently on the cheek, promised to pray for her and to return again before Christmas. Relieved that the religion topic had not caused contention, Dolores returned the hug and kiss, mumbled gratitude for the prayers, and half-whispered, with a tear coming to her eye, her hope that Christmas would come soon.

Then Cristina added, as if an afterthought, "Oh, I almost forgot. I've got something to give you." She quickly unlocked the car, sat down in the driver's seat, reached into the glove compartment, and extracted a sealed envelope. "Here, *Mijita,* open this after I've left." Without another word, she started the car and slowly drove down the driveway past the guardhouse, through the gate, and out of sight.

Dolores watched the car leave, tears now in both eyes. Then she opened the envelope. It contained two items. One was a Miraculous Medal on a chain. The other was a newspaper clipping, with a large photo of--*the Chairman!* She gasped. During her visit she had never mentioned him nor her work for him. *How did Cristina know that I'm working for the Chairman?*

Then she read her Aunt's handwriting across the bottom of the newspaper clip,

> *"Dolores, this man is very dangerous. He will try to control you. I beg you, stay away from him. Love, Cristina."*

(2)

The Honest Debate Society had reconvened at Pat Greene's apartment in Rosslyn. One prior visitor, Joanie Atkinson, had not come; but a new member had appeared, Father Kanek's brother, Jerry. Potato chips, cheese dip, coke, beer, ale, and chocolates lay on the coffee table in front of the sofa.

"Ladies--I mean, lady--and gentlemen, and children of all ages," began Pat, with his usual pretended pomposity, "we have a new member of the team, the Honorable Jerry Kanek, brother of our esteemed chaplain. Enlighten us, distinguished Sir, as to your background and your reasons for attending this noble gathering."

"Well, I don't know if my title should be 'Honorable,'" responded Jerry with a smile, "since I'm not a Judge. But I am an attorney and a fact-finder. I work for the government in law enforcement. I'm here to protect my kid brother, Father Mike, from falsehood, non-apple pie, and anything not the American Way."

"What he means," interposed Father Mike, with a grin, "is that I invited him, figuring the topic would be of interest."

"Maybe I could use your services," said Vanni, again in loose fitting blue jeans and a light grey sweatshirt. As at the earlier meeting, this one also had lettering across the chest, a different saying, *Abstinence Makes the Heart Grow Fonder.* "As the only girl surrounded by all you macho men, I might need protection from a certain investigative reporter"--she winked at Pat--"who might try to drag me kicking and screaming to the altar."

"That's the real reason Father Mike's here," retorted Pat, without missing a beat, "--to perform the ceremony once those chocolate cremes I've spiked with an aphrodisiac take effect."

"You're bluffing, buster," said Vanni, "and to prove it I will gobble up my usual supply of calories," she picked up a chocolate, "and I betcha they won't raise my level of lust even one milligram. In fact, since the rest of you may not have noticed the Hope Diamond here on my finger, I'll announce that Pat and I are now engaged--*but*--" she added solemnly, as she pointed to her sweatshirt, "as you can tell from today's motto, Pat is going to have to suffer before he gets the prize."

"When's the date?" asked Jerry.

"We were thinking of December 31, 1999," said Pat, "if Ms. Blonde Bombshell can control her desires that long."

"Or control *yours?*" asked Father Mike.

"Well, maybe. But I have to admit, Vanni and I do see eye to eye on that. I am looking for a 'one-life stand,' not a one-night stand. I can wait less than two years to have her as my wife for the rest of my life."

"How come you chose December 31, 1999?"

"Well, I could be facetious and say that with the Millennium Bug question, if all the lights go out that night because the power grid goes down, it would be an interesting way to start a honeymoon."

"Actually," said Vanni, "Pat and I have to grow together a bit, on the religious thing, and both of us figure that the next two years could see some big changes in the world. We have to get to know each other better and figure out how to deal with those changes."

"Right now, however," said Pat, moving the discussion away from personal plans, "the topic is one which, I admit, I am thinking of working into one of my newspaper articles...and I need the input of wiser minds than mine."

"Thanks for the compliment," said Father Kanek, "if we qualify as 'Wiser Minds.' You told me on the phone you wanted to explore the potential and the implications of computer chip surveillance."

"Right."

"O.K. Shoot--give us a working proposition to debate."

"I can do that," said Jerry Kanek, "provided that *nothing*, absolutely nothing I say here tonight, will be attributed to me. In other words, my name never appears in print, and is never mentioned even orally outside this group. Otherwise, as the CIA people say, 'I'd have to kill you.'" The remark was clearly meant as a joke, and they all took it that way; but they also realized he was serious about anonymity.

"Killing the Talkmeister is against the Rules of the Honest Debate Society," rejoined Pat, smiling, "and besides, Father Mike can prove to you that the End does not justify the Means. So you can't."

"No, but you might suddenly fall asleep"--Jerry punched his right fist into his left palm--"and wake up exiled on a desert island somewhere. That would pass muster with the Principle of Double Effect."

"If you promise to dump Vanni onto the same island, that's O.K. with me!"

"Hey, gang," interrupted Vanni, "I'm not going to any island where there aren't any chocolate cremes and I've gotta do my aerobics alone! Besides, I found a gym that has some Stairmasters, and I climb to the top of the Empire State Building twice a week. Couldn't do *that*, on a desert island. So come back to reality, boys, and let's get on with the topic."

"Right; I'll cut the jokes. Jerry, the answer is: you have my word. As a serious journalist, I protect my sources anyway. I promise not even to say something about a government law enforcement guy--I'll just say 'reliable parties,' or some such."

"O.K. Reliability is subjective, Pat. Subjectively, I am reliable. Whether what I think is objectively correct, you'll have to confirm from whatever other sources you have. But--here's your proposition: *The chip technology is now in place to permit anyone who wants to use it, to track every person in the world.*"

"Why do you say that?"

"Let me try an answer," said Father Mike. "From what I know, it is now possible to put a computer chip in such places as your car license plates, your telephone, or even your television set and know where you are, or overhear what you are saying. And you probably wouldn't know anyone was listening." They all glanced uneasily at the TV sitting in the corner of the room.

"Wouldn't the logistics of that be, well, unbelievably complicated?" asked Vanni. "I mean, there are over two hundred fifty million people in the United States alone--sure, half of them are kids--but that still leaves well over a hundred million adults, all driving cars or making calls or watching television. Seems to me it would take as many people *listening* as there are people *being listened to.*"

"Twenty, thirty years ago, that was the case," said Jerry. "But today a computer chip the size of a penny can do over a trillion--that's a *thousand billion*--calculations in less than a second. All you gotta do is target the people who fit a certain 'profile,' and use a word-recognition computer program."

"I get it," said Pat. He took a sip of *Pete's Wicked Ale.* "You digitally record on a disc the target's conversation and, when he uses certain key words, you isolate that conversation and determine if he has said anything incriminating." He was mentally taking notes for a possible article.

"Right, and then you run your disc back a few minutes to when he called and pick out the numbers dialed. That way you find out who he called too," said Jerry. "Or, program it another way: set it up so that whenever Mr. X, your target, calls anyone, you get a computer reading of the ID of every person he talks to. Then you tap them in turn."

"O.K., you geniuses have convinced me," said Vanni. "But why would anyone want to go to all that trouble? Maybe the technical side is possible, but who would *use* it?"

Father Mike had been rereading all the recent books of prophecy and his mind turned to warnings in those by John Leary. "It is possible," he said, trying not to sound melodramatic, "that a would-be dictator would want to 'tap' everyone's phone early in his reign, before he had solidified control, to locate his remaining rivals or those people most likely to resist the police state he is about to impose."

"Ability to tap their opponents' phones would have made seizing power even easier for Lenin and Hitler back in their time," added Pat.

"Father Mike, you mentioned putting computer chips in license plates, phones, televisions...How about in a credit card, like the new 'SmartCard'?" interjected Vanni.

"Sure. Goes without saying. The thing does have a little chip in it. That's one reason I'm not going to take it, though maybe the mega banks won't send one to a Jesuit priest, who has a vow of poverty. It's not 'the Mark of the Beast' that the Bible warns against, but in my opinion it still has too much evil potential."

"You have a VISA card, Father?" asked Vanni. The priest nodded in the affirmative. "Yep, for air travel, mostly."

"Then you're on their list," said Pat. He summarized his exchange with Morgan Janley at Atlantic Bank earlier that week.

Jerry looked at him with a frown. He saw a worse possible abuse. "Let's say that each of us did accept that SmartCard thing, and we each had it in our wallet or purse right now. Let's say, further, that the damn thing is more than a little file drawer of your medical, driving, and bank info, but that it is also a *surveillance device*--so that it sends a signal which somehow these towers we see going up everywhere enhance and beam up to a satellite..."

"Which re-transmits to some central computer, like in the National Security Agency or the White House," continued Vanni.

"Or," added Father Mike, "as far as, say, a computer in Brussels or Rome."

"Whoever controls that computer can, within twenty seconds, know who came to this meeting, and, if the thing is also a listening device, know what we talked about," said Jerry. "Since everybody in the country will have one of these babies, the Government could listen in on *any* meeting *anywhere!*"

"By the way," said Father Mike, "the only solid information anybody has about the new Chairman of the Council of Europe is that he's a big computer expert."

"My God!" exclaimed Pat. "He could put an end to privacy, to freedom of association, and to freedom of speech! And," he added with a touch of despair, "most Americans won't even question it."

At that remark, Vanni's usual bubbly optimism deserted her. She stared at the TV set without really seeing it and heard herself saying, "George Orwell's *1984*...only in 1999."

(3)

John and Susan DeSanto sat on the sofa in their farmhouse outside Peoria, watching the television weather report. They had spent the day loading boxes of dehydrated food staples into the basement and sending out audiocassette tapes on the End Times to anyone who responded to the newspaper ads they had placed in the Catholic press around the country.

John didn't much care for television news. It was canned, the doctored product reflecting a truncated world view of elitist commentators and "anchormen" who were high paid propagandists for secular humanism. The networks almost always portrayed ministers as money-grubbing frauds and priests as hypocritical spokesmen for chastity who carried on secret affairs with female parishioners. He also had found that one could learn far more about the true state of the world by reading *Remnant Review* and *The McAlvaney Intelligence Advisor* along with the books Father Mike had given him, than a year of watching Tom Brokaw or Dan Rather. So he rarely watched TV news.

Nor did Susan. The baby took a good deal of time, but the chief reason was her reaction to John's explanation of what the near future probably held. She had not wanted to hear it, because more than anything she wanted to be a wife and mother and raise a large family in a stable setting. But she had taken the time to read most of the books John brought home and had just finished Sadie Jaramillo's *THE GREAT SIGN: Messages and Visions of Final Warnings*. Now she turned the TV off and read the Bible or prayed the Rosary.

But tonight they took time out for the weather special, a documentary on the country's travail. They both had relatives in various parts of the country sweltering under the unnatural heat.

The report was worse than they had heard earlier that afternoon. Parts of Florida were still smoldering; widespread fires had broken out in sections of Texas, California, and Oregon; the heat wave was spreading, like a toxic plague, northward into Kansas and Nebraska, and if substantial rains did not come soon, much of the corn and soybean crops would be ruined. For the first time in their lifetimes, they heard a public official, the Secretary of Agriculture, remark--cautiously--the possibility of food shortages.

Following a forecast of another week of 100-degree-plus heat across most of the country, the cameras returned to Florida, to show dark menacing clouds sending out countless sky-to-ground lightning strikes, which started new fires.

"Are you thinking what I'm thinking?" she asked.

"Yup. If you have in mind what I told you about that vision driving to Chicago in that horrible thunderstorm a few months ago: this awful weather is part of the punishment for our sins.

"That's it," she said. "And one other thing: the lightning--the TV people talk about it as if it just happens--you know, some sort of blind chance--but the fact is, if a sparrow does not fall from Heaven without God's knowledge, then lightning does not scorch the earth without God's permission."

"You're right, honey. But not one American in a thousand, and maybe not one Catholic in a hundred, makes the connection between the fires and our country's sins."

(4)

Father Sean O'Bannon held in one hand a FAX of a page from *THE JERUSALEM POST*, which a fellow Franciscan had sent him from the Holy Land. The other priest had circled a news article about an inexplicable phenomenon that had occurred over Jerusalem the night before: *green lightning.*

In the other hand he held a phone. He was finishing a brief call to Father Michael Kanek, who had authorized him to read "that manuscript we discussed."

"Mike, before we hang up, I have one question, which may or may not be relevant to anything we've discussed...Do you know anything about a phenomenon, which the *JERUSALEM POST* reported over that city two days ago--*green lightning...!?*"

"Not that specific occurrence. But I can tell you that at least one of the mystics who receive frequent messages from Jesus and Mary was told a couple years ago in effect, that when you see green lightning, know that the time of Antichrist is near."

CHAPTER X

(1)

It had not been a good week for Pat Greene. First the babe at Atlantic Bank had insisted he accept a SmartCard when the bank introduces it in a few weeks. Now another problem: Franklin Moorehead, his Editor at the *New York Tribune*, insisted they would *not* publish his expose on the HAARP project.

"Let me get this straight," he said, straining to keep anger out of his voice. "You find nothing wrong with my article, but you won't print it...?"

"Nothing 'wrong,' Pat, in the sense that it seems you've got your facts straight and you state your conclusions in a responsible way," said the voice on the other end of the line.

"Then why the Hell won't you print it?" snorted Pat, his anger going up a notch.

Moorehead decided to try to be conciliatory. He liked Pat Greene and respected his work. When the *Tribune* decided to engage him as a Contributing Editor, they knew he "pushed the envelope" sometimes; but his treatment of controversial themes was invariably fair and balanced. "Pat, you gotta understand; this decision does not change our relationship: we will still pay you for submitting one solid article per month. And we will pay you for this one on HAARP."

"But what's wrong with my article?" Pat repeated. He didn't mind the offer of his $8,500.00-per-article stipend, but if he accepted the money and shut up, what commitment to principle did he show? Just one more reporter who gets bought off.

"I've been told that any article on HAARP could compromise national security."

"National security! Frank, there's nothing in there that's not public knowledge--or at least available to the public if they wanted to check things out and put two and two together. Look, I was tempted to try to break into BDR's offices, but I didn't. I was tempted to try a lot of things that, if I got caught, could put me in jail--but I didn't. All I did was check out the twelve patents these guys got, interview some scientists employed by a subsidiary of ARCO, get in touch with a fellow in Alaska, talk with a big expert on Nicholas Tesla, and surf all over the Internet to find people who also worried about this fool experiment. Just stuff that any good reporter would do. All the information is already out there. I simply put it together.

"Anyway, you journalistic purists didn't worry about national security when you published *The Pentagon Papers* twenty-five years ago. 'The public's right to know,' you said, was more important. Don't you think the public has a right to know, today, that a bunch of Dr. Strangeloves are zapping the ionosphere with enough gigawatts of energy to destroy the ecology of the whole damn planet?!"

"Pat, personally I would be inclined to agree with you. But it's not my decision alone. We work closely with the Government on evaluating articles that might, just might, compromise national security...and our Government contacts who have reviewed your essay think we should hold it indefinitely."

Pat was really fuming now. "So, what you're telling me, if I may rephrase it, is that the Government acts as *censor* of controversial articles in a major American newspaper. What about *my* First Amendment right of freedom of speech? For that matter, what about *your* right of freedom of the press?"

"It's not really censorship, Pat. Censorship occurs when Government puts criminal penalties on the publication of an article, so that if a newspaper did, the author and the paper's editor would be fined or thrown in jail. Or when they get an injunction against printing it anywhere. Here, you are free to take your article and sell it to some other paper. Of course, if you say that's what you'll do, we won't pay the $8,500.00--and if no one else takes it, you've lost $8,500.00."

"And maybe get blackballed with any big paper or syndicate after my year's contract with you guys runs out?"

"Well, Pat, that wouldn't be my preferred way of handling this. But you know how the corporate world is: ruffle too many feathers, and the big birds want to kick you out of the nest. So I guess it could happen."

"O.K., I get the message. I'll take it under advisement. I want to get some advice on what to do, so I won't decide right now. I'm the kind of guy who puts principle over pragmatics--so, to live with myself, I just might have to swallow the loss. But on the other hand, my dad always told me to ask that old Marine Corps question, 'Is *this* the hill you want to die on?'"

"Good. Cool down. Give it some thought. If you want, come on up to New York next week and I'll buy you lunch; we can discuss it some more then."

"Thanks for the offer. I may do just that--and if I do, I'll give you a couple days notice. But...just one question, *who* was the guy in the Government that put the kibosh on your printing my article?"

"I'm probably not supposed to reveal any names, but, Hell, you're reliable and we're kicking you around a bit here...The fellow is somebody new at the Treasury Department, who was big in banking up here in New York. He's the Deputy Undersecretary of Treasury; his name is W. Carleton Mason II."

Pat wondered, *How the Hell does a guy at Treasury have his fingers in the 'national security' pie? Isn't that a job for State and the Pentagon?* but he decided not to ask.

(2)

Cardinal Eugenio Cassendi watched his computer printer spew out pages of names--all the Cardinals, then all the Bishops, then all the Monsignori, then all the priests in the world. Once this task was done, he would print the lists of all the religious order priests in the world, starting with the Fathers General or other worldwide superiors, then working down through the heads of monasteries and the presidents of universities and the pastors of parishes under the leadership of order priests.

He planned to compare his list with a shorter one which the Chairman had faxed to him. His own list was simply factual: who was assigned where. The Chairman's list was political: an "enemies list." These were the ones the Chairman wanted removed.

"Removal" could take either of two forms. Had the Chairman his way, they would receive the same treatment Stalin gave dissidents in Russia: purge, pogrom, Siberia, "liquidation"; but even the Chairman recognized the present limits of his power and, being preoccupied with moving toward complete political control, had agreed with Cassendi that he could effect "removal" in a way more congenial and less blatant: reassignment.

To ensure accuracy in his targeting, Eugenio Cassendi had hit on a simple stratagem to supplement the Chairman's list. He hoped it would reveal which priests were likely to be most resistant to the New Church he planned, once he was Pope. He engaged a marketing psychologist to construct an "attitude and orthodoxy survey,"--a phrase he kept to himself--by which all the priests in the world were to fill out a questionnaire, one half of which was a self-description and the other half descriptive of other priests. The questions included doctrinal matters, such as belief in the Real Presence and the inerrancy of Scripture; and one's position on controverted issues, such as the evolution of humanity or democracy in the Church.

He planned to use the orthodox ones' habitual commitment to truth against them: they would reveal themselves because of the firmness of their convictions. Then, when the time was ripe, he would force the elderly ones to retire, reassign the younger ones to some "Siberia" where they could do little harm to the New Church and, indeed, because of their frustration, where they might leave voluntarily. Then, through the new bishops he would appoint, he would replace them with lay "parish coordinators." These would take over the CCD and Adult Education programs and make sure that the laity were indoctrinated in New Age jargon and practices.

Just like running a corporation after a hostile takeover. That was all the Catholic Church would be: a captured corporation. A body without a spirit. A zombie without a soul.

(3)

At its headquarters near Fairfax County Parkway fifteen miles outside Washington, D.C., the CEO of BDR Corporation, Martin Toller, took the call from W. Carleton Mason, III, recently appointed Deputy Undersecretary of Treasury. They had been acquainted back in college but had lost track of each other until now. Toller always welcomed a call from a high government official, since it could lead to more business. As a "beltway bandit" company, his firm lived largely on Federal contracts. Though they had a good many, they could always use one more.

"Marty, this is Carl Mason. Remember me?"

"Sure do. How are things going? Bring me up to date."

They exchanged highlights of personal histories, and then Carleton Mason turned to the reason for his call.

"Marty, Treasury is assembling a Task Force from the private sector to advise us on Y2K compliance problems as well as on a variety of other electronic improvements in law enforcement, currency protection, and so on. I understand BDR has a contract with BATF right in the middle of that field. So I'd like to invite you to a preliminary meeting of our Task Force, so you can get to know some of the other people on the team and maybe decide to join us."

"I'm honored. Naturally I'm interested. When's the meeting?"

"Three weeks from today. Seven p.m., at a private room at the Hay-Adams."

"Damn! That date's not so good. I'll be out of the country that week. But--" he wanted to show genuine interest because this might lead to serious money from the Feds--"I wonder whether I could deputize my Executive Assistant in my place."

"Sure," answered Mason. What's his name?"

"It's not a *he*; it's a *she*. Her name is Marilee Van Niesen."

(4)

The angel came to Cristina Montalvo in her sleep. "Come with me," he said, "and I will show you the center of Evil."

Obediently, she rose, wearing only a long nightgown which came down close to her ankles. He took her left hand in his right. She did not see more than an indistinct outline of her guide, but she could feel his presence.

"You are wondering who I am," said the angel. "I am your Guardian Angel. The Lord wants you to understand the battle as we approach the climax."

They rose through the ceiling into the air and began to move rapidly northeastward in the darkness a few hundred feet above the ground. As they left the room, she glanced down and saw, to her amazement, *her own body lying on the bed*, apparently still asleep! "Do not be afraid," said the angel, again reading her thoughts. "You have read the life of Catherine Emmerich and other mystics; you know it is possible for the spirit to leave the body. Your body will remain safe. It is under the protection of other angels."

An ordinary person might well have been terrified by this experience, despite the angel's reassurance. But Cristina Montalvo had moved far in the spiritual life, and saintly people, such as her role model Catherine of Siena, develop a union with God which translates into such practical virtues as courage, faith, and abandonment to divine providence. She had determined that if she were to be an instrument of enough grace to save Dolores, she must be totally obedient to God's will.

They sped like lightning across Spain, through France, and into Belgium. She felt no wind to indicate speed, but she could see the lights of cities and towns approaching, then below her, then receding behind her--all as if she were in a rocket flying five thousand miles an hour. In less than two minutes they reached a large office building in downtown Brussels. They descended to a deserted sidewalk. She saw a clock on the building; its hands indicated 1:15 a.m.

"In this building there are two things you must see," said the angel. He stepped forward through the wall and she accompanied him; they penetrated solid substances the way light goes through glass. Past two more concrete-and-steel walls and they stood, alone, in a cavernous basement room, one whole wall of which was covered with small blinking lights arranged in a dozen patterned clusters, most of them with work stations and light green TV monitor screens. It made a low humming noise. It was some sort of machine.

"This," said the angel, "is the largest computer in the world. It can do things no other can duplicate: link with satellites, create holographic images and transmit them to various points, locate specific persons by monitoring a chip they carry, record and analyze millions of telephone conversations, even send the same image to every television set and Internet site in the world."

"Why do you show me this?"

"Because, in combination with other electronic devices, it is the ultimate evil *thing* in this world. You--and others the Lord is choosing--must pray against it. When enough people pray, God will force it to malfunction and ultimately to break down.

"Now come. I must show you something else."

They rose quickly to the top floor of the building. They stood in a wide, lavishly carpeted and ornately decorated hallway. On the walls were Mideast symbols such as pyramids and mosques. "Within that room," the angel pointed toward the end of the corridor, "is the ultimate evil *person* in this world. He is having a meeting. We will join them."

"Won't they know we are there?"

"No, though you will also see some demons there. But we are under the protection of the Holy Spirit: we will be invisible to them. Have no fear. Come."

They walked through the closed doors and stopped at the foot of a long conference table. It had seats for ten, plus the seat of honor at the head. Six of the ten seats were occupied, one by a woman, the other by men. At the head of the table sat a broad-shouldered man in middle age, caucasian but darkly tanned, with sharp nearly black eyes and Middle Eastern features. Having already seen his face in a vision some months earlier, and then in the newspaper, Cristina recognized the Chairman. She felt a clammy coldness in the room.

Behind each of the six seated persons crouched man-sized creatures with glinting eyes, each a different horrible shape. Each had a humanoid face, but one looked like a huge toad, another a wolf, a third an immense spider. The others had unrecognizable ugly forms. She gasped at their ghastliness and recoiled as she felt pure evil emanating from them.

The angel held her hand tightly. "Do not be afraid. You see the results of sin: once they were angels, just as I am. Now they are demons."

"Why isn't one of these demons standing behind the Chairman?" she asked, regaining her composure.

"Because his demon is already within his body," came the answer.

Hidden under the mantle of the Holy Spirit, they listened intently for five minutes. The Chairman was summarizing his plans. He wanted strict obedience and split-second timing, once he gave the signal. He punctuated his remarks with occasional blasphemies. The others, clearly cowed, asked few questions. Cristina paid close attention, her anger at his words mounting. At the Chairman's third blasphemous comment, Cristina's anger exploded. *You ingrate!* she thought. *Jesus died even for you, and all you can do is abuse His name!* She could not contain her anger any longer; spontaneously she thrust her arm straight out, pointed at him, and spoke in a strong voice which, had they been in the material order, would have filled the room, "*By the Blood of Jesus, shut your dirty mouth!!*"

Instantly the Chairman coughed, as if something stuck in his throat. He coughed again, tried unsuccessfully to clear his throat, and groped for a glass of water just beyond the papers lying on the table before him. After a moment, the water restored his voice and he resumed his discourse. But the blasphemies stopped. He continued in a more restrained tone.

"We must leave now," said the angel, a few minutes later. Still holding her hand, he walked her quickly to the back of the room, through the closed door, and out into the corridor.

"You are thinking," said the angel, reading her mind, "that when you awake tomorrow morning, this may all seem to be a dream."

"Yes," she answered, wondering why he made the point.

By now, they were out on the sidewalk once again and he said, "Come across this street." In a moment they were standing at the edge of a small city park, next to an old wrought-iron fence, ornamented with small metal balls soldered atop every other vertical iron picket. He put his left hand around one of them and broke it off. "Remember what I did here," he said.

Then they rose into the air and with the same speed as before rushed back above France, into Spain, and in scarcely two minutes, were back in her room. "Lie down and go back to sleep," he commanded, pointing to the bed where her body lay. Obediently, she sat on the edge of the bed, swung her legs up, leaned back, and stretched out in the place of her body. He touched her forehead gently and she fell asleep at once.

The next morning when she awoke, lying on the bed table next to her alarm clock was a golf-ball-sized round metal fence ornament.

(5)

Thunder. Crashing loud thunder. In the darkness.

At midnight it began. The first rumble exploded like a bomb in people's ears. It started at the International Date Line in the Pacific and moved westward like a sonic tidal wave, hitting each new country and territory exactly at midnight. The thunderous explosions continued repeatedly, again and again and again, like shells bursting in an artillery barrage. In some places the sound was loud, in some places soft; in some places it was near, in some places far.

But in all places the crashing explosions were continuous. *Thunder...thunder...thunder.* And the day stayed dark.

Initially people thought the sounds presaged a heavy rainstorm. But as the noise continued through the night and on toward dawn, many looked out to discover, to their shock, that there were no clouds in the sky--nothing there to suggest any rain.

Initial amazement turned to worry. Worry quickly turned to fear. The sound continued with no break for exactly twenty-four hours. For those who did not know why this was happening, fear merged into terror.

Long before this terrifying day ended, terror had reached the threshold of panic. The thunder had lasted the whole day.

(6)

John Paul II knelt motionless in prayer. In front of him on the shallow desk part of his kneeler was a large wooden cross with an exquisitely carved figure of Christ. Spattered here and there on the figure were drops of water. Tears.

In his mind he saw the state of the Church. Bishops, perhaps half of them or more, no longer faithful to the ancient teachings. Seminaries turning out social workers who had no time to pray. Vocations drying up in most dioceses. Nuns wanting to be priests.

Surveys in industrialized countries showing that less than half the Catholics believed in Christ's Real Presence in the Holy Eucharist and a low percentage attended Mass regularly. Equally troubling, most "good" Catholics in the West seemed paralyzed, unable to affect public events or even speak out about the abortions or the moral collapse of their society.

He knew it had to come. The fulfillment of Scripture. The third Secret of Fatima. The great Apostasy. The setting of the stage for the Man of Sin.

But he had never surrendered. As long ago as 1979, he had realized it was coming; but he had decided, with the resoluteness that had marked his character during all his years, that he would do all he could to postpone it, to mitigate it, to prepare the Faithful for it.

His critics never understood what he was up to. Or perhaps a few of them knew all too well. But with most, their spiritual vision was too blurred; indeed, some of them had slipped into total spiritual blindness. They wanted "modernization," they wanted priestesses, they wanted to change the rules on life and death, sex and family. Some wanted to elect their own bishops. They all wanted Power.

They did not want to understand that Truth can never change. They did not want to admit that man cannot change evil into good by voting upon it or decreeing it from on high, whether the "high" was the Congress of the United States, the Council of Europe, or the Papacy itself.

But he had resisted the *Zeitgeist* and the leaders of his own Church who embraced it. He had intensified his prayer, spending up to six hours a day wrestling with powers and principalities and spirits of the air. He had traveled hundreds of thousands of miles, to leverage his own charism and the anointing God had given him into greater influence for the traditional Gospel in dozens of different countries. He had preached; he had written; he had prayed--and, with Our Lady's gracious help and bolstered by the prayers of the Remnant Faithful, he had led the mystical resistance to the inevitable. For some years they had held it off, as God the Father, moved by their prayers and the pleading of the Virgin Mary, extended the Era of Mercy.

But time was running out. The agents of Evil had intensified their activities as well. They had performed at least one Black Mass somewhere in the Vatican itself; members of their secret societies had infiltrated the Episcopacy; they had set up witches' covens and Satanic worship in most major cities; they had neutralized governments in the fight against moral evil by installing amoral men and women as the governors; they had spread the miasmic New Age philosophy throughout the world until a functional Paganism dominated Western man's thinking.

He looked at the Figure on the Cross. "I am sorry, Lord," he said half aloud, "but we do not pray enough. The salt has lost its savor."

Then he heard the thunder. Unlike so many others, he was not frightened by it. He had been forewarned in a vision that there would soon be extraordinary physical events. He sighed. *Adam lost everything in a Garden next to a tree; Jesus regained everything in a Garden and on a tree. Now mankind must go back into that second Garden to recapture, through Jesus, the right to live once again in the first Garden. The Garden of Gethsemani.*

"Your Holiness." He recognized the voice. He had heard it once before, at the University of Stuebenville. He looked up.

Standing just within the closed door was a tall, powerful figure. "Your Holiness," the figure repeated, respectfully. It was Michael the Archangel. "It is time. Evil must have its hour. The Lord wants you to come with me."

(7)

The 191st meeting of the American Astronomical Society included learned papers and reports on a range of stellar phenomena, from coronal mass ejections on the sun to the effects of an asteroid hitting the Atlantic. According to newspaper accounts, the treatment of the last topic included the effects of a tsunami wave generated by a three-mile-wide asteroid hitting the Atlantic Ocean. A computer simulation showed that the entire eastern seaboard would be affected, with floods swamping the East Coast as far as the Appalachian mountains. Delaware, Maryland, and Virginia would be inundated. The same computer calculations using a smaller impactor--one perhaps five hundred yards across--would send a wall of water over three hundred feet high toward the coastlines of the ocean. Such a tidal wave would be higher than a twenty-story building.

CHAPTER XI

(1)

Father Michael Kanek had finished glancing through the current issue of the country's leading "liberal" Catholic newspaper. It had printed a long speech by Cardinal Eugenio Cassendi, titled "Love the Church and Work to Make Her Loved," a lecture that was part of a series in the Diocese of Rome in preparation for the Year 2000 Jubilee. It was a media event which took place at the very site where Pius XI and Mussolini had signed the Lateran Pact. He knew little of Cassendi, but it appeared he was a very powerful prelate, the Secretary of an important Congregation.

One of Kanek's conscious intellectual habits was his skill at sorting through polysyllabic doubletalk, identifying straw men, and dissecting false logic. Thus this lecture by Cardinal Cassendi caught his attention. Indeed, it was a red flag.

The theme of the talk was the Church's "need" for ongoing reform. On the one hand, the Cardinal spoke of the necessity of maintaining tradition, and he used impressive quotations from St. Vincent of Lerins. On the other hand, he cited and praised Modernist theologians like Jacques Mondar and Franz Jung. It was Mondar who favorably referred to the Second Vatican Council as a "counter-Syllabus," alluding to Pope Pius IX's famous "Syllabus of Errors" of 1864.

Cassendi's speech reminded him of the warning by St. Pius X of how the Modernists operate. In the encyclical *Pascendi*, Father Kanek recalled, Pius X taught that the tactic of Modernists is to mingle both traditional and progressive statements in their writings. The Pope had said, "...in their books one finds some things which might well be approved by a Catholic, but on turning over the page, one is confronted by other things which might well have been dictated by a rationalist."

The Cardinal's address contained a curious composite of traditional Catholic terminology, Vatican II lingo, trendy language such as "concerns for the environment" and even a New Age reference to the world as a "Global Village."

Yet the prime reason for Michael Kanek's concern was Cassendi's favorably quoting the radical "theologian" Franz Jung. He quoted a section from one of Jung's recent books and claimed that it contained "beautiful pages dedicated to the Christian mystery," and called him--without qualification--"the German Catholic theologian." Cardinal Cassendi knew quite well that the heterodox Jung was stripped of the right to call himself a "Catholic theologian" by none other than Pope John Paul II. Indeed, mused Michael Kanek, in Jung's most famous book, *The Essence of a Christian,* he had denied the Divinity of Christ, dismissed the miracles in the Gospel, denied the bodily resurrection of Jesus, denied that Christ founded an institutional Church, and denied that the Mass is a re-presentation of the Sacrifice of Calvary! *How can this guy be called a "Catholic theologian"?* wondered Kanek.

The Cardinal's brazen reference to Jung as "the German theologian" raised an important question in Michael Kanek's mind: is the Cardinal a calculating Modernist or just one more confused prelate caught up in the spirit of the age? Cassendi's praise of Jung could be no slip of the tongue: he spoke from a carefully prepared text. Is the upper echelon of the Vatican bureaucracy, led by men like Cassendi, now acting as if the Pope were already dead, his condemnation of Jung consigned to history? Does Cassendi have in mind a rehabilitation of Jung and a host of other radicals during the next pontificate, to which he may well aspire?

Then another concern struck him. As a priest begins to forget the Source of his spiritual power--and it slips away--desire for political power often rushes into the vacuum. As he takes on a political mindset, he often takes on a political style. Part of the politicians' style is to "signal" to one's followers through an ambiguous public pronouncement acceptable enough to the hesitant but with lines the "insiders" can read between. The Communists had used this device many times.

Was a would-be Pope communicating to would-be revolutionaries that he was ready to lead them?

(2)

John DeSanto was giving a talk to about fifty lay people at Our Lady Queen of Apostles parish in Glenview. Though the pastor had first resisted the idea, John's brother Matt, a member of the parish and sizeable donor to its building fund, persuaded him at last to permit a lecture on something as old-fashioned as Marian apparitions.

John finished by quoting the Message of October 13, 1973, at Akita, which the Bishop later, in April of 1984, after years of extensive investigation, declared was of supernatural origin, was reliable, and worthy of belief:

"...if men do not repent and better themselves, the Father will inflict a terrible punishment on all humanity. It will be a punishment greater than the deluge, such as one will never have seen before. Fire will fall from the sky and will wipe out a great part of humanity, the good as well as the bad, sparing neither priest nor faithful. The survivors will find themselves so desolate that they will envy the dead. The only arms which will remain for you will be the Rosary and the Sign left by my Son. Each day recite the prayers of the Rosary. With the Rosary, pray for the Pope, the bishops and the priests.

"...The work of the devil will infiltrate even into the Church in such a way that one will see cardinals opposing cardinals, bishops against other bishops. The priests who venerate me will be scorned and opposed by their confreres (other priests). Churches and altars will be sacked. The Church will be full of those who accept compromises and the demon will press many priests and consecrated souls to leave the service of the Lord. The demon will be especially implacable against souls consecrated to God. The thought of the loss of so many souls is the cause of my sadness. If sins increase in number and gravity, there will be no longer pardon for them.

"...Pray very much the prayers of the Rosary. I alone am able still to save you from the calamities which approach. Those who place their confidence in me will be saved."

(3)

Dressed to resemble Swiss Guards, four men with guns drawn smashed into the Papal apartments. They rushed across the sitting area and slammed against the closed bedroom door. It burst open and the leader's flashlight illumined the bed. It was empty.

They expected to find the Pontiff asleep. They stopped and looked at each other in amazement and the leader, a man named Malin, shouted, "Where the Hell is he?"

He ran to a closet and swung wide its door. Only the usual clothes and robes a bishop's closet would contain. He tapped the three closet walls and carefully scrutinized the floor, to see if there might be a secret exit, a trapdoor perhaps. Nothing.

Another man quickly rushed to the window and brushed back the heavy drape-like curtain. No, there was no one standing behind it. Feeling foolish, the third knelt to look under the low bed; as he expected, nothing there but a pair of slippers and a day's worth of dust. No space for a man.

"He has eluded us," snarled Malin, in a frightening tone of anger and hate. "No matter. We will continue with the plan. We can find him later. He must be somewhere in the building."

While Malin watched, the other three returned to the hallway outside the suite and carried in a large wooden crate, three feet in both width and depth, roughly six and one half feet in length. To judge from the strain on their muscles, the crate weighed over 250 pounds. They laid it on the floor next to the Pope's empty bed and pulled back the single blanket and sheet.

They removed three metal straps wrapped around the crate, pried open one side of it, and carefully lifted out the body of a dead man. With unaccustomed gentleness they placed it on the Pope's bed with the head on the pillow, in the position of a man sleeping on his back. Their care indicated they wanted it to appear no violence had caused the death. Dressed in a white cassock such as the Pope wears, it was the body of a man killed only hours before, Giovanni Petrone.

(4)

Already skittish because of the inexplicable day of thunder, Wall Street investors had little emotional reserve to handle more disturbing events. So when word of the American attack on Saddam Hussein hit Wall Street, the stock market exploded in a frenzy of panic selling.

The market lives on emotion and buying is based on optimistic expectation; when bad news hits, that optimism disappears like a pricked balloon, and the herd stampedes for the tall grass. There is nothing more frightening to investors than war, especially in an oil-rich area such as the Middle East.

The American attack on Saddam triggered events the President and his advisors, of whom almost none had prayed for guidance, had not foreseen. Saddam had smuggled many of his biological and chemical weapons to Libya and hidden others in hillside caves, not in the numerous palaces the Americans believed he was using. Thus he could have permitted unlimited inspections. But he enjoyed tweaking the American President, whom he considered a buffoon well out of his element, by playing the on-again-off-again game of permit-then-refuse inspections.

Saddam's strategy was simplicity itself. He realized that he had lost the Gulf War because President Bush had put together a strong coalition of allies who supported the American initiative, whereas he, Saddam, had acted alone without the backup of friendly nations. *This time,* he had vowed, *he* would have the coalition of supporters; and the American President, drunk with over-confidence, would be the one acting alone. He, Saddam, would turn the tables. He would make it look like the Americans were the aggressor. And he would have Muslim friends to back him up, while the Americans would be isolated.

When the Chairman of the Council of Europe called and informed Saddam secretly that Europe would not back the United States if it attacked Iraq, Saddam decided to call the President's bluff and terminate further U.N. inspections. Having ordered a massive military buildup in the Persian Gulf, the President in turn concluded that he had to act, lest America--that is, the President--be humbled by a "two-bit tin-pot dictator." So he ordered massive air strikes against all of Saddam's palaces. This was the first time in its history that the United States had attacked a nation that had not first attacked it or one of its allies.

To the amazement of the President and his advisors, Saddam's military did not fire back. Instead, the next day he went on television and told the rest of the Muslim world that he was a man of peace. He said that the Great Satan the United States was the aggressor. He pointed out that Russia, China, and united Europe all opposed the

American aggression. He appealed for Muslim unity against the Great Satan by showing the mangled and bleeding bodies of women and teenage children who, he said with a measure of truth, had been working as innocent civilians in the target buildings.

Of all the ethnic groups in the world, the Arabs and other Muslims, such as the Iranians, are perhaps the most volatile. In the oversimplified Muslim worldview, any western nation which is not Mohammedan is Christian and must be converted or conquered. This hostility dates back to the us-versus-them mentality inculcated by Mohammed himself. Not all Muslims are fanatics, by any means; but those who are remember very well, even if the post-Christian Europeans and Americans have forgotten, the battle of Tours, the Crusades, Ferdinand and Isabella driving them from Spain in 1492, losing their fleet at Lepanto in 1571 and half of Europe in Vienna in 1688--all turning-points favoring the Christians, save the Crusades, whose results were initially mixed, and ultimately Muslim successes. The desire for revenge still burned bright, tempered only by the temporary willingness of Saudi Arabia and some of the smaller countries to swallow their principles for oil-generated dollars.

So tens of thousands of stock owners, small and large, rushed to their phones and, for the nerds among them, to their computers, and sold, or attempted to sell, their holdings. Busy signals and mysterious glitches impeded many among both groups, but thousands did get through, shouting in unison: "Sell!"

During each hour of trading the market dropped over 100 points; at the end of the day, it had dropped 697 points, even more than the Black Monday of August 31, 1998.

By 8:00 p.m., the Administration's Plunge Protection Team and its Working Group on Financial Markets met in emergency session. The "Team" was set up after the Crash of '87. It is headed by the Treasury Secretary and has as members the Federal Reserve Chairman, the head of the SEC, head of the CFTC, the head of the Federal Reserve Bank of New York, the head of the President's National Economic Council, the Chairman of his Council of Economic Advisors, and the Comptroller of the Currency.

They met at the Old Executive Office Building, next door to the White House. Those members who had been out of town returned to

Washington on private jets chartered by the FBI. They were rushed into downtown D.C. in government limousines, and to maintain complete secrecy, they were chaperoned by the Secret Service from the Hay Adams hotel, following, in reverse, the same underground route Dolores Montalvo had used some weeks earlier to escape from the White House.

Because the Undersecretary of the Treasury, who should have been present with the Secretary, was sick, his deputy, W. Carleton Mason, was directed to appear in his place. It was the same evening as the planned meeting to which Mason had invited Martin Toller, whose prior overseas commitment had made him substitute Marilee Van Niesen.

Washington's afternoon rush hour had been especially congested that day, and Vanni's Afganistani cab driver professed, in nearly unintelligible English, that he could not find the Hay-Adams Hotel. As they meandered around northwest Washington, Vanni became frantic about how gauche she would seem coming in late when she was the stand-in for her boss. Then she hit on a successful stratagem: give the Afghan poobah behind the wheel five dollars every time he turned in the correct direction. Thus she managed to get to the hotel only twenty minutes late and thirty dollars lighter.

All in vain, it turned out. Because of the international emergency, the meeting had been cancelled. But she had the sense to check at the registration desk, where a clerk gave her a handwritten note from Mason:

> Dear Ms. Van Niesen:
>
> My apologies for your inconvenience. The President called an emergency meeting because of Iraq matter. I do want to meet with you. Please wait in the lobby of the Hay-Adams, if necessary until 11:00 p.m. In the interim, have dinner at the hotel on me.
>
> Sincerely,
> Carl Mason

She was impressed with his thoughtfulness. That a busy man in the middle of an emergency would take the time to write such a note! But she was irritated, as well, that he would tie up the rest of her evening, maybe until eleven o'clock. Yet she also felt an intuitive suspicion; so she went to a pay phone and called Pat Greene to tell him what was up.

(5)

Father Michael Kanek was speaking about Catholic prophecy at St. Jude's parish church in McLean, Virginia. His talk, which started at 7:00 p.m., had gone one hour, when he stopped for questions. He was soon to discover that not all the hundred or so in attendance were enthusiastic about his message.

"Father," opened one questioner, her voice tinged with anger, "you recount a bunch of visions and messages that say God is likely to punish us with horrible devastation. That may be *your* God, but it's not *my* God! *My* God is a God of mercy, of love, of forgiveness!"

"Madam, may I say first, that neither you or I are fiction writers, who can choose to characterize 'our' God as we might want. We have to describe God as He is. Second, if you look at both the Old and New Testament, you see that the same God who destroyed Sodom fed the Israelites in the desert, the same Jesus who forgave the woman taken in adultery also drove the money-changers out of the Temple. God has *both* mercy and justice, both compassion and anger.

"Third and finally, I do not make up the messages I have told you about. Neither do the persons I quote. Deeply spiritual priests have studied them and examined the messengers, whether John Leary, Christina Gallagher, Maria Esperanza, Sadie Jaramillo, or the others I mentioned--and these priests have concluded that these people are not hallucinating or tricking themselves or us. You are free not to believe that God spoke to them about punishments if you want--but I would suggest you first study exactly what they said and take note of the sins in the world, which do call to Heaven for punishment."

Another hand went up. "Father Kanek, isn't it true that the Church--not just a few individual priests--has not yet approved Leary, Mrs. Gallagher, Mrs. Esperanza, and most of the others? Until the Church speaks on a matter, I don't see why lay people should have to believe it."

"May I ask you a question, as prologue to my answer to your inquiry?" responded Kanek. The man said Yes. "Are you or anyone you know, among those Catholics who want more democracy in the Church, perhaps going so far even as to desire that the parishioners could choose their pastors or Catholics of a diocese could elect their Bishops?"

"Yes. I think democratic forms would improve the Church immensely. In my opinion, it's too authoritarian."

"Well then," answered Father Kanek, "why do you not permit lay people to evaluate for themselves whether the visions and messages I have cited are genuine? Why do you suspend your judgment so much that you refuse to take the evidence at hand and come to your own conclusion? Why wait for the Church? And if the Church ended up approving these messages, would you then accept them? If lay people are smart enough to choose their Bishop, why are they not smart enough to evaluate the evidence they would have their Bishop evaluate for them?

"And, in any event," he concluded, "the problem is that most bishops take a very long time to investigate and come to any firm conclusion. In my opinion, we cannot wait ten years or more before we publicize information and teaching which could well be from Mary or even Jesus Christ Himself. I prefer not to keep it secret but to give it to all of you and let you make up your minds."

Another hand went up. This one turned out to be on his side, and she said something he had wanted to say but feared that, coming from a priest, it might be offensive. "May I comment on the last two questions?" she began. When he nodded Yes, she continued, "You people who find fault with these messages make me sick!

"I think you are just looking for an excuse not to pray more. Even if these messages are not true, what harm is done if we think they are? We still pray more, and try to amend our lives. But if they *are* genuine, we are in plenty of trouble and we *better* get on our knees fast, and spend our time praying instead of arguing."

(6)

"What do you mean, you still can't find him!" The Chairman almost shouted. He resisted the impulse to throw the phone against the wall. "You fool, he's an old man. Did he *outrun* you and your men?" he added, with deliberate sarcasm.

"Sir, with all due respect, I swear to you he wasn't there when we broke in," answered Malin. "We have to be discreet in searching the building, since most of the Swiss Guards are loyal to him and know nothing of what we're doing. You *do* want us to maintain secrecy, don't you?" It was the debater's trick of asking a question to put his opponent off balance.

"Of course I do," responded the Chairman, calming a bit. "But the reason I engaged you is your reputation for never bungling a murder or a kidnapping." The Chairman's voice started to rise once more as his anger again surfaced.

"Sir, the drill went off like clockwork. *You* gave us the script and we carried it out to the letter. You got the result you wanted: everyone thinks John Paul II is dead. They believe it was a heart attack. There is no evidence anywhere, to the contrary. I cannot help it if somehow--I don't know how or why--he chose to go somewhere else, secretly, earlier in the day."

The Chairman paused and pondered. He was a brilliant man and his plans benefited from the brilliance of invisible forces working with him. An unwanted thought flashed through his mind and he shivered slightly. *Michael. It must have been Michael.*

"All right. I will pay you one million dollars, to cover your costs and what you owe your men. The other nine million will be paid when I have proof that the real John Paul is dead. But if there is one word of publicity about his death when it actually happens, you'll receive not a penny!"

It was the other's turn to pause. Malin felt his own anger mounting. "You promised *ten* million dollars. Give me only *one*, and I myself make nothing on this deal. I risk my life for nothing! You wanted John Paul out of the way so the Cardinals would call a meeting and elect your man to the Papacy. Once that happens, it does not matter if the public finds out, after his death, that John Paul died last night or dies a week from now.

"I want the full ten million *now*," Malin added, firmly. It's not *my* fault he's still alive. If you want me to search the Vatican, or Rome, or all of Italy, or all of Europe--that's another assignment, for a separate stipend."

"If he eluded you amateurs once, he probably will again," sneered the Chairman in response. "*I* have the means to find anyone, anywhere; and *I* will find him. He's probably in a monastery somewhere. When I locate him, I will call you and you can finish the job. But until then, one million is all you get. Be happy I do not put a contract out on *your* life."

"All right...I'll wait for your call." said Malin, in pretended acquiescence. But he was thinking something quite different. *You promised ten million. You insult me. No one crosses me and gets away with it. You will regret that remark.*

CHAPTER XII

(1)

POPE DEAD!

said the *New York Post*

JOHN PAUL II DIES IN SLEEP
Pontiff Found by Aide Early
Today. Funeral Planned Soon

said the *New York Times*

HEART ATTACK CLAIMS PONTIFF
Failing Health Leads to Death
In Sleep. Millions Mourn

said the *Chicago Tribune.*

* * * * * * * * * * *

Father Michael Kanek stared for a long moment at the newspaper. He sighed, remembering how he'd met the man only a few months earlier. Then he closed his eyes. He thought about the Pope's letter, about being a closeted Bishop, and about what his next move should be. He stood up, left the room, and walked quietly down the corridor toward the Chapel. *As Churchill said at one point in World War II,* he thought, *if we are not at the beginning of the End, we are surely at the end of the Beginning.*

* * * * * * * * * * *

The President got the news at breakfast. An aide entered his private dining room, approached, and suggested he might want to turn the television on, because the Pope had just died, and he might want to catch public reaction. The President did not care much whether the Pope was alive or dead, since most American Catholics were politically asleep and their supposed religious beliefs had little impact on their politics. He had found the Pope to be too inflexible, a quaint throwback to an era where people seemed to believe in principles worth dying for. He ordered the aide to turn on the set.

* * * * * * * * * * *

Marilee Van Niesen heard about the Pope's death during her noontime lunch break. Work at the company precluded any discussion of it until her scheduled Bible Study meeting that evening. There one of the participants, while giving lip service to John Paul II's good qualities, made some negative comments about Catholics not being "true Christians" and Papal authority not being Biblical. Being a new Christian, she had not heard many such comments. *How could Father Mike, his brother Jerry, and John DeSanto--men she admired as completely honorable and, she had every reason to believe, dedicated to Jesus--how could such men not be true Christians?* She assumed the Cardinals would elect another Pope and the Church would go on as it always had.

* * * * * * * * * * *

Cardinal Eugenio Cassendi struggled to prevent a smile of relief when a Swiss Guard, almost in tears, met him in the hall with the news. He expressed rehearsed shock and dismay and pretended that the convening of the College of Cardinals to elect a successor was quite secondary to the necessary funeral arrangements with appropriate honors for such a great Pontiff.

* * * * * * * * * * *

Theodore Patrick Greene watched the television news closely. The Pope's death troubled him, because he considered John Paul a colossus in his time and doubted an adequate successor could easily be found. He watched the images from Rome--interviews of mourners, all saying the same thing; speculation by anchormen about the election of a successor, etc. and he noted something puzzling. When the camera zoomed in on the deceased Pontiff lying in state, the announcer assured the viewers that what they saw was the deceased John Paul *exactly as an aide found him.* Pat Greene wondered *how could it be that John Paul lay down, alive, in his cassock?* It would be more natural to lie down in one's pajamas or a night shirt. *There's something wrong here!* he thought.

(2)

Father Michael Kanek sat in his room at Georgetown University, looking at the English text of the Apostolic Letter the Pope had given him a couple months earlier.

This Apostolic Letter was unlike most Encyclicals, Papal "letters" to the whole Church on political, social, moral, or religious matters. The usual practice had been for a Pope to ask one expert--*peritus*, they were called--or a small committee, to draft a statement along lines of the Pope's known views on some complex matter. Then the Pope might make comments and suggestions, a committee would hash out the nuances, and a final draft would come back to the Pope, some months later, for his final approval. Something like the task of speech-writers for a national leader, though taking longer.

This Letter was clearly the work of the Pope alone. The Pope had written it in Latin; the angle of the letters was different on different pages, intrinsic evidence that he had not composed it in one sitting or that his mood changed more than once as he proceeded.

Kanek had gone to his word processor and typed in the exact Latin text that the Pope had written. If he needed help with translating a certain passage, he decided, he could go to one of the many linguists at the University; but he could not show them the original, because the European script was too obvious. As it was, he might have to excise certain words or phrases lest they give away the author's identity. He locked the original in a strong box in his closet and used the printed Latin manuscript for translation. He had now finished the English version except for the footnotes. He reread it as a whole:

"To the bishops, priests and deacons, men and women religious, all the lay faithful, and men and women of all faiths or none:

"I have chosen to send you this letter at the close of the Century and my Papacy, as a final reminder of ultimate truths we all need to acknowledge and embrace.

"'You shall know the truth and the truth shall make you free.'"[1] This axiom is so pervasive in our lives that one is surprised that many modern intellectuals object to its application in ethical and religious areas. In fields as disparate as designing and building jet planes that fly safely, to the surgeon operating on heart or eye, we humans must first discover the intrinsic dynamics of the being we are working on, and only then can we--working *within* its natural structure--proceed to a successful end. In other words, there is a natural order in all things, and we depart from the demands of that order at our peril.[2]

I. Questions about Evolution

It has always been surprising to me that many scientists and others who profess commitment to 'the scientific method' of laboratory investigation and careful effort to replicate a successful experiment under controlled conditions--that such actual or potential scientists, so committed to finding the intrinsic natural order within the object of their investigation, then go out to the public arena and tell ordinary citizens that there is no fixed order in the universe, but that it all is 'evolving.' In their work they affirm natural law, but in their words they deny it.

The unreflective belief in generalized 'evolution' between species, or of apes into men, despite the sincerity of its adherents, is belief in a lie. Though in a letter as short as this I cannot lay out the objections in detail, I will mention a few concerns that may give pause to the apologists for the evolutionary theory.

First, after diligently searching for over a century, no one has found even one *demonstratively proven* 'missing link'; but if thousands of men and women came forth from thousands of ancestral apes, one would expect to find dozens, even hundreds, of such 'links.'[3]

Second, since the earth's electromagnetic field has a 'half-life' of roughly 1400 years, i.e., it deteriorates by fifty percent in that period, then it would follow that the field was twice as strong, in the year 600, as it is now; four times as strong in the year 800 B.C., as now; eight times stronger in the year 2200 B.C., and so on. Regress to 10000 B.C. and the electromagnetic field would be so strong that nothing on earth could live. How then could evolution *of complex living organisms* have been going on for millions of years?[4]

Third, the Second Law of Thermodynamics shows that the *direction of observable change* is not from chaos to order but is from order to chaos. Things break down; they do not spontaneously change to the better.[5]

Fourth, the essence of the scientific method is to use controlled data in laboratory settings and then, when a theory seems proved by one experience, to replicate the experiment to observe and confirm that the theory is a 'law.' This scientific method has never been applied to the theory of evolution, which has not been proved in the laboratory and has not been proved by common observation.[6]

Fifth, though there are small changes *within* species--e.g., men and women are generally taller today than in the Middle Ages--these minuscule modifications are irrelevant to finding examples of *one species transmogrifying into a different species*; no one has ever found cats turning into crows, or even into dogs. There is stubborn consistency within each species: despite endless laboratory experiments, the effort to create a hybrid animal which can sexually reproduce itself invariably fails. One may wonder, if animals were readily evolving over centuries, why it is that once they reach a certain level of development they suddenly *resist* further evolution? The evidence is overwhelming that living things struggle to remain what they are, not to change into some different living thing.[7]

Sixth, a century of efforts to find even a measure of persuasive proof having failed, some proponents have now and then resorted to deception--e.g., the invention of such frauds as 'Piltdown Man'--or 'refining' the original theory of Evolution into its direct opposite--e.g., 'Punctuated Equilibrium.' This last concoction seeks to explain the sudden appearance of new species as a 'jump' that just 'happens,' perhaps because of cosmic radiation. So the old theory of gradual small changes is saved by invoking a new theory of sudden large changes! The ancient Greeks would

call this an example of *Deus ex machina*; I would call it
"Creation," but under another name.[8]

All in all, modern men and women should not accept the
unproven *theory* of evolution *because to believe this theory
takes too much faith.* The theory is widely accepted because
of constant repetition in universities and the media. But
repetition of an untruth does not make it 'evolve' into truth.
It is also accepted because to admit the only other
alternative, Creation, is to grant the existence of a Creator.
To grant that the Creator exists is to admit, at least tacitly,
that He can make demands on us, because we are *creatures*.[9]
Evolutionism is the religion of atheists. Thus it should not be
taught in the public schools of those countries whose courts
have outlawed the teaching of religion in those schools.[10]
Evolutionism is the theological 'security blanket' of God's
Prodigal Sons and Daughters who do not want to admit they
are ruining themselves and should return to their Father's
house. [11]

II. Human Origin, Sin, and Redemption

God created Adam and Eve and from them came the whole
human race.[12] He put in them and in all of us, the basic sense
of right and wrong--conscience. But because Adam, with
Eve's agreement and encouragement, chose to disobey God,
our human nature became infected with such moral weakness
and spiritual myopia that, by and large, we find it terribly
difficult to recognize the right thing with our intellects and
choose to do it with our wills. Indeed, so rare is it that we
humans can, over a long period of time such as a lifetime,
consistently choose the good and avoid the evil, that one may
say that without God's special help, all men and women
would commit serious evil.[13]

As evidence of this point, look around you. Listen to the
daily news on the radio or television: half of it is accounts of
murders, thefts, sexual abuse, and other crimes.

Further, because God created Adam, Eve, and all of us,
He has the right to claim allegiance, obedience, worship. "I
am the Lord thy God; thou shalt not have strange gods

before Me"[14]. When Jesus was asked to sum up the commands of God, He boiled them down to two, of which the first is, "Love the Lord thy God with thy whole heart, whole mind, whole will, and all thy strength."[15]

The Second Commandment is "Love Thy Neighbor as Thyself."[16] In other words, all we are supposed to do in this life in order to obey the Creator is to love Him--which means, keep His Commandments[17] and love our neighbor. We are measured by the degree to which we accept and embrace these Commands, by the degree to which we love God and our neighbor daily.

The "Final Examination" for humanity as a whole and for each of us has only two questions: During your life, how well, how often, how consistently, how unselfishly, did you love God and love your neighbor? This question will be asked of each of us, face-to-face, by Jesus Christ Himself at our personal Last Judgment.[18]

Just as the modern world has invested considerable resources in persuading people to believe the theory of Evolution, it has also invested much in trying to persuade people to disbelieve the *historical fact* of Jesus Christ. Yet there is greater historical evidence that Jesus Christ existed than of any other ancient or medieval figure: the four Gospels; the statues and paintings; the writings of pagan historians such as Josephus, Tacitus, and Suetonius, all conversant with the period; the actions of tens of thousands of people--the martyrs--accepting horrible torture and premature death, all for belief in Jesus.[19] [This point is demonstrated in greater detail in my Apostolic Letter of November 14, 1994, *Tertio Millennio Adveniente*.]

So one Man, who came out of obscurity at age thirty and spent only three years preaching, who was rejected by the religious leaders of his country, whose appeal to the masses was so shallow that their 'Hosannas' of Palm Sunday could be turned into 'Crucify Him!' on Good Friday, who was executed on a cross in a remote province of the mighty Roman Empire, inspired thousands and eventually millions to change their lives radically, to embrace self-restraint and virtue, to risk loss of property and family and life itself, and--the missionaries among them--to set off for distant lands, as did Paul and many of the other apostles, and in their footsteps thousands of dedicated men and women, all leaving family and home to preach the Good News to strangers in dangerous lands. The Good News, the Gospel, is really very simple:

All men have sinned against an infinitely good God. This sin closed Heaven to us. Justice required infinite reparation to make up for sin's infinite evil. Since no collection of humans could ever add up to the infinite, mankind was boxed in to a situation we could never escape on our own. So, out of infinite mercy, God sent His Son to *take our place.* He was "made sin" for us,[20] and took upon Himself the punishment reserved for us. He was tortured and nailed to the Cross *in our place.* His death being of infinite value, He erased our infinite debt. God's justice was perfectly served and the Gates of Heaven were reopened. At the same time, having lived a perfect life and given us perfect teaching on how to imitate that life, Jesus Christ provided all who would listen the means of finding limited happiness in this world and perfect happiness after death. He proved His claim to be God through His Resurrection from the dead.[21]

III. Modern Rejection of the Benefits from the Redemption

This message, this belief, this *truth* became the basis for a whole civilization. It was a civilization that developed hospitals and orphanages and old peoples homes, serviced by men and women who, like Mother Teresa in our time, freely gave their lives in daily unremunerated service to others; a civilization in which men and women knew right from wrong and most tried to do right; one that limited the powers of governments because no King was above the 'higher law,' God's law; one that respected the rights of the weakest and poorest, including the right to life itself--because all were children of God and had the same Father in Heaven. It is no exaggeration to say that Christian Civilization, or Christendom, was *qualitatively* different from all others, whether ancient, medieval, or modern, just as Jesus Christ Himself was *qualitatively* different from all other men.[22]

But now, as history slouches to the end of the Twentieth Century, modern man has, to a large degree, rejected the Christian Civilization that gave birth to his freedom and prosperity in this world, the promise of happiness in the next world, and to meaning, purpose, value in both time and eternity. The phrase, "Post-Christian Era," has had much currency at least since World War II. It is a phrase which, sadly, is especially apt. Many modern men and women, particularly those who believe the falsehood of Evolution, welcome the ascendancy of this phrase from the realm of rhetoric to the world of reality. What they will not face is the fact that when one rejects the source of the good in his character his character loses that good itself.

They believe that once they effectively purge Christianity from the earth, they can build a New World Order with "humanistic" values replacing Christian teaching. They believe that they will introduce a 'New Age' wherein, somehow, Almighty Man will build a world without God but unified economically, politically, and even religiously.[23] In their writings and seminars, some go so far as to predict that Man will evolve to some mystic 'Omega Point,' and some even say we shall be as gods.[24] There is enormous excessive pride in all this.

We have heard it all before. In the Garden of Eden, the Serpent lied to Adam and Eve and told them 'You shall be as gods.'[25] At the tower of Babel, the unified economic-political-religious world power sought to mount up to Heaven, again pursuing godlike capabilities.[26] So one might say that far from evolving in a straight line up to some superior ultimate, mankind has come full circle back down to the ancient starting point. As we enter the Twenty First Century we face the same question as did Adam and Eve: Will we obey God or disobey Him? Will we try to be 'as gods' through our own finite efforts or will we accept our creaturehood and let the infinite *God* raise us up to His level through Jesus?[27]

IV. The Deception to Come

Pride goes before the fall. In the near future, my children, a certain man will emerge who will tell you that you can be 'as gods' if you only follow him. He will offer you peace and prosperity, jobs and food, in return for total allegiance. He will play on your fears of economic chaos and war, both of which, quite possibly, were engineered by him and his secret followers to panic you into giving him the unlimited power over you that he desires.[28] At first he will seem only to be a brilliant, charismatic political leader; soon he will show his true colors: he aspires to be a religious leader, but one different from all who came before. For he will at last demand not just allegiance, but *worship*. All of this has been foretold, in outline, in the Bible (c.f. Daniel, 2 Thessalonians, Revelation). This man will be the Antichrist.[29]

This man may seem to have marvelous powers. He may work apparent miracles. Remember, pagan sorcerers had power, from the Devil, to work apparent miracles. But whenever there was a contest, God's power prevailed.[30] This man will propose and later demand that everyone take a certain "mark" on his forehead or his right hand. This "mark" will have multiple purposes, one to allow buying and selling and another to show allegiance to this world leader. The Scriptures have warned us of this trap, and so I tell you solemnly, if you voluntarily accept this "mark," you have doomed yourself to a hellish life on this earth and to Hell itself at your death.[31]

This man will establish a world government and he will be, in effect, the dictator of the world for a short time. During this period, you should go into hiding, like Joseph and Mary when Herod sought to kill the Infant Jesus.[32] The Antichrist will be assisted by a world religious leader whom mystics have often called the False Prophet. Like John the Baptist, who prepared the way for Christ, this man will prepare the way for the Antichrist. No one will know the identity of these men until they reveal themselves, but Our Lord has provided a useful way to judge:[33] "By their fruits you will know them."[34] If you understand the truth, you will recognize falsehood; if you are committed to the genuine good, you will avoid evil. If you know what true doctrine and good morals are, you will recognize their counterfeit.

So, my brothers and sisters in pilgrimage, I call upon you to discern the spirits, because not all spirits are from God.[35] Expose the wolf in sheep's clothing. Resist his lure of bread, for not by bread alone does man live.[36]

V. The Key to Reaching the Promise

Mankind will go through an "Exodus experience" during the final days.[37] Those who live in the final days will go through a "desert," in which only God can preserve them. As the Hebrews of old, so those who would reach the Promised Land of the Era of Peace that God has promised us: we must rely on Him for food and on His angel for guidance in the night.[38] The key to spiritual and even physical survival will be an intense life of faith and prayer.

So I urge you to take to heart the truths I have summarized here. If you have prayed little, begin now to pray much; if you have wasted countless hours in mindless entertainments mesmerizing with image and sound, sports spectacle or computer, cast those worthless amusements aside as you would last week's newspaper or worn out clothes that no longer fit.[39] To the priests of the Church, I say: it is no longer a time for mediocrity, but a time to gird yourselves with the armor of faith, put on through the exercise of continual prayer.[40] To the lay people of the Church, I say: exorcise yourselves of the false belief that you can float downstream on the tide of paganism as long as in your hearts, for an hour on Sunday perhaps, you bring your physical body into the presence of the Lord.

And to all men and women of good will, I say: God will indeed give you an opportunity to choose Him and, in that decision, to choose eternal life for yourself. But that opportunity will not last long, and the powers of evil will make superhuman efforts to persuade you to throw away the last opportunity. I plead with you, cast off the shackles of hedonism, materialism, and atheism, and join with me in extending our arms out widespread and saying, "Come, Lord Jesus!"[41]

For He is coming soon. And you must be ready.

John Paul II
Rome

CHAPTER XIII

(1)

Pat Green and Vanni were driving from her work, intending to have an early evening dinner. They were heading out Route 66 through Fairfax County toward a country restaurant.

"So this guy Carlton Mason asked you to wait *until 11:00 at night* for him to show." Pat wondered whether this Mason character was a wolf on the prowl, who saw Vanni as his next meal. He had also heard the name before, from his newspaper editor, as the person who'd blocked publication of his HAARP article. So the more he could learn about the guy, the better. But he did not like the idea that his girl, his *fiancée*, should be railroaded into spending half an evening with a New York banker who thinks he's running both Treasury and Defense.

"Yep, I told you that when I called night before last--that he asked me to stay that long," she said. "But he got there a little after ten."

"Still, it strikes me as a bit presumptuous."

"Me too, and I wouldn't have stayed except that my Boss sent me as his stand-in, and my Boss is big on slurping up to Government types who can hand out cushy contracts to us Beltway Bandit corporations," she answered.

"Well, you got a point. There's the 'Golden Rule: He who has the gold makes the rules.' I guess I probably would have done the same thing. Hope you got a free dinner on his tab."

"I did," she smiled, "and I managed to get a chocolate sundae for dessert before he showed up."

"Means more Stairmaster for you, my dear!" he kidded.

"Not on your life, big boy; when calories realize whose body they're in, they run away, just out of fear of having to deal with a determined babe like me. Next time we're in New York, I'll race you up the stairs to the top of the Empire State Building."

"Hey, Supergirl, I'll chase you anywhere--but not straight up a thousand feet of stairs--unless we're there on December 31, '99, and the Millennium Bug has all the elevators stuck in transit--but then it would make more sense to run *down* the stupid steps if the 'Bug' blacks out the whole city."

"Anyhow, Pat," she came back to the topic, "I'm going to level with you, because this fellow Mason is a smooth operator."

"And I bet he's warm for your form," added Pat.

"Maybe. But if I give him a Round Two, he definitely will be," she said.

He paused, dodged a swerving semi that was crowding his lane, downshifted from fifth to fourth, then, as red tail lights popped up everywhere ahead of him, shifted again to third and hit the brakes. The distraction gave him a chance to think.

"Honey, I'm a candid guy. I take it this fellow is single. I know it's flattering to a woman for any guy, especially a smooth bigwig, who's probably handsome and suave--for any guy like that to take an interest in you."

"It is," she said simply.

"But, Vanni, you *are* a 'blonde bombshell,' so we should be surprised if the guy were *not* impressed with your looks.

"In this case, though," he continued, "you and I are engaged. So my strong preference would be, that you not meet with Mason, unless I'm along--and I can't see him being enthusiastic about that, unless the pretense for his meeting with you is to talk Beltway Bandit business, only business, and nothing but business. Of course," he added, "then he could say I should not be there because the discussion is confidential."

"He invited me to dinner next Sunday."

Pat frowned. "Did you accept?"

"No, I told him I was busy. But I think he'll call and ask again, or think up something for a different day."

"During the time you were with him, did he see your engagement ring?"

"He must have. He came into the hotel restaurant as I was finishing my ice cream. He sat down and we talked for about a half hour. I gestured with my left hand deliberately, I picked up the water glass with my left hand, I reached for my purse with my left hand. If he didn't see the ring, he needs a seeing-eye dog."

"So he wants to hit on an engaged woman, and he has the gall to invite her to dinner and make a play that will steal you away from the man who gave you the ring he's disregarding."

"That sums it up accurately," she said, "and I don't like the position he's put me in."

The traffic started to open up again, and Pat wound up through the gears. His sports car bolted forward into a clear lane.

"Let's figure that one out," he said. "If we both have the same handle on your feelings, then the problem, at least in part, is that any noncooperation with Mason will get back to your boss, and maybe jeopardize your job."

"I think so."

"Second, I bet this Mason guy not only wears red ties; I bet he's sharp, worldly, poised, self-assured, probably late thirties--just old enough to give the impression of macho maturity--yet young enough to have a good supply of sex appeal. Any woman find him attractive."

"Well, I do--but not as attractive as you might think. Even if we weren't engaged, I would be hesitant about him. Sometimes we women can read a man quicker than men read us, and he strikes me as a lot like the 'singles scene' guys I was getting sick of around the time we met. I think that by the third date he'd be saying, 'Your place or mine?'"

Pat hit the brakes again, as a teenager in a red Acura coupe with boom box booming at 100 decibels shot by and cut into his lane.

"Then here's what I'd like you to do," Pat said. "Keep everything honest. Head him off at the pass--by which I mean, go to your boss and tell him you met with Mr. Mason, tell him whatever business stuff you and Mason discussed, and then--before the boss figures he can get on the good side of the Treasury by making *you* Mason's 'escort' whenever he wants--tell the boss, in no uncertain terms, that your personal life is off limits--and that if Mason needs a female dinner companion, your firm can get him one, if they want, through a 'temp' agency."

"Gee, you're tough," she said. But inwardly she was pleased.

"Well, I've been listening to Father Mike on lots of different things--and I notice that he has a habit of cutting to the quick. You know, he'll analyze the ethics of a problem, figure out what's the right thing to do, and then commit himself wholeheartedly to it. No beating around the bush. No hemming and hawing and trying to have it both ways..."

He slowed the car to take the exit ramp onto state route 15, and they both were silent for a few moments, as he approached the stop sign at the crossroad. He turned left, crossed back over Route 66, and accelerated onto a commercial boulevard in a small town. The restaurant was a couple miles ahead on the right.

"Let me add a footnote," he said, "and then we can get off this topic, unless you want to pursue it...I think the time to break off a dangerous relationship is right at the beginning, before it wraps around you like a boa constrictor. I think that if you give this guy any hint of romantic interest--or do anything that he *interprets* as interest, whether *you* meant it that way or not--then he will pursue you aggressively, *and* tie his interest in you to government favors for your company--which means that your Boss will try to help Mason get his hooks in you."

She looked serious and slightly worried. She loved Pat and, except for their not seeing spiritual matters from the same point of view, would have set a marriage date much earlier than she had. She hadn't fully realized, until he pointed it out, the danger she might be walking into.

As he parked the car, he glanced to his right to measure the parking space and saw her worried look. "Promise me," he said with a twinkle in his eye, trying to lighten things up a bit, "you won't challenge Mr. Mason to chase you up the stairs to the top of the Empire State Building! He might just do it!"

"I know he would, if I dress like I used to before I became a Christian...Say--I bet that's the answer!" she exclaimed, as if she'd opened a cookie jar and found a diamond. "I'll make him chase me to the top after he eats a big dinner--he'll have a heart attack--and then we won't have to worry!"

(2)

Cardinal Eugenio Cassendi and other Vatican plenipotentiaries worked feverishly to put together the Consistory, the meeting of the Cardinals from around the world to elect a new Pope. Cassendi believed he had the votes, but some of the traditional Cardinals, such as the ones from Africa, could be an obstacle. On a secure phone line he discussed his concerns with the Chairman of the Council of Europe, who assured him that some of those men would have an "accident" on their way into Rome and would not be in attendance after all.

(3)

Father Michael Kanek had been invited to the Healy Hall office of the new Acting President of Georgetown University. He was also the new Superior of the local Jesuit community.

The new man was an unknown to Kanek, but the scuttlebutt on him was, from Kanek's perspective, not good. His name was Father Wilton Johnson; he was from the New England Province; he had spent much of his time in theological studies in Rome, and later sociology studies at the University of Michigan. He had authored one pop sociology book in cooperation with an unknown associate of Father Anson Grady in Chicago. It was well written and clever, but its editorial message was that the Church should teach what the people do: the Church should continually adjust its doctrines to reflect changing mores. He had never asked to say Sunday Mass and preach at some local parish--and he apparently had never done *anything* to promote spirituality among the students he taught or the laity he hobnobbed with. In fact--Father Kanek tried to dismiss the harsh thought--except for the priest's black suit which he wore occasionally, there was nothing external that would give the proverbial "man from Mars" reason to believe that the Reverend Wilton Johnson was a Catholic priest rather than, say, a Unitarian minister. Kanek tried to dismiss the question, often asked about religious pretenders, "If the police accused you of being a Christian, would they have enough evidence to convict?"

"Father Kanek, how are you?" Wilton Johnson met him at the office door. He reached out to shake Kanek's hand, and the latter noted that the grip was not firm. "Do come in. Have a seat." They both sat down, at diagonals from a coffee table set at one end of his large office. Father Johnson made a few pleasant comments and small talk and Kanek, recognizing this was just setting the stage to something quite different, went along with the convention. Finally, his host came to the point.

"As you know, the Church is in transition, what with the unfortunate demise of John Paul II and with the election of Cardinal Eugenio Cassendi as new Pope." Father Kanek nodded agreement and listened warily. "Fortunately for the prospects of effecting necessary reform rapidly," continued Father Johnson, using the cliched idiom of the modernists, Kanek thought, "the new Pope has appointed a new Father General for the Society of Jesus. He in turn has sent to all the Provincials, and thus to university presidents, a questionnaire which he wants us all to fill out and return within a week." He brandished a four page monograph in his right hand.

"Fine," said Father Kanek, with as much enthusiasm as he could muster, "I'll look it over."

"Beyond that," continued Father Johnson, "I might be able to help you in the transition that is coming."

Kanek wondered why he needed help, but decided to play along. "I am sure all of us would welcome a way to make our lives more stable in a turbulent era," he said, using words that he knew really had almost no meaning. He tried to keep any tone of sarcasm out of his voice.

The other priest brightened, perhaps believing Kanek's use of jargon reflected his own mental confusions, and continued. "I'm glad we agree. What I have in mind is, that there probably will be some reassignments and I wouldn't be surprised if you might be one of them."

"If that is so, then this questionnaire that you have--I presume it has to do with a man's suitability for certain assignments--why is it pertinent to me? If my Superiors have already decided to reassign me, it would seem the questionnaire is moot."

Father Johnson could not prevent a slight frown from crossing his face, because he realized that the other man was very incisive and he did not want to lose control of the conversation. The use of raw power--demand obedience--was not his style. He always wanted a non-confrontational relationship.

"I can see why you say that, on first glance. But in your case I felt, if you are to be reassigned, that there might be some leeway--you know, some room for your own choice and preference. This questionnaire would probably help us to assess the relationship between your subjective preference and the objective situations we might choose among."

Kanek could not quite follow the logic of this newest burst of gobbledygook, because the easiest way to figure out where he should be assigned would be to tell him the options available and then *ask* him which one he wanted. The superior could always override his wishes; but at least he would have the benefit of discussing the subordinate's proposals. The Order had done quite well in four hundred years without using industrial psychologists as intermediaries between superior and subordinate. Francis Xavier had made it to India, Isaac Jogues to the Iroquois, and Arnold Damen to Chicago, without the benefit of filling out multiple-choice answers on a survey!

But he was beginning to suspect that there was an ulterior purpose in this questionnaire thing--did they want to know where he would like to be assigned, and then they would send him somewhere else? Or, because of his own low profile stance on campus, was it that they were not sure where he stood on the issue of the American-Church-versus-the-Roman-Church struggle?...and wanted a way to confirm their suspicions?

"O.K.," said Kanek, without emotion, but trying to resist the temptation verbally to pin this wishy-washy circumlocutor, or at least ask him bluntly what assignments might be in their minds. Obviously, he reasoned, if they wanted him to know that *before* he returned the survey, they could tell him right now. "I'll look this thing over and get it back to you promptly."

The other seemed relieved. He always felt that small triumphs over his subordinates would grease the skids for greater ones and he believed Kanek's noncombative response was a surrender. They agreed that this interview had been productive and Kanek departed. *Is this the management style of the "new" Church,* Father Kanek wondered, *the style of a corporate bureaucracy? What ever happened to the Church of the Saints and Martyrs?*

(4)

John DeSanto sat in his study at the farmhouse. In his hand was a book of visions and messages by a seer, known only as Julia of C. The book's title was *JESUS CALLS US.* He opened to page 40 and read,

> *"So speaks God the Father, God the Son and God the Holy Ghost: "All that, in My Goodness, I undertook until now upon the Earth, has been cast aside and crushed by My administrators. I, Myself, am trampled in the souls of My faithful. Because of this, I will crush the unfaithful Earth, together with her administrators, and I will rise up on My Earth, and My Wisdom will rule on it until My Time.*

> *"In this time, the people live far from Me, according to their own cleverness. My Wisdom and My Humility are derided on the Earth. Therefore I will transform the Earth and it will be new, according to My Law. The people whose lives I spare will revere My Holy Name. Their hearts will be shaken by My Voice, which they will hear after the Great Trial. All I have done on the Earth was good, but man, My creature, has changed all into evil. I will show the Earth My great Power: I will rock her foundations and will cause the hearts of men to shudder. The play of My Anger over My disobedient children will be terrible. I wait and endure the evil upon the Earth for a very long time, but I will do what is necessary that which belongs to Me, will not be lost. The ears of many people are closed to My Voice, as if I were not the Lord of My creatures. All that exists in nature serves Me, only man has turned his back on Me. But to whom will you go if you leave Me? You have no choice other than darkness and the father of lies, Satan, who runs behind you, to ruin you and to win you to himself--then you are forever lost. O miserable Earth, what a black*

conscience you have! If you would only have wished to see My Day, darkness would not have engulfed you. Every work, once begun, must at some time, have an end; also all this that is happening must have an ending, so that I do not also lose those who are marked with My seal. The Earth has gone deaf to My Words, so it has become a slave of darkness and its own empty glory, which leads into the darkness of the abyss, into the precipice of eternal agony; My Heart cries over you, O Earth, and over the injustices with which you offend Me."

John DeSanto closed the book and started to pray.

(5)

The major astronomical observatories and the Department of Defense are linked together by computer. It is rare that they send DOD any important information, but defense planners always worry about the possibility of a nuclear missile attack and are eager to track the whereabouts of other nations' satellites. Thus any data from any source are welcome.

Captain Robert Crane, U.S. Air Force, assigned to Data Collection, stared at his computer print out. Then he punched a few buttons and sent urgent E-mail messages out to all the observatories. His message went as follows:

"We have received information from one of the observatories in our network that a comet or asteroid has been discovered on a course likely to intersect the earth's orbit in 30 to 45 days. Please describe the size and speed of this comet and calculate the mathematical chances of its hitting the earth. Your immediate response is urgently requested."

(6)

"Cristina." It was the voice of her Guardian Angel.

"I am here," she said simply. She could see only the outline of a man-sized being. He reached forth his right hand in a gesture as if to touch her forehead, though he stood a few feet away. From his hand flowed a gentle stream of soft white light. She felt a mix of peace and strength.

"I will place some images into your imagination, and then I will explain them."

Immediately she saw a Titan 4A rocket, towering twenty stories high and weighing almost two million pounds, standing on a launch pad at Cape Canaveral in Florida, which she was well aware is part of the United States on its Atlantic coast. Then, as she watched, the rocket went into ignition/lift-off stage, and billows of smoke and red-orange flame burst out from its bottom, it shuddered, and slowly began to rise into the air.

Then, as if one fast-forwarded a television movie, a new scene appeared. The rocket had reached orbit point and had deployed a huge antenna with a diameter bigger than the length of three soccer fields--more than 1,000 feet. Attached to it by long tubular wires was a receiver, a reflector, two solar panels, and, at the bottom, a small satellite dish which, though she did not know it, was a "downlink" dish.

"You are wondering why I have shown you these scenes," said the figure standing a few feet away.

"Yes." She was perfectly calm, for her prior experience with this Angel had taught her many valuable lessons. One was that he was entirely in control; another, that if she was patient, all would come clear in due time; the third, that in dealing with the Angel she was, in reality, dealing with God.

"The rocket you have seen will be launched in one week. If it functions properly, the deployment of the antenna in orbit will take place as you saw in the second image.

"This is called an Advanced Vortex Intelligence Satellite. It can intercept broadcast transmissions from radios, cell phones, radars and other electronic communications systems, even down to simple hand-held radios. Its makers claim it has a legitimate American national security purpose, but it will be taken over by the Chairman and used for evil--unless God intervenes."

"What do you want me to do?"

"For the next week you must pray an extra hour per day, pleading the Name of Jesus and the Blood of Jesus, that the Father will intervene. During that hour, you may choose any form of prayer you wish, but include the Rosary."

"May I ask you another question?"

"You may."

"Did the Blessed Mother send you?"

"God the Father authorized the Blessed Mother to deal with this satellite. She sent me. Also, you are not the only person to whom the Blessed Mother has sent angels to request prayer. But the prayers of all of them are essential."

"Please tell my Mother I will happily do as she wishes."

CHAPTER XIV

(1)

John DeSanto put the Learjet into a gentle ascent away from Chicago's Midway Airport, on a gradual climb up to Flight Level 150 or fifteen thousand feet on a course east by south east toward Washington, D.C. On board were two precisely calibrated metal refrigerators. They contained, carefully preserved and wrapped, two living human organs, a heart and a liver. The coolers were strapped to hooks bolted to the floor and rested atop eighteen inches of foam cushion padding. Both had to be delivered as quickly as his jet could take him, to Reagan National Airport and thence, by local medical courier, to the surgical transplant team at Washington Hospital Center. This valuable cargo could mean the difference between life and death for two needy recipients.

For a pilot of his skill, this should have been routine. He had made this kind of run half-a-dozen times in the last two years--to the Mayo Clinic in Minnesota, to the Ochsner Clinic in Louisiana, to Johns Hopkins in Maryland, and to other medical centers with organ transplant capability. In the last few months, however, foundation work limited his time; so he would take assignments, as he did this time, only as an emergency when no other qualified pilot was available.

Unbeknownst to John DeSanto, on a railroad siding in northern Indiana, forty miles southeast of South Bend, stood an apparently abandoned flatcar, carrying a bulky load covered with a dark green tarpaulin. Next to it on a dirt road half-concealed by a small cluster of trees, stood a nondescript jeep-like truck. On the flatcar, under the tarp, were armed launchers for four early model Soviet-made surface-to-air missiles. In the truck, dressed in army fatigues but wearing no insignia, sat two east German artillery men. Two others leaned next to the truck talking.

These soldiers were part of a much larger multi-national force surreptitiously brought into the United States beginning in 1993. There were small Chinese units in Texas, German Luftwaffe pilots in Arizona, east Europeans in Colorado, and Russian units in Georgia, Pennsylvania, Louisiana, and other states. By and large, the public knew little of the fact that foreign military units were training and encamped on American soil. Where the public did take notice, as with the Luftwaffe in Arizona, spokesmen for the official line quickly laughed off the fears of the old-timers: it was only a matter of mutual training programs, like a military version of college student exchange. Indeed, when some citizens in Louisiana inquired why Russian tanks were being unloaded from ships on the docks near New Orleans, the Government's straight-faced response had been that the tanks were here to be painted! No one seemed to wonder whether it might be easier to send the paint to Russia.

The men at the Indiana rail siding snapped into action when they heard their radio crackle alive. In guttural German came a quick description of John DeSanto's Lear, with the command to destroy it. The four-man crew had no idea why, nor did they care; the commanding officer had been briefed on the general purpose of this type of mission: to test their ability to control the skies in this sector, to interdict any commercial or private flights, when the signal for the Takeover came at last. But a man in Brussels knew precisely why: during a random review of American pilots who also were Catholic, his computer had cross-referenced key data: fifty-three Catholic former Air Force or Navy officers were still flying, five of them this very day, of which two would pass within range of the Indiana missile crew. He ran a profile of each and settled on John DeSanto as the target: educated at Notre Dame, member of NRA, subscriber to *The Wanderer*, distributor of books and tapes on Marian apparitions--all in all, one who must eventually be eliminated. Might as well do it now, and get the added bonus of practice for the SAM crew and, if the later NTSB investigation discovered traces of missile residue, create further justification for extreme police powers against "terrorism."

So they hastily tore the tarp off the launcher, and with a rapid rotating motion of a large wheel that two of them rushed to turn, moved the launch mechanism into a forty-five degree upward tilt. They pointed it toward the north, turned a key in a lock, pulled a foot-long lever marked, in German, "Arm-Ready," and awaited the signal to fire. At eight thousand feet, John DeSanto's Lear jet was coming any moment, the perfect target for a heat-seeking missile.

The Woman peered into a golden globe and saw clearly the Lear in flight and the ready launcher on the ground a few miles away.

She spoke a single word. "Michael!" Instantly the Archangel appeared at her right hand, "Yes, Blessed Lady?" he asked. "Save him," she said firmly, pointing to the jet. He asked her a second question, to which she answered in the affirmative.

A nanosecond later the Archangel entered the cockpit of the Lear jet and, invisible, sat down in the empty copilot seat. Ten seconds after that the ground crew launched the missile.

"DeSanto, you have a lock! Repeat, you have a lock--at three o'clock!!" Michael spoke in a dimension where sound and thought are the same. In the voice of John DeSanto's old wing commander from his carrier days, the words penetrated his mind like a vivid memory. Years of training rushed back as conscious and subconscious became one. He reacted instantly.

Reflexively, he pushed the throttle forward to full power, banked sharply to the right, and headed the plane into a steep climb straight into the brilliance of the sun. He wished he had after-burners.

The missile sped on, closing on the tail of his plane. It moved at 1300 m.p.h.; the best he could coax out of the Lear in its fight against gravity was a mere 500.

"Now, close the throttle and go over the top!" came the thought from the same voice, commanding a somersault backwards toward the missile. It was a maneuver F-4 pilots developed in Vietnam. *Down there, in that grove of trees, is the enemy. Your target."* John DeSanto looked out the side window and, sure enough, a smoke streak from the rear of the missile led right back down to the trees and, half visible, a railroad flat car with launcher aimed at his sector of the sky.

As he had expected, the sudden disappearance of the jet's engine exhaust confused the missile's guidance system. With the jet's hot trail gone, it locked onto the heat of the sun as its target. It took twenty seconds of fruitless flight for the missile's computer to adjust for the anomaly that it could not cut its distance to the sun. John DeSanto had gained precious space.

"Now, go full throttle and dive toward the target." With a grim smile, John looked back at the missile, by then inexplicably turning to resume pursuit, and then down at the men on the ground. They were

gesticulating wildly as their captain shouted panicky orders to fire a second shot. But they would be too late: now he was in a steep dive--the men below thought it was suicide--straight at them, with the missile closing rapidly right behind him.

He wished he could "go to guns" and take those bastards out, but of course the Lear was unarmed. But there was a better way to get them: he had studied the tactics of World War II Stuka pilots, even met two old timers among them early in his flying career, and picked the brains of the by then ancient aviators who had, in their own war, pioneered dive bombing. Whenever he had the chance, he had practiced the maneuver in F4s and other Navy jets. The Archangel sitting invisible next to him knew all this.

Aware that miscalculation would mean death, he held the dive till the very last possible second, hoping the missile would be only a few hundred yards from his tail, and he could pull out sharply. A witness to this maneuver would think the plane bounced off the ground like a huge winged tennis ball.

Michael was fully aware of the timing, the physics, the strain on the wings, the speed of the missile. Faster than any computer, even the Chairman's in Brussels, in a simple mental glance that calculated it all, he grasped what had to be done. He reached over with his left hand, placed it atop John's on the stick, and took control.

Their hands interpenetrated. The Archangel and the man pulled the plane out of its dive less than 50 feet above the flatcar. Three seconds behind the Lear, the missile, its dive speed up to 1,600 miles per hour, could not change course.

It slammed into the launcher with a horrible red-orange explosion. Jagged lumps of hot steel shot out in all directions, like a huge holiday firecracker. Fragments of burning metal killed all four men instantly. The Lear jet sped back up, trying to outrun the shock wave. It shuddered violently for a couple seconds, but Michael surveyed every molecule of the plane in a glance and determined there was no structural damage. At the same time, he deflected the burning chunks of metal shooting up.

As he climbed, John DeSanto gave a final relieved glance down at the charred debris smoldering below. "I didn't know I was *that* good," he said half aloud with a trace of a grin.

"Alone, you aren't," he heard in his head. And he remembered a song his parish sometimes sang at Mass: *I will raise you up--on eagle's wings...*

(3)

John DeSanto touched down at Reagan National Airport only three minutes behind the ETA in the Flight Plan he had filed in Chicago. The medical courier team was ready and transferred his valuable cargo quickly. The head of the team signed the Receipt document and John was free to go. As an independent contractor with Federal Express, DHL, and UPS, he had the option to wait 24 hours for a return flight cargo opportunity. If he could avoid dead-heading back to Chicago, he could earn a second fee. Besides, he needed to talk with reliable people about what had happened.

Civilian pilots are required to report to FAA any serious suspicious or untoward events during flight. This is an ASRS, or Aviation Safety Reporting System, report. The FAA distinguishes between an "accident" and an "incident." In theory, the FAA cannot use information in the ASRS to jeopardize the pilot's license. But many pilots fear that it might. John figured that what he ran into qualified--in spades!--as an incident to be reported. Then too, low-orbiting surveillance satellites probably picked up the explosion. They may have photographed the attack, his evasive maneuvers, and his luring the missile back down to destroy its own launcher.

DeSanto surely was not going to lie about what had happened. But he realized that the Government might not want to make public what he went through. He had no idea who had fired at him and if he had not read the private revelations of various mystics, who recounted some messages that foreign troops were hidden around the U.S., he would have been certain that somehow some fool Infantry ground-to-air missile team had, for Heaven knows what stupid reason, been stationed on that railroad siding--and some crazy tried to kill him--or some incompetent hack had launched the damn thing accidentally.

But the words in his mind--*"Down there, in that grove of trees, is the enemy. Your target"*--if they were from God, gave the lie to these explanations. Unless all four of the soldiers were in on a plot to kill him--or someone else flying by--God would probably not use the missile to destroy innocent Americans along with the crazy or the hack.

He knew he had to file that report with FAA, and if he described *everything* that happened--leaving out the words in his head--it was almost certain that he would be an embarrassment to the Government. If some damn fool incompetent off-the-deep-end-nut American had tried to kill him, Congressional hearings would drag the Army through endless pain. If, God forbid, it was a *foreign* military unit, well, the FBI, CIA, and NSA would wallow in the same pain.

He went to the nearest airport pay phone, called Pat Greene and Father Mike Kanek, and confirmed that they could arrange an emergency meeting of the Honest Debate Society. He wasn't sure he wanted Vanni there, but he would leave that up to Pat. He definitely did not want Joanie Atkinson present, because he didn't think she had the depth to handle the topic. He especially hoped Jerry Kanek was in town, if Pat could find him, since he believed Jerry was either FBI or CIA, and in any event, he was cut out of the same mold as Father Mike, with the added advantage of understanding whom to trust, if anybody, in the Government. Once he had his plans clear, he called Susan.

"Hi, Honey, it's me, John," he said to her from the pay phone. "Yep, I'm O.K. Got here just about on time."

"I'm relieved," she said. "I had the strongest feeling in early afternoon that you were in danger, so I kept saying *Hail Marys* and the prayer to Saint Michael the Archangel the rest of the day."

"Your prayers may have made a difference," he said, "but I can't explain right now. Listen, I'm going to stay here tonight. Till about midnight you can reach me at Pat Greene's--you got the number--after that I'll be at the Key Bridge Marriott or the Best Western in Rosslyn. One of them will have a room. If they don't, I'll call again and tell you where I am."

(4)

Lake Maggiore straddles the border between Italy and Switzerland high in the Alps. The largest town at the Swiss end of the lake's long and narrow expanse is Locarno. Twenty kilometers outside the town, halfway up Mt. Madone, was situated an expansive ski lodge, which had been closed for two months for thorough renovation. Three years ago, the elderly owners, a traditional Catholic couple whose ancestry went back to the middle ages, had given the property to their only daughter as an engagement present. It was the place where her fiancée had proposed. But when the young woman's husband-to-be died a few months later in the tragic TWA Flight 800 crash, she retired in grief to seclusion at their family home in Bern. Soon she decided, because her parents were financially secure and she herself did not want to be reminded of the place where she had become engaged, that she would give the property to the Holy Father. This transfer was effected by the family lawyer without the slightest publicity, using an offshore trust on the Isle of Mann as the apparent owner.

One of the guest rooms in the lodge had been converted into a chapel. In this room there was a small altar, and on it a golden monstrance was positioned, with a white Host in the upper center. On either side were some small lighted candles. A white haired heavy set man sat motionless and alone before the monstrance with its Host, his lips moving in continuous quiet prayer.

Stationed outside at the corners of the main building, invisible to any being on earth or under the earth, stood four angels almost as tall and powerful as Michael the Archangel.

CHAPTER XV

(1)

"The Honest Debate Society hereby convenes," announced Pat Greene with less than his usual ebullience. "Our soul brother and esteemed erstwhile aircraft carrier fighter pilot, John DeSanto, has called this august body into Emergency Session. The topic is not a proposition to debate but a problem to analyze--and probably counsel to offer."

Present were the entire group, except Joanie Atkinson: Pat Greene, Vanni, John, Father Mike, and his brother Jerry. On this occasion Vanni's light grey sweatshirt had blue letters saying, *No Earth Pain Now, No Heaven Gain Later.* On the table before them were the usual refreshments. It was 8:30 p.m. and a driving rain fell continuously outside.

"Since you guys are here at my request, on a rainy week night and on short notice, I'll summarize quickly, so I can get your input," John DeSanto began.

"This afternoon I was flying out of Chicago with a medical delivery for Washington Hospital Center. It should have been routine. But--now I want you to understand, whether you believe I had a vision or message from God during that big storm outside Chicago a few months ago, what happened today was all physical--visible to the naked eye." He paused and took a swallow of Coke.

"Go on," said Pat.

"I was over northern Indiana, southeast of Notre Dame, and *someone manning a missile launcher on railroad flat car fired a surface-to-air missile at me...!*" For the moment, he did not mention the voice that warned him. They looked at him with mixed shock and amazement.

"Who would do *that*?" asked Vanni. "How did you avoid getting shot down--killed?" asked Jerry Kanek. They spoke simultaneously.

"One at a time! I don't know who, Vanni, but that question is one reason why we're here, because I have to do a report for the FAA, and I need some advice...But, I'll get to that in a minute." He looked over at Jerry, sitting in an easy chair diagonally across from the sofa and to Pat Greene's left. "How I avoided it, Jerry--well, for a few seconds I thought it was my own skill--I used standard evasive tactics, roll over, head into the sun, back-flip toward the missile, so that the thing's heat-sensors will lose touch with their actual target--my exhaust--and it will try to attack the sun. In vain, of course.

"But I did something else that was really a stroke of genius: a voice sort of popped into my head--maybe it was from my subconscious--but I got the idea to dive at the missile battery and lure the missile into following me down and hitting *it* instead of me."

Father Kanek had a hunch. "Let me guess," he said, "I'll bet you have reason to believe it was not just your own mind--it was the Archangel Michael!"

John DeSanto looked at him in surprise. "You're right," he said. "My wife, Susan, told me when I called her later that she had a strong feeling in mid-afternoon that I was in danger, and she prayed a lot of prayers to Mary and Michael the Archangel."

"Hey, guys, I don't want to push you to digress much, but the firm of Van Niesen and Greene, Skeptics-at-Law, need to cross-examine on that point," interposed Pat.

"Sure, this is not a monologue by a crazy Navy Wannabe-Top-Gun," said John pleasantly, relieved that they could "discuss" a bit and not just react to his experience. "Ask away."

"Well, John, you know I'm open-minded, but I have a hard time buying the idea that an angel--or an archangel, whatever the difference is--intervened to save you. Got any proof?"

"Proof? Well, if he was there, he sure didn't leave his calling card. So, candidly--no, I don't. Except maybe the coincidence of Susan's feeling and the way she dealt with it. Plus the fact that the dive I made, to try to elude that missile and trick it into such a power-dive of its own that it couldn't pull out before it blew up its own launcher--that dive had a chance of success of, maybe, far less than one in one hundred thousand.

"So, no matter how skilled the pilot, to pull a plane out only feet above the target without crashing himself--well, there were too many variables way beyond my control. And they all had to fall perfectly in place."

"I don't get it," said Vanni. "What variables?"

"Well, just to name a few, because we are getting into a cul-de-sac and I'd like to stay on the main road, but--first, something warned me--I didn't look out until after something *told* me the missile was on its way. Second, I got the idea of exactly what to do so forcefully it was like my copilot was shouting it in my ear--except I didn't *have* a copilot. Third, the maneuver I took confused the missile, but not every missile would be confused; it depends on the quality of its heat sensors. Fourth, something told me to look exactly where the attack originated and I had banked the right direction--coincidence?--so I was positioned to have a straight run down at the thing before the missile repositioned and caught up."

"How fast do those things go?" asked Father Mike.

"Depends on the make and model. Most do at least 1,300 miles per hour. That's twice as fast as I could get the Lear to go, except in the power dive, where I probably hit Mach 1."

"So the timing, you diving from--what?--8,000 feet?--down to the ground--the missile going twice as fast as you--yet its closing on you so near that when you pulled out its speed was too great for it to pull out--yet it not catching you before you had a chance to pull out--so the timing was...*supernatural...?*"

"I think so. And add to it, even though the shock wave and shrapnel from the blast travels for a few seconds, from point of origin, faster than the plane--it seems it didn't get any dents. No damage. Another miracle."

"O.K.," said Vanni. "The firm of Van Niesen and Greene--you will note, Greene suggested Van Niesen is the Senior Partner--order of importance, you know--our firm accepts your answer and will take the motion under advisement. That is, speaking for Pat, because I want to get back on the main topic, we can agree for the sake of argument that God sent an angel to save you. We Evangelicals have no problem believing that."

"I still do, a little," said Pat. "But I gotta admit, these discussions are wearing my doubts down a bit. In this case, though, Archangel or whatever, I would normally doubt that there would be a *missile launcher*, for Heaven's sake, sitting on a railroad siding in, of all places, northern Indiana!"

"Anyway," said John, "let me tell you the rest of the story. I've got to file a report with the FAA--I've already called them and put on the record that something extraordinary happened, and I'll give them the details tomorrow. In fact, once I got out of there, I radioed a quick summary to the nearest control tower."

"So, that doesn't sound too big a problem," said Vanni. "Just tell them what you just told us..."

From the moment he heard the summary of the missile attack, Jerry Kanek's mind had been racing, considering possibilities, measuring risks, speculating on levels of likelihood. "I dunno, Vanni; I can imagine a number of scenarios that led to this attack, and some of them require a lot of prudence to talk about without getting your rear in a sling because you stepped on the wrong toes!"

"How so?"

"I'll get to that in a second. But first, John--and everybody--do you remember when the Government burned down that cult compound in Texas, that immediately after they roped it off and bulldozed the whole place?" A couple heads nodded agreement, the looks of others suggested no memory. "Again, do you remember when that federal building was bombed, how the Government again roped the whole place off and bulldozed it down to look like a gravel parking lot?" Again, some nodded in the affirmative.

"Well, I'm going to toss out a 'worst-case scenario,'--worst, that is, from the point of old-timers like me, guys who went to Catholic schools and cry when they sing *The Star-Spangled Banner* and get all choked up when they see men like you, John, sitting in the cockpit of your fighter plane on a carrier and giving the 'thumbs up' sign and flying off to fight a Saddam Hussein, like in the Gulf War eight years ago. In other words, I'm a patriotic American and love this country.

"But let's assume that *some* people in our Government have an insider agenda of their own and that missile launcher was part of it.

Assume, just for the sake of argument, that they had it there for some eventual use. Say, maybe you just happened by, John, like a practice target. Or maybe the idea is to convince Americans that there are terrorists everywhere, so they can bulldoze Congress into passing more of those so-called 'anti-terrorist' laws which, as an attorney and a guy familiar with law enforcement, I can tell you are eroding our constitutional freedoms a Hell of a lot faster than 'global warming' makes you sweat in August."

"Jerry, I follow you, and I've got another hunch," added Father Mike. "I feel that the same thing that happened with the cult and the federal building, after the fact, will happen here."

"Great minds run in the same channels, little brother," smiled Jerry Kanek. "Keep on with my hypothesis: say that some group in Government was behind this. Hell, even if the launch was a genuine accident, they wouldn't want the public to know that they had a stupid missile launcher sitting in the backyard, almost, of Notre Dame University, shooting up innocent Americans flying a necessary heart transplant to a hospital! The bad publicity would outweigh, I think, the benefit--from some people's perspective--of stirring up further fear of terrorists."

"I think I've got the makings of another investigative feature article for the newspaper," said Pat. "*If* I can get those chickens to think for themselves and not swallow the line some bureaucrat gives them about 'national security.'"

"Sounds like you've got something on your mind we ought to talk about, Pat, but right now let's stick to John's mini war today," said Jerry. "You guys should know, I think the cleanup crews used a crude but effective form of what I call *damage control*. They sent in a team of specialists to remove all the evidence that might reveal misconduct on their part or support an explanation different from the official line as to what happened."

"Hunch number three," said Father Kanek. "Soon, all the evidence at the location of the flatcar and the launcher, or what's left of it, will disappear. Especially anything that suggests foreign involvement."

Pat Greene was thinking of whom he might interview. "John, Jerry mentioned Notre Dame. Do I remember correctly, that you were a student there?"

"Yes, I was. For you folks who measure time in football seasons, part of my four years there overlapped with Joe Montana's. I didn't play varsity football, though, because, well probably I wasn't good enough, not at Notre Dame--but I was in NROTC and wanted a chance to become a Navy pilot, and I had to work my tail off to get straight *A's* in some tough scientific courses. Why do you ask?"

"Do you know any Notre Dame grads who might still be living in that part of Indiana?"

"Only one, a guy who was on the team. We were roommates in first year, because he didn't go out for the team till he was a sophomore. A guy with an appropriate nickname for a tackle, 'Tank' Majoreski. Heck of a nice guy. I think he still lives on a farm in that area, a farm his dad ran."

"Polish fellow?" asked Father Kanek. "Played tackle, huh? Those Poles are tough." The others smiled.

"Well," Pat continued, "let me suggest you call him, *right now*, and see if he can do you a favor and check out the site, or knows anybody who was near that siding or saw the launch or heard the explosion--anything to prove, with a witness, that it actually *happened.*"

"Of *course* it happened, Pat," said Vanni. "John's an experienced pilot--it was daytime--he wouldn't make this up. The missile destroyed a railroad car, killed some men--there will be plenty of evidence lying around, you know, a big hole in the ground, pieces of their uniforms, twisted metal, even--dead bodies." The last two words she forced herself to add.

"Sure, Vanni, there *would* be, if the 'damage control' guys don't get there first!" observed Father Kanek.

"Who *are* the 'damage control guys,' Jerry?" asked Vanni, who figured his background in federal law enforcement gave him an inside track on information of this type.

"I don't know for sure," he answered. "I've heard some bothersome rumors, though. I don't think it's any old-line agency, like FBI or CIA. I think it's FEMA."

"Who--or what--is 'FEMA?'" asked Vanni.

"The Federal Emergency Management Agency," answered Pat. "It's a new bureau that was cooked up a few years ago--I don't know whether by law or Executive Order. Anyhow, it started out more or less under the control of Congress; but recently the President transferred it to the National Security Agency. So now it's part of the Executive Branch--which means Congress doesn't know all it's doing--if they give a damn."

"Well, there sure have been enough emergencies in the last few years to keep them busy," said Vanni. "Hurricanes, floods, fires...an earthquake," she added.

"True enough. But they have a very broad mandate, and in practice they have put together a small fleet of planes and a network of detention centers around the country," said Jerry. "Some of them they call 'Federal Transfer Centers.' Outside Oklahoma City, for instance, there's a new one that can hold over six hundred prisoners. They claim the purpose is to hold terrorists."

"You don't mean to say, do you, that some FEMA guys launched that missile?" asked Vanni.

"No, I don't, 'cause I just don't know who launched it. I'm only saying that it would be my guess that if the evidence disappears, and the Feds act as if nothing happened, and even challenge John and question his honesty or his eyesight--well, I would say *someone* was involved in 'damage control'--and my guess is it would be FEMA."

"Let's go back to the basic question," said Pat. "As Talkmeister, I have the duty to keep us on track. I think we're here not primarily to speculate about, say, FEMA--but to give our advice, for what it's worth, on what John tells the FAA."

"You're right, Mr. Talkmeister," said Father Kanek, "without reflection, I'd suppose we all would recommend simply that John should tell them the truth, the whole truth, and nothing but the truth."

"Sounds pious, Father, and normally I would agree without any qualification," said John. "And I sure wouldn't lie, but--"

"But sometimes," Father Mike interrupted, "a person has to *package* the truth in a way that he lives to tell the whole truth another day, in a safer forum."

"Lying is not smart," said Pat, "for pragmatic reasons--as well as the state of his soul, Father Mike," he added, looking at Kanek. "The pragmatics are simple: you got to figure that the Feds already *know* what happened, and their interest in your story is *not* to find the truth, but to find out about *you*--how much you know about who launched it, how much you insist on going public with it--getting some maverick like me to write it up for a million people to read--and how pliable you might be to incentives, or if need be, to threats to keep quiet."

"That's really cynical, Pat," said Vanni. "You make me want to pig out on chocolate cremes, to distract myself from such cynicism."

"If that's your plan, I'd recommend a six-pack of *Pete's Wicked*," rejoined Pat. "Your mind will fog up faster...But let me give a few reasons why I think they do know what happened: first, they've got a zillion reconnaissance satellites up in the sky, with camera ability to read a car license plate from twenty miles. So, when that missile exploded, it's almost certain some satellite recorded it. The late night shift at CIA are probably pouring over the pictures right now.

"Second, it's hard to believe that a *missile launcher* that needs a railroad flat car to mount it can be smuggled into the U.S., complete with crew--"

"There were four guys, dressed like soldiers, but I didn't get more than a glance," said John DeSanto.

"--a crew, like I said...of four men, and nobody knows about it. Maybe they jumped from a sub off Delaware and hitch-hiked to Indiana!--but it's more likely they had help, a 'cover.'"

"You're assuming they were foreigners," said Father Mike. "What is there to rule out their being Americans?"

"I guess I just don't want to believe that four of our own military guys would, for no reason, try to shoot down a civilian plane here in our own country," said John.

"How about an accident?"

"It would be a first. We've had SAM missiles since Vietnam, but we've never shot down one of our own planes! But, Father Mike, even though an accident is tremendously unlikely, let's say they didn't *want* to shoot me down, but somebody made a mistake. Still, what were they *doing* there, in the first place? A SAM battery, of all things!"

"If someone can analyze the debris, they can probably tell what kind of missile it was, who made it, and so on. Possibly the same with the soldiers' uniforms--if anything is left," said Vanni.

"I think that if the 'damage control' guys do show up, and clear the area of clues, you've got every reason to believe there's a rogue group inside some agency, that has its own high-tech weapons, and is not afraid to use them--or test them--by killing American citizens," said Pat.

"Well, maybe," said Father Mike. "That's the hypothesis I lean to, but--playing Devil's Advocate--why couldn't the damage control guys clear the area just to prevent panic--you know, if people thought enemy soldiers were sneaking around their Indiana farms, looking for targets, they'd get pretty worried."

"Just protecting us from ourselves, huh Father?" asked Pat, with a touch of sarcasm. "Big Brother knows what's best for ordinary Americans, and it's *not* to know that someone is stalking them with surface-to-air missiles! So that if a newspaper wanted to print this whole story, they would be abusing the freedom of the press--because 'national security' or some other shibboleth means the people are more secure if they *don't* know what's going on!" he added, bitterly.

"Wow, Mr. Talkmeister, *you* sure need a six pack of *Pete's Wicked*! Lighten up, man!" said Vanni.

"Sorry, Vanni. You know I feel pretty strong about freedom of the press. I've taken my own licks recently, in that boxing ring; but we can't go into that now."

"Let me refine my comments about telling the truth," put in Father Mike. "There's no ethical obligation to *interpret* the truth in a way that makes you a suspect or calls attention to your suspicions. I think John can just say something like this: 'I was flying at such-and-such altitude...I saw this streak of smoke rising from the ground and heading at me...Because of my Navy training, I interpreted it as a missile...instinctively I took evasive action as best I could in a Lear...I dived down toward the source, where it launched...It followed me...When I pulled out of a steep dive, it didn't...It blew up what looked like a railroad flatcar.' Period. End of statement."

"Footnote," said Pat. "My advice is, first, make this in writing. But they probably will want an oral briefing, too, so they can ask you questions. Be really terse in answering. Second, have a tape recorder with you and insist that they let you tape your statement and the Q-and-A. And, third, have a witness there, preferably an attorney." He looked at Jerry Kanek.

"Sorry, Pat. I'd like to help. But the rules I work under wouldn't permit it. I do have three or four attorney friends, though, who once worked for the Government and now are in the private sector." He got up and walked toward the kitchen, to retrieve a phone book. "They're still around here. I'll get you the numbers. Maybe you could call each of them tonight until one agrees to go with you."

"Wouldn't the bigwigs at FAA be annoyed if I come in with an attorney?" asked John.

"No doubt. But their annoyance is less important than your protection. Remember, these guys can revoke your license to fly, and they might be told to discredit *you*--the old approach: if you don't like the message, kill the messenger.

"I have to add," he said over his shoulder, as he reached below the microwave stand to grab the phone book, "the odds on that are low, I think, because of your Navy record. But 'whistleblowers' these days don't get rewarded, they get canned, so you've got to figure it could happen."

"While you guys are rummaging around for phone numbers," added Vanni, "why don't you get Tank Majoreski's number right now and put him on the trail of some hard evidence?"

"I second that," said Pat. "And tell him you've got a friend who's a newspaper writer--me--and your friend has a contingency fund. I'll pay his expenses and a stipend of one hundred dollars per hour up to $1,000.00 for his time. It will be $2,000.00, if he comes up with solid evidence this thing happened just as you've described."

(2)

The Warning.

It happened at two p.m. on a Thursday. How long it lasted, none of those who survived the later cataclysms to discuss the question could answer. It was the event foretold by many prophecies, an event so extraordinary that nothing like it had ever happened before in the entire history of the world.

Time stood still.

Time stood still--*everywhere.* The earth stopped rotating and all planets, including earth, stopped in their orbit around the sun. The continuous flows of transient energy on the earth, such as winds and rivers, all simply stopped. And every bird, every animal, every insect, every fish--all ceased their motion. Everything, including humans, "froze" in one place. Planes, automobiles, railroad trains, boats--all suddenly "locked" in static position, like statues.

But there was no damage. Had the spinning earth "stopped" like an automobile hitting a wall, every creature on it would have been killed by the impact. But because the Cause of the immobility was the power of God Himself, and God did not intend to harm any of His creatures at this time, that same power preserved them all physically and intact, as if nothing had happened.

God took a "snapshot" of our world and, for an indefinable moment--who knows whether it was a minute, an hour, or a week?--*He replaced our moving world with this immobile "photograph."* Every finite being in the universe was suddenly immobile within this "photograph." His purpose was to give every man, woman, and child a personalized Warning.

During this universal pause, every person had his own Vision. He or she saw exactly how they stood before God. They saw themselves as God sees them. They saw past, from the first day they had the use of reason, down to every detail of yesterday, up to the very present. They saw actions, they heard words, they saw--or somehow heard--their thoughts.

Each saw his life in all its details, the moral or immoral decisions highlighted, all the sins of commission or omission, spread out before him. Like a video tape on fast-forward, a person's life rushed past his mental vision--but with a terrible, frightening difference: he saw each action *in itself* and *he saw the state of his mind when he did the actions*; he saw the immediate impact on another person--say, a murderer saw and felt the pain of his dying victim--and he saw *the secondary effects of his evil act*--the murderer saw the pain and loss in the victim's wife and children, he saw them growing up without a father, he saw the trouble and evil they engaged in, prompted often by the lack of a father in their lives.

Every person discerned the direction of his life: whether the path he had voluntarily chosen would take him to Heaven or to Hell. He saw what would happen were he to die *right now.*

It was an interim Judgment. It was the Last Judgment in miniature; but like a mid-term exam, it would tell the person tested whether he was heading for a good grade or sliding down toward Failure. There still would be time to change--if the person wanted. But for many, the time would be short.

CHAPTER XVI

(1)

For Dolores Montalvo, the Warning was a crushing experience. She had been lounging on her villa deck, sipping a goblet of white wine, and pondering whether to go back to Zurich to get the rest of her money. Suddenly her vision blanked out. The things around, the sliding glass door behind her, the privacy fences to either side, the pole on the table holding the umbrella above, the beachside lights in late evening along the boardwalk near the now dark Mediterranean Sea--all seemed to evaporate as if they were enveloped in a dense black mist. Every single thing just disappeared.

In the place of all these material pieces of secular reality appeared a glowing yellow-white globe brighter than the sun. It rushed toward her like a comet coming at lightning speed and, before she could gasp for a single breath, she found herself *in* it. *She was now standing on the very edge of a stage, and in front of her--was herself!* She was like the Director of a play watching the Final Rehearsal in which she herself was cast in the main role.

She saw scene after scene from her own life--from the moment, around age six or seven, that she began to grasp Right and Wrong. She saw herself many times, vamping her father to get a favor, candy or something, she didn't deserve; and a Voice, a powerful terrible Voice, washing over her like a huge wave, *You lied to him.* She saw herself preening before a mirror, hundreds of times, admiring her own beauty at different ages; and a Voice, *Your beauty was My gift, not yours; why were you so proud?*

She saw her many acts of disobedience to her mother and her governess; and that awful Voice, saturating her being like water a soggy sponge, *Your disobedience of them was rebellion against Me.* She saw her momentary devotion at her First Communion...and later, her many cursory Communions, her mind wondering what man would notice her walking up the church aisle, and then her wandering thoughts about later entertainments after Mass was over; then those days in her late teen years when she simply stopped attending Mass, stopped praying, and simply drifted away. These scenes were accompanied by that penetrating Voice, *Mass is not a fashion show...I came to you expecting love, but you didn't even show Me courtesy...*

Compressed like a thousand three-dimensional pictures in an enormous family scrap book, the scenes moved to her twenties. She saw all the churches she should have entered but never did; she saw gifts of Grace like beautiful wrapped boxes of Christmas presents, unopened, untouched, because ingrate Dolores was too busy pursing fame and sex to find time to pray. *I could have made your spirit as beautiful as your body; instead you chose to be ugly.*

She saw her adult life, parties, beaches, movie studios--always the beautiful Dolores showing too much cleavage, too much thigh--and the men, the lust in their hearts, and the evil they would do, or want to do, which destroyed at least one marriage and sent three other men down a rapid immoral slope. And the Voice, again, *For a moment's pleasure, you destroyed some men for eternity.*

She saw all the petty little plots she had engaged in to start her acting career, the little tricks, the half-broken promises, and once she had a measure of stardom the threats and demands that only egotistical people make to impose their wills on lesser mortals.

She saw all the secondary evils like eddying ripples spreading out from a stone tossed into the surface of a pond: teenage girls sopping up lurid details of tabloid accounts of Dolores' conquests, stories exaggerated for sensationalism but with a large grain of truth--and some of those girls using her as a model and, to a lesser but still self-destructive degree, imitating her lifestyle. And thus committing sin after sin after sin. *Woe to the person who scandalizes My little ones--it would be better for him--or her--to be cast into the Sea with a huge stone tied around her neck.*

She felt that corrosive moral acid of pride and hate spreading through her heart, radical Feminism, the unnatural hostility toward men that she had nourished through anger and self-pity that the men in her life were, or seemed to be, exploiters of women. She realized for the first time that disdainful hatred of *all* men is the same thing, psychologically, as a white man's racist bias against all Blacks, and the Communists' irrational condemnation of all Capitalists. *Whoever hates his or her fellow human, hates Me.*

Shaken by the searing revelation of her inner corruption, she tried to turn her head away, but wherever she looked the Vision was before her. "No, no!" she cried out loud. "I don't want to see it! Stop! STOP!!" But relentlessly the pictures continued, three dimensional as before, concretely, immersing her in a multi-dimensioned mix of sound and sight and thought.

And then came a scene more terrible than any previous. *The abortion.*

The Vision took a sudden change: instead of generic events in a pattern, she saw the moment she seduced a man, a fellow actor, one evening after film shooting for the day was over. She became pregnant that night. Of course, she'd told herself, she could not have a baby; it would stand in the way of her career! So she got advice from other experienced women her age, and found a qualified doctor--there are many, these days, who deny the scientific fact that the unborn child is a human person--who for a modest fee would rid her of "the problem" when she was four months pregnant.

And now, in her Vision, she saw *the child forming in her womb*: the tiny perfect little hands, the head and face with eyes and nose and mouth, the beating heart. Then she saw the surgeon's instrument enter and tear apart that little body. *Yet the child's face formed into a that of a one-year-old little girl, then a two-year-old, then three, then four--and it spoke to her:*

> *"Mommy, why did you kill me? I wanted to sit in your lap and hug you. I wanted to play with you at the beach. I wanted to kiss you on Christmas day."*

She clenched her fists. She tried to close her eyes. She heard herself scream, "No, God, no!" But the child quickly grew older, and as a young teenager continued to look into her eyes and speak to her:

> *"Mommy, I would have been as beautiful as you. I could have used my beauty for good. You would have been proud of me when I graduated from school."*

Dolores buried her head in her hands. But the Vision would not stop. And her hands could not block it; it was in her mind, in her heart, exposing the horrible evil she had done.

"Mommy, I needed love and protection so I would blossom as God intended. In my twenties I would have married. I would have had three good children. "

Dolores groaned. This was so terrible. She was sinking into an ocean of guilt. It washed over her head; it poured into her mouth; it saturated her being. She flailed her arms in useless effort to rise to the surface.

Then the Vision became even worse! Suddenly she was standing before Jesus Christ on the Cross. She was alone. The dying Jesus looked into her eyes. He was horribly disfigured, raw flesh hanging loose where the scourging whips had rent His body, blood dripping out of the nail wounds. It was a scene far worse than she had ever seen in the churches. His eyes penetrated her soul.

"I am dying here, with these nails through My hands and feet, with these thorns piercing my head, with this horrible thirst I feel--because of the sins you, Dolores, commit. You are crucifying Me!"

She collapsed to her knees and sobbed. She bent lower and lower until her face, covered by her hands, almost touched the floor. *I want to die!* she heard herself say out loud.

The Vision responded to her plea. Instantly it changed. *Now she saw two long stairways, each beginning at ground level, one leading gradually up to a bright soothing white light; the other descending gradually down to a doorway of fiery crimson light.* She understood that the first was the path to Heaven; the second, to Hell. She did not want to look but the Vision held her hypnotically.

She saw a person moving down the second stairway. It was a beautiful woman in a long gown. But as she descended, a blank look on her face, her beauty slipped away. The woman changed, gradually but really, to an old hag and the dress became torn and tattered...then, as she approached the end of the stairs, she looked like a witch, her dress scarcely more than rags, and she began to move faster. Dolores got the strong impression that the changes were not just due to the passage of age: each downward step by the beauty-turned-hag-turned-witch symbolized one cf the woman's immoral choices. Dolores understood that the corruption of this woman's beauty was not external but was within her soul.

The woman proceeded to within five or six steps from the entrance to the fire. As she came closer, it loomed larger. Now the doorway to the fire was huge, like a blast furnace in a steel mill. She could see inside the door a vast sea of fire. Plunged into the flames were demons and lost souls as if they were red hot coals, transparent and black or bronze-colored in human form, which floated about the conflagration, burned by the flames that issued from them but not consumed. They floated, without equilibrium, and shrieked with sorrow and despair.

But despite this horror, still the woman proceeded, still she seemed not to care, still there was that blank look on her face. *"Stop!"* Dolores heard herself yell, *"Or you'll go to Hell!"*

The woman, who had seemed vaguely familiar to her but whose identity somehow had been concealed, turned to stare at the person calling. In some unexplainable way, *now the woman on the steps at the edge of Hell was Dolores herself--and the woman watching, who had called to her to stop, was...Cristina Montalvo.*

(2)

Dolores Montalvo was only one of the billions of people who saw themselves in the Warning as God sees them.

No one was exempt from the Vision. The huge golden ball of light absorbed every person in the world. Each was alone. Each saw only the state of his or her own soul. Their reactions ranged across the spectrum of human response to any serious bad news that is caused by one's own conduct. But in this case the revelation was infinitely greater; for there was nowhere to hide, no shading, no pretense, no excuse--and the subject was not something of high or low price in this world, like a death in the family or financial loss, something enormously important at the time but not essential to the person's eternal destiny. Rather, the subject *was* that destiny. And each human being realized, within that blazing light, that *he or she was fully responsible for every iota of evil he or she had ever voluntarily committed.*

Each realized that to continue on the good or evil path would bring him or her to Heaven--or to Hell.

Each realized that he or she had to repent of all the evil and recommit to and intensify the good.

Each realized, most for the first time, that Christianity is true: that Jesus Christ did die a horrible death on the cross, for each man and woman who ever lived.

Millions of demons exited Hell and rushed into the world to find victims to confound. They whispered a dozen excuses, tailored to the temperaments and belief-systems of their targets, to convince them that the Warning did not happen or, if it did, that it did not matter. The level of spiritual maturity of most people was infantile; they tended to accept the demons' bogus explanations, except in those cases where a Christian friend or relative intervened by personal explanation or private prayer.

With few exceptions, the liars, the murderers, the adulterers, the pornographers, the abortionists, the corrupt politicians, the blasphemers, the voluntary addicts, the prostitutes and pimps, the child abusers--indeed, a majority of all the people who had nurtured a *habit* of self-indulgent sinfulness--these resisted their Warning.

Some scoffed and laughed it off as a trick.

Some told themselves it was a bad dream.

Some said to themselves, "So what? I'll take my chances!"

Some chose to reject the mercy in the Warning, the chance to erase all the evil they had done by genuine contrition; they told themselves in self-chosen despair that they were going to Hell anyway, so they might as well enjoy the time they had left.

Some even recognized the Warning was from God but their hatred of Him was so great that they screamed at Him, aloud or in their minds, "I hate You. I don't care what You want to tell me. I would rather rule in Hell than serve in Heaven!"

The time to repent was immediate. The longer the habitual sinners temporized, the lower the chances that the Vision, which was gradually fading from their minds, would move them to change their lives' direction.

Except for a few small stations, the powers of the world control the television media. Thus they sought to dispel fear, dilute the message, deny its Source. Talking heads on the Sunday discussion shows vied with each other to invent "explanations" which fit their naturalistic assumptions.

"Mass hallucination," some said. "Atavistic throw-back to pre-cognitive times when humankind was shackled by superstitious fears of divine retribution for failing to placate imaginary gods with appropriate sacrifice," social anthropologists from politically correct universities opined. "Electronically induced disorientation from solar eruptions bombarding the earth with negative-charge electrons," astrophysicists counseled. An attorney from a local "civil liberties" chapter hinted that Pat Robertson's TV satellite had broadcast subliminal images to all the television sets in the world.

By Monday afternoon, however, the masters of electronic and print media decided that any further publicity of the Warning, whether discussion of its origin or photo stories of long lines leading to confessionals in Catholic churches, would only serve to convince fence-straddlers that the experience had actually happened and did require a decision. Better to black it out. So they turned their cameras and commentators to other political and economic distractions concocted by the would-be masters of the world. So for many the Warning became a non-event.

A small percentage found the Warning so horrific, the ugliness of their souls so wretched, like modern replicas of *Dorian Gray*, that the emotional shock was too much: the sheer terror from seeing their visible descent to the door of Hell itself was so crushing that heart attacks and strokes killed them at once. But it was their own moral turpitude, not God, that directly caused these deaths.

As God had foreseen, in a world populated with six billion people, hundreds of millions did wake up. Many agnostics, like Theodore Patrick Greene, who harbored a secret kernel of faith, rushed to priest or minister and sought Baptism or, in Pat's case, absolution. Many backslidden Protestants pleaded with God for forgiveness. Many fallen-away Catholics who had convinced themselves they were living good lives, called the parish rectory and asked, even demanded, that priests hear confessions, *now, not tomorrow, not Saturday afternoon--now!* And most priests obliged.

The Warning shook priests the most. Generally, there are three groups of priests in the Church in America, with their counterparts in other countries: the Angry, the Confused, and the Faithful.

Priests saw the state of their own souls; all were troubled, shocked, or even terrified. Except for a few who were only mildly shaken--some old monks, some African bishops, and a rare ascetic, the Warning shocked all of them, because every man makes excuses for himself and seeks to minimize his own faults.

But with priests, the shock was qualitatively different from what lay people felt: priests make a formal commitment to God, a covenant to be *alter Christus*, a promise to pursue souls, to preach and teach the Gospel "in season and out of season."

The medical profession heals, but some doctors kill through abortion; the legal profession seeks justice, but some lawyers counsel perjury and obfuscate the truth; politicians promote the Common Good, but some use their office to enrich their private selves. So it is with priests: their profession is to save souls, but some lead souls astray. These suffered the greatest pains from the Warning. Hypocrisy is a greater sin when one's formal profession itself is a pretense.

The Angry priests realized they had given their heart to the whore of new age Modernism. They saw their lukewarm Masses. They felt the pain they inflicted on Jesus in the Eucharist for hiding Him in little boxes on plain walls in tiny rooms instead of enthroning Him in a golden tabernacle where the people would be motivated to pray to Him. They felt the anger and frustration of faithful lay people, who had sat through so many droning social gospel sermons, politically correct excuses for tinkering with the Bible's language, and concocted liturgies designed to entertain but not to uplift. They were shown many souls falling into Hell, a Hell they never had preached on, a Hell many taught the laity to understand could not exist because God--"*She*"--is too merciful.

The Confused priests suffered less than the Angry ones. Still, their lukewarm Masses, lukewarmness to the Eucharist, tolerance for perversion of language and liturgy in Bible and worship--God's view of these forms of quiet sacrilege and His disgust with it they felt as did their brethren who, in their anger, had aggressively sought to change the Church.

And, Angry or Confused, those priests who practiced virtue in public but practiced vice in secret saw they were rushing toward Hell at breakneck speed. Those who made a mockery of the vows of poverty, or chastity, or obedience came to understand, in that blinding light, that sacrilege angers God and that a priest who deliberately and habitually breaks his vows is a living sacrilege.

The Faithful priests saw their flaws and their failings but were emboldened to work harder at sanctity by seeing the fruits of their fidelity: that God was pleased with their efforts, since He looks more at intentions than at results; and that their prayer, to which they had been faithful, pleased Him greatly.

One would think that such a searing experience would convert every priest who endured it. There were indeed many conversions among the Angry and the Confused. But a very large number of them had invested too much psychic energy in heresy, had enjoyed too many accolades from the secular world for their "independence of thought," had resisted too many earlier and less dramatic promptings of grace, had resented John Paul II's traditional teachings for too many years.

So the majority of the Angry priests rejected the Warning and chose to cast their lot with the "reforms" of Eugenio Cassendi, the new Pope Julian.

(3)

Saddam Hussein's bold finesse--not shooting back at the attacking American planes--and his eloquent television complaint about the unjustified military aggression by the Great Satan, America, had their desired effect. In the streets of Iran, Iraq, Syria and other Middle East nations huge mobs rioted, shouting, "Death to the Great Satan America! *Jihad, Jihad!!*" This was the moment the bloodthirsty leaders of these countries had waited for, the chance to destroy American military might, to put its President in his place, and to seize the opportunity to achieve the Final Solution to the Problem of Israel.

Because its President had departed from America's historic policy of fighting only *defensive wars against unjust aggression,* the country would suffer unimaginable devastation.

The Muslim counterattack took two immediate routes. Within days of the U.S. strikes on Saddam's palaces, the air forces of all Muslim nations united in a combined retaliatory attack on the American Sixth Fleet in the Persian Gulf. The American carrier pilots and battleships put up fierce resistance to the powerful assault against their vulnerable ships and managed to hold their own, with minimal damage.

But they could not entirely neutralize a second strike by land-based medium-range ballistic missiles from Iraq, Iran, and Syria, using guidance systems purchased from the Chinese Communists, which launched half a dozen tactical nuclear weapons at the American fleet. Defensive countermeasures destroyed four of them before they reached their targets. But two of them got through. The result was disaster.

When strong winds blew aside the mushroom clouds, *there was no trace left of an aircraft carrier, three destroyers, and two escorts. They had been sunk or vaporized.* Many carrier-launched fighters already in the air did find ground bases for landing, but in some cases their new hosts were hostile. On the sea, in one battle, the Americans lost half as many men as were killed in the entire Vietnam War!

Part of the battle group positioned on the outskirts of the flotilla, and two submerged nuclear submarines, did survive largely unscathed. But their commanders put them into a full speed withdrawal, not out of cowardice but out of simple calculus of probabilities: without the carrier they could fight only a defensive engagement and the captains of the submarines wanted to be in deeper water if the President ordered them to fire nuclear missiles of their own.

(4)

The Chairman watched the TV news reports of the military debacle with euphoria. Saddam had done just what his second phone call, a few days earlier, had urged. *The chess game proceeds toward checkmate!* he mused, with overweening self-satisfaction.

He turned to the computer station in his office. A few clicks of the modem and he had sent an E-mail directive to what he called the "T-Team" in the United States. It had four sections, one each in Los Angeles, Chicago, Atlanta, and New York.

Within a week, he told himself, *the United States would be under Martial Law.*

(5)

Tank Majoreski pulled his pickup truck onto a dirt road running parallel with a railroad spur track. He moved cautiously at five miles an hour looking carefully toward the roadbed of the tracks on his right. He was fully aware that he might run into men who did not want him to see what they were doing.

After about two miles, he saw a cluster of trees in the distance and a large van parked just off the road near the tracks. There were two men standing on the tracks. One held some sort of tool that looked like a shovel.

A man in the van opened the door, climbed down, and started walking toward Tank's pickup, which was now creeping forward. This man, like the two on the tracks, was dressed in a dark brown military-style uniform. All of them had pistols at their hips. Tank did not recognize which branch of service the uniforms represented.

"Whatcha looking for, Mister?" asked the man approaching. *That's a question I should ask you,* thought Tank. But he decided to be conciliatory. He stopped the truck and leaned out the window.

"Nothin' special. I live in this area. Just driving by. Don't usually see soldiers around here. Can I help you guys with something?"

"No need," said the other. His unsmiling face suggested irritation that someone had discovered him and his men. "We're doing fine on our own."

"What *are* you doing?" asked Tank.

"Mister, it's none of your damn business," he said with a frown. "And I think you should just keep on going before you get in trouble." He put his hand on his gun.

Controlling his football instincts, Tank glanced again at the two men on the track and his adversary standing in the road. He again noted they all were armed. He decided discretion is better than valor. He also saw that none of them had any stripes or shoulder patch to indicate rank. Their van was entirely unmarked.

"Sure, sure," he shrugged, "No problem. Like I said, I was just moseying by." He put the truck in gear and slowly started around the man standing in the road, who chose not to back off to permit him easy passage. The man glared at him.

As Tank passed, he glanced at the place where the two stood on the tracks. There was a blackened patch, as if something had recently burned and the weeds and tall grass were trampled down between the black patch and the van.

CHAPTER XVII

(1)

Three days after the Chairman had sent a command to the "T-Team," explosions in four cities shattered the early evening calm. Each blast occurred in the post-dinner evening hours, one in New York on Monday, a day later in Atlanta, then in Chicago, and finally in Los Angeles--all timed to dominate the television news later that night. In each case the explosion, which people first thought was a small nuclear device but turned out to be an enormous amount of dynamite, destroyed everything within a city block and rained debris a half mile out in all directions.

In New York the bomb obliterated office buildings a few blocks from Wall Street, in Chicago the railroad yards, in Atlanta the city's major water works and reservoir, and in Los Angeles the primary expressway interchange near the downtown area.

At 10:00 p.m. on Friday, the President appeared on national television. He looked grave.

> "My fellow Americans, the events earlier this week are great tragedies in our history, ranking, I am saddened to say, with the attack on the *Lusitania*, before World War I; and Pearl Harbor, which began World War II. But in each of those regrettable events, the indomitable American spirit, coupled with superlative political leadership, eventually triumphed over the forces of evil--and so shall it be in our own day. But we should not delude ourselves that the task will be easy or the foe is irresolute. Just a few days ago, Saddam Hussein and his allies used nuclear weapons, violating all rules of international law and common sense, to destroy part of our fleet in the Persian Gulf. Here at home, as the news reporters have told you, in four major American cities, terrorists have detonated large bombs, or clusters of bombs, and caused death to hundreds of innocent citizens, the destruction of hundreds of millions of dollars of property, and the disruption of necessary services, such as water supply and electricity for upwards of a million people. Thousands of innocent Americans have been injured, and I must assure you, that I share the grief of those who have lost loved ones,

your distress at our national loss, and your desire to bring the perpetrators to justice.

"Though no group has yet claimed responsibility for these terrorist bombings, the FBI and other law enforcement agencies inform me that, in their judgment, it was religious fanatics, either sympathizers with Saddam Hussein or radical anti-abortion extremists seeking to cause disruption of abortion services but cloak their illegal actions under public concern over the military situation in the Middle East. But I want to assure you, my fellow citizens, that this Administration will not sit idly by and let such terrorists cause death, destruction, and disruption with impunity. Rather, we will act vigorously to pursue the perpetrators and to establish a system of security for our citizens that precludes anyone's imitating terrorists in the future. Consequently, to deal with the obvious terrorist threats we now face, by Executive Order I am declaring a State of National Emergency and instituting Martial Law. For those of you who are law abiding--and this is the overwhelming majority of Americans--your lives will not change significantly, except for minor inconveniences, such as security check points on the highway, where your identification will be required. For the few of you who deem yourselves outside the law, your lives will be severely restricted, because law enforcement will have the tools to identify, pursue, locate, and apprehend you before you do any more harm to innocent adults and children.

"Because many of our military are in the Middle East, Yugoslavia, the Pacific, and other parts of the world, I have determined that we do not have, from our own armed forces, sufficient trained troops to implement Martial Law without being supplemented by others. Consequently, by agreement with the leaders of Germany, Russia, and other countries, I have arranged that contingents of their armed forces be located within our borders to assist with law enforcement tasks as needed. I am confident that you will cooperate fully with them so that their and your own safety and security are heightened during these difficult times."

The President concluded with some platitudes about national unity and redundant assurances that he would do everything in his power to avenge the victims and protect the country against future attacks of this type. Riveted by his words and preoccupied by the events that necessitated his speech, most Americans failed to notice, amid the welter of television images of Presidential speechifying and bomb-blasted cities, that he studiously kept his right hand out of camera range.

(2)

The Honest Debate Society convened once again at Pat Greene's Prospect House apartment. As usual, out the east window from the tenth floor they could see jets coming down diagonally every two minutes, left to right over the Potomac River, to eventual landing at Reagan National Airport. Life seemed the same as usual; but they knew it wasn't.

"The topic tonight, Vanni and gentlemen," intoned Pat, his wonted light humor absent from his voice, "is the death of the Pope, the events in the Middle East,"--a euphemism for the most horrible American defeat in their lifetimes--"and the President's decree of Martial Law."

On first glance it seemed their lives were the same. Father Mike, in his standard black clerics, maintained his usual calm. Pat had his bottle of *Pete's Wicked Ale* and on the desk in the corner lay an envelope with a hefty check from a publisher. Jerry Kanek still looked like a lawyer, though without a vest; so far his job had not been changed. Vanni, whose regular employment also had not changed, tonight dressed in slacks and the usual grey sweatshirt, was curled up in an easy chair; on this occasion the dark blue logo across her shirt said, *When All Else Fails, Read the Directions--the Bible.* John DeSanto was back in Illinois.

"I'd like to open the discussion," offered Pat, "with the observation that, in my opinion, something fishy's going on, not only in the U.S., but also in Rome. Look--"

He pressed buttons on the TV remote and the VCR under it began to play a video tape of It was a series of excerpts from recent television news broadcasts.

"Look closely at the Pope. Watch especially when they zoom in and you can see him close up." They all stared at the screen.

"I taped most of the news reports. Then I had a guy who videos weddings do a little editing, so you won't have to listen to the talking heads tell you 'what it all means.'" He kept the television voice low and continued, "It might take three or four minutes, and I'm not going to tell you what to look for..." He turned up the commentators' voice.

They watched for a few minutes. Finally Jerry Kanek, whose mind was more attuned to the surreptitious, said, "Pat, pause it, would you?" Pat complied. "Run it back a few seconds--to where they show the Pope lying there." Pat did so. "I don't know if you saw what I saw, but--well, the anchormen keep saying they found him in his bed and that *this*--what we see--is exactly the way he was when they found him." "Right, that's what I noticed," said Pat.

"Then there is something strange. Let me ask my esteemed brother a question: Mike, is it normal for priests to sleep *in their daytime clothes?*" The others chuckled.

"Hardly. We're like anybody else. We priests own pajamas and I for one use them. Besides, a priest's business suit, like a pilot's or an attorney's, is too formal and uncomfortable to sleep in, unless you're in an airport at midnight."

"Well, I guess it was a stupid question, but it had a point--because the talking heads keep saying the Pope died in his sleep, *but they show him dressed in his usual daytime robes.*"

"So you think someone put those robes on him *after* he died?" asked Father Kanek.

"Yes, I do," said Jerry. "And I do too," said Pat. "And I don't know what to make of it."

"To add to your suspicions," said Father Mike, "I've been blessed with what people call a photographic memory, and I had the honor of meeting personally with the Pope not too long ago. I've got to tell you--now that we all scrutinized this video--that *I don't think this man's face is the face of the Pope I remember!*"

"Wow!" exclaimed Vanni, popping a piece of chocolate into her mouth. "You guys are way ahead of me! Are you saying the dead man is *somebody else!!??*"

(3)

Jerry Kanek logged onto CompuServe and looked at his e-mail. He had an encrypted letter from the Director of the FBI. He decoded it and read: "Dear Agent Kanek: Because of recent events, I am reassigning you immediately to our Anti-Terrorism Task Force. Please report to our Washington, D.C. headquarters, Room 4-10A, at 10:00 a.m., Thursday of this week."

(4)

A week had passed. *The Woman peered into the golden globe. She saw a huge rocket lift off from southern Florida. "Michael!" she said. Immediately the Archangel stood at her right hand. She pointed to the rocket and gave him a command.*

A second later the Archangel, as tall as the rocket itself, approached as it thundered up and out over the Atlantic. He lifted his immense sword but paused for a moment. In an instant, he estimated the speed of the rocket, its distance from populated areas, the strength and direction of the winds, and the location of some small fishing and pleasure boats off the Florida shore.

Forty-two seconds after lift-off, Michael struck the rocket once and it immediately heeled over. Two seconds later he struck it again. It blew up in a spectacular explosion visible for dozens of miles in Florida. Brightly burning bits of solid rocket propellant and other debris rained down in sweeping arcs into the ocean, and the rolling booms from the blast set off car and house alarms as far south as Cocoa Beach. As he had calculated, no one was injured.

The Archangel returned to Heaven. Ever humble, the Woman thanked him for his help. In return, he bowed and thanked her for the assignment. He had enjoyed it.

(5)

Windsor, New York, is a small central New York town a few miles north of the Pennsylvania border and west of the point where the Delaware River forms the northeast border of that state. The town's older section predates the Civil War and contains neat bungalow houses row by row close together on tree-laden narrow streets. One of those houses is the family residence of an outspoken anti-abortion activist, Rendoll Berry.

Berry had concluded years ago that abortion is murder, for the scientific evidence is incontrovertible that the fetus is a human being, which within only a few weeks of conception has a tiny beating heart, measurable brain waves, visible fingers and toes, and all the other physical elements that humans, however small, display. Unlike the overwhelming majority of Americans who do not follow Judeo-Christian morality, and unlike most apathetic Christians, Rendoll Berry realized that the systematic extermination of helpless innocent human beings is a national crime descending to the level of the Holocaust. He decided long ago that he had to do what he could to stop the murders.

So he picketed abortion clinics, distributed leaflets showing pictures of unborn babies, set up sidewalk counseling groups, addressed those church and civic organizations willing at least to listen, wrote dozens of articles, and when the opportunity arose debated on radio and television. He tried to stay scrupulously within the law and cautioned his followers against any kind of violence.

But pro-abortion activists worked with sympathetic lawmakers in many states and in Congress to draft dragnet-type wide-reaching laws which defined, in many cases, what they were doing as illegal. These laws and their continuing activism spawned numerous civil and criminal legal actions against them, many of which were motivated solely by desire to "bleed" them financially with lawyers' fees. Still, the pro-life activists remained a thorn in the abortionists' side. All that was about to change, as the government took a different tack in its fight against them.

Around two a.m. a medium-sized grey van that looked like it belonged to the telephone company rolled into this neighborhood and parked across the street from Rendoll Berry's home. The van was loaded with complex electronic equipment, much of it not available to the general public. A small panel behind the driver's side window slid open and a telescope-like instrument protruded a few inches and took aim at the point where the telephone line entered the house. Besides the driver, the vehicle concealed a computer expert, who sat before a console complete with monitor and keyboard. As soon as the van had parked and the little telescope was extended and pointed at the home, the expert booted it to operational mode and inserted a disc into the "A" drive.

The disc was titled "Rendoll Berry--Illegal Activities."

(6)

His motorcycle beside him, a burly police officer stood on the shoulder of the ramp fifty yards short of the stop sign at the top of the hill. As cars rolled by, now and then he stepped to the edge of the shoulder and raised his hand in a *Stop* gesture, and as the surprised motorist started to brake, the officer waved him or her onto the shoulder. Then he walked up and asked for the person's "papers." He was about to run this drill with an attractive young blonde as target.

The cop was firm but polite. But his message scared her.

"I'm sorry, Ma'am, but your papers are not in order." He stood by the side of her car. In his hand was her Driver's License and Vehicle Registration form. Normally these were all a police officer would ask for.

"What do you mean? They're current," Vanni answered.

"I know--but they're not complete. You need the SmartCard as well. Do you have it?"

She started to rummage in her purse, knowing full well the Card was not there, but trying to think of something to say. Finally she asked, "How come this is necessary? And how come you stopped me? I was well within the speed limit."

"It's a new rule the State DMV has put in," he answered. "The stop is part of random security checking," he added. "You're right, you weren't speeding. But with this new rule, it's an infraction if you can't produce your SmartCard when an officer requests it."

"I never heard of that rule," she said, trying to contain her irritation. "When was it passed?" She kept rummaging, pulling from the purse lipstick...notepad...pencil...second set of keys...tiny box of tissue...and laying them one at a time on the passenger seat next to her wallet. She wondered if playing the Dumb Blonde role would work.

"Last week," he said. He saw she was getting flustered and enjoyed her momentary discomfort. He thought she was quite cute. But he was just doing his job and did not really like the rule either. "Actually, the President imposed it by Executive Order and the DMV simply issued guidelines on enforcement."

"Well," she said, turning the purse upside down and shaking it, an action which produced only two sticks of gum, a small coin purse, a mirror, a few credit card receipts, and her company ID card, "it looks like I don't have it. Maybe it's at home. Guess you'll have to jail me for an 'infraction,'--unless you'll let a poor little ol' dumb blonde off for good behavior." She batted her eyelashes at him pretending to flirt, knowing he would see through the pretense.

"Miss Van Niesen," he said with a smile, handing the license and registration back to her, "I'm permitted to use discretion. You get a pass this time. But, I've got to tell you, the rule is that I have to enter this 'Warning-of-Infraction' into the computer. The next time an officer stops you, you better have the SmartCard with you."

"What if I can't find it?"

"Maybe the bank will issue a new one. The President has decreed that anyone who doesn't have the SmartCard after the first warning will lose his--or her--driver's license."

(7)

The President's declaration of Martial Law did not sit well with a vocal minority of citizens. The Cardinal of New York, who rarely spoke out on political matters, went on the radio to point out that the Church condemns violence against innocent persons and that the President' tarring the anti-abortion cause with the same rhetorical brush as he condemned supposed Iraqi terrorists was a gratuitous slur on good citizens, unsupported by any evidence, and merely pretext to provide other Americans with a target for revenge, since the Iraqis, if they were involved, were out of reach. He demanded that the President withdraw the Order creating Martial Law.

In the Congress, the Chairman of the House Judiciary Committee spoke out in the same vein in a nationwide television interview. He pointed out that in the twentieth century, those who imposed Martial Law rarely gave it up, that four explosions in four cities--the evil work of probably no more than a few dozen people, if that many--was not grounds to rip away the constitutional rights of two hundred fifty million Americans. He noted that foreign troops from such countries as Germany and Russia were the *last* people to endow with police powers over ordinary Americans: the militaristic cultures they grew up in did not promote the same sense of Due Process of Law and respect for citizens' rights that Americans had a right to. He too demanded that the President withdraw the Martial Law Order.

Some television commentators, a few Senators from western states like Utah and Montana, numerous "libertarians" on both the Left and the Right, many small businessmen, many small newspapers, and quite a few Evangelical leaders spoke out, in different forums, to the same effect.

A few days later, the intimidation, harassment, and arrests began. By and large, they were done very quietly, so as not to cause public outcry or generate third party resistance.

The Congressman received a late-night knock on the door. When it was opened, three burly men in dark suits, displaying what purported to be law enforcement identification cards, informed him that there had been terrorist threats on his life and, in the interest of his personal safety, he should come with them to a "safe house." Though suspicious, he felt there was no other option, for the men were insistent. He disappeared into a waiting Cadillac sedan.

Other supposed plain clothes police came to the Cardinal's office late in the afternoon, produced the same kind of identification, and offered the same rationale for His Eminence to depart with them. The Cardinal remonstrated that he preferred to leave his safety in the hands of God, but the visitors insisted and almost dragged the protesting churchman outside, down the stairs, and into a waiting limousine.

The Government dealt with the television commentators in ways more subtle: the Chairman of the FCC, acting on the orders of the President, called the CEOs of each network employing a recalcitrant anchorman and made it clear, in no uncertain terms, that he should shut up or the network would be in deep trouble with the Government. The supine CEOs dressed down the anchormen for their temerity in attacking the President in this time of national crisis and insisted on support for the Martial Law decree. All but two caved in. Those two were summarily fired.

The critical Senators received threats on the lives of their wives, children, or grandchildren. As with the Congressman and the Cardinal, law enforcement personnel delivered the threats, in the guise of information about likely kidnapping attempts and none-too-subtle warnings that they "could not be responsible" for what might happen if these lawmakers kept speaking out. All the Senators got the message and chose silence except two: one had an "unfortunate accident" driving home a few nights later and was found, dead, in the twisted rubble of his car. The last one committed suicide, it was determined later by the Park Police who found him in underbrush near the George Washington Parkway, by shooting himself in the head three times.

The other public critics of the President's move lacked any national forum. Though their protests kept the flame of freedom psychologically alive in the hearts of some, they had no practical way to organize effective resistance. Thus their outcry only served to identify them to the President's list-keepers, who planned to give them priority treatment when it came time to implement Executive Orders #11000 and 11004.

Normally these events would be headline news, but the press was itself intimidated by what it saw happening to such prominent persons. And there was plenty of other news, most of it bad, for the papers to splash across their front pages. The loss of half of the Sixth Fleet, the four bombings, and the instant crash of the Stock Market, which had followed these events, preoccupied the press completely.

The Market had dropped like a skyscraper elevator broken loose from its moorings. In four trading days, the Market lost over 2,600 points; it seemed nobody wanted to buy and everyone wanted to sell--those who got through the busy signals by punching redial constantly.

(8)

Soon after his first talk with Father Kanek, John DeSanto began making a Holy Hour every day. Because the pastor of his parish church did not want to leave it unlocked after sundown, John looked for other quiet places. Sometimes he walked near his home; often he merely retired to his room. When the church was open during the day and he was in town, he would go there.

During a recent visit, a strange thing happened. His surroundings seemed to fade out. He no longer saw the pews before him, the statues on the far sides of the altar, the altar itself, or even the gold tabernacle in the center of the sanctuary area. In their place he saw a vision of a huge rocket standing on its launch pad at Cape Canaveral, then rise up into the air, reach a point a few thousand feet above the shore, roll over and then--explode in a ball of red flame. Then he heard a Voice say:

> *This launch would have put into orbit a satellite designed to track and control innocent people and to serve the purposes of evil men. It was destroyed by the power of prayer. Do you realize that you can change the WORLD by never leaving your homes or your churches or your convents or your parishes? You can pray down the evil leaders, those who are bent on destruction. You can even pray down the length of time the Anti-Christ will be in existence. But pray, you MUST pray, and NOW!! This should be your commitment and priority. It is your responsibility. The WORLD is your responsibility. Are you ready to help Us save it through your prayers? When you see harm being done, a wrong being created, atrocities committed, pray IMMEDIATELY in unison with Us for that person or persons and then SEE how changes will occur. Yes, even your bad laws can be changed in this manner. It costs you nothing except your commitment to PRAY. And the cost is a commitment of time. Who has given you this time?*

The vision faded. The church surroundings returned. John knew he had heard the Voice of Jesus. And that the message was not just for him alone, but for all Catholics who would listen.

You can pray down the evil leaders...You can even pray down the length of time the Antichrist will be in existence.

CHAPTER XVIII

(1)

The Woman peered into the Golden Globe. It now was a kaleidoscope, showing every single person in the world, including their spiritual condition. Those who were faithful to Jesus were golden white; the most holy among them had an aura of bright gold encircling their heads. Those who were unfaithful and had rejected the Warning were reddish black and had flames around them. Arrayed before the Woman, and not visible in the Golden Globe, were ranks of tens of millions of angels, a segment of the Heavenly Host. From above and behind her, the Voice of a Man spoke to the Woman. It was full of power and authority. "It is time to send them," said the Voice.

The Woman was pleased to hear the command and hastened to carry it out. For many years she had prayed earnestly for this moment. She stepped forward and looked out over the ranks of angels. "Go!" she said, "and mark the foreheads of all you meet who are worthy of the Lamb!"

(2)

The Chairman reacted to the Warning with characteristic arrogance. He too had received a vision of all his sins, and a special insight into the overweening pride that underlay them. But he quickly dismissed the entire experience and the certainty of Hell unless he repented, as the last-ditch effort of a weakening God to trick him into giving homage. He told himself there wasn't any Hell or that if there were, *he* would not go there. He told himself that *he* would conquer earth and then rise to Heaven, and if God were there, *he* would hurl that God down into Hell and take God's place. If denial of reality is the primary mark of people who are mad, the Chairman was the most insane man in all the world. But even madmen can rationally pursue their tactical goals.

For the Chairman, the Warning sounded an alarm: it meant God would put into high gear His last-ditch campaign to win as many souls as possible to allegiance to Him; so he, the Chairman, would accelerate his program as well. We will see who conquers more souls!

So, with America under martial law...the financial markets of the world plummeting as the Middle East conflict simmered...the banks in the United States, Europe, and Japan suffering "runs" by thousands of citizens who wanted--but could not get--their cash, and the "Millennium Bug" computer crash looming on the horizon, the Chairman decided it was The Moment for his "First Announcement."

From his office atop a major bank building in Brussels, the Chairman went on world television. With the cooperation of the networks, he preempted a prime time slot. He also considered but rejected for the while, the idea of using his supercomputer to flash his face and his speech onto all the computer screens of the world, through the Internet. He could do that the next time, after the fools were conditioned to accept him.

"Citizens of the World!" he intoned majestically. "It is I, the Chairman of the Council of Europe...I am here to help you solve a serious group of problems.

"As you are painfully aware, there has been a tragic downturn in the fortunes of the peoples of the world. The system of nation-states, which served humanity well for the last two centuries, has finally run its course.

"Its collapse is all around us. Some nations are fighting each other, as the Middle East countries and the United States. Some nations are near economic collapse, as their banking systems feel inordinate strains, partly caused by other nations. The nations of the world will not be able, individually and often locked in internecine feuds, to address the looming 'Millennium Bug' problem, that many computers will malfunction at the end of the year 1999.

"All of these doleful events, and others I could mention, threaten your peace and prosperity. All of these events require concerted activity by a World Authority that can take into account the interests and needs of all of us, the need for jobs, the need for food, the need for a stable business system, the need for military security against the prospect of war, the need for lasting peace.

"The time is ripe, indeed the moment is urgent, that we, the people of the world, take control of our destiny...that we create a common political and economic structure that is capable of addressing these many problems, and will put us once more on our common path toward lasting peace and universal prosperity.

"This is a concept that thoughtful people have been urging for much of this century. Indeed, some of the most far-sighted thinkers in the world have even addressed this matter in writing, through such documents as *A New Constitution for the World*. But the time has now arrived to move from thoughtful discussion to effective action. So, in cooperation with my friend, the President of the United States, and with the other leaders of the G-7 and other United Nations members, we have agreed to establish an Acting Directorate, to coordinate our nations' efforts to deal with the threats to peace and prosperity.

"While our various diplomatic representatives iron out the details of modifying outmoded notions of sovereignty and streamlining appropriate flow of tax revenues to the Directorate, I will take all suitable steps to prevent further decline of the equity markets, the banking system, and the military security posture of each country. The central committee is drawing up a detailed program, which I will announce to you shortly.

"My friends and fellow citizens of the world, we stand on the threshold of a new era. Our collective response to the challenges will succeed. We will usher in a new age of such peaceful prosperity that those few reactionaries who might oppose these developments will wonder why they ever doubted.

"Indeed, our economic cooperation will enhance our political unity; our political oneness will set the stage for a fellowship of all peoples united in a New Humankind, casting off the superstitions of the past, and marching forwarded together, united in a common faith in Humankind. Working together we will demonstrate our ability to create our own destiny through concerted, unified action under a single leadership undivided by petty individualism, outworn nationalisms, and divisive creeds."

He smiled broadly. His dark eyes flashed compellingly, almost hypnotically. A tape played synthetic audience applause. Subliminal messages, broadcast at a speed too fast to be noted by the conscious mind, appeared on the screen saying, *Give all power to the Chairman. The Chairman is God.* A billion demons burst out of six secret entrance holes to Hell, one on each continent except Antarctica, to roam the earth, repeating the subliminal message again and again to anyone who did not deliberately drive them away with prayer, holy water, Scripture verses, appeal to Michael and his angels, and the Name of Jesus.

The picture of the smiling Chairman remained on the screen, the subliminals continuing, for twenty seconds. Then the networks swung to their national stations, where secularized pundits were ready with a documentary on the Chairman punctuated with fawning adulation at his brilliance and uncritical assertions that Mankind--"Humankind"--would be safe under his leadership.

(3)

The parade began innocuously enough. Eugenio Cassendi, now Pope Julian, rode easily in the open limousine through the streets of Rome. Though he felt the repetitive gesture of blessing the cheering faces along the parade route was so much wasted time, he enjoyed the pomp and applause. He believed that superior human beings such as himself should be honored by lesser human beings, such as, in his opinion, virtually everyone else in Rome. Thus he had approved an elaborate winding parade route ending, at last, in St. Peter's, where he planned to read a directive to the whole Church loosening its rules on sexual morality and repealing the strictures on women priests. As a matter of fact, he even had the parade route published in the local papers so as to ensure a larger crowd.

His plans would have worked well, except for a lone gunman who had secreted himself in an empty hotel room overlooking one of those many traffic circles in Rome where everyone must wind three-fourths around 360 degrees in order to continue on his original boulevard.

The window of the room provided an unobstructed view of the approaching line of cars as they slowed to enter the circle.

The gunman stood by the window and waited patiently. A tiny portable radio, volume turned very low, broadcast news of the coming parade and its eminent passenger. The gunman carefully pulled from his suitcase a rifle stock, barrel and trigger mechanism, laser scope, and silencer. He assembled them quickly and jammed a seventeen-bullet clip into the stock.

Malin was an expert marksman.

(4)

Father Michael Kanek wondered about the TV set in the corner of the recreation room at the Jesuit residence. He felt like unplugging it or facing it to the wall. But he did not have the authority to do so and he knew that if anyone with the power did this, some of the community would complain. As he pondered how to be rid of this electronic Trojan Horse, his portable cell phone rang.

"Father Mike? This is Pat. Did you see the Chairman's presentation a few minutes ago?"

"Sure did, but I'd rather not talk about it right now." The priest had concluded that *everyone's phone is monitored* and that the Chairman's supporters would use voice-recognition technology to analyze all conversations that occurred shortly after his talk, and then target anyone who was suspicious or critical.

"Let's find our friends and meet ASAP," he added.

Pat, ever talkative, wanted to analyze the Chairman's remarks right then, but the firmness of the priest's response made him hesitate.

"I'll pick up the blonde bombshell and see you at my place," he said.

"And I'll try to reach the others," said the priest. Actually, it was only his brother. He found himself trying to mislead anyone who might be listening.

(5)

The Chairman called on the secure line to the President. "Tell your people at HAARP to send up the most powerful beam their equipment can transmit. Have them repeat it again and again, twice a day, for a week!"

"You know that's sure to disrupt the weather, maybe over the whole world," responded the President.

"Of course I do, you fool!" snarled the Chairman. "The more disruption the better. Let them panic at the blizzards, the tornadoes, the heat waves! When I come, I will calm all these storms. By then, they'll be even more susceptible."

"All right, I'll do it. But I want something in return."

"What!? You would bargain with *me*...!?"

"Mr. Chairman, please be calm," responded the President, trying to use his most charming tone. "Compared to what you are asking of me, it is nothing..." The Chairman was silent. "I have finally recalled what happened the night you sent me that woman, Dolores Montalvo, and I had a stroke..."

"Why, Mr. President," the Chairman said with a touch of sarcasm, "Ms. Montalvo is indeed beautiful, but I did not think her charms are so great that a man of your...ah, skill with women...would grow faint in her presence."

"She had some sort of weapon. If it didn't sound like science fiction, I would say it was a ray gun. She tried to kill me with it, but--" he strengthened his tone to sound macho--"all it could do was put me to sleep for a few hours."

"And how do you know her intent was not simply to put you to sleep for just a few minutes?" rejoined the Chairman, implicitly contradicting the President's assertion of strength.

The President did not detect the Chairman's second foray into sarcasm, and continued: "I want you to send her to me, but without her weapon, of course. I want to deal with her myself. Privately."

"Of course, Mr. President. Revenge is a worthy purpose in a man of your prominence. I will see what I can do. But if she does come, you will have her on my terms, since she works for me."

"And those are?"

"When I command it, she is returned to me--unscathed. Her beauty intrigues me. And she has a certain independent spirit--doubtless you perceived it--that will be a pleasure for me to break."

"All right. It is agreed. Are we finished now?"

"One more thing," answered the Chairman. "Mr. President, have you ever heard of a man named Malin?"

"No."

"He is the best assassin in Europe. He is a former East German commando. In your country, he would have been a Navy Seal. He is a superb marksman. He relishes getting at targets who think themselves well protected. On occasion, I give him an assignment."

"Why do you bring this up?"

"Because I want to help you overcome the temptation to doublecross me. I expect obedience. You *will* comply on HAARP and on returning Ms. Montalvo unscathed. And you must move our Timetable along rapidly. Or Malin may come looking for you."

(6)

W. Carlton Mason III, strode up the long cobblestone walkway that led from the circle in front of the mansion where he had parked his car in the last space available. He did not like being late, but all these damn meetings dealing with the market crash and counter-terrorism surveillance made it impossible for a man to keep any schedule.

He did not know quite what to expect, but the invitation, cryptic and oral, had implied that he was joining some sort of inner circle. With his experience in the banking community and international finance, he had long suspected that there was a group of men and women in Europe and the U.S. who were pulling the strings. He had hoped to work his way into their inner councils, because that was where the power was. But his divorce from Vicki had put his ambitions on hold. Now, however, that the distraction had blown over and he was part of the Washington elite, it seemed time to get back on the fast track to power. So he had welcomed the invitation.

He was met at the door by a powerfully-built man who seemed out of his element dressed, as he was, in a butler's tux and tails. The man produced a list from his pocket, glanced at Mason's driver's license, and beckoned him to enter. Mason assumed the butler doubled as security. But despite his aura of toughness, the man was cordial enough and ushered him down a wide corridor to a large dining room. There a dozen or so well-dressed men and women sat quietly around a large rectangular oaken table. The recessed ceiling lights operated on a dimmer and were turned down to their lowest. The main light in the room came from five red candles, each about six inches high, set in the middle of the table in the form of a pentagram. In front of the candles and at the opposite wall facing the doorway, sat, with her eyes closed, a very attractive brunette in her mid-forties.

Carlton Mason and his companion stood momentarily at the doorway as latter scanned the group looking for an empty chair. "Who is she?" whispered Mason to the man.

"Kimberly Sherref," answered the other in a whisper even lower than Mason's. "She is a psychic. She has a spiritual name when she goes into a trance." Mason looked carefully at the woman, who seemed about to speak, though her eyes were still closed.

"It is the name of her Spirit Guide," added the man, as he gestured to him to take an empty chair at the end of the table and opposite the side where the Sherref woman sat, "Chaka Krishna."

Mason said nothing and sat down. The others scarcely glanced at him, so focussed were they on Kimberly Sherref. He had no faith in spirit guides, because he had no faith in anything he could not see and touch; but the concentration and apparent opulence of the guests impressed him.

Her eyes still closed, the Sherref woman spoke. "Is that you, Chaka Krishna?" she asked in a low husky voice.

"It is I," came the response in a different, masculine voice. "I bring you greetings from the Council of Ascended Masters." Mason was dumbfounded. Unless this woman were a clever ventriloquist who could alter her voice and pretend to be a man, *there were two people in one body!* He had absolutely no idea how such a thing could happen. As his mind groped unsuccessfully for an answer, the masculine voice continued.

"The Ascended Masters have determined that the time has finally come to intervene directly in the affairs of humankind to save you from self-destruction. We have a Plan to bring peace and prosperity to mankind. We will begin to implement it in the near future, through the cooperation of enlightened political leaders including the President and the Chairman of the Council of Europe."

The people in the room--Ph.D.'s, attorneys, bankers, high government officials--nodded approvingly. None of them, usually so astute in professional dealings, wondered *who* the "Ascended Masters" might be...or *whether they might have an ulterior purpose.*

(7)

Over the last two hundred years, the Woman had appeared in hundreds of places around the world: at LaSalette, at Lourdes, at Knock, at Fatima, at Garabandal, at Akita, at Cairo, and at dozens and dozens of less famous spots, including many in the United States. Indeed, counting the chapels and churches where she had given messages to visionaries and locutionists, sometimes without becoming visible, she had graced countless locations throughout the world.

A week after the Warning a mysterious event occurred: *a luminous white Cross appeared in the air* a hundred feet above each of these locations. From whatever distance it was viewed, it seemed to be fifty feet high, three-dimensional, solid, and visible both day and night. Light seemed to flow out of it. The News organizations quickly discovered the phenomena and their television crews showed them on the evening News. Because all the Crosses showed up on radar, some governments sent military jets to try to destroy the Crosses to test the reality of what many thought was an illusion.

In vain. The first time a plane flew at the Cross, it went right through, but nothing changed with the plane's passage. The second time a pilot tried to dispel the vision by flying through it, or firing at it, his plane exploded as if he had hit a brick wall.

At first the television networks found these events newsworthy. But within a couple days they stopped covering them, as if an order had gone out to disregard the Crosses. Few realized that the indestructible Crosses marked places of Refuge for people fleeing religious persecution.

(8)

The document was titled, *"Interim Treasury Report on SmartCard Dissemination."* The President did not like what he read.

Couched in the usual bureaucratic mumbling, tortured syntax, and self-serving excuses blaming policy failure on vague sociological conditions and demographic anomalies, a simple fact stood out: Americans were not rushing in droves to embrace the SmartCard.

Though the Decree had gone out requiring all citizens to apply for the SmartCard or else forfeit one's Driver's License, less than half the population had done so. And Talk Radio was buzzing with hosts and callers agreeing that this "National I.D." violated personal privacy rights and could accelerate the coming of the Big Brother Police State. Some callers even suggested that the Card might be a surveillance device, which indeed it was; and maybe even a listening device, which indeed it could be activated to become.

To counter such an unfortunate outbreak of truth, the President had dispatched his Cabinet members and Party leaders to calm public fears and deny any nefarious purpose. He also planted some questions at his Press Conferences, so that he could exercise his considerable skill in doubletalk, further to assuage public concern. Being a dissimulator second only to the Chairman himself, the President enjoyed some success with this tactic. Still, libertarians were picketing banks and federal buildings and holding "Burn-the-Card" rallies. Popping up on placards everywhere were pointed slogans such as, *"Your American Repress Card: Don't Leave Home With It."*

The President calculated that eventually he would have his way, especially with the quiet "house arrests" of leading opposition political figures he had surreptitiously undertaken. But with the Chairman breathing down his neck about the Timetable and the need to move rapidly to the next stage of the Plan, he decided he had to do something more drastic. One has to help Evolution along now and then. Or as Lenin had remarked, one has to break a few eggs to make an omelet.

He decided to order the immediate introduction of the Microchip. But to do so, he needed a pretext.

(9)

John and Susan DeSanto had finished packing three knapsacks, one for each of them and one for the baby. They had squeezed in everything they could think of and could carry: a change of clothes, warm gloves and boots, wet wipes and toilet paper, natural food bars, canteens of water, flashlights, Swiss army knife, and so on. When they finished, they looked at each other with dismay. Both realized that, naturally speaking, these things would keep them alive about a week. That was all.

John wondered whether to take his pistol and some ammunition. He kept debating in his mind two conflicting perspectives: on the one hand, "Vengeance is Mine, sayeth the Lord"...on the other, a man should always protect his family, and the decision to disarm himself could permit roving vandals to steal his little supply cache or harm his wife. He pondered the dozens of private revelations that he had read over the past few months. These had uniformly urged that people in the Remnant Church take sacramentals such as Rosary, holy water, scapulars, and pocket-size Bibles, but said nothing about weapons.

He finally decided that he would not use force against the Chairman's agents, should he encounter them, but leave his defense to God. But the robber or rapist would meet a hail of bullets. John hoped God would approve.

That night as they slept, an invisible being like a man appeared in their bedroom and scrutinized them closely; seeing what he was looking for, he leaned over their beds for a moment, and then reached out to touch their foreheads with his thumb. In a gesture similar to the priest's on Ash Wednesday, he marked their foreheads with a cross. Unlike the cross of ashes, *this cross was visible only to those they would meet who themselves bore the same cross.*

CHAPTER XIX

(1)

Jerry Kanek stepped into the room, his finger to his lips. "Shhhhhh," he whispered to the others. From his coat pocket he produced a device that looked like a TV remote. Quietly he circled around the room, aiming the device behind curtains, into a flower pot, down the wall and floor air vents, and everywhere else that could be "bugged." The others realized he was doing a "sweep" of the apartment.

Satisfied the place was not under surveillance, he went to his briefcase, which he had left next to the front door, and retrieved a telephone, complete with cord. He quickly walked to the kitchen, removed Pat Greene's own phone from the wall, and hooked up in its place the one he had brought. Then he handed Pat's old one to him, with a prewritten note, "Please take this phone to your store room in the basement." Pat nodded, took the phone, and exited. Jerry returned to the living room and unplugged the portable television set in the corner and carried it out onto the balcony. As he reentered, he pushed the sliding glass door all the way closed.

Finally, while the others held their breaths, as it were, Jerry spoke. "I don't think this place is being bugged, but there is no way to be absolutely certain."

"What was the deal with the phone exchange?" asked Vanni, as Pat came back in.

"The regular phones in this building are all post-1990. Most contain a transponder chip that can transmit conversations to a listening center. Can't prove that was happening, but better safe than sorry. The phone I put up in the kitchen is an old one from the early 1980s. No chip in it."

"I want to thank Jerry for his help," said Pat. "In gratitude for his efforts, I would like to ask him to open the discussion. He sat down in his chair and poured some *Wicked Ale* into a glass.

"Well, Pat, I didn't call the meeting and I don't know if I should set the agenda. But obviously, if you've kept up with the news the last few days, civil liberties are going down the tube fast. The

Chairman of the Council of Europe has concocted a world government plot that the President has bought into...our Government is trying to pin the bombings on the Right to Life movement...the President's SmartCard scheme didn't catch on big with Joe Sixpack, and the President is mad as Hell and probably cooking up something even more intrusive..."

"And a cop stopped me the other day for no other reason," said Vanni, "than to 'check my papers'--by which he meant, to see if I had the SmartCard. I didn't. I don't have one. He gave me a pass, but said that next time I lose my license."

"Well, on the good side," said Father Kanek, "big, indestructible crosses made of light have appeared in the air over dozens of spots in the world."

"More than dozens, Father--hundreds and hundreds," said Vanni.

"The more the better!" responded the priest. "But how do you know it's so many?"

"The company I work for has consulting contracts with DOD and CIA. We provide technical support and *ad hoc* expertise to these agencies whenever they want something that they haven't got the money for, or cannot put together quickly through regular channels." She stopped, her cheeks flushed, and she thought rapidly. "What I'm telling you," she then resumed almost in a whisper, realizing that she had momentarily forgotten that except for Jerry Kanek, the others did not have her level of security clearance, "is classified. I hope you will keep this completely confidential--especially you, Mr. Hard-Charging Investigative Reporter," she added, looking at Pat.

"My dear," said Pat, who wanted to lighten the conversation, "your wish is ever my command. My passion to expose our government's depredations is not as strong as my desire to put a wedding ring on your finger before the clock strikes two thousand. Besides, I don't think you said anything classified--and even if I tried to write it up, my ever-cautious editor at the *Tribune* would deep-six it the way he did my article on HAARP. So don't worry."

"Good." She swallowed some 7-Up. "So I'll just get to the point. DOD and CIA both asked us to help them figure out what is causing those crosses. They sent us photographs of hundreds of them. Also pictures of planes flying *through* them, planes *crashing into* them, and air-to-air missiles fired *at* them--but all with absolutely no effect *on* them!"

"I have a hunch," said Father Kanek, "that if the pilot simply wanted to satisfy his curiosity, his plane went right through, without any damage...but if he wanted to *destroy* the cross, his plane or his missile would itself be destroyed. There is a Biblical principle--what you sow is what you harvest--evil that you do will come back to you--which these crosses will impose on their assailants. Or, I should say, God will."

"So what's the bottom line?" asked Pat.

"We haven't come up with any natural explanation," said Vanni, "except that my boss thinks it's some kind of hologram transmitted from a satellite, or somewhere, with a technology that we don't have in our country yet. One of our analysts actually thinks the crosses are tied in with extra-terrestrials. Neither of them has any proof at all."

"You mean little green men from other planets?" asked Pat, with a slight sneer.

"Right," she responded.

"Extra-terrestrial, all right," said Father Kanek, "but not the physical kind. Doesn't anyone realize the crosses might be *from God?* So many people want to invent absurd theories when common sense would explain the facts."

"It does take a bit of faith--or at least an open mind," declared Pat.

"Pat, many private messages from God predicted this exactly. They said that shortly before the End of the Age, crosses would appear at every location where a genuine apparition of the Virgin Mary had taken place."

"Why?" asked Jerry Kanek.

"Probably three reasons. One is to endorse the appearance itself--to stamp approval on the message and messenger at that spot. Second, to raise Christians' morale, to show that God is still in control. Men shoot their best weapons at the crosses and nothing happens! Third, to indicate the position of places of safety--refuges--during the turmoil to come."

"Places to hide?" asked Vanni.

"Yes." He saw a troubled look cross Pat's face. "I know that kind of news is a mixed blessing. Most of us would rather not have to go into hiding--but, if we do, we sure would like to know where to go."

"It's becoming a real possibility," said Jerry Kanek. "Someone tried to shoot down John DeSanto; the President ordered this SmartCard thing; it is quite likely somebody in Rome is pretending the Pope is dead, so they could engineer the election of a successor--"

"--Whose writings and speeches show," interrupted Father Kanek, "that he does not see the world through the same orthodox eyes as John Paul II."

"Right. And I can tell you--" he glanced at his brother--"that experiments on violent prisoners, with a microchip inserted under their skin, turned them into walking listening devices and quasi-robots who couldn't resist the commands of their captors when low-frequency electrical current was beamed at them."

Vanni squirmed in her chair. "Could they do that to you just through the SmartCard?"

"It's likely they could calculate your location or listen to your conversations--but no, the electrical beam wouldn't disorient a person unless the receiver--the Chip--were under his skin. That would connect it straight to the central nervous system through the body's conductivity," said Father Kanek.

(2)

At that moment, the phone rang. Pat took a few quick steps to the kitchen and answered on the third ring. It was a tenant in the same building. They talked for half a minute and then Pat hung up and returned. "It was my neighbor, Harry Mannington," said Pat. "He's retired military. Was a full Colonel. He sees the world the way I do. He wanted to tell me that it's just been announced that the President is coming on television in a minute with a major statement. He figured I would want to hear it."

They agreed it would be good to watch, so Jerry retrieved the television set and plugged it in. The picture showed an anchorman prepping the audience. As they watched, the picture faded to the President sitting behind a desk in his White House office. He began:

"My fellow Americans. As you recall from my recent speech, our country is working closely with the Chairman of the Council of Europe and other world leaders to put together concerted international efforts in the pursuit of peace and prosperity.

"Unfortunately, agreements among nations cannot do the job alone. The world economy faces some major challenges: the banking system could deteriorate rapidly unless effective steps are taken to shore it up. And the computer- based infrastructure of society could suffer serious disruptions caused by malfunctions at the Year 2000, or indeed before that date.

"Your government has been working energetically with leaders of the banking and computer communities to develop a solution to these problems. Fortunately, the far-sighted leadership of this Administration and these private sector specialists has created a new electronic system that will be invulnerable to computer malfunction and which can significantly strengthen our banking system. Universal adoption of this electronic system will assure economic prosperity here and abroad.

"The enthusiastic adoption of the SmartCard here in the United States was an excellent first step in the right direction. But our Administration has been besieged with complaints from citizens who either lost the card, inadvertently left it at home when they needed it later at restaurant or airport, or had it stolen. It is clear that the SmartCard's function is in great demand; but it needs improvement.

"Our scientists have developed a harmless microchip that can perform all the functions of the SmartCard. It can be inserted under the skin of the forehead or the hand, where minuscule changes of temperature serve to keep it charged. For the purpose of buying at the store, the hand is better, because it can be conveniently swiped across a scanner. Attached under the skin, the microchip cannot be lost, left at home, or stolen. [The camera fades to a fifteen-second video clip of a pretty customer at Safeway quickly walking through the check-out line and swiping her right hand across a scanner. The actress-customer smiles into the camera and says, "I *love* this. It's *so* much better than old-fashioned cash or credit cards!"]

"When all Americans have this chip implant, our banking system will be safe against counterfeiters. Heightened speed of transactions will save countless man-hours, thus enhancing productivity. And--because the microchip will *not* be networked into the existing noncompliant computer systems, which could well fail in less than a year--our entire financial system will do a successful 'end run' around the Millennium Bug problem. Thus we will avoid the cataclysmic loss of jobs and money that many futurists have predicted.

"So, to expedite this process, I have signed Executive Order 2000FFF, which directs all banks and post offices to process citizen acceptance of the microchip. At all these locations, trained medical professionals will be available from 10:00 a.m. until 4:00 p.m. every day, to assist each of you to obtain a microchip."

(3)

Even as the President spoke, in an unrelated development, telescope computers confirmed the appearance of an asteroid or comet heading on a trajectory straight toward earth. The computers calculated its known speed, the gravitational attraction of nearby planets like Jupiter and Mars, the even greater gravitational pull of the sun, the speed and direction of the earth in its orbit, and all other conceivable variables.

The composition of this hurtling ball was an anomaly: although it was solid, made of various metallic elements, mostly iron, it nonetheless was encased in ice which reflected the sun and it gave off a tail of ice crystals which made it doubly visible in the sun's rays. It seemed to be an immense craggy ball of metal coated with a sizeable quantity of ice. It was *both* a comet and an asteroid.

Preliminary reports, issued within hours of each other by the three largest observatories in the Western Hemisphere, were not good. Their unanimous conclusion was that unless something dramatic were done to deflect or destroy the solid comet, it would soon hit somewhere in Europe, the north Atlantic, the United States, or the northern Pacific.

(4)

The President had finished his microchip speech. The members of the Honest Debate Society sat in stunned silence. For a minute, no one spoke.

Jerry Kanek half-consciously reached under his left arm and touched the bulge near his armpit. He wondered what good his gun would do in the face of the trap the President was putting together. He stood up, unplugged the set again, and carried it back to the balcony.

Father Mike stared into space, the palms of his two hands together, fingertips touching his chin. The others did not know whether he was thinking or praying. They were busy with their own thoughts.

Vanni looked at her engagement ring, thought about marriage plans that might be shattered, and wondered when the Rapture would take place.

Pat Greene took a long, slow drink of ale and pondered the odds that he and Vanni would have a normal future. He wondered whether the publishers' checks he had not yet cashed would be any good if the government imposed a whole new financial system.

Finally, Father Mike broke the silence. To no one in particular, he half mumbled, "This has all been predicted. Even the suddenness of it all. But I'm surprised it's so tightly compressed. It's as if time is an accordion. Things you might expect would happen months or even years apart are all happening in the same week!"

"Father Mike," said Pat, "remember the first meeting we had?--how Vanni asked you for a private seminar on some of this stuff, and you said O.K., if Talkmeister-the-Bonbon-Supplier came along?" Despite their worries, the phrase caused them all to smile. "Well, we never got around to that. But I think it's time for it, or the equivalent."

"I don't want to give a lecture," said the priest. "But questions are fine..."

"Good. My first question is, these events seem like a transition. If they are predicted, is the final outcome predicted too? What is the final chapter...?"

"After some very hard times, there will be an Era of Peace. That's the bottom line. Those who live in that period will think they are in the Garden of Eden. There will be plenty of food, interesting things to do, an idyllic life. There will be no disease, no wars, no lawbreakers, no bad weather. Even the animals will be tame. People will sense--and sometimes see--God walking with them."

"I'd like that," said Vanni. "Right now I have to look over my shoulder when I go to get my car out of the office parking garage. Some of those dangerous animals are two-legged."

"Well, Little Red Riding Hood, that's because when you're not in jeans and a dumpy sweatshirt you naturally attract wolves," said Pat with a smile.

"Hey, buster, thanks for the compliment, but flattery will get you not one inch farther than your honorable intentions. Let's keep my skirmishes with Big Bad Wolves out of the discussion right now. I want to ask about those 'very hard times' Father Mike just glossed over. What about the Rapture?"

"Vanni, the Rapture is a scripture interpretation by many Evangelicals that says Christians will be taken out of this world before really bad times hit. Within the Rapture camp, there are different divisions: some are 'Pre-Trib,' some 'Post-Trib,' some in the middle--that is, some think God will snatch Christians away before the Tribulation, or at the end of it, or halfway through it."

"Right. We agree. So why worry? God will take us out."

"Are you saying that because you believe it or because you are a good devil's advocate?"

"I *think* I believe it," she answered. "But I've been a serious Christian for scarcely a year, so I never picked up this idea by osmosis as a child, from my parents or the preacher. So it doesn't have a strong emotional hold on me--but I *hope* it is true."

"We could spend the night analyzing Scripture and arguing the point," Father Mike responded. "But right now events are coming like an avalanche, so I'll just give you my take on the whole idea, so we can turn to the practical side of what to do about the President's newest edict...

"The Rapture," he continued, "as most Evangelicals understand it, does not really appear in Scripture. In my opinion, they take texts that refer to the Second Coming of Christ and invent what can only be called an Intermediate Coming, which thus adds a Third Coming, the final one. The people who do this are usually very sincere and holy. But their subjective goodness is irrelevant. The fact is, the early Fathers of the Church did not teach a pre-Trib Rapture, nor did such Middle Age theologians as Aquinas or Bonaventure. And Scripture itself seems to contradict the idea. The Bible says that 'those days'--the tribulation period of world wide upheaval, the reign of Antichrist, etc.--'would be shortened *for the sake of the Elect.*'

"Now *if the Elect were no longer in the world, there would be no need to shorten the days for their sake.* God would not have to shorten the time, if the Elect were not still here."

"What about the Book of Daniel, where we are told that the Antichrist will reign for seven years?" she countered, sincerely puzzled.

"Granted that Daniel's symbolic descriptions, a Beast with seven horns and the other allegorical passages, do apply to the End Times and the reign of the Man of Sin, we still have the fact that the Scripture is a covenant, a contract, between God and man--and God

Himself put in His right to modify the hard things He imposes on us humans--to shorten the number of days."

"This reminds me of basic contract law," put in Jerry. "A contracting party can waive conditions that are onerous to the other party without voiding the contract. He simply gives the other person a better deal than the person had agreed to. In this case, God can say, 'I was going to allow you to go through seven years of pure Hell,' but for the sake of some of you--the Elect--I will shorten that down to...' well, to less."

"And, to come back to Vanni's original question," said Father Kanek, "I think that the Elect are going to stay here, on earth--somewhere on earth but maybe not where we are right now--during the final conflict. The private revelations in the last twenty plus years are consistent with this position."

"O.K.," she said. "That makes sense. Pat may think I'm a dumb blonde," she said, smiling in his direction, "but it seems sensible to me to prepare for the worst. Then if God surprises us and does pull a Rapture, we win anyway. Next question: where do we stand right now?"

"Knee-deep in alligators," said Pat. The President's declaration that everyone must take a microchip rekindled his anger at Atlantic Bank trying to force the SmartCard on him. And he was mad that some cop had stopped Vanni to tell her she had to carry the damn thing or lose her driver's license...and that when someone tried to expose this kind of crap, as he had with the crazy HAARP experiment, his article ends up in File Thirteen.

As these thoughts raced through his mind, he said, "I'm disgusted with most Americans: they all just sit on their duffs, watch Monday Night Football, and applaud when the President hands their country on a silver platter to the Chairman, because he mouths Pavlovian words, 'Peace and Prosperity,' and all the lazy dogs can do is salivate."

"It's pretty sickening," agreed Jerry Kanek. "But we can complain about it to each other all we want. Doesn't kill any alligators or get us out of the swamp."

A Prophetic Novel of the End Times

"Right, Jerry," said Father Mike. "So I'll just add a footnote to answer where are we right now. The private messages seem to be from God, which it might be prudent to take seriously, tell those who would listen that they better 'head for the hills,' you might say, when six events take place."

"Which are--?" two of them asked.

"First, John Paul II is no longer Pope. Second, the Warning takes place. Third, a false or imposter Pope takes over the Catholic Church. Fourth, stock market collapse causes economic chaos. Fifth, the Antichrist reveals himself. Sixth, governments try to force everybody to take the Mark of the Beast. Not necessarily in this order. And perhaps some of these occur within weeks of each other."

The furrowed brows on each showed intense thought. Father Mike sipped his Coke and waited for them to absorb what he'd said. Finally Vanni spoke. "Here I go again, getting us off the track, but...Father, one of the claims of the Catholic Church which offends most Protestants and makes the Church attractive to a few is that 'the Gates of Hell shall not prevail against' the Church--and that the Pope is infallible..."

"In faith and morals, not poker or the stock market," said Pat.

"Right. Faith and morals," she repeated. "A few Evangelicals like me actually like it that way: our Protestant world is sliced up into maybe five hundred different sects. We don't present a unified witness. We can't pretend to teach the pagan world because we have no single voice, no teacher who speaks with any more authority than any other. It's anarchy."

"I think I know where you're going," said Pat. "The blonde bombshell is going to throw a logical bombshell at Father Mike."

"Not maliciously," she said. "I just see what you Catholics call a scandal coming and am wondering, sincerely, how you will handle it."

"Fair enough question, Vanni," answered Father Mike, evenly. "You're absolutely right. That's the problem: if the Catholic Church really *is* the true Church and *does* have the Holy Spirit guiding it so that it always teaches truth, then how can an any Pope start teaching false doctrine and loose morals, as I think we will see the new Pope doing soon, maybe this week."

"That's it," she said simply.

"Let me try to defuse your bomb," offered Jerry Kanek. "If Pope John Paul II is not dead and if he did not voluntarily resign, then the new guy is an imposter. He *seems* to be Pope but he's not. Like counterfeit money, what he teaches will *seem* to be real but will not be. He won't have the authority to teach. The new guy will be a counterfeiter. What he teaches might *look* genuine but won't *be* genuine."

"Actually," said Pat, "it is not so much the subtle differences between the money the counterfeiter prints and the genuine stuff--it's the fact that he does not really have the *authority* to print it."

"You're right, Pat," said Father Mike. It's a question of legitimate transfer of authority...Even if John Paul *is* dead," he continued, "there were too many procedural irregularities and suspicious events in the process of electing Pope Julian. For example, some of the African Cardinals didn't even get there at all--their planes had mysterious mechanical failures. And two traditional Cardinals were killed in an auto accident on their way from the airport to the Vatican. It could be argued that the election was not legitimate."

"But if the people, most of them anyway," rejoined Vanni, "take the new guy to be the rightful Pope, won't they follow him? And thus won't whoever is behind him--I suppose that at root it's the devil himself--win anyway? So the Gates of Hell prevail, after all, by deception."

Father Mike sighed. "Yes, there will be a schism. Two churches. In the United States people will have to choose between the 'American church' and the 'Roman Catholic Church.' Hell will prevail against those who follow the false Pope, though it will not prevail against the traditional Church or those Catholics, a remnant, who stay faithful to the ancient teaching. I hope you won't think this is hair-splitting, but Jesus' promise was to His *Church*, as an institution--not to the individual members, some of whom want to change His Church to conform to New Age thinking. The Church remains the Church, even if it loses three-fourths its members to schism."

"I never thought of that," said Jerry Kanek. "But it makes sense. If I recall some history I learned in college, at the time of the Arian heresy, the Church lost a majority of its bishops. A lot of lay people, too! If Jesus' promise were to all the *individuals* who are members of the Church, He would be guaranteeing their personal salvation and orthodoxy despite what doctrines they change or immoral actions they commit. That passage, about the Gates of Hell, has to refer to the institutional Church."

"You get a base hit again, Father Mike," Vanni said. She put a potato chip into her mouth and thought for a moment. "I guess I got us off the conversational track. So I'd like to get back on. The prior question was along these lines: what are these hard times--swamp full of alligators, as Pat said--and how do we get out of the swamp?"

"In my opinion, there's a police state coming," said Jerry Kanek bluntly. "When cops stop innocent women on expressway ramps and ask to see their 'papers,' you have government run amok. I've heard some FBI agent has found terrorist plans on the computer hard drive of a pro-life activist named Rendoll Berry; but I think that guy, or some other agent, planted them himself.

"And those experiments on prisoners violated federal law, but somebody on the federal level had them done anyway. And when banks tell customers they *must* accept a card that nobody knows what's in it, just because some bank in Switzerland says they can't use a bank without it--you've got more government without the consent of the governed."

"My hunch is, that's just for openers," said Father Kanek. "You notice the President said nothing about any *sanctions* beyond loss of your license, in case the people don't run out to get their hands punctured with some mysterious gizmo. Most people have no idea what's inside it or what it will do to their health."

"History shows these things go in two steps," said Pat, pausing to sip a bit of ale, "incentives first, then punishments for those who don't swallow the bait. I bet that when you enter your bank next week, you'll see big signs promising fifty or even a hundred dollars added to your checking account if you accept the Chip before the end of the month."

"Fifty or a hundred?" asked Jerry. "AT&T sometimes offers that much just to get you to switch back from MCI or Sprint!"

"They'll offer whatever they need to," said Pat, "to get the lemmings to run over the cliff. Those of us who say, 'Hell no, I won't go,' will feel the wrath of Government. Voluntary first, then compulsory."

"Right. Punishment if you don't take it. To make things look legal, they'll pressure Congress--it's already a spawning ground for lemmings--into passing some laws that say you're a felon if you don't take the Chip. They'll call you an enemy of the State, though maybe they'll use a sanitized euphemism." Jerry Kanek was as angry as Pat. "Then guys like me will be told to go out and arrest people like you."

Seeing the men were getting uptight, Vanni tried to inject some lame humor. "Do you think they'll take away my chocolates?" she asked with an Oh-No-Not-That! tone. The others did smile, but continued in the same serious vein as before.

"Remember," said Father Kanek, "we have one advantage: all this has been predicted, and we know the predictions. The six steps I mentioned are the starter's gun going off for the race to safer ground. Some people use the word *underground.*"

"Where would we go?" asked Vanni. "I've been a city girl all my life."

"I don't know where we should go," said Father Kanek. "But God does. Don't think I'm making light of your perplexity, Vanni," he quickly added, observing her unhappy expression. "But we have three logical possibilities: first, take the Chip and avoid punishment from the Government--"

"But get punishment from God, which is worse," said Jerry.

"Much worse. This chip thing is the Mark of the Beast. The people who accept it won't have peace and prosperity for long. There are terrible punishments coming, right here on earth. And when they finally die, they'll go to Hell. Not a good choice!

"Second, stick around. Pretend nothing has changed. Go to work and live at home. Lie low. Try to buy food from friends...until the bureaucrats' computer burps your name out as a Resister or Felon or Enemy of the State. Finally get arrested for sure...and imprisoned in a Detention Center...and, when the heathen really get drunk with power...probably undergo torture." Vanni and Pat scowled; Jerry tried to remain impassive.

"Third, leave the areas where surveillance is heaviest and ride out the storm in hiding. This will be like an extended camping trip in the wilderness. Nobody will enjoy it. Unless we pray constantly for God's help, we'll get caught or we'll starve."

Vanni wanted to joke about stuffing herself with chocolate right now, so she could later hibernate like a bear, but she couldn't bring herself to pretend there was any humor at all in this. Finally she said, "Father Mike, this is horrible. Besides the Era of Peace you mentioned, is there *any* reason to be cheerful? If I weren't a Christian, I think I'd jump off a bridge!"

"Believe it or not, Vanni, every message that describes the evil days to come also says 'Fear not, I will take care of you!' Again and again, God says, I will feed you, as with Manna from Heaven...Fear not, I will give you Spiritual Communion...Fear not, I will send Michael and other angels to protect you...Fear not, I will confound those electronic devices searching for you...Fear not, just when the Man of Sin thinks he has won, I will cast him into Hell..."

"So the key," she said thoughtfully, "is that we have to trust in God and have the faith to keep asking Him for help." Then her mind hopped to another point in the President's speech. "Hey, it just occurred to me--the President said this new Chip computer system will *not* be part of the non-compliant computer network we now have, which will probably crash on January 1, Two Thousand..."

"And you're wondering what it will be tied into?" asked Pat. She nodded affirmatively.

"My guess is to the Chairman's supercomputer in Brussels."

(5)

The Kanek brothers had left and Pat was driving Vanni back to the Falls Church townhouse she shared with Joanie Atkinson. They talked about what to do right away. She told him she was quitting her job and wanted to move to her grandmother's house outside Charlottesville. He suggested he pick her up after work tomorrow, her last day. Then she suddenly took the conversation in a different direction.

"Pat, what did you do when the Warning hit you?"

"For a little while, I panicked," he said slowly. "I saw what a rat I'd been. It really shook me up. I saw how I had kidded myself about the Church and about God. I decided I had to face the truth. After all, I make my living exposing the truth, and now the truth *about me* had been exposed--in my mind. So I sucked it up and went to Confession."

"To Father Mike?"

"No. He's a great priest, really solid. But we're close friends. I know all about the Seal of Confession, but, somehow, I like the anonymity of the sacrament. You can go to any priest."

"So you just walk into any church and say you want to see a priest?"

"Not exactly, though it amounts to that. If it's an emergency, you go to the rectory and ask for a priest. Most of the time, you find out when they're hearing confessions and go to the church and stand in line outside the confessional. It's a little room like a walk-in closet, that has two parts. The priest sits behind a screen; you kneel or sit on the other side; he can hear you but he can't see you. I went back to my high school parish. There's a very holy old priest there. I figured he'd ask tough questions but that with a young priest, I might be tempted to gloss over something. I couldn't fool an old one. Might as well take my medicine."

"Did it take long?"

"The lines were long. Lots of submarine Catholics unsubmerging and coming back, like me. But it was only five or ten minutes actually talking to the priest. He was very kind. It didn't hurt--I mean, hurt my ego, as much as I was afraid it would."

"I'm glad you came back to God," she said simply. They were getting closer on the religious thing. The Catholic Church was having a good influence. She could sense the changes in him. She liked them.

He pulled the car into the space in front of her townhouse. They got out and walked up three steps to the landing in front of the door. She handed him her key and he inserted it into the lock. He did not immediately turn it to open the door.

Instead, he took her in his arms and for a long moment they kissed intensely. Then she pulled her head back. As their lips separated, he whispered, "I love you. Why don't we move that wedding date earlier?"

"Maybe so, big boy," she said pertly. "But let's figure out how we get through the swamp first."

At that moment, in the dim moonlight, they each saw a small cross appear on the other's forehead.

(6)

Near the church of San Marcos in the northwest quadrant of Madrid, a tall woman dressed in a plain dress, her head covered with a dark blue shawl, slowly approached the steps leading up to the heavy double doors. Her skirt came almost to her ankles and revealed only a scuffed pair of low-heeled shoes. She carried a worn leather purse and she limped ever so slightly.

The woman's right hand grasped the thick metal handrail that ran diagonally down the middle of the steps and, with an effort, she slowly mounted the stairs, pausing briefly halfway up the steep eighteen steps.

When she reached the landing at the top, she hesitated, as if catching her breath. She rubbed the sleeve on her right arm across her forehead. Then she struggled to swing open one of the two big bronze doors. Finally successful, she disappeared into the gloom of the foyer of the big old church. If anyone noticed, they would think that Cristina Montalvo, who came here at this hour frequently, had returned for her daily prayers.

An accomplished actress, the woman who entered the church was Dolores Montalvo. Inside the building, secreted in a small room near the confessional, Cristina Montalvo waited, praying the Rosary. In the confessional, reading his breviary under a single lightbulb, sat an old Dominican priest.

CHAPTER XX

(1)

The headlines on the mainstream newspapers looked like the supermarket tabloids.

COMET TO HIT EARTH!
President Urges Calm

COMET COMING FAST
Air Force Ponders Missile Strike

Other articles began with such headings as **Financial Collapse as Markets Panic...Chairman Blames Christians...Chip Implant Program Slows...Thousands Besiege Stores...Atlantic Impact Likely...Tidal Wave to Hit Coast.**

(2)

When an unknown assassin hit Pope Julian with a single shot, the new Pontiff slumped backward in his car, blood spurting from the chest wound. The bullet severed an artery near the heart. In the hospital later that afternoon Eugenio Cassendi, the new Pope Julian, died. Or seemed to.

When he got the news, the Chairman immediately went on television. Again the subliminals urged *Take the Chip at Once...the Chairman is God...Worship the Chairman*. Again his dark eyes flashed hypnotically. And this time he added something new: using a computer program of his own design, he inserted into the transmission low-frequency electrical impulses and subdued oscillating green lights. The program also overrode any Internet on-line activity on all the computer screens in the world, so that computer monitors showed the same picture as all the television sets. The Chairman's face was broadcast into every home and every office. The effect was mesmerizing. Those who had taken the Chip faded into a trance and began to mumble worshipful praise of the Chairman.

The Chairman's message was brief. Once he moved beyond expressions of grief at the loss of his good friend, Pope Julian, he made, with minimal elaboration, only two points.

The Chairman has been sent by God, he told the world.

He, the Chairman, would go at once to the hospital and raise the Pope from the dead, he told the world.

And everyone who was in the world and of the world believed him.

(3)

That same night, and continuing nightly for a week, in hundreds of thousands of homes around the world, angels appeared in the rooms of sleeping people who had a Cross marked on their foreheads. "Get up!" they commanded. "I am your Guardian Angel. You must wait no longer to go into hiding. Come with me."

Different angels took people in different ways. Some they told to walk, some to ride bicycles, some to take the angel's hand and he would transport them, some to get into their cars and follow him--though the angel would warn that automobiles, unless very old, could be traced electronically, so the people would have to abandon their vehicles before reaching their destinations.

Where married couples were of one mind, the angel would lead them together to the same place, often a cave or a refuge where the Virgin Mary had once appeared. But where one spouse refused to leave, the angel did not force the issue. He and the other merely departed without the recalcitrant spouse.

Even this division had been foretold in Scripture.

(4)

By and large the authorities could not prevent this quiet exodus. They were too busy controlling the urban food riots, maintaining the flow of preprogrammed personalized computer chips to banks and post offices, and using their computers to identify Enemies of the State whom they wanted to round up into Detention Centers set up over the years by Presidential Executive Order.

There is a streak of rebellion and independence in the American temperament. Despite years of welfare state dependence and the siren

Huddled on an old sofa along the back wall sat a man and a woman clutching each other. The woman held a child. None of them had the Chip.

The soldiers looked around. *The room seemed empty.* They could not see the people who sat, in plain view, twenty feet away. The squad leader strode to the bedroom door, peered in, and decided it was empty too. "If anyone ever was here," he said, "they've gone."

After the soldiers left, John and Susan DeSanto breathed a sigh of relief and whispered a prayer of gratitude.

Their Guardian Angels put their swords back in their sheaths.

(7)

"Father Michael Kanek, I *insist* that you accept the Chip. I command you under the Vow of Obedience!" declared Father Wilton Johnson, somewhat pompously. "In this time of civic crisis and near anarchy, it is essential that we priests support the government and give good example to the students."

"Sorry, Father, no can do." Kanek had never imagined he would directly disobey the command of a Superior, but he owed his first allegiance, as St. Peter had said in *Acts*, not to men, but to God. Besides, the Superior of a religious community did not have higher rank than a Bishop. Perhaps that was why the Pope had secretly ordained him to the episcopacy, he thought, so he would not worry about disobeying such a command.

"You realize, don't you, that when you go outside that door"--Johnson gestured towards his office door--"and leave this campus, the police are sure to apprehend you. You probably will end up in a Detention Center. You will be branded a Traitor--an Enemy of the State."

"I am the King's good servant, but God's first," responded Father Kanek, quoting Saint Thomas More. "Have you read that little piece of paper they give you to sign, just before they insert the needle with the Chip?" asked Kanek. "They make it crystal clear," he continued, "that if you take the Chip, you abjure your Faith."

"Words, mere words," said the other. "These days everybody signs things they don't mean. You can sign it, but withhold assent. That way you have the best of both worlds."

"The only way I can *show* I withhold assent is *not* to sign it," Kanek shot back.

"But this directive is not just from the President. It is from the Pope himself," rejoined Father Johnson. "Here--" he held up a paper, "he states plainly that he wants all priests and religious to accept the Chip."

"He can 'state plainly' that the Chairman is God--I don't care, it's not the truth," snapped Kanek, getting angry. "I am tired of all this hypocrisy. I'm sick of all these games. Why did you join the Order, Will, if for you it is only the ecclesiastical arm of the ruling political Party? We are supposed to witness *against* the Apostasy and *for* Jesus Christ--not *join* the Apostasy and *betray* Jesus!!"

Before the other could think of an answer, Mike Kanek strode out the door and slammed it behind him.

(8)

After a half hour in the Confessional, Dolores Montalvo finished. The old Dominican priest absolved her, she recited a heartfelt *Act of Contrition* and accepted her penance, and after a minute to wipe her tears she left the little room. There in the main church knelt Cristina, praying.

The two women saw each other and, out of respect for the Blessed Sacrament, walked wordlessly down the side aisle and into the vestibule, where they threw themselves into each others' arms and hugged.

"Oh, Auntie," began Dolores, her voice hoarse with emotion, "you've pulled me from the jaws of Hell! How can I thank you?" She sniffed, and tears again formed in her eyes and began to slip down her cheek.

The older woman felt strong emotions as well, but she controlled them better. She cleared her throat, forced back the beginning of a tear, and answered, "It was not I, my dear. It was Our Lady. *She* asked me to pray for you. I prayed a bit. *She* sent you the grace to listen to the Warning."

"She must get me another grace," said Dolores, retrieving a handkerchief from her small purse and wiping her eyes. "The Chairman has ordered me back to the United States to work for the President. I am sure he wants revenge for something I did to him."

"Do not go," said her Aunt firmly. "Instead, go to Garabandal. You have managed to get here without detection. Continue to be the actress and secretly go there, where you will be safe during the Purification. Do penance there, like Mary Magdalen, and ask God to shorten the days of Purification. The Three Days of Darkness will come very soon."

After Dolores left, Cristina returned to the church to give thanks. A female Voice in her head assured her, *"You have done well, my daughter. Dolores will be safe. Now intensify your prayers against the Chairman's computer, as your Guardian Angel showed you in Brussels."*

(9)

Jerry Kanek knew he had one week before they would come for him. The new FBI Director had decreed--everything was done by Decree these days--that all Agents must have taken the Chip by the end of the month, and today was the twenty-third. Meantime, he had one advantage: the multiple police forces that seemed to be everywhere did not stop cars with Government plates. He had a black Crown Victoria with Government plates, extra aerials, and driver's side spotlight--the whole works--and he intended to use it to save his brother.

They met outside the rear parking lot entrance to the Best Western in Rosslyn, the same place they had begun their trek to find privacy the day he flew back in from LAX, so many weeks ago. At Jerry's insistence, Father Mike carried a small suitcase. They sat in his car and talked for a half hour. Gradually Jerry brought Mike around to his way of thinking.

Then they went inside to the restaurant, had a quick soup and sandwich, and, when finished, headed downstairs to the men's room one floor below. They entered separate toilet stalls, took off all their outer clothes, and exchanged these garments over the divider wall between the two stalls. When they emerged, the priest looked like the FBI agent and the agent was dressed like a priest. Everything had been exchanged, including wallets, except one thing: Father Mike insisted that Jerry keep his gun.

They drove a few blocks to Prospect House in Arlington, site of Pat Greene's apartment. Jerry stayed in the back seat, hidden by the car's dark tinted windows, and Father Mike, looking like a trim, middle-aged lawyer, entered the front lobby and brusquely flashed Jerry's FBI credentials in the face of a startled daytime desk clerk. Because the Honest Debate Society meetings had always been after dinner, this clerk had never seen either Mike or Jerry Kanek. "FBI. I'm here to interrogate one of your tenants, a--" he looked at a small notebook as if checking the name--"a Theodore Patrick Greene."

The clerk did not want to mess with the FBI and readily buzzed open the inner door, which led to a bank of elevators. "Tenth floor, Suite 1008," he said obsequiously. The "FBI man" disappeared into the inner corridor and stepped into an elevator. Five minutes later he and Pat Greene emerged; not quite in tandem with Pat in the lead holding a briefcase, they strode through the lobby and out to the tarmac and the Crown Victoria.

"Give me the keys to your apartment and your car, Pat, then drop me off a few blocks away," commanded Jerry, as Father Mike and Pat climbed in. "I'll stay at your place for awhile. You two guys find Vanni and then get the Hell out of here. Go to her grandmother's or somewhere. With no more food coming in, D.C. will go up in flames in a few days--and the tidal wave will put them out!"

This was all an emotional roller-coaster for Father Mike. "Jerry, they're going to kill all the priests who don't take the Chip. They'll kill you," he said, his voice cracking, "or you'll drown!"

"Then, if you do what I tell you, little brother, they *won't* kill *you*," Jerry answered forcefully. "Isn't that what this Christianity thing is all about--one man dies in someone else's place? But don't worry, I'll get through this. I'll see you on the other side, when it's all over!"

CHAPTER XXI

(1)

At last! he had located John Paul II. A loquacious workman at the ski resort had let slip that it had a distinguished visitor and wondered aloud how there could be *two* Popes at the same time. Now he, the Chairman, would call Malin to have him finish the job. Later he would have Malin killed.

"Mr. Malin, it is good to speak with you again," began the Chairman in a friendly tone. There was silence on the other end of the line. So he continued.

"I believe I was too hasty in withholding the other nine million dollars you earned on your last assignment."

"And so," said Malin, his suspicion and his greed in tension, "you will wire it now to my Swiss bank account? To what shall I attribute this sudden change of heart?"

The Chairman sensed Malin's suspicion and the sarcasm in the question. But he had his purpose firmly in mind and could wait until later to put the man in his place. "I will wire four million dollars now, to show my good faith; then, when you finally kill John Paul II, I will wire the other five million."

"So you know where he is?"

"Yes. A ski resort in Switzerland, near the Italian border. One of my aides will fax you a map of the area along with plans for the building he is in."

"All right. I'll do it. But there are *four* bank accounts, in different countries. When I receive the map and plans, I will fax you the bank names, the routing numbers, and the account numbers. Send a million dollars to each. When I am able to withdraw the money, I will go to Switzerland and finish the assignment. Then I will fax to you five more account numbers in as many different banks. Send one million to each of them."

"Agreed," said the Chairman. "It is a pleasure to work with an honorable man."

(2)

The chaos in America intensified...Supermarket shelves quickly emptied, and truckers bringing food to the cities refused to come closer than the outlying suburbs, lest hungry mobs attack them...The President's paramilitary forces set up random check points on major highways to apprehend the citizens who still had not accepted the Chip...Ferocious thunderstorms erupted everywhere, mile-wide tornadoes appeared out of nowhere, and unseasonal temperature drops froze unharvested fruits and vegetables...Brownouts and blackouts spread across the convulsing society...The urban welfare underclass, deprived of their free food and subsidized electricity, rioted in a dozen big cities...Looting spread from the downtown areas toward the suburbs...A crush of automobiles clogged the westbound highways out of Boston, New York, Philadelphia, Washington, and indeed the whole East Coast, as people struggled to exit coastal areas and find high ground. Few brought enough food, and with the bizarre temperature changes spiking up to the 90's and then down to sub-freezing almost every other day, few had adequate clothing. All in all, it was worse than if someone shouted "Fire!" in the proverbial movie theatre--*but the "theatre" was the entire East Coast.* Inconvenience turned to suffering.

Amid all this, after a worrisome meeting with the top technical people at NASA and DOD, the President returned to his office and considered his options. As usual, his first thought was himself. He could go to the secret Underground Command Center in Bluemount, Virginia, a small city-within-a-mountain in Loudon County that the National Security Agency had set up over two decades. Or he could take off in Air Force One on some pretext and go to a safe place--Colorado perhaps, or Switzerland. Or he could stay in Washington and act presidential: tell the people to be calm and to think of others in this crisis...crack the whip over his Cabinet heads and law enforcement people to expedite the Chip program...continue to oversee the purging of his political enemies through house arrests and contrived disappearances. As he pondered, he remembered his directive to the European CIA headquarters, to find Dolores Montalvo; because he felt the Chairman was taking his good sweet time in sending her back, he had decided he would send his own agents to get her.

The phone rang. Once again, the staff aide who took the call informed him it was the Chairman, who on this occasion was in an expansive mood.

"Mr. President, the Plan is now working perfectly. I have created the ultimate computer program to deal with the comet. I have done multiple redundancy test runs." The Chairman had decided not to destroy the thing. "If your people can provide me weapons that work, I can easily deflect that comet away from the earth!"

The President felt the Chairman was overconfident. The man was a megalomaniac. "That's wonderful news, Mr. Chairman," he said, trying to inject belief into his voice. "Our space-trajectory analysis people at NASA told me this morning that the comet will hit in the Atlantic three to four hundred miles offshore and due east of Washington--unless we destroy it."

"And *you*," said the Chairman as if reading his mind, "have doubts whether even I, with all my expertise, can conquer this pebble that so frightens you."

"Mr. Chairman, no one respects your expertise more than I," he responded. "But we have only one chance, and if something goes wrong--on *our* end, as you say, with the weapons--then, well, then a tidal wave hundreds of feet high will drown everyone still in the coastal cities from Boston to Miami."

"And the thought just happened to sneak into the back of your mind that the tidal wave will hit Washington, D.C., where *you* are." The Chairman's sarcastic bent reared up.

"I owe it to the American people to continue to provide them leadership in this time of crisis," said the President, sounding as if he were making a campaign speech. "And I owe it to *you*, Mr. Chairman," he quickly added, groping for a way to avoid admitting his cowardice, "to stay alive so that we can complete the Plan. If I were to drown, I am of no use to you."

"True enough," said the other. "So I have a proposal for you. Come to Brussels. I am calling a meeting of all the new Directors. It is time to assign Directorates. You have first choice--but you must be here. As for the comet, even if flaws in your weapons should cause us to fail, the British Isles will block the tidal wave from reaching

Belgium." Because the President did not instantly agree, the Chairman tossed in an additional incentive. "Oh, by the way, I have located Dolores Montalvo. She is as beautiful as ever. I will have her waiting for you after our meeting."

This offer was an outright lie, but it was a proposition the President could not refuse.

(3)

"The great and terrible Day of the Lord," the Bible had called it. An understatement, thought Father Michael Kanek, as he and Pat Greene maneuvered the black Crown Victoria through side streets, probing the neighborhoods for access to a relatively uncrowded boulevard.

They met Vanni as planned and began the journey toward Charlottesville. Driving an unmarked police car, wearing dark business suits, conservative ties, and stern demeanor, the two men in the front seats looked the part of determined Federal agents. No local police bothered them at the two check-points they encountered. In each case Father Mike flashed Jerry's wallet ID; an officer gave it a cursory glance and waved them on. Most random checking was done at night, anyway, and it was now only late afternoon. So far their cover had held.

* * * * * * * * * * * *

Jerry Kanek, dressed in a priest's black suit and reversed white collar, stood just inside the door of the chapel, a small wooden church, on the compact Marymount College campus in north Arlington. The College was closed and the campus deserted; with growing social chaos, he doubted there would be people around if and when the school reopened. He had come here to try to refresh his spirit and steel himself for what he knew would eventually take place. He had been a devout Catholic all his life, but the "slings and arrows of outrageous assignments," as he had once remarked to his brother Mike, had eroded his zeal for prayer and devotion. True, he frequented the sacraments and often, if not daily, prayed the Rosary. But to his mind, these rudimentary spiritual efforts were not heroic. And now he wondered about changing places with his brother--whether he was ready for martyrdom.

He picked his way gingerly through the rubble of the ransacked little church. He had lived in the area ten years earlier for a year's assignment in Washington, D.C., and he had come here often in the early evening when the sun's last golden rays streamed through the stained glass windows and competed with the red tabernacle lamp for the believer's attention. In those days he had nurtured a deep devotion to Jesus really present in the Blessed Sacrament.

Once on a retreat he had read a short biography of some saintly fourth-century Christian in Spain, who had watched in horror as a man, having just received Holy Communion, yielded to influenza and, unwittingly, vomited up the Sacred Host onto the floor. Shocked that the man left the Host in a puddle of vomit, the other had rushed over, put the Host into his own mouth, and swallowed. The story concluded with his reward: God decreed that for his faith in overcoming natural repugnance, he would never again suffer the slightest sickness.

Jerry Kanek wondered why that memory had come back to him as he surveyed the wreckage. The place was a shambles. Along the side aisles next to the pillars, the ornate wood-carved Stations of the Cross were broken on the floor, some split in pieces as if axed. Some pews were hacked and spray-painted black graffiti profaned others. He walked up the messy main aisle slowly, his mind a jumble of questions, his heart a mix of grief and anger. Who would do such a thing? And why?

He reached the front and saw that the altar, a heavy wooden table, had been chopped with an axe as well. One of its thick legs had cracked and it leaned at a rakish angle, as if a slight shove would cause collapse. Scattered on the floor, between the shattered altar and the open tabernacle, lay its contents, including a pyx, a monstrance, and *three white Hosts.*

As he stared in disbelief, a harsh voice spoke from the doorway he had entered two minutes before, said, "Come back to see what we've done to your shitty religion, have you, Father?"

Kanek looked Jesuit, but his instincts were FBI. He knew that he had to turn to his left, so that in reaching for his gun his right hand was not directly visible. He also knew the man was probably armed and might have companions. As he turned slowly, he spoke in a loud, controlled and unemotional voice, "Do you mind my asking why you did this?" Half turned, he could see there were two men in the doorway and one was, indeed, pointing a gun at him.

"We had our orders. But it was a pleasure. You people follow a god who died a long time ago." *You're right; He did,* thought Jerry Kanek, *but after three days He rose again--so He's still alive*; but, as he glanced at the three Hosts on the floor, he did not say it.

"And why did you come back to the scene of your crime?" asked the apparent priest with a force that took them aback for a moment.

"Because we thought maybe we missed something, like those so-called 'Sacred Hosts' you Catholics think are so important," said the man in the doorway, the strength in his voice comparable to Kanek's. But in his inattention, he had lowered his gun just slightly.

In that instant, Jerry Kanek sprang forward to land behind the partly tipped altar where two of the three Hosts lay, pulled his gun, grabbed the first wafer with his left hand, thrust it into his mouth, and rolled to fire two shots at the armed vandal forty feet away. One hit him in the left shoulder. Surprised by the priest's acrobatic move and gun play, the other man fired wildly. But his companion drew his gun and ran in a half crouch four steps over and quickly scurried up the side aisle, using the pillars as a shield.

Jerry Kanek snatched the second Host. He thrust it into his mouth. Five shots, from two different locations, cut into the pew and the tilted wooden altar. None hit him.

The third Host lay further away. Jerry dived for it. In a split second, he gulped the third Host into his mouth. Just as he swallowed, three bullets tore into his body, one in the shoulder, one in the neck, and one in the head.

(4)

It was night and, fortunately for his plans, clouds concealed the moon. Dressed entirely in black, Malin cautiously approached the main building. He avoided occasional patches of snow, leaving no tracks. Through his night vision goggles, the building loomed an eerie greenish before him. But he had been on these missions before and the surreal aspects of it did not daunt him.

As he neared the building, he wondered where security was. At one point he paused and crouched behind a clump of bushes for almost ten minutes. Hearing nothing, he moved closer. Perhaps there were no guards. Perhaps the people here wanted to maintain the pretense that there was no one important enough to guard. He could not see a tall angel watching him.

At last he reached a flight of wooden steps at the rear. He grabbed the railing tightly with his left hand, to make sure no ice on the steps might cause him to slip. In his right, he held a .38 caliber German Walther pistol, silencer attached. On his back was strapped a powerful semi-automatic rifle. The pistol would do the job; the rifle was for defense. Catlike, he moved upward quickly and to a covered porch that encircled the three story frame edifice. The wind had picked up and the eaves above him groaned and whistled like a hoarse flute, sounds that served to cover the creaking of old floor boards underfoot as he made his way along the wall, looking for the fifth window. The angel still watched but did not act.

He reached the fifth window, pulled a glass cutting tool from a pocket, drew a circular cut near the window lock, and with a small suction cup extracted the cut glass. He reached in carefully and unlocked the window. It creaked slightly as he raised it, so he took his time until, after five minutes, he had inched the window high enough to step in. He found himself in a storage room. By now the clouds had passed and pale moonlight spilled in through the window behind him, casting enough light for his night vision glasses easily to pick out objects to avoid and a door to access the inside corridor. Two minutes more and he found the room the Pope used as a chapel. The angel stayed invisible next to him.

His plan was simple: do not search the building and risk rousing a guard or an early-rising servant; wait for the Pope to come to say Mass. Kill him there. So he returned to the storage room, piled some old towels and rags into a mound, ascertained that the room could not be locked from the outside, and stood a broom and a bucket behind the door in a way that anyone entering would cause them to topple with a crash. He intended only to doze, but as a precaution he set the timer on his watch to awaken him in two hours. He lay down on the floor, with his head on the pile of towels. Because of his military training, at any sudden sound he could spring instantly out of sleep to deal with an intruder, who he was certain would be unarmed.

Malin's plan progressed without a hitch. Footfalls on the creaky wooden floor just outside the room awakened him minutes before his watch would have sounded. He guessed, correctly, that three or four people were going to the chapel. He waited five minutes, then followed. When he got to the open chapel door, he saw that the Pope was at the little altar, facing six short rows of pews. A young man stood at the side to act as altar server; and two women who looked like nuns knelt in the second row.

Malin slowly lifted his Walther and aimed. Instantly the angel, still invisible, raised his sword over Malin's head. But a Voice spoke to the angel: *Do not stop him; John Paul must receive the Martyr's Crown. But allow no harm to the others.*

Malin squeezed the trigger. *Whhhzzzuttt!* The bullet hit John Paul in the left side of his chest. He looked up in shock and pain, whispered a half-audible prayer, then toppled forward across the altar. Malin determined there should be no witnesses and aimed at the altar boy and fired. To no avail. The angel was quicker: he caught the bullet in flight and hurled it back at the assassin. It hit him just above the right ear.

Police ruled the two deaths murder-suicide.

(5)

They approached Charlottesville without incident. It was dark and there were few cars on the road. The President's check-point crews used computers linked to little aluminum boxes filled with electronics installed at random points along major highways during the last few years. These scanned for SmartCards and later would be programmed to detect the Chip or, for those citizens brave enough to disobey the President's decree, the absence of the Chip. However, as spot gasoline shortages began and traffic thinned, the authorities removed their crews on Route 29; and Father Mike, Pat Green, and Vanni slipped through the net on Interstate 66. She stayed low in the back seat, out of sight behind tinted windows; and the two "federal agents" in a police vehicle with government license plates caused no suspicion.

By now Vanni had to help navigate as she knew the area well. When her grandmother still lived here, she had visited often. After declining health forced the old woman to move to Ohio to be near her son, she had given the cabin to her three grandchildren, and Vanni had come here a few times to clean up, sort out memorabilia, and talk with a real estate agent about selling the property. A two-bedroom, one-bath large cabin on a hilly dirt road leading to a non-working farm did have some charm and, because of its back porch view of a small lake at the bottom of a steep hill, might have been marketable. But Vanni and her brothers had decided to keep it for the time being. Then, when social upheaval began, the real estate market declined. Half hoping that a buyer might still miraculously come along, and half expecting that she might need the isolated house, she had left the furniture, some canned goods and dry food in the little pantry, towels in the bathroom, and blankets on the beds. For the same reason, she kept the electricity on.

They bumped their way to the end of the road, parked, and quickly entered the cabin. "Does this place have any water?" asked Pat, looking around the living-dining area.

"There is a well. It has an electrical pump. We'll have water until the electricity goes," she answered. She took off her jacket and tossed it over a chair; underneath it she was wearing her *Abstinence* sweatshirt.

"It will when the comet hits," said Pat.

"Right. So I'm going to store some water while I can." She walked into the little kitchen and opened a cabinet, revealing a row of empty plastic bottles.

"Vanni, do you have any duct tape?" asked Father Mike. She told him to look in the storage shed, off the back porch. He followed her direction and, with relief, found the tape and some empty buckets. In a moment he was taping the cracks in the window jambs and around the door. He also pulled down the shades on every window and taped each secure to its sill. Pat filled the buckets, reconnoitered outside, brought in some firewood, and climbed the ladder to the loft to cover a small window there.

These elemental precautions complete, they locked and bolted the doors, sat down at the table, and prayed for twenty minutes, sometimes aloud, sometimes silently. Then under a single dim bulb, Vanni put together a small cold supper. They did not know whether the power company monitored electricity flow to every individual home so that sudden use would alert the authorities to their presence. They decided to use only candles from then on.

On the shelf above the fireplace stood a small battery-powered portable radio, which Vanni had given her grandmother to use in case an ice storm caused a power failure. She turned it on now and tuned in a news station. "Let's agree," said Father Mike, "that if the Chairman comes on, we turn it off right away. He has hypnotic powers." The news broadcast stated that the Chairman's advanced computer had interlinked with NASA's launched missiles and would shortly destroy the comet and save all humanity. It sounded like government propaganda. They responded with an hour of silent prayer.

Finally Father Mike opened the suitcase he had left just inside the front door. He extracted a chalice, a liter of red wine, a prayer book, various cloths, and cruets. "I'm going to say Mass before the comet hits" he said matter-of-factly, "but don't feel you need to participate." He did not know the state of their souls and, with the stress they all were under, did not want to press them to participate in Mass. "The dresser in the small bedroom will work just fine."

Vanni stood up and walked a few feet to the adjacent bedroom doorways. She looked in one, then the other, then at the supper table. Then she said, "Father Mike, I suppose you wonder what sleeping arrangements we are going to make..." Before he could answer, she continued, "Don't worry, I still believe in what my sweatshirt says."

"Well, Vanni," the priest said, smiling, "it's your house. And keeping abstinence in mind, there seems to be only one possibility. We have two separate bedrooms and one sofa in this room."

"Easy enough," said Pat cheerfully. "Vanni gets the big room, because a double bed is more comfortable and it's her house. Father Mike gets the small room and the single bed. I get the sofa out here. No problem. I defer to beauty and sanctity."

"There's another possibility," said Vanni, watching Pat's face. "Father Mike, you can say the Mass at this table rather than in the bedroom, and while you do"--she took a long breath and glanced at her engagement ring--"could you perform a marriage ceremony for Pat and me? Then," she added, "Father Mike can keep his small room--but nobody has to sleep on the sofa."

The two men were dumbstruck. After a long pause, Father Mike found his tongue first. "I've performed dozens of marriages for former Georgetown students," he began, "and I pretty well have the words of the ceremony memorized. So the answer is--yes."

As the priest spoke, Pat came to his senses, bolted across the room, took her in his arms and kissed her, mumbling something about wanting the wedding date earlier but never having *this* in mind. But she gently pushed him back and said, "Hold it, buster, there's plenty of time. I've got one more thing to say." The two men wondered what new bomb she had ready.

"Father Mike, I think it's important for a married couple to have the same faith. Though Pat doesn't know it, I've been doing a lot of reading and praying. Before you marry us, will you accept me into the Catholic Church?"

(6)

The Chairman sat at the master console in front of his immense computer in the Brussels bank building. Monitor screens provided visual interface with NASA's Mission Control and telescopes locked onto the fast approaching comet. Millions of bits of data poured in from hundreds of sources, the heat of the space crafts' engines on the launching pads, the wind speed aloft, the direction and speed of the comet, the influence of gravity on its trajectory, and thousands and thousands of other facts. The computer whirred in short bursts of activity, punctuated by almost inaudible *ka-glunkk* sounds as it concluded layered analyses and transmitted action recommendations to the next level of sophistication.

It had been two days since NASA had launched six armed space probes in quick succession, three from Vandenberg and then three from Kennedy. Under the Chairman's computer guidance, they would form a crescent-shaped cluster of missiles, aimed all to one side and slightly ahead of the target. He planned to explode them in a sequence designed to exert maximum blast impact all from one side of the comet's path. It would bounce off the force field and be deflected diagonally away from earth.

The Woman approached the Throne of God. Next to her walked Michael the Archangel. Slightly behind them, as an honor guard escort, walked two more angels, powerful in their own right but smaller than the Archangel. Michael carried a globe-like blue, green, and brown sphere. Once arrived before the Throne, the Woman and her entourage stopped. They bowed. Michael handed her the colored globe. Within it one could see the prayers, fasting, and sacrifices of twelve mystics on earth. The Woman held it out, a gift to God the Father, and made a request. As He always had, when she could bolster her request with enough prayers from people on earth, the Father granted her request. She was now ready to deal with the Chairman's computer. At once she dispatched Michael to Brussels.

The Archangel had looked forward eagerly to the day when he could enter the center of evil on earth. This was a major step in what he wanted to do, to avenge the good God for all of Lucifer's insults...

Two demons on guard at the Chairman's computer center were no match for the angry Archangel, who would brook no delay in carrying out his task. He hurled them back down to Hell with one powerful blow, then did his work quickly. Seconds before the Chairman could enter the command to detonate, Michael cut the maze of cables and wires that provided primary electrical power to the boards and circuits for the programs controlling the missiles. Before the auxiliary generators could switch in, he burnt them out in a massive short-circuit, with ten million volts from his sword. At once, one-third of the Chairman's computer power vanished.

When he entered the command to detonate, nothing happened.

CHAPTER XXII

(1)

At Vanni's suggestion, Father Mike put a few drops of red wine on the door post above the front door, saying a prayer that this symbol of the Blood of the Lamb of God would serve to protect them from the intrusion of evil. Then he blessed one of the filled buckets and its contents became holy water. Pat Greene eyed him quizzically.

"This is one more small preparation for what I think is going to happen," he said. "The Three Days of Darkness." Pat and Vanni both had blank looks. Father Mike sat down in the corner chair and Pat and Vanni plopped onto the sofa, and he put his arm around her.

"I don't think we've discussed this much," Kanek began. "But I might as well tell you, since it's the Grand Finale."

"'Three Days Darkness.'" Pat repeated. "I guess the lights go out," said Vanni.

"You're right. But there's more to it: they go out all over the world. And no artificial light will work, except blessed candles. So everybody will be in darkness so thick that they can almost feel it. Demons will roam the earth in visible forms, looking for people with the Mark. It will be their final harvest, their last chance to gather up all the souls they want to take down to Hell."

"So demons will be visible," said Pat. "Is that why you wanted all the windows covered?"

"That's the main reason. If demons swarm around outside, I don't want to yield to the temptation to look at them."

"Hey, Father Mike," said Vanni, "of all the people I know, *you* should be able to handle something like that."

"Thanks for the compliment, Vanni," he said, "but I've learned not to rely on myself. The secret in avoiding temptation is to nip it in the bud. Most spiritual evils, maybe all of them when you get right down to it, are beyond an ordinary human being's power to control. When we admit how weak we are, then God can act through us--or, here, protect us from something we cannot handle on our own."

"You mean just *seeing* these things would--well, would knock us for a loop?" she asked.

"Quite possibly. I don't know. But the messages that predict the Three Days of Darkness uniformly say, "Don't *look* out and don't *go* out.""

"Any idea why?" asked Pat.

"My hunch is, and I think this is confirmed in some of the messages, that the sight of these beings will be so horrible that we would be terrified. Terror is an emotion. And emotion makes people do stupid things."

"I can think of another possible reason," said Vanni. "Deception."

"Good point," said Father Mike. "To get us to open the door, they will imitate the voices of a loved one--Vanni's brothers, or my brother Jerry--and the voice will plead to be helped or to be let in. If we look out, a demon may be able to disguise himself temporarily to look like one of them, just long enough to trick us into opening the door."

"But why don't they just come in on their own?" inquired Pat. "Look, they're fallen angels, but they *are* angels, which means they're pure spirits and they can pass through walls."

"You'd think so," said Father Mike. "I can't tell you for sure why that's not the case here, but perhaps it has to do with a rule God has laid down: in tempting men and women, the devils need some cooperation on our part. Generally speaking, they cannot just force themselves on us. There is a line to cross, a boundary, and we have to invite them across."

"And the door is literally that boundary," she said.

"That's it. They don't get in unless we let them in."

"Well then," she responded, "let's agree that we won't open a door or look out a window--and if one of us starts to, the other two will pull him back."

"Or pull *her* back," added Pat.

"Hey, Mr. Investigative Reporter," she rejoined, poking his shoulder with her fist, *"you're* the guy who will want to write an article next month on what they look like!"

"I think," said Father Mike, sticking to the topic, "that we have to recall the angel's command to Lot and his wife when they were about to escape from Sodom: don't look back."

"This all reminds me of Paul's epistle," she said, "--where he said that we struggle not against flesh and blood, but against powers and principalities, and spirits of the air."

(2)

The Chairman snarled a profanity and slammed his fist against the console table so hard that it cracked. Then he slid his chair twenty feet over to a different bank of computers and screens and pushed, almost pounded, a half-dozen buttons on the nearest keyboard. The monitor lit up and a second later its screen showed the comet. He let out a long string of curses as he watched the armed space probes hurtle past the incoming comet harmlessly and recede into the vastness of space.

Again his fist hit the table, this time not as hard. He could still take command of the situation. For the goal, he told himself, was *control*, and even without one-third of his systems, he still had enough computer capacity to control of the world.

He strode out of the room, passed two human guards outside in the corridor without nodding to them, and hurried to the elevator. He pushed the button for the top floor and considered how to handle the people who would be waiting in the penthouse conference room. He would have to alter his plans slightly. Just a tactical shift.

He swept in with a wide smile on his face. The ten guests, two women and eight men, one of them the President, all in expensive business attire, grew quiet as he approached the portable lectern at the head of the table. He shook hands with no one except the President, who had a place nearest the head of the table; nor did he kiss either woman's hand. Aloof and commanding, as was his style, he raised his hand and gestured them to be seated.

"Ladies and Gentlemen," he began, forcing himself to act cordial, "I am pleased that you have had the opportunity to renew old friendships and, for some of you, to begin new ones. I was delayed, as you know, by the need to oversee the steps the Council of Europe, under my leadership, and the United States have taken to dispel the threat from the comet. It gives me great pleasure to inform you," he lied, "that we have been completely successful."

Applause broke out around the table, along with whispered comments, "I knew he could do it!" "There never was any doubt." None of them dared to ask him, if they thought to, why they had not been permitted to view the explosion on the television screen.

"I have a short three-point agenda this evening. The first topic is a matter of great import, and one in which you will take great satisfaction. We have accomplished a specific goal our movement has worked over two centuries to achieve." He paused for dramatic effect. "The Catholic Church has been destroyed."

Loud applause around the table was punctuated with "Good riddance!" and "Now at last humanity can progress!" and "Death to superstition!" The Chairman beamed and let them enjoy the moment.

Finally he continued. "I will summarize the specifics. First, we have either killed or persuaded to come over to our side, over ninety-nine percent of the priests in the world. The remaining few are in hiding, but we have the means to track them down and we will do so.

"Second, Pope John Paul II is indeed dead." More applause around the table, subdued because they could see he wanted to continue. "As you know, he had left the Vatican and gone into hiding. But because of our superior logical powers," he lied again, "we were able to deduce where he must have gone. I sent one of our men to finish the job."

"Third, and perhaps most important because it means that the monster cannot arise from its grave...we have killed, or forced to abjure their faith, every orthodox Bishop in the world!" Again, applause and comments akin to those when he announced the Church had been destroyed.

"I should tell you," he continued, "that during his travels, John Paul II had secretly ordained a number of Bishops. That old man was brilliant in his own way, but he was no match for *me*. I imagine he expected that we would round up all the known Bishops who were not in our camp, but he would leave the Church with some secret ones in reserve who could carry on the Apostolic Succession. He was mistaken."

"Now, to the second point of my agenda," he continued in a businesslike way. He stepped to the side and pressed a button on the wall. A panel slid upward, revealing a large television screen. He pressed two other buttons and the screen filled with an ominous green light. He stepped through a door in the corner into a smaller room behind the main conference room and, a moment later, his face and upper body appeared on the screen before them. Above them, in each corner at the front of the room, were two mounted devices which, if they noticed them at all, his guests might have thought were security cameras like those found in banks. They were not. They were transmitters.

His eyes flashed hypnotically; the screen filled with a mysterious green light behind him, bathing his features in a strange glow that somehow was compelling, controlling; the two transmitters hummed out a low-frequency electrical beam wide enough to reach the right hand of every person seated at the table--the hand and the *Chip* that each had voluntarily accepted under the skin. *Worship me; I am God. Worship me; I am God. Worship me; I am God*, he kept repeating. The beam disrupted their brain waves: reflective thought was impossible, their wills were mush, their energy drained. Half in a trance, half yielding assent to the lie they did not recognize and could not find the will to deny, in unison they repeated, again, and again, and yet again, "You are god. We worship you. We give you thanks. We praise you." The hum, the face, the words, the beam--all continued for a few minutes.

The Chairman relished his ultimate triumph over the leaders of the world he had conquered. They belonged to him, their countries, their minds, their bodies, their souls. He could do with them what he wished. He had total control. Compared to these helpless little people, *he*, the Chairman, was indeed god!

So he turned to the third and last point of his agenda. He pressed buttons again. The screen faded. The hum stopped. The hypnotic picture blurred and disappeared. Again he was standing at the lectern; they seemed to come back to their senses. Like a woman who has voluntarily allowed herself to be ravished, they felt guilt, vague distaste for what they had done, for what they had set in motion weeks earlier when they took the Chip. They knew they had sold their souls to the Chairman, but they could not find it in themselves, even now, after the obscenity of worshipping this man, to resist. It was far too late to retreat. So their avaricious thoughts turned instead to the Directorates the Chairman had promised. The President wondered, too, how ten people could share the ten sections of the world, when he had been promised three. And he thought about Dolores Montalvo.

"I thank you for your affection," the Chairman began. "And now it is time to name who shall rule the Ten Directorates." He picked up a piece of paper and studied it for dramatic effect. They leaned forward eagerly.

Then his eyes narrowed and a sinister look came across his face. Hatred welled up in him and the Devil looked out from his eyes. "I have decided to rule the Ten Directorates *myself*, without you!" He pushed a button. The side doors flew open. A dozen soldiers in black uniforms, pistols drawn, broke into the room.

Later, behind soundproof steel doors in the sub-basement of the bank building, under the giant computer room, ten once mighty people spoke curses, complaints, sobs, demands, shouts, angry screams and wails. Pride, rebellion, and greed had brought them to this unlikely way-station on their journey to Hell.

(3)

As if driven by an unseen hand, *the comet actually increased its speed.* Already ten times larger and brighter in the night sky than Venus, it rushed closer, larger, and now hurtled into the earth's atmosphere. Its ice casing burnt off. The craggy metallic surface burst into flames from friction with the atmosphere. But because of its density, size, and extremely hard outer shell, the flames consumed very little of its substance. Now the monstrous burning boulder looked larger than the sun. People in the eastern United States and Canada as far west as Pittsburgh, Knoxville, and Atlanta watched in horror. People in Boston, New York, Washington and every coastal city watched in sheer terror.

"The great and terrible Day of the Lord" was upon mankind. The moment of ultimate punishment. The necessary cleansing for all their sins. The final catastrophe, compared to which all previous floods, earthquakes, hurricanes were trivial. The end of *the Chastisement.*

The monster crashed into the Atlantic at fifty thousand miles an hour, over ten miles *per second.* On a slight diagonal path, sky to sea, east toward west, on a line pointed toward but short of the U.S. mainland, it punctured the ocean surface like a bullet through jelly and knifed down to the ocean floor. The impact had the force of a thousand hydrogen bombs. It ripped through layer after layer of rocky tectonic plates as if through so much paper. It drilled on ten miles toward the inner earth. The entire globe shook violently.

A huge wave taller than the Empire State Building rocketed up toward the sky. Billions of tons of displaced water pounded out in all directions from the point of impact. Blocked by the ambient water, the wildly crashing wave pressed *up and over* the resisting water it met, like an avalanche overrunning boulders in its path. The extra weight of the fast-moving wave mounting the stationary water compressed it down and out, quickly doubling, then quadrupling, its weight. So compressed was the water that it seemed almost *solid.* The immense weight was far too much for the ocean floor to bear. It cracked, again and again, as the now roaring tidal wave, gaining strength from the incalculable weight it sought to dispel but could not, powered its way toward shore.

The first impact was far stronger than a "ten" on the Richter Scale. The moving tidal wave, crushing and cracking the ocean floor like the tires of a huge truck speeding across plywood strips, added after-shock and after-shock, as in dozens of places the ocean floor buckled and collapsed. Transfer of kinetic energy at the speed of sound rushed through the ocean, the rocks on its floor, and the ocean floor itself.

Billions of tons of water poured into thousands of fissures and cracks in the ocean floor. Dormant volcanoes came to angry life. They spewed and spit hot molten lava up and out, adding to the chaos in the elements. And on land, on every continent new and revived volcanoes awoke with angry thunder.

The immense mountain range of water roared on toward shore.

(4)

When the comet hit, the three fugitives were in prayer in their dim Charlottesville cabin. One blessed candle flickered on the table. Father Mike had given a short explanation of the Mysteries of the Rosary and of Spiritual Communion, so that Pat and Vanni would have some additional ways they might want to pray.

The impact shook their house violently as if it were hit by a huge truck. Plates fell from cupboards. The beds, sofa, and tables bounced like deck chairs on a ship caught in a tropical storm. The earthquake knocked the three inhabitants to the floor.

Somehow the lone blessed candle on the table did not topple. The noise outside rose, as layered earthquakes felled trees. Winds howled. No! it wasn't the wind; *the howling was demons spreading over the earth searching for their prey!* Then there was pounding on the door, an insistent intruder demanding entrance.

"Keep praying!" shouted Father Mike. Already on the floor, he knelt and braced himself with his left hand. He faced the door and lifted a small crucifix. "I command you, Satan, in the Name of Jesus, *be gone!"* At his gesture and words, the three invisible Guardian Angels with them in the shaking room exited temporarily. The screaming and curses outside grew louder for a moment. Then the noise faded into the distance. The angels reentered, still invisible.

It went on this way during all the prolonged night. Waves of shaking, then calm, then shaking again; thunder and lightning; volcanic ash seeping in through the chimney; howling demons outside; the roof pelted with sleet and hail; sharp drop of temperature. Pat Greene crawled along the pulsating floor to the back door and prayed against the evil at that portal; Father Mike brandished his crucifix near the front door and repeated, constantly, exorcism prayers. At one point Vanni crawled to the bedrooms, grabbed the blankets, heaved herself to her feet, stumbled back to Pat and then to Father Mike, and threw a blanket over the shoulders of each. The priest shouted to her to get under the blanket with Pat, as the temperature plummeted down to freezing. She started back toward the kitchen when she saw, slithering out of the fireplace opening, a huge snake *with the face of a man!* She screamed.

Father Mike turned and saw the serpent moving toward her. He grabbed the inside doorknob, pulled himself to his feet, and dove to the corner of the room where the bucket of water stood. In one continuous move he grabbed the handle and threw the blessed water at the approaching reptile. When the holy water hit the snake it emitted a blood-curdling scream of rage and pain and reversed itself at once, disappearing back up the chimney.

Father Mike and Vanni looked at each other, sweat glistening on their foreheads, their hearts pounding wildly. "Keep praying, Vanni, and we'll beat these monsters!" Again the room shook and the cacophony outside intensified.

It went on this way for three days.

(5)

The seventy-second hour came at last and the noise suddenly stopped. Exhausted from stress and the effort to pray constantly, they had huddled together in the main room, facing three different directions, and two would pray while one would doze. After two hours, they'd waken the sleeper and another would doze. When the noise did stop at last, the three fugitives collapsed into a fitful sleep, Pat and Vanni next to each other on the floor, Father Mike ten feet away near the cold fireplace.

There was a loud knock on the door. They all sat bolt upright. They had slept in their clothes. Grabbing whatever furniture lay nearby, they pulled themselves erect. Light seeped in past the drapes. They looked at each other quizzically, surprised but somehow, they knew not why, not fearful. The knock came again.

"Who is it?" shouted Pat.

"Michael the Archangel," responded a strong male voice.

Pat and Vanni looked at each other in astonishment. Father Mike recognized the voice. Memories of the meeting in Steubenville rushed back, and in his mind's eye he saw the Pope stand firm before the apparition and "test the spirits," as Scripture directed.

"If you are Michael, come in without opening the door," said Father Mike, rubbing his eyes.

Immediately, three feet inside the closed and locked door, a tall man-like figure appeared, dressed like a Roman gladiator. He had blonde hair, broad shoulders, and a strong square jaw. An immense sword hung from his belt. Light radiated from his body and a balm of peace and joy poured over the weary humans. He had a broad smile on his face. He pointed his right hand at the two front windows; instantly the heavy drapes parted and warm yellow sunlight flooded the room.

"Please come with me," said the archangel in a pleasant respectful voice. "I wish to show you some of the New Eden. Later the Lord Jesus would like you to join Him and many others for dinner."

* * * * * * * * * * *

EPILOGUE

Time seemed to fly as they journeyed through the beautiful landscape. The trees, the flowers, the carpeted greenery dotted with manicured shrubs and exotic red and yellow and purple vegetation, were all so much more vivid, more lush, that by comparison a Disney fairyland would seem painted in drab grey, black, and white. Jungle animals now tame grazed near blue brooks and streams and lakes, adding glory to the park-like setting. The air was so clean it felt as if one was breathing pure oxygen. The survivors of the Tribulation were exhilarated, but not tired, like an Olympic runner who has won the Gold in a great race, then showered and returned reinvigorated by the applause, the energy of the crowd, and the congratulations of his loved ones.

At one point Vanni wondered why the greatest Archangel was spending time with *them*, an Evangelical-become-Catholic girl, a lapsed-but-now-returned Catholic layman, and an ordinary priest. And Father Mike found himself wondering what had happened to Jerry, John DeSanto, the false Pope Julian, the Chairman, and Pope John Paul II.

Michael read their thoughts and addressed them: "There are questions in your minds which I can answer briefly," he said. "Jerry Kanek is in Heaven. John DeSanto survived, as you did. Cardinal Cassendi and the Chairman are chained in Hell; the Lord Jesus put them there and I myself bound them. Pope John Paul was martyred and is in Heaven."

He paused and looked at Father Kanek. "I am here with you," he continued, "because the Blessed Virgin has asked me to accompany for a time, the only living Bishop in the world--the new Pope."

The Woman walked slowly up the ramp toward the Throne of God. To either side were her usual two angelic escorts. With her perfect mix of dignity and humility she moved forward, excitement and joy in her heart. She and the two angels bowed. Then, erect again, she spoke: "Thank You, Father. Thank You, Jesus. Thank You, Holy Spirit."

As she stood there one could see, beneath her heel, the crushed head of a serpent.

DAY of INIQUITY
A Prophetic Novel on the END TIMES

By William A. Stanmeyer

This gripping End Times novel will deepen your Faith as you see the final scenario unfold through the eyes of memorable characters in a world under demonic assault:

- "The Chairman," mysterious world leader
- Dolores Montalvo, amoral actress, agent of theChairman
- Fr. Michael Kanek, expert in Tesla electrical theory, traditional priest in a "modern" Church
- Theodore Patrick Greene, agnostic, investigative reporter exposing secret government plans
- Marilee Van Niesen, Christian career woman with a sense of humor
- Jerry Kanek, F.B.I. agent suspicious of a "rogue agency"
- Eugenio Cassendi, the "imposter Pope"
- John DeSanto, ex-Navy pilot, visionary, target of secret foreign military in the U.S.
- Cristina Montalvo, Spanish mystic

And others, both good and evil, whom you already know.

A techno-thriller plot with profound spiritual insight, the story exposes such imminent developments as mandatory "smart cards," the Y2K crisis, universal satellite surveillance, the microchip "Mark," and other events predicted by current visionaries and the Bible.

The section on The Warning is unforgettable. This book has multiple themes, sudden reversals, and personal redemption and its amazing plot rushes to a powerful surprise ending.

A fascinating novel that helps one to understand the times we are in. A perfect gift to awaken those you know to discern the "signs of the times."
Maureen Flynn - Editor, Signs and Wonders Magazine, Co-author of "Thunder of Justice"

Only $13.95
-plus $3.95 shipping and handling for each book.
Canada add $5.00 additional for each book shipping and handling.

Order from Signs and Wonders of Our Times
PO Box 345, Herndon, VA   20172-0345
Phone: (703) 327-2277 Fax: (703) 327-2888

THE GREAT SIGN

Messages and Visions of Final Warnings

A Powerful book on God's warnings and great mercy to prepare us, His children for a new Era of Peace. His greatest act of mercy will be a universal warning or illumination of souls, accompanied by a miraculous luminous cross in a dark sky.

This is a book you must read if you want to learn how:

✞ The Mother of All Humanity warns her children.

✞ Priests must inform and prepare God's people, with faith, hope, love, prayer and sacrifice.

✞ The thunder of God's justice will resound and nature will mirror the fury of God's anger, bringing mankind to its knees.

✞ Worldwide economic and financial collapse will far surpass anything that has ever happened.

✞ The Church and the Pope will be attacked.

✞ **The GREAT SIGN, a miraculous, luminous cross in the sky,** will accompany **the warning or illumination of souls**

✞ Forces of Antichrist will impose worldwide order and the sign of the beast.

✞ The Holy Rosary is a most powerful weapon to strengthen and protect.

✞ Christ will end the rebellion and bring a glorious, new Era of Peace for His Father's remnant which remains true.

Order Form

☐ **Yes**, I would like to receive **THE GREAT SIGN!** Please send me ___ copies for $14.95, plus $3.95 shipping and handling for each book within the U.S. Canada add $5.00 additional for each book shipping and handling. Please call for exact foreign shipping rates.

Check or Money Order enclosed. U.S. funds only.

☐ MasterCard   ☐ VISA   ☐ Discover   Expiration Date _____

Card# ☐☐☐☐☐☐☐☐☐☐☐☐☐☐☐☐ (Include all 13 or 16 digits)

Signature (required for credit card orders) _____

Name/Recipient _____

Address _____

City _____ State_____ Zip_____

Please make checks to **SIGNS AND WONDERS** for Our Times
PO Box 345,Herndon, VA 20172-0345.
For immediate attention, call our Order Department at (703) 327-2277 or
FAX (703) 327-2888
Thank you for your love and support.

Tribulations and Triumph

The End of An Evil Era and the Dawn of a New Glorious Time...

Now, a new voice from the American Midwest is added to the Chorus. The Lord is giving an American housewife, Joanne Kriva, words of warning and pleas for peace—and imparting details of events that will soon overtake the world. Joanne's new volume focuses on the messages she received from Our Lord and Lady between February 1995 to August 1996.

Read and Learn:

- why the apparitions of Our Lady are about to close;
- the dangers that threaten Pope John Paul II—and his placewithin the Divine Providence;
- how the Antichrist is alive and plotting to fully exert his power in the world;
- how destruction will be unleashed on a scale never before witnessed in human history;
- what glorious era awaits those who remain faithful during these troubled times.

Tribulations and Triumph

Joanne Kriva   Volume 2

REVELATIONS ON THE COMING OF
THE GLORY OF GOD

Read Tomorrow's News TODAY!

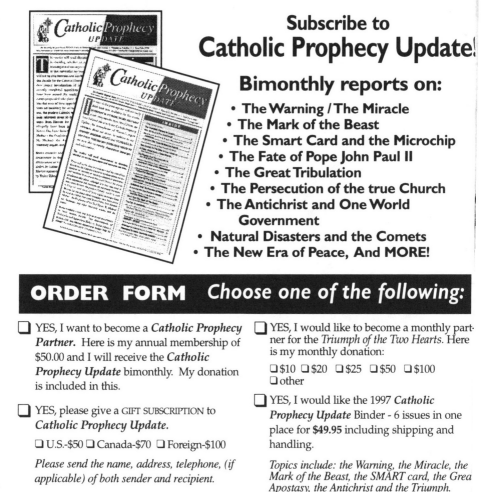

Subscribe to
Catholic Prophecy Update!

Bimonthly reports on:

- The Warning / The Miracle
- The Mark of the Beast
- The Smart Card and the Microchip
- The Fate of Pope John Paul II
- The Great Tribulation
- The Persecution of the true Church
- The Antichrist and One World Government
- Natural Disasters and the Comets
- The New Era of Peace, And MORE!
